PRAISE FO

"Both heartbreaking and mesmerizing."
—Lisa Wingate, *New York Times* bestselling author of
Before We Were Yours

"Stirring and romantic, a sweeping novel about first loves and second chances."
—Sarah Pekkanen, author of *The Opposite of Me*

"An absorbing, intelligent novel about retracing one's steps to recover what was lost, and about coming to terms with the mistakes of the past in order to rediscover a future. Peter Golden reminds us that going back is sometimes the only way to move ahead."
—Elizabeth Brundage, author of *A Stranger Like You* and
The Doctor's Wife

THEIR
SHADOWS
DEEP

ALSO BY PETER GOLDEN

THEIR SHADOWS DEEP

A Novel

PETER GOLDEN

LAKE UNION
PUBLISHING

Published by Lake Union Publishing, Seattle

www.apub.com

Amazon, the Amazon logo, and Lake Union Publishing are trademarks of Amazon.com, Inc., or its affiliates.

ISBN-13: 9781662525971 (paperback)
ISBN-13: 9781662525988 (digital)

Cover design by Shasti O'Leary Soudant
Cover image: © Alexandre ROSA / Alamy; © Simon Herrmann / Getty
Interior image: © Denys / Adobe Stock

Printed in the United States of America

For Molly and Benjamin,
with best wishes from the past
and hope for the future.

And for Annis, with love.

When you are old and gray and full of sleep,
And nodding by the fire, take down this book,
And slowly read, and dream of the soft look
Your eyes had once, and of their shadows deep.
—W. B. Yeats

PART I

CHAPTER 1

Greenwich Village
December 1959

Caitlin Russo was being watched. The man was across MacDougal. His fedora and topcoat with the upturned velvet collar were out of place among the Saturday-night parade of beatniks, students, and assorted lunatics swarming past him in Salvation Army castoffs. But he was staring at her. Caitlin's maiden name was Gallagher, and willowy Irish girls with a cascade of reddish-brown hair and electric-blue eyes knew about getting stared at.

As the man cupped his hands to light a cigarette, Caitlin started walking. Christmas lights shone in the shop windows, and bursts of music leaked from the coffeehouses. She was supposed to meet her husband at Café Bohemia, on Barrow Street. Miles Davis was in town, and Gabe was a jazz fiend and had become friends with Miles after the war. Gabe had been working narcotics in Midtown then, and Miles had gotten busted copping heroin outside the Three Deuces before playing his set. Gabe had collared the dealer and let Miles slide. The quickest way to Barrow was up Sixth Avenue, but Caitlin wanted to find out how serious the man was about watching her and decided to take him through Washington Square Park.

He was walking along with her on the other side of MacDougal. Staying on her side of the street, Caitlin walked up to the corner of

MacDougal and West Fourth, waited for two cars to pass, and then darted into the park. Up ahead, an old woman with long white hair was sitting on a bench with a blanket over her shoulders. Caitlin looked back. His hat was pulled low, so she couldn't see the man's face. A trio of coeds in raccoon coats staggered drunkenly past him, singing "Do You Wanna Dance?" After they turned onto West Fourth, the man was gone.

Still, Caitlin would take the long way through Washington Square. *You can't be too careful.* Caitlin's mother repeated that warning so often, with her pink-beaded rosary in her hand, that it might as well have been part of the Apostles' Creed. Caitlin gave the old woman on the bench a dollar. The woman gazed up at her with eyes as vacant as the night sky. Caitlin remembered nursing her mother and her mother looking at her as if she were a stranger. Caitlin liked to think that her mother had recognized her before she died.

Faith, Hope, and Charity. Caitlin believed in all three.

CHAPTER 2

Manhattan

"Where did you get this shit?" Jack Kennedy asked.

He was on the phone with the author of a Kennedy-family biography scheduled to be published in the spring. The writer had sent him the galley proofs, and Jack had finished reading the pages in his penthouse duplex at the Carlyle Hotel.

The author, a freelance writer, said, "From an interview I did with your father in 1945."

Jack felt as if his head would explode. "After the Nazis got done murdering millions of Jews?"

"Yeah. That's why I didn't pitch the interview to any magazines."

The galley was on his lap, and phrases Jack had underlined jumped out at him:

Honestly, I'll tell you, I'm not a fan of some Jews, but I don't want them thrown into gas chambers.

If Jews would quit talking about everyone hating them, people wouldn't hate them so much.

Jack said, "My father knew you quoted this garbage in your book?"

"Senator, your father's been helping me."

Jesus, what was his father thinking? He had been just as tone deaf when he had served as ambassador to Great Britain in the run-up to

Peter Golden

World War II and he got going on his isolationism rants and tried to convince Roosevelt and Churchill to cut a deal with Germany.

Jack removed his reading glasses. "Get rid of my father's comments on Jews."

The author's voice shot up an octave. "The publisher's ready to print."

"Tell him to get unready."

"Senator, it'll cost a fortune."

"It'll cost a lot more when I get my father to sue you silly bastards."

The author was still talking as Jack slammed down the receiver. A slice of chocolate layer cake was on a room service cart. He was shoveling the last bite of it into his mouth when the phone rang. Jack knew it was the ambassador.

"Hiya, Dad."

"That writer called. Why you giving him the business? He's a poor mick living in some town in Arizona and just trying to earn a buck."

When it came to politics, Jack thought, Joe Kennedy could be brilliant. It was the ambassador who had convinced him, four years ago, that the country was ready to put a young Catholic war hero in the White House. And his father had backed up his optimism with millions of dollars for his campaign. Yet here was his other side, a baffling tactlessness, and Jack was slow to reply because his father was unaccustomed to his children criticizing him.

"Dad, if those quotes come out, I can forget about the Jewish vote. I'll lose New Jersey, Illinois, Florida, maybe New York, and definitely California—Nixon grew up there."

"Jack, I call 'em like I see 'em. With Jews, wops, the coloreds, and my own kind. You know how many shamrocks I bought drinks and the SOBs threw up on my shoes to say thanks?"

"Can't we lay off the Jews? And the Italians, Negroes, Hindus, or anybody else you feel like telling off."

"I've never said a goddamn word about Hindus."

Jack laughed. "I need a favor."

6

"What now?"

"My friend Gabe's wife knows Julian Rose. Gabe's going to ask her to set up a meeting with me, you, and Bobby."

His father snapped, "Julian and his gangster pal Longy Zwillman, those sheeny bastards hijacked a shipment—"

"Longy hung himself ten months ago, so let's skip the good old days of Prohibition."

"I know, Jack. You think I'm too old to read the newspaper?"

"All I think is that except for FDR, New Jersey usually goes Republican, and Julian can help turn that around. That's sixteen electoral votes."

"Don't expect me to come north and freeze my ass off. Tell Julian I'll see him in Florida. Is that all, Jack?"

"I love you, Dad."

"You should," the ambassador said and hung up.

Jack knew his father believed every move he'd made since the end of the war had been done in his son's interest, so butting heads with him left Jack feeling guilty. He wished his sister Kathleen was alive. Kick had a way with Dad. She had a way with everyone. Jack remembered the scowling old man in a hunting cap who collected seashells on East Beach. All the kids had been frightened of him until Kick dropped a handful of periwinkle shells in his pail and treated him to one of her dimpled grins. His eyes had opened wide, as if he were offended by her forwardness; then he'd broken out in a toothless smile. That was Kick's gift: a talent for improving anyone's day.

A knock sounded on the door. Jack stood, his lower back throbbing. Opening the door, he found a young blonde in a tight, salmon pink dress before him—just what the doctor ordered.

"Please," Jack said, stepping aside. "Come in."

CHAPTER 3

Gabe was double-parked under a streetlamp outside Café Bohemia. Caitlin was shivering when she got into the Chevy Bel Air.

He cranked up the heat. "You OK?"

"Some creep—"

"Where?"

Caitlin turned to Gabe. His father's family were Jews originally from Madrid, and with his black hair curling out from under his tweed cap, dark eyes, and features as precise as a wood carving, Gabe could have passed for a Spanish nobleman. There was something thrilling about his face, an alloy of feral intelligence and restrained fury, which made Caitlin feel as if nothing could hurt her.

She said, "I dropped off our deposit for the apartment, went for a cup of coffee at Caffe Reggio, and when I came out, he was on MacDougal watching me."

"What'd the creep look like?"

"Fedora, expensive topcoat."

"That's the best you can do? C'mon, Cait. You used to be a cop."

Caitlin heard a note of fear in his voice and regretted mentioning the creep. Even though Gabe was thirty-seven, nine years older than her, and had been a detective and a marine decorated for bravery fighting the Japanese on Okinawa, he was a worrier—a tendency, he conceded, that he shared with his mother, who had come to America from Kyiv as a girl and never lost her conviction that the Jew-hating Cossacks had followed her to Brooklyn. And lately, Gabe worried more than ever. It didn't help that they were residing in his parents' apartment in Flatbush. Gabe had moved back in to look after his ailing mother and father, who'd died within months of each other. That was a year ago, and Gabe couldn't bring himself to leave his childhood home. Caitlin blamed Gabe's anxiety mainly on his new job. *Running errands for the State Department* was all he'd say about it. Caitlin didn't believe him. She suspected the work was dangerous and he didn't want to scare her with the details. It paid well. Gabe shopped at Brooks Brothers now and had bought her a diamond-and-emerald wedding band and agreed to rent a bigger place in Greenwich Village. But he traveled frequently and returned from his trips quiet and distant, sitting by the window, watching the people on Ocean Avenue, and chain-smoking Camels. His silence worried Caitlin, and when she would finally ask him what was wrong, he'd brush her off with a quip. "The Dodgers moved to Los Angeles," he'd say and grin.

Now, Caitlin said, "If I remember anything about the guy watching me, I'll tell you."

Gabe frowned and started driving uptown. "I've got to make a stop."

Caitlin leaned against him, and he put his arm around her. "What time do we have to leave for Washington next Sunday?" she asked.

"Été's plane gets in from Paris at two, and we'll pick her up and go."

"Her novel was terrific."

"That's why I volunteered to drive her down. You want to be a writer. Maybe she can help. And we're going to Joe Alsop's. I told him about you. Besides his column for the *Herald Tribune*, he writes for the *Saturday Evening Post*. Joe says he's got an idea for you."

On Seventy-Ninth Street, Caitlin spotted a woman standing between two children with her arms over their shoulders while they looked up at a whirl of snowflakes, and suddenly, she missed her mother. "There's room for a baby in the new apartment."

Gabe grinned. "I noticed. Want to hop in the back seat?"

They were stopped at a red light. Caitlin put a hand on his thigh and massaged the pinstripe flannel of his trousers.

"That's a start," Gabe said.

At night, traffic was sparse on Riverside Drive, and as Gabe backed into a space across from the park, he said, "I've got to see a guy."

"Who?"

"Just a guy."

Caitlin, annoyed by another one of his secrets, changed the subject. "What's Jack Kennedy like?" Gabe had been with the NYPD in 1950, when fighting broke out in Korea and the marines recalled him. For some inexplicable bureaucratic reason, he had been shipped to French Indochina to guard the American legation in Saigon, and Kennedy, hoping to run for the Senate and wanting to buff up his foreign affairs résumé with a tour of the Middle East and Asia, stopped in the city. Gabe had given him his take on the war between the French and the Indochinese Communists. They became friendly and had kept in touch. Caitlin assumed Kennedy had helped him get his new job, though that was another thing Gabe wouldn't tell her.

Gabe said, "Jack's smart and funny. He'll be at the party on Sunday."

Caitlin smiled. "He's very handsome."

He arched his eyebrows in mock horror.

"Not as handsome as you."

"That's better," he replied and kissed her. "Be right back."

After taking a briefcase from the trunk, Gabe crossed Riverside to a dingy brick apartment house and entered a vestibule. He pushed the button for 901 and was buzzed in. The apartment was across from the elevator. Victor Diaz, in a zebra-striped dressing gown and velvet slippers, was waiting for him in the doorway.

"Hola, Gabriel." Victor was about forty, a wiry Cuban as blond and blue eyed as a Swede. He had been a pimp in Havana, then relocated to Miami Beach, where he'd discovered arranging to smuggle American small arms was more profitable than renting out women.

"Buenas noches," Gabe said, stepping past Victor, who closed the door. Other than an easy chair by the window and a dim pole lamp, the room was empty.

Gabe asked, "You find that film we talked about?"

"*Tu amigo*, he is worried?"

"Forget my friend. You're doing this for me."

Victor's tongue darted out to lick his lips. Gabe hated snakes, and Victor reminded him of one. "No luck. I keep looking."

Gabe doubted Victor was telling the truth. Probably figuring the longer he stalled, the higher the price. Gabe gave him the cordovan briefcase. Victor popped the clasp and appeared surprised when he pulled out a Sunday edition of the *Journal-American*. He was even more surprised to see the High Standard automatic with a silencer that Gabe was pointing at him.

"I got a lead on the film," Victor said quickly. "A guy named Ruby."

Gabe lowered the pistol. "First name or last?"

"*No lo sé*. Yenchi Baylin, down in Miami Beach, might know." Victor dropped the newspaper on the floor. "And my money for the shipment?"

"Shipment's canceled," Gabe replied and put three .22-caliber slugs in Victor's head, stepping back to dodge the blood splatter.

Gabe pocketed the shell casings. The marines had trained him to kill, and he'd gotten good at it firing at waves of Japanese soldiers. During his six years as a cop, he'd killed one man. Gabe had been at the Horn & Hardart in Times Square when a nut had entered the Automat, firing a shotgun, wounding a woman and her child before Gabe shot him.

Gabe could live with his past: it was his present that troubled him. After retrieving the briefcase, he dropped the pistol inside it and took the stairs to the street.

CHAPTER 4

Washington, DC

On a Sunday evening in the old tree-lined neighborhood of Georgetown, a flock of the local elite gathered at the home of columnist Joe Alsop. Between martinis as clear and cold as winter starlight and spoonfuls of terrapin soup, the women talked about children while the men discussed the nation's future.

Following dessert, the men left the table to continue their discussion, and on this evening, three guests trailed Alsop into his garden room: Allen Dulles, the director of the Central Intelligence Agency; Ben Bradlee, Washington-bureau chief of *Newsweek*; and, moving with a slight limp, Senator Jack Kennedy, who was exhausted from stumping across the country.

Jack settled into a Queen Anne armchair next to Alsop, who was fitting a cigarette into a ceramic holder identical to the one used by his distant cousin Franklin Delano Roosevelt. Alsop wasn't as genteel as FDR. He was a hawkish cold warrior and flayed anyone who disagreed with him. His latest victim was President Eisenhower. In his column, syndicated to over two hundred newspapers, Alsop had echoed Jack's charge that Eisenhower's cuts to the defense budget had forced the country to fall behind the Soviet missile program. Criticizing this missile gap, Jack thought, was in the national interest and astute politics. Ever since Russia had launched its *Sputnik* satellite in the fall of 1957 and beat the United States into space, Americans had grown nervous about the Soviets obliterating them with their new technology.

Now, Alsop stared at Dulles through his tortoiseshell glasses and declared, "I daresay Castro might do good things in Cuba."

"That's ridiculous," the CIA director replied. "But you are impressive—talking out of your ass while you're sitting on it."

The director's response pleased Alsop down to his cap-toe shoes. His standard gambit was to make an outlandish statement and convert his guests' rebuttals into quotes for his column.

Alsop lit his cigarette with a gold Dunhill lighter. "Care to explain, dear boy?"

Dulles puffed on his pipe. "Our information is that Castro put Che Guevara in charge of dispensing revolutionary justice, and Che has the firing squads working overtime. And Castro has been a bad boy—stealing all the land, bank accounts, and businesses he can."

Ben Bradlee knew this information was off the record, but Dulles would call him the second *Newsweek* could use it. "Do you regret we didn't help Batista survive the revolution?"

Kennedy said, "Why should we have helped that prick?"

Dulles, with his white hair, wire-rimmed glasses, and tidy mustache, looked every bit the aging Princeton gentleman until he scowled at Kennedy, and his face revealed another version of the man, the amoral maestro who had been credited with the overthrow of governments in Iran and Guatemala. He considered Kennedy too callow for the presidency. His talk about the missile gap was nonsense. It couldn't be publicly refuted by Eisenhower because the proof came via photographs from the CIA's classified U-2 spy plane, and violating the airspace over the Soviet Union was an act of war. The missile-gap criticism had infuriated Eisenhower, yet Dulles had to be cautious with Kennedy. He would make an appealing candidate and, if he won, could fire him. So in the dry tone used during his years as a Wall Street lawyer, Dulles said to the senator, "We might have assisted Batista because he worked with us."

Kennedy stiffened. "Fulgencio Batista was a dictator who set up a corrupt police state, let the mob bring in casinos, and murdered thousands of his own people. And we gave him the weapons to do it. Now the bastard is living it up in Portugal with our money that he stole."

Dulles said, "The CIA believes Castro is a Communist, and he should be dealt with."

Bradlee was studying Kennedy. "What is it, Jack?"

"If I were Cuban, I would've been with the rebels."

Siphoning his contempt for Kennedy's naivete from his voice, Dulles said, "We all read your speech in the papers, and I'll concede your main point: the desire of nations to be free and independent from the West or the Soviets is more potent than capitalism or communism. Except Che is an educated Marxist who wants to unite Latin America. If he hasn't converted Castro yet, he will, and then Cuba will be a problem for us. And, Jack, I doubt characterizing us as Western imperialists on the Senate floor will win you the White House."

Politically, the speech had been reckless, but Jack had believed in it, and identifying with rebels wasn't a new feeling for him. In 1951, he had gone to Saigon to see how France was faring in her war there and left convinced imperialism was finished. Ho Chi Minh and his forces might have been Communists, but they were also nationalists, and Jack could see himself joining them to throw out the French colonizers. And Jack knew why he felt this way. His father, despite his wealth, had never recovered from growing up Irish in Boston, where the Brahmins had acted as if the Irish should aspire to nothing higher than scrubbing the toilets on Beacon Hill, and the father had passed his resentment on to his son.

Even so, Jack's resentment of Dulles went deeper than inherited rancor. The director was too blasé about the violence required to overthrow governments. Jack's older brother had died in the war, and Jack had come close. Dulles had spent the war in the safety of Switzerland, directing a spy network, and Jack disliked know-it-alls who hadn't been under fire. Guys like that could get people killed for nothing.

The doorbell chimed, and Alsop said, "Ah, the evening's pièce de résistance."

With a bounce in his step, the columnist departed, and in his whiskey-and-cigarette growl, Bradlee asked Jack, "What the hell's he doing now?"

Jack answered his friend with a smile he'd been working on since the age of three, when his parents had put him in a sanatorium to recover from scarlet fever—a smile he'd perfected during a childhood and adolescence of chronic illness and pain—that celebrated Jack Kennedy smile, so very Irish and American, wide and bright, the smile that was the wall Jack had built between himself and the world.

CHAPTER 5

Her pen name was Été. She was the twenty-seven-year-old daughter of a French banker and a Vietnamese doctor who had died from dengue fever treating villagers outside Saigon. With her long straight black hair, her large dark eyes, and a complexion as pale gold as the scotch and soda Joe Alsop was handing her, Été was an exotic sight in an ao dai—a snug purple silk tunic over white slacks. She stood in the living room greeting the wives in English until Jacqueline Kennedy said, "*Enchanté de faire votre connaissance*," and Été replied in French.

Having delivered the guest of honor, Caitlin and Gabe sipped martinis by the fireplace. Caitlin was wearing her black dress from Saks Fifth Avenue, but seeing Jackie Kennedy made her feel like a peasant at a cotillion. She was even more stylish in person because her walk and gestures were as elegant as a ballerina's at the barre. Now, Jackie was speaking to Été in English about the influence of Colette's autobiographical fiction on Été's novel, *Au Revoir, Papa*. The novel had won the Goncourt Prize, the most prestigious literary award in France, and in English translation it was that unique bestseller lauded by critics.

As the men filed in from the garden room, Alsop introduced them to Été, who kissed each one on both cheeks. The wives watched, stone faced.

Gabe swallowed a laugh. Keeping his voice low, he said, "Joe's a troublemaker. He meets Été at a dinner in Paris, finds out she's coming to New York, and invites her here to tease his pals. Her novel—"

"You didn't read it."

"I read about it—and the theory that it's more real than invented. Either way, some of those guys could've come right out of her book."

Gabe was no gossip, but he did tell her about Dulles. The married CIA director, notorious for his mistresses, had allegedly expanded the definition of *foreign affairs* by making love to the queen of Greece in his office. And Gabe was right—powerful men appeared everywhere in *Au Revoir, Papa*. In interviews, Été refused to confirm or deny her novel was a memoir. But the narrator is a teenager mourning her Vietnamese mother and fighting with her overbearing French father. To end her nights of opium and wild young men, her father sends her to a boarding school in Switzerland. The narrator runs away to Paris. She has affairs with her father's business associates and his uncle, a former minister of finance. When her father learns of the incestuous liaison, he beats her so badly she has to be admitted to a hospital, but she sneaks past the nurses and sets out for the Riviera, hoping, as Été wrote, "to find what I had been seeking all of my heartbroken life, a voice that would be mine, and mine alone."

"Here you are," Joe Alsop said. "Gabriel, Jack wanted to chat with you. And I'd like to speak to your lovely wife."

As Caitlin watched Gabe go, the columnist said, "Not much in common, those two. The Jewish ex-cop and Catholic rich boy. I wonder what they have to discuss."

"My husband doesn't talk about his work," she said, which was true and, in this case, misleading. Gabe had asked her to call Julian Rose to see if he'd meet with Jack. During Prohibition, Julian had been a top lieutenant to Longy Zwillman—New Jersey's Al Capone. Unlike Longy, Julian had avoided the IRS, FBI, and Senate investigations by quitting the rackets and building a real estate empire. Caitlin had called Julian at home. Gabe didn't say why Jack wanted the meeting, but to get to the White House, a candidate needed backing from local political bosses, and in New Jersey most of those predatory glad-handers owed Julian a favor.

Alsop said, "Gabe told me you had been a policewoman, and now you want to write. That's an interesting transition."

"I used to be an English teacher." Caitlin's life, as far as she was concerned, had been a muddle of accidents. Her desire to be a writer began around the time she taught herself to read, and ever since her twelfth birthday—when her mother, Maggie, took her to the Broadway musical *On the Town* and Caitlin departed the Adelphi Theatre humming "New York, New York"—she longed to exchange her small town for the roaring city across the Hudson. Yet when Caitlin graduated from Montclair State Teachers College, her mother was so far gone she could seldom recall her daughter's name. Caitlin lived with her on their side of the duplex, teaching high school English in Maplewood and paying one of their tenants to care for Maggie during the day. After her mother died, Caitlin rented out her half of the house and moved to a basement studio in Greenwich Village. The rental income was helpful, but she needed a job. She was tired of teaching, so when she heard on the radio that the police department was seeking college-educated women, she sat for the civil service exam. Caitlin was hired and began corralling runaways and checking on families until seeing what a father could do with his fists and a mother with a pan of boiling water made her ashamed to be human. Six months ago, after two years on the force, she quit and married Gabe and decided to chase her dream of becoming a writer.

Alsop said, "I mentioned your police work to Reed Howland, my editor at the *Saturday Evening Post*. He thinks your experience would make a fine piece."

"That was kind of you. But I've only reviewed *Summer and Smoke* and *The Iceman Cometh* for the *Newark Evening News*. I'm not ready for the *Post*."

"Let Reed be the judge of that." Alsop looked over her shoulder. "It appears your presence is required."

Caitlin turned. Gabe was waving for her to join him.

Alsop handed her his business card. "I've written Reed's number on the back. And no obligation, but the presidential campaign is going to be a doozy. If you hear anything—"

"I understand." And she did. Alsop had offered her a meeting with an editor as bait for information Gabe might pass along to her. That's how it went in Washington, she supposed. Caitlin didn't know if she wanted to play his game, but to keep her options open, she gave the columnist her prettiest noncommittal smile.

◆ ◆ ◆

Jack Kennedy was inspecting the porcelain figurines of flamenco dancers on a wall shelf when Gabe led Caitlin into the garden room and introduced her to him. With all the pictures of him in the press, the senator was a familiar sight to Caitlin—tall and slim with tousled chestnut hair and a college-boy face as bright and poignant as a fall afternoon. What surprised her was that in his gray suit and tie, and with lines at the corners of his greenish-gray eyes like gouges in smooth wood, he seemed weathered beyond his years and, somehow, fragile.

"Good to meet you," Jack said and held out his right hand.

His handshake was firm, not the dead fish men frequently reserved for women, but he winced when he stepped toward her, as though it hurt to move. His bad back was famous. Caitlin had read about his wartime injury in the *New Yorker*, when his boat, *PT-109*, was sunk by a Japanese destroyer, and he swam for five hours towing a burned crewman by clamping his life belt strap in his mouth. A few years ago it was all over the news that he lapsed into a coma following an operation on his spine, and a priest was summoned to administer the last rites.

"I enjoyed your book," Caitlin said, referring to *Profiles in Courage*, Jack's bestselling, Pulitzer Prize–winning portrait of eight senators he admired for their political bravery.

With the remote politeness of a candidate working a Rotary club, Jack replied, "Nice of you to say. I hope Mr. Rose shares your opinion. How do you know him?"

"My father was friends with him."

Jack studied her as if he knew she could say more and chose not to. He didn't seem put out by her choice, only curious, and his curiosity was appealing. Gabe was like that, always trying to figure her out. But Caitlin hadn't even told Gabe the whole story about her father. In 1931, Longy Zwillman and Siano Abruzzi, the premier bootleggers in Newark, had a disagreement over who would supply the bars. Her father owned Gallagher's Tavern and bought from Longy. In December, six months before Caitlin was born, the Abruzzis beat her father unconscious and torched his bar. He died in the fire, and his murderers turned up dead in the Passaic River—put there, according to Caitlin's mother, by Julian. He also looked after his friend's widow and daughter—purchasing the duplex for them, getting her mother a job in the cafeteria at Beth Israel Hospital in Newark, paying for Caitlin's schooling, and hiring her in the summers as a secretary. Julian didn't mention her father until she was in college. Caitlin was dropping the mail in his office when, out of the blue, he said, "Your dad was a sweet man. I was in his bar that night. If I hadn't left early . . ." He glanced at the mail on his desk. "Don't wrestle with the past, Cait. You can't win."

Jack said, "I'm hoping Mr. Rose will meet with us in Florida."

Caitlin replied, "He says maybe he'll see you and your father in New Jersey."

Jack flashed his boyish smile—the one magazine editors loved plastering on their covers—but he didn't appear amused. "Dad hates the winter up north."

"Julian mentioned that."

On the phone, Julian had referred to Joe Kennedy as an antisemitic SOB. Her mother had told her that before the war, Julian and his gangster buddies used to beat up American Nazis at their meetings. Longy had been close to Julian, and, along with his tax troubles and a charge of bribing jurors, Longy had been subpoenaed by the Senate Rackets Committee shortly before he killed himself. Jack had served on that committee, and his brother, Bobby, had been the chief counsel. Jack had to know some of this but still thought her making the call could help persuade Julian to meet with him. He was wrong, yet Caitlin, aware of how much Gabe liked Jack, didn't want to be the one to tell him.

Gabe said, "Jack, a guy like Julian, you got to ask him yourself. Call his office."

Jacqueline Kennedy materialized in the doorway. "Jack, we ought to be going."

Her voice was more authoritative than Caitlin had expected—the voice of a wife who wanted to go home. Now.

The senator didn't budge. "Jackie, you remember Gabe. And this is his wife, Caitlin."

"Nice to see you both," she said.

After clapping Gabe on the shoulder, Jack grinned at Caitlin. Jackie glared at her husband, and to Caitlin it felt as if someone had thrown open a window and let the winter in.

Outside, Gabe said to Été, "My company rents an apartment for me by Rock Creek Park. We can drop you."

"Thank you, no. Mr. Alsop phoned the Mayflower, and the concierge sends a car."

Gabe went to retrieve her suitcases from his trunk. Caitlin asked, "Was it worth the trip?"

Été let out a bubbly laugh. "I have the impression Mr. Dulles believes he can divine the mysteries of the Orient by removing my clothing." Something quirky flared up in her eyes, as if people, in all their flamboyant complexity, existed for her to transform into prose.

This was the quality, Caitlin thought, that had produced *Au Revoir, Papa*, and Caitlin envied it.

A station wagon pulled up. The driver, in a bellman's uniform with gold buttons, got out to take the bags from Gabe. Été put a hand on Caitlin's arm. "I apologize for falling asleep riding here. We were to talk about your writing."

"There's not much to talk about."

"I must go to Los Angeles to discuss the movie. Later in January, I am at the Algonquin Hotel, in New York. You call me, yes? I know no one there."

"You know Gabe and me."

Été hugged Caitlin. It was the hug of a lonely child, reminding Caitlin of how she felt when her mother was dying in the fog of her forgotten life. Caitlin held on to her, feeling her tremble, until, at last, Été got into the station wagon and was gone.

CHAPTER 6

Jack gazed down at his sleeping daughter. Caroline was on her side and smiling as if she knew her father was in the nursery watching her. He wanted to hold her, a reliable cure for the emptiness and sense of impending doom that had plagued him for as long as he could remember. But the surgeries on his back hadn't done a damn bit of good. The pain was constant. Bending over was impossible. Jack kissed his fingertips, then touched them to his daughter's forehead.

In the bedroom, Jacqueline sat on a chair in the light of an antique hurricane lamp, inspecting swatches of drapery fabric. No use fighting about her spending again. Jack knew his wife had her reasons for being angry at him, and his nickel-and-diming her on her decorating their house was at the bottom of her list. Behind her elegance, she had a vengeful streak—no hysterics, just a brooding silence that drove him nuts and made him feel helpless. So his most politic move, he decided after swallowing a codeine tablet and changing into his pajamas, was to keep quiet.

Murmuring a prayer, Jack crossed himself, then got under the quilt and drifted off to sleep, a mixed blessing because that dream was back. The night the *Amagiri*, a Japanese destroyer, rammed his patrol boat. A fireball lighting the sky, sailors bobbing in the sea, the hours of Jack swimming from island to island. Even after saving his crew and receiving the Navy and Marine Corps Medal, Jack felt waves of guilt for the two men under his command who had died. And the dream persisted.

Jack had resigned himself to living with it. Like he lived with Addison's disease, his disintegrating spine, the stubborn infections, and the excruciating ulcers and colitis, all of which reminded him that every breath had its price.

Tonight, though, the dream shifts to a cool blue afternoon. Jack sits on a beach and looks out to sea. The South Pacific islands are gone. He's confused. Then he realizes this is Hyannis Port. Sailboats skim across Nantucket Sound, and a woman walks out of the water in a white bathing suit. She has the same open, honest face and gold brown hair as his younger sister Kick. Jack feels elated. Kick was his closest friend and the most rebellious of the nine Kennedy children. Her marrying a Protestant British lord had outraged their pious mother. During the war, Kick worked for the Red Cross in London, and a month after her older brother Joe, a navy pilot, died on a bombing run, Kick's husband was killed by a German sniper. Kick remained in Britain, and in 1947, when she and Jack were in Ireland, Kick shared her big secret: she was in love with another royal Brit and Protestant, a married man who planned to divorce his wife and marry her—this last fact guaranteed to send Mother around the bend.

Yet this woman can't be Kick. In 1948, her plane had crashed in France, and her in-laws, the Duke and Duchess of Devonshire, had buried his radiant sister in an English churchyard.

Standing over him, the woman says, *You missed my funeral, Jack.*

His sister's voice startles him. "Kick?"

The duke and duchess gave me quite the Catholic send-off. At the Farm Street Church, in Mayfair. Enough stained glass in that joint for two cathedrals.

Jack mumbles, "I couldn't take seeing you like that. I prayed for you at Saint Francis Xavier."

Kick grins. *Did you go to confession?*

Jack returns the grin. "Not enough time."

Kick laughs, like God tells her jokes no one else can hear. *You're married, Jack. And still chasing girls. You won't have enough time to confess unless you quit the Senate.*

Embarrassed, Jack digs his fingers into the sand.

Your wife is beautiful. So why all this girling?

Jack lets the sand fall between his fingers. "I don't know. I can't stop."

Aren't you happy?

"When I see Caroline."

She's a gem.

"Kick, I miss you every day."

We'll be together again, Jack.

"You don't believe that, do you?"

I do. God calls us all. He's calling me now.

"Don't go, Kick."

Gracefully, the way he recalled Kick gliding across the dance floor at the Stork Club, she spins around and walks into the sea. Jack tasted salt water on his tongue and opened his eyes. Jackie was sitting on the bed, smoking a cigarette.

"You're restless," she said, stubbing out her Salem in the ashtray on the nightstand.

"I saw Kick in a dream."

"That girl—Caitlin. She resembled Kick in her pictures."

Jack wiped his eyes with a pajama sleeve.

Jackie said, "Go to sleep, Bunny. I'll turn out the light."

Then the room was dark, and his wife was beside him. Jack stared into the darkness for a long time before he fell asleep.

CHAPTER 7

Greenwich Village
January 1960

This, Caitlin thought, wrapping herself around her husband. *Just this.* The main event. Gabe was a master of the prelude, kissing her neck, a drizzle of fingertips on her thighs. He was excruciatingly patient. Caitlin sometimes resented his patience. It revealed the depth of her need for him. And her hunger for this—the slow, relentless rhythm winding her up. The nuns' warnings about prurience a far-off joke as she met Gabe's thrusts with fiercer thrusts of her own. Under her eyelids, a white light, a summer memory, the hot sand at Lavallette, the scent of the sea and the suntan lotion on her baking skin. Caitlin was going away into that light, aware of nothing beyond the tightness at the center of her until the long unwinding began, and Caitlin cried out and Gabe stiffened against her, his muscles under her hands as hard as marble.

After they broke apart and lay side by side, Gabe whispered in the dark, "You think we made a baby?"

"No."

"Why *no*?"

Caitlin said, "Because I'm pregnant."

"You are? You're positive?"

"My period's a week late, and you can set Greenwich Mean Time by my cycle."

In a glimmer of moonlight through the curtains, Caitlin saw worry lines creasing Gabe's forehead. "You gotta see a doctor, don't you?"

"I found an obstetrician in Manhattan. I'll see her eventually."

"We should buy a baby-name book." His tone implied that if they didn't purchase one immediately, their child would go through life nameless.

Caitlin stifled a laugh. "Brentano's isn't open now."

She slid closer, feeling his body along the length of her, and later, a languid moment away from sleep, she heard Gabe say, "We better get that book."

That morning, Caitlin woke up alone and, after digging out a robe and slippers from one of the mover's boxes, went to find Gabe. She had planned to tell him about her pregnancy on New Year's Eve, but they weren't done packing in Brooklyn, and the next day they moved into a five-story, red-sandstone building on Grove Street. Caitlin had fallen in love with the third-floor, light-filled three bedroom as soon as the rental agent had shown it to her—the high windows overlooking the narrow triangle of Christopher Park with its trees looming over a statue of Union hero General Philip Sheridan.

Caitlin was going to use the smallest bedroom as her study, and that was where she found Gabe. He was kneeling on a drop cloth and dipping a brush into a can of stain to touch up the brown-maple rolltop desk he'd refinished for her.

"It's gorgeous, Gabe. Thank you."

"It'll be dry tomorrow, so you can start that article for the *Saturday Evening Post*."

"I'm just meeting that editor, Reed Howland, when he comes up from Philadelphia. We spoke on the phone for ten minutes, and he didn't ask me to write anything."

Gabe set the brush on top of the can. "Alsop told me he will, and writers write, don't they? It can't hurt to start."

"I have to go to South Orange and fix a leaky toilet."

"Caitlin." He used her full name only when he was annoyed with her. "You're having a baby; you shouldn't be doing that. Call a plumber. Or let me drive you."

"I like to read on the bus." If Gabe didn't calm down about her pregnancy, they'd both be ready for the loony bin by her ninth month. "Sweetheart, I'm pregnant. Not sick. Let's have breakfast. I'll make french toast."

"The coffee's made, and I got the papers. They're on the counter. Jack announced he's running for president."

In the kitchen, Caitlin whisked eggs, milk, cinnamon, and vanilla extract in a bowl and told herself that she rode the bus to New Jersey every six weeks because she was a conscientious landlord, performing the routine maintenance on her duplex she'd taught herself to do as a teenager to spare her mother the expense of a handyman. This was partially true. The other part of the truth went back to an evening four years ago. Her mother's mind was gone, and her body wasn't far behind. Caitlin was sitting on her bed. Maggie was under the covers staring at her.

"Pretty girl," she said.

"I look like you, Mama."

"Will you go get me a pack of cigarettes?"

"Tomorrow, Mama." Maggie hadn't smoked in a year, but the request cheered up Caitlin. It was a sign that her mother knew she was talking to her daughter. In the evenings, if Maggie ran out of Pall Malls, she used to send Caitlin to the police station in South Orange Village to buy a pack from the cigarette machine.

Her mother gazed at her. "Why do you call me *Mama*?"

"You're my mother."

Maggie shut her eyes. "Yes."

The *yes*, Caitlin liked to believe, proved that her mother had recognized her. Maggie was gone by midnight. Even before phoning the funeral home, Caitlin decided she had a duty to hold on to the memory of their life together. That was why she'd kept the duplex. Perhaps she'd sell it after her baby was born. Once Caitlin was a mother, her own mother would be with her whenever she fed or bathed her child. Every mundane act of love would be a restoration. Mother and daughter would be alive in the same body, making it impossible for Caitlin to lose her again.

CHAPTER 8

South Orange, New Jersey

Caitlin's reward for installing a new flapper in the toilet would be a stop at Gruning's. It was a short walk. All along Cottage Street, tinsel-laced Christmas trees were out on the curb with the trash. A green sports car was idling at the end of the block. Sports cars were as rare as chariots on Cottage Street. As Caitlin approached the car, it took off around the corner, and she glimpsed the driver through the rear window. Like the man who had been watching her on MacDougal, the driver was wearing a fedora and an overcoat with the velvet collar turned up. Caitlin was frightened, but it didn't last. There was no reason she knew of that anyone would be tailing her. Those hats and coats weren't uncommon, and except for Gabe, nobody knew where she was going or had followed her off the bus.

Gruning's, in the middle of South Orange Village, served as a meetinghouse for young and old. Caitlin remembered the crowds outside when President Roosevelt died and the following August, when World War II ended. Inside, a soda fountain was across from a long glass case of handmade chocolates and jelly slices arrayed on doilies like sugared rainbows. Past the candies were red leather booths, and up a few steps was a room where teenagers listened to the jukebox and boys practiced smoking cigarettes like James Dean. The primary draw was the ice cream, made in the factory out back, and among its biggest fans was

Julian Rose, who was paying the cashier at the register when Caitlin came through the doors.

"Coffee chip," Caitlin said after standing on her tiptoes to hug him.

Julian picked up the string handles of a takeout bag. "How'd you know?"

They laughed. When Caitlin had worked for him in the summers, Julian had sent her to Gruning's every Friday to bring back a quart of coffee chip, which they ate for lunch.

Julian said, "Tell Gabe I'm seeing the Kennedys next week."

"I will." She wanted to tell him about the baby. He was the closest thing Caitlin had to a living parent. It would be more prudent to wait another two months. An article in *Redbook* claimed that 80 percent of miscarriages occurred in the first trimester. But when Julian asked, "What's up, Cait?" she couldn't resist.

"I'm pregnant."

Her father, a friend of Julian's, had been murdered twenty-nine years ago, yet here was Julian, no stranger to violence, his eyes glistening. Caitlin tried to combine the two pieces of the man. They didn't fit, and her only explanation was the poetic wisdom of Walt Whitman—*we contain multitudes.*

"That's wonderful, Cait."

Julian put on a happy face, but he must've still been thinking about her father, because when he left, one hand was holding the bag while the other brushed at his eyes.

Caitlin sat in a booth, eating a scoop of coffee chip with hot fudge and whipped cream and thinking about something Gabe had said—*writers write, don't they?* His implied criticism that she wasn't working rankled her. Then he'd suggested that it couldn't hurt to get started. It sure as hell could hurt. Suppose her dreams exceeded her talent?

Only one way to find out, Caitlin could hear her husband reply, and to shut up the imaginary Gabe, Caitlin pulled a marble-cover composition book and ballpoint from her leather courier bag. In her exquisite handwriting, a legacy of her Catholic-school education, she wrote:

> I met my husband because a self-defense instructor at the Police Academy, a bruiser with an IQ equal to his shoe size and the conviction that women were unqualified for any duties beyond crossing schoolchildren, strangled me.

Not bad. The test? You wanted to read the next sentence. Caitlin kept writing:

> The bruiser, Sgt. Heany, let me go. I collapsed. Heany looked at me as if a puppy had made a mess on the floor. The gym was packed with recruits and instructors at the Police Academy.

Caitlin remembered her humiliation as she'd left for the day. The department had considered it pointless to offer self-defense training to the seven female recruits, and Heany had been out to demonstrate just how pointless it was.

> "You want to learn to defend yourself, I'll train you."
> I turned and saw Detective Gabe Russo. He had been temporarily assigned to the Academy to lecture on interrogating suspects. During his lecture, I thought he was clever and handsome, but I had no plans to date a cop and asked him, with more than a trace of sarcasm in my voice, what sort of training he had in mind.
> He gave me an index card. "I'm not much for double entendres. That's the address. You want to train, be there at five tomorrow."

The address was for a boxing gym in Chinatown, and for three hours every evening except Sunday, Gabe taught her how to deal with an attacker. There was no small talk, and Gabe didn't ask her out. Two weeks later, Heany selected her to play the victim.

> Seeing the light reflecting on his shaved, bullet-shaped head was so alarming I forgot every move Gabe had taught me. Then Heany was pressing his thumbs into my neck. I ducked under his arms, stepped back, and escaped. He smirked, grabbing my sweatshirt and pulling me toward him. I kneed him between his legs. Gabe had warned me: this was no guarantee a guy would go down, and Healy didn't. He did bend over, though, and I drove the heel of my hand into his nose. He staggered back. I kicked his right knee, and Heany fell. He was on all fours, staring up at me, blood trickling from his nostrils.
>
> Gabe was waiting for me in the hallway. I thanked him again and asked, "Why'd you help me?"
>
> "Lady cops should be able to handle themselves. And—" Gabe glanced down at his wing tips as if making sure his shoes were shined before he said, "You're beautiful, and I didn't want anything to happen to your face."

Caitlin reread the pages. Not a bad start. She paid the check and went out. The streetlamps were on, and snow sparkled as it fell past the gaslights. She crossed South Orange Avenue to the bus stop. She had her pages, a husband, and a baby on the way. She felt a happiness that had always seemed beyond her reach.

Caitlin wished her mother were alive so she could tell her.

CHAPTER 9

South Orange, New Jersey

Three Kennedys were in Julian Rose's oak-paneled library, and, as far as Jack could tell, not one of them was happy to be there. Jack, the most curious Kennedy, was the least unhappy. He had never met a well-read ex-gangster.

"I was sorry to hear about Longy," Joe Kennedy said.

The ambassador was seated on a Danish modern couch, with his sons on either side of him. Julian faced them from a chrome-and-leather sling chair. Jack could picture Julian playing an aging cowboy in the movies. A Gary Cooper with dark hair graying at the temples and an unnatural stillness that gave him a vaguely menacing air.

Julian said, "A shame your boys didn't get to grill him in front of their committee."

Bobby, who had been the chief counsel of the Senate committee, snapped, "Mr. Rose, we were investigating labor racketeering. Your friend Longy earned his subpoena."

Jack admired Bobby's pugnaciousness, yet his altar boy's faith in his own virtue was irritating, and because Jack was here to ask Julian for a favor, he glared at his brother, signaling him to shut the fuck up.

Julian gazed at Bobby. "He did earn it. And I told my friend: when you questioned him, he should mention your father selling him and his partners his liquor distributorship in 1946. Right before Jack's first run for Congress. I heard a suitcase of cash was involved. Is that correct, Joe? Any of that cash get funneled into your son's campaign?"

No one spoke. At last, the ambassador gave Jack's knee an affectionate pat. "My boy wants to be president."

"So does Mrs. Nixon's boy," Julian said.

His expression revealed nothing. Jack had had his staff compile a report on Julian. He'd read about his fighting with the Office of Strategic Services in France and a story of his interrogating a Nazi general before the war crime trials began at Nuremberg. They were in an interview room in the Palace of Justice, and when the general denied any knowledge of the death camps, Julian slammed his head against a wall. Jack could see Julian with the same expression the instant before he rang the general's bell.

Joe loosened his tie. "I gave Dick money for his Senate campaign, and if the Democrats don't nominate Jack, I'll vote for him. But Jack will make a better president. Because, like Jack says, 'He's got ideals but no illusions.'"

Julian startled the Kennedys by chuckling. "Which means he'll know the right thing to do but won't do it?"

Jack said, "It means I'll do what I have to do to win."

Julian stretched out his long legs. "That doesn't tell me why you'd be better than Nixon."

Jack walked over to the wall of bookcases. Contrasting himself with Dick wasn't easy. The two men had come to the House in 1947. While they were from different parties, they agreed on so much, especially that the United States could never back down to the Soviets or their Communist allies, foreign or domestic. Jack believed that Dick was as smart and tough as anyone in Congress and would one day sit in the Oval Office. In 1950, Dick made it to the Senate. Jack caught up to him two years later, but by then Eisenhower had selected Dick as his vice president, and Dick distinguished himself as an effective stand-in for Ike when he was sidelined by a heart attack. Jack had to concede that Dick, with his hardscrabble boyhood in rural California, understood most Americans in a way that he did not. Their worries about piles of unpaid bills and their children dancing to that sex-crazed rock 'n' roll; their resentment of taxes going up, up, up and politicians who didn't give a tinker's damn about them; their fear of an incomprehensible future, all while the Soviets were poised to reduce their country to nuclear ash. Nevertheless, Jack wasn't without his advantages. A Harvard-educated war hero with the looks and poise of a matinee idol, a father who could finance his run, and a coterie of young mavericks to help him. But his ace in the hole was that Jack knew what people seldom admitted to themselves: every hour aboveground was a gift. His brother and sister had been killed in their twenties. Jack had been sick forever and had received the last rites four times. He didn't worry about the future because he wasn't sure he'd have one. Nor did he mistake his attitude for courage. It was his acceptance of the fact that everyone was headed to the grave. That was the source of his ironic humor and his talent for inspiring people to set aside their fears and be better than they ever imagined.

Taking a book from the shelf, Jack looked at Julian. "I saw this when we came in. Max Weber's lectures. I read it in college. Weber writes that we can't achieve the possible unless we attempt the impossible, and to do that requires a leader with—"

"Charismatic authority," Julian said. "Hitler had that in spades."

"So did Franklin Roosevelt." Jack put the book back on the shelf. "Mr. Rose, Dick Nixon would be a competent president. That's not enough, not today. The world spins too quickly. The speed scares people, and when people are scared, they freeze. A president has to get them moving. There is too much poverty here, and we have to get involved with poor nations everywhere—it's how to beat back the Communists. We need more schools and science programs to keep pace with the Soviets, and we have to explore outer space—someday our national defense will depend on it. We need the same spirit that won the war, and that's what I can do. Inspire Americans and create that spirit."

Jack couldn't tell whether he was persuading Julian, who appeared to be sleeping with his eyes open. "Mr. Rose, there are Americans who think if a Catholic is elected president, the pope will rule the country. I doubt they think any better of Jews. You disliked my father's isolationism. So did I. And my family did its share in the war—we lost my brother and brother-in-law fighting the Nazis, and I'm lucky to be alive. There's no shortage of Catholics in New Jersey, or Jews, Negroes, and immigrants. Those are my voters, and I hope you'll help me win this state."

Julian said, "New Jersey also has no shortage of Republicans."

The ambassador had stayed out of the conversation and hadn't reacted to Jack bringing up his isolationism because he didn't want to antagonize Julian. Now, softly, he said, "Bobby, what'd you find?"

Bobby, who had resigned from the Rackets Committee and become his brother's campaign manager, removed a notebook from the inner pocket of his suit coat and opened it. "The Republicans are in the farm districts and the suburbs, but the cities have more votes, and they'll go for Jack. There are twenty-one counties in New Jersey, and if he wins Essex, Hudson, Mercer, Middlesex, Passaic, and a couple of the smaller ones, he'll win here."

Julian studied Jack. "And you'd like me to talk to the mayors and county bosses?"

"I would, Mr. Rose."

Julian stood. "I'll be in touch."

The Kennedys had taken a limousine from Manhattan to New Jersey. After they sank into the back seat, the ambassador drew the black curtain across the partition separating the chauffeur from the passengers.

Bobby asked, "What'd you think of him, Jack?"

"He'll call because he said he would. But he's still pissed off at Dad. And he looks like he could kill somebody without breaking a sweat."

"He's had a lot of practice," the ambassador said. "Which is why I wanted you fucking idiots to stay off that committee and leave the mobsters alone."

Jack and Bobby had heard this harangue before, and they were not inclined to suffer through a replay. Bobby said, "There's no way to pressure Rose to help us. I got ahold of his FBI file. Not much in it. And he doesn't need any of Dad's money."

The ambassador grinned. "That makes him different than you two."

It was intended as a humorous swipe at his boys, who lived off their trust funds, yet Jack and Bobby knew their father was still put out they had ignored his advice.

As the limousine emerged from the Lincoln Tunnel, the ambassador asked, "You'll have dinner with me at Le Pavillon?"

The restaurant, located in the Ritz Tower Hotel, served excellent French food. Bobby agreed to join his father, but Jack said, "I'll skip it. I feel like taking a walk."

"A walk?" His brother snorted. "It's freezing out, and yesterday you were on crutches."

Jack knew Bobby suspected he was going off to meet a girl, and ordinarily he found his brother's holier-than-thou act more amusing than annoying. Yet the codeine was wearing off, and his lower back was on fire. Jack was in no mood for it and jabbed at Bobby's piety. "I'm cured. I drank a vial of holy water from Lourdes."

The ambassador folded his arms across his chest. "Jesus Christ, Jack. A gossip columnist writes about you shaking the sheets with all those babes, you can forget about the White House."

His father had had scores of affairs, and Jack smiled at him, saying, "Dad, you don't qualify to give that lecture."

"Goddamn it, I'm not the Irish Catholic running for president. When the priests read about it, they'll cut your balls off, and the church biddies will vote for anyone except you."

Jack wanted neither to fight nor to hurt his father by telling him the truth. Three years before Jack announced his candidacy, he had been on the road speaking to groups and meeting local officials, and sometimes, when he was racked with pain, quitting was tempting. With his health problems, how many years did he really have left, and did he want to spend them in Wisconsin diners and West Virginia coal mines and wherever else he had to campaign to win a primary? He'd rather watch Caroline grow up and have more children with Jackie and go sailing and chase his side action without worrying about gossipmongers, Khrushchev and Castro, and the thermonuclear flashes of World War III.

The limousine pulled over on Fifty-Seventh Street, outside the Ritz Tower. "Talk to you both tomorrow," Jack said, then climbed out of the back seat and got into a taxi.

"Fifty-Nine West Forty-Fourth," he told the driver and glanced at his watch. He was supposed to be at the Algonquin Hotel an hour ago, so upon arriving, he'd have to endure another tirade about his bad manners.

Été hated it when he was late.

CHAPTER 10

Greenwich Village

"Do you have to carry all the time?" Caitlin asked.

Gabe holstered his .38 Detective Special on his right hip and put on a heathery sport jacket. "It gives me an excuse to show off my new Harris Tweed. What do you think?"

Caitlin was sitting on the bed, brushing her hair. Her expression indicated that she couldn't have cared less if he were wearing a bowling shirt. "I don't believe you work for the State Department. That creepy Dulles character was looking over at us at Alsop's party, and he knows you, I'm sure of it. You work for the CIA."

In Georgetown, Gabe had thought that by avoiding Dulles, Cait wouldn't notice any connection. That was wishful thinking. His wife was a goddamn radar station.

Caitlin stopped brushing. "New apartment, new rules. Tell me the truth."

Gabe bent over the bed and snapped his suitcase closed. "Don't you have your lunch today with that *Saturday Evening Post* guy?"

"Yes. And don't change the subject."

Gabe went with a half-truth. "I handle security for a private company, Q&D Relocation Services. Our government houses people around the world. I check that they're safe."

"You work with spies?"

"With Ivy League sissies who want to be tough guys. Like last month, I saw that a bunch of them had hired these young, good-looking maids. I'm thinking the guys will wind up in bed with them and talk too much. And somebody could pay the maids for that information."

"Like the Russians?"

"Cait, stop being dramatic."

"Dramatic? Why? Because I want our child to have a father—not what I had, a grave to visit at Mount Olivet Cemetery?"

Gabe winced at the thought that he would leave their child fatherless. A little defensively, he said, "All I did was tell those guys there are plenty of gray-haired grandmas who need the work." Gabe had skipped the part about investigating the bank accounts and contacts of the CIA men to make sure the Soviets or Cubans hadn't turned them into double agents. He didn't mention that he'd been paying Victor Diaz to smuggle arms to Castro's opposition in Cuba, and that he had graduated to assassin, and that the CIA had set up a phony company for him so no intelligence service could connect his activities to the government.

Gabe kissed her. Her lips responded—slightly. "I'll call when I find out my schedule. And don't worry. My job's safer than walking a beat in Brooklyn."

With the sun shining through the window, her blue eyes glimmered like sapphires. Gabe could've looked at her face forever, but instead he grabbed his suitcase and, in the living room, turned back. Cait was staring at the floor and looking as though she was waiting for the ceiling to collapse.

His Chevy Bel Air was parked on Waverly Place, across from the triangular brick Northern Dispensary, a medical and dental clinic. Gabe tossed his suitcase into the trunk. A Checker cab stopped alongside the dispensary. The driver, with a Greek fisherman's cap on his head, eyed the Chevy. Gabe froze, his right hand going to the grip of his .38.

The taxi drove off. Gabe leaned down into the trunk and opened his briefcase, then removed the pistol with the silencer. He hid it behind the spare tire that was stored in a well on the right side of the trunk. If his .38 bothered Cait, he'd hate to hear what she'd say about the High Standard automatic.

Fact was, his job scared him. Victor had needed to go, but Gabe hadn't planned on being the one to relocate him. He'd been hired to babysit a bunch of innocents who could quote Aristotle but had never met a pickpocket, and now he had developed a fear of taxicabs. A feeling that the drivers were tailing him. Cait had claimed she was being watched. Was she imagining it? Or could the CIA be shadowing her in order to keep tabs on him? Or the Soviets? Possibly. The KGB had agents in the city. Gabe hadn't felt such dread since Okinawa, with the Japanese artillery rounds exploding around him. Back then, he'd seen death as a remedy for his fear. He didn't have that luxury now, with Cait and the baby. As a cop, Gabe would've hauled down ten grand a year—tops. The CIA paid him twenty. He wasn't going anywhere.

Taking the briefcase, Gabe headed to Prince Street, where an artist friend of Cait's lived in a loft above Fanelli Cafe. Cait had met her after relocating from Jersey. Her nickname was Winkie, due to a condition that caused her to blink constantly. She must not have minded, because that was how she signed her artwork. Before asking Winkie to give him a hand, Gabe made her swear not to tell anyone. It wasn't foolproof, but it beat hiring a stranger who might run his mouth.

"Hey, Gabriel," Winkie said, sliding back the loft door. She was Cait's age, but with her coppery helmet of hair, her freckles, and the gray sweatshirt and overalls she was wearing, she could have passed for a teenager.

"How'd it go?" he asked.

"Come see." Winkie crossed the cement floor to a worktable cluttered with sketch pads, pencils, and etching tools. In the center of the table was a silver cigar box. Gabe had bought the humidor at Tiffany, and Winkie had engraved an inscription across the lid: **To Premier Fidel Castro from the People of New York City, September 1960**

"Beautiful," Gabe said.

"How do you know he'll be here in September?"

"That's when the United Nations General Assembly meets. Castro will give a speech."

Winkie looked up at him, her eyelids fluttering. "Cait called yesterday. Congratulations on the baby."

"Did you tell—"

"You told me mum's the word, but she's wigging out, not knowing what you're up to. And man, this inscription knocked me off my ledge. What's with you and Castro? He just wants what's best for Cuba."

"Right," Gabe said, slipping the silver box into his briefcase. He took four one-hundred-dollar bills from his pocket and put them on the table.

Winkie said, "I told you, no charge."

"The money's not for the engraving. It's for keeping quiet."

The legendary Danny Cohen. Cops would be talking about him as long as bartenders poured drinks. The storytellers seldom failed to mention Danny didn't look like a cop. He was a wiry Jew from the Lower East Side with a blond crew cut and dreamy brown eyes. He was thirty-three but looked ten years younger, with a face you could call *pretty*. With that face, and being Jewish, Danny had a lot to prove. Irish cops were half the department. Their opinion: Jews would rather read than fight. Gabe they left alone. He was built like a longshoreman, and with the last name of Russo, they made him for a wop. But Cohen? That was like waving a red cape at a bull. A dumb Irish prick once tried out a joke on Danny, asking him if he knew the difference between a pie and a Jew. Before Danny answered, the prick said, "A pie don't scream when you stick it in the oven," and Danny, a strong, crafty practitioner of the sucker punch, broke the comedian's nose.

This was the background music to the legend. The main theme: Danny Cohen was maybe the bravest, toughest cop ever to serve the good citizens of the city. Gabe had been his partner, working narcotics in Midtown, gangs in Washington Heights, and homicides in the Bronx. To Gabe, Danny wasn't brave or tough. He was out of his fucking mind.

For example: One day, a whacked-out glue-sniffer was on a roof with a hunting rifle, shooting up 156th Street. Danny and Gabe had just finished lunch next door, and as Gabe ducked behind a truck to help a little girl who'd been hit in the leg, Danny walked through the bullets snapping past him and entered the building. Minutes later, the glue-sniffer pancaked on the sidewalk. Danny came out with the rifle and said to Gabe, "He slipped."

Now, Danny was a captain and the commanding officer of the Sixth Precinct, which policed Greenwich Village, and one of the reasons Gabe stopped at the Charles Street station house. Danny was at the food cart outside, buying a hot chocolate.

"You want something?" he asked.

"I'm good."

Danny said, "Cait sent a postcard with the new address and phone number. I was gonna touch base and see if you wanted to get a drink at McSorley's."

"There's closer places in the Village."

"But McSorley's is men only, so I can't meet another of my future ex-wives."

Danny had a habit of falling in love at first sight, getting married, and discovering, much to his chagrin, that his bride expected him to be home before midnight in a state of relative sobriety. Danny was four years younger than Gabe, but he had two marriages behind him and a third awaiting the guillotine in court.

Trying to sound casual, Gabe said, "Last April, when Castro was in the city, you were on that security detail watching him."

"For his trip to the Bronx Zoo. Kids mobbed him like Santa Claus had dropped in early."

"Castro's no Santa. He's coming here again in September. You know any cops who'll be handling his security?"

Danny sipped his cocoa. "Why you asking?"

Gabe felt ashamed for even broaching the subject with his former partner. "Curious."

Danny squinted at Gabe as if he were a suspect bullshitting him. "Cops pull a lot of stunts. But we don't whack anybody over his politics."

Gabe backed off. "Who's asking you to? I came by because I need a favor. A couple weeks ago, Cait thought a guy on MacDougal was following her. My new job's got me on the road a lot. Could you send a car past our apartment once in a while?"

"What's going on, Gabe?"

"Nothing."

Danny tossed his cup into a trash can. "I'll send the car."

CHAPTER 11

New York City

At twelve thirty, the tables in the Bar Room at 21 were crowded with men in impeccably tailored suits and women straight from the pages of *Vogue*. There were conversations everywhere, soft as candlelight, with flare-ups of laughter lit by scotch, bourbon, and gin.

Caitlin studied the model boats, toy trucks, stuffed animals, ballet slippers, and football helmets dangling from the ceiling, all of them donated by famous patrons of the restaurant. "First time here?" Reed Howland asked.

Caitlin felt as if a teacher had caught her daydreaming. She had been nervous about meeting the editor, and being surrounded by sophisticated New Yorkers wasn't helpful. "Is it obvious?"

Howland smiled as though he was concerned that he'd offended her. "First-timers can't help it. This place is a circus, but I have a weakness for their chicken hash, so when I'm up from Philadelphia, I can't resist."

Caitlin watched him drink his old-fashioned. She guessed he was forty. His fair, wavy hair was as thick as a teenager's and curled over the collar of his olive corduroy suit jacket, but his face—which may have been the best-looking face in his prep school yearbook—was webbed with lines around his eyes and mouth. It was a captivating face, and Caitlin thought there must be a story behind every line. Yet instead of talking about himself, Howland had drawn her out. Spurred on by a martini, Caitlin had talked about her life until, worried that she was rambling, she stopped and stared at the peculiar collection on the ceiling.

Howland set his empty glass on the red-and-white-checkered table-cloth. "You didn't mention why you resigned from the police force."

That wasn't an oversight. Caitlin was unsure what he'd think of her after she told him.

The waiter brought their lunch. The creamy chicken hash was served over wild rice and topped with spinach and a crust of cheese. Caitlin had lost her appetite. Howland dug in with gusto. If she wanted to sell an article to the *Saturday Evening Post*, Caitlin would have to tell him. She ate enough to be polite, then said, "It happened when I was assigned to the Youth Division."

Howland put his fork on his plate.

"Kevin Walsh. He was eleven years old, red hair, freckles. His parents couldn't decide whether to murder each other or drink themselves to death. The city put Kevin in an orphanage—Saint John's in Queens. He'd run away, and I'd find him in the playground by Holy Cross Church. It's in Hell's Kitchen, his neighborhood. I assumed he missed his friends. The third time I found him, I asked if there was a problem at Saint John's. He says, 'No, I came to get my mom. Dad's gonna kill her one day. She sometimes goes to Mass.' I suggested we go by his parents', and Kevin says, 'I did. They got kicked out for not paying rent. I can't find them.' His mother didn't show. He was trembling, trying not to cry. I took him to Tad's in Times Square for a steak dinner. He hugged me when I returned him to Saint John's. After I left, I was a mess. I hadn't cried like that since my mother's funeral."

So softly it was barely audible above the chitchat in the Bar Room, Howland asked, "What happened?"

His eyes, Caitlin noticed, were green. "I did some digging and got his parents' address, thinking I'd go by with Kevin when he ran away again. A few weeks later, he did. Except Kevin wasn't in the playground.

I wondered if he'd located his folks. So I go there. A building behind Port Authority with plywood over half the windows. Inside, people are standing in the hall, and I hear shouting. An old man says, 'The Walshes are at it again. My wife just called the cops.' I follow the shouts, bang on the door, and it opens. The lock's broken. I go in. Kevin's sitting on the kitchen floor holding his arm and crying. His mother's in a housecoat by the stove, with a saucepan in her hand. Her red hair's up in curlers, and she has a bloody lip. The father's by the table. Short guy with big shoulders and a beer gut. 'Arrest that bitch,' he says. 'She threw boiling water on Kevin.' The mother screams, 'It was an accident! You punched me. The water was for you.' I say, 'Let's relax; Kevin's hurt.' The father explodes, 'You won't handle her; I will!' He grabs a baseball bat off a chair. I order him to drop it, and he cocks the bat like I said *batter up*. I reach into my purse for my pistol and point it at him, and his wife yells, 'Don't shoot him!' and she pulls a butcher knife from a drawer."

The waiter arrived and cleared their plates. "Coffee? Dessert?"

"Give us a few minutes," Howland replied.

When the waiter was gone, Caitlin said, "I used to do extra hours practicing at the NYPD firing range, but I never thought I'd shoot anyone. Not until Kevin's mother runs at me, raising the knife. I throw up my arm. The knife cuts me above the elbow, and I shoot her in the knee. She's screaming and rolling on the orange linoleum. Kevin crawls to her. The husband swings the bat at me. He must've been drunk and misses by a foot. The department issued women .32-caliber pistols. Not enough stopping power for a guy his size. Shooting him in the knee won't work, so I aim at his head and say, 'I'll kill you.' That's when two officers show up. They arrested Kevin's parents, and after the department ruled my shooting the mother was justified, I resigned. I didn't want to stay until I killed someone. Worst part was afterward when I tried to talk to Kevin, he wouldn't even look at me."

The waiter returned. Howland said to Caitlin, "Coffee?" She nodded. He held up two fingers, and the waiter went away.

Not wanting to talk about Kevin anymore, Caitlin turned the conversation toward Howland. "How did you become an editor at the *Post*?"

"By accident. I'd graduated college and gotten married and was working at the State Department when Pearl Harbor was attacked. My boss wouldn't let me enlist. I spent the war in DC and London. When it ended, I traveled through Europe writing reports on how we could assist countries with their recovery. Then I worked in our embassies in Moscow and Paris. Marjorie, my wife, was with me in France. She was diagnosed with cancer, and that's where she died."

"I'm so sorry."

"Thank you. It was an ordeal. Marjorie was a take-charge gal, and I was lost without her. I'd been raised in Philadelphia, and I went home and wrote a series of articles on postwar Europe. The *Post* published them just as an editor job opened up, and they offered it to me. Only downside is that I hate the cold. Every chance I get in the winter, I go to the Caribbean. My favorite part of the job is helping new writers. I'd like to help you. You have a compelling story. You seem hesitant, though. Why is that?"

The waiter delivered their coffee. Howland drank his black. Caitlin added a drop of cream. "I always wanted to be a writer. My mother was a brave woman. She taught me to work hard and take care of myself. She forgot to mention that dreams can come true. Hers never did."

Howland put his coffee cup in its saucer. "You don't have to be an aristocrat like Edith Wharton to be a writer. Lillian Hellman's father sold shoes. Anyone can try, including Irish girls from New Jersey. Why don't you write me some pages and send them along?"

Caitlin had edited and typed the pages she had written at Gruning's and stuck them in a manila envelope. She wasn't sure if she was committing a faux pas, but she slid the envelope out of her courier bag. "I made a start."

Howland smiled. "Very good. I'll read it on the train."

CHAPTER 12

Washington, DC

When Gabe first saw the CIA building complex on E Street NW, he wondered who had attached the CENTRAL INTELLIGENCE AGENCY sign to the chain-link fence out front. Probably the same mastermind who didn't care that the parking lot was visible through the fence, so anyone could write down the license plates and track the cars. Gabe had pointed out the security lapse to Director Dulles. Nothing had changed, which was why Gabe parked a half mile away from the complex.

Today, Gabe had an early meeting with the director. Accustomed to the rigid command structure of the marines and the NYPD, Gabe found it odd that Dulles served as his case officer, defining and supervising his assignments. Not that Gabe blamed him. Managing field operations had to be more interesting than keeping pencil pushers in line.

"Mr. Russo," the director said, glancing up from the blueprint on his desk. "Take a seat."

In their last phone call, Jack had told Gabe that he'd bumped into Dulles at the Occidental Grill and that the director was obsessed with erecting a legacy to himself, a CIA campus in Langley, Virginia.

The director, reaching across his desk to a pipe rack, selected a corncob. "I saw the New York papers had little to say about the demise of Mr. Diaz."

"Victor had priors in Miami for running prostitutes and knocking them around. New York detectives would've seen his sheet and told reporters the city was better off without him."

Dulles filled the corncob from a plaid tobacco pouch. "Our agent who recruited Mr. Diaz trusted him. Do you know why he went bad?"

"Victor was a criminal. Criminals tend to be too enterprising for their own good."

The deal with Victor had been simple. The CIA had trucked small arms and ammunition to a warehouse in Florida, and Gabe paid Victor to arrange for the munitions to be smuggled into Cuba for Castro's enemies. It had gone smoothly until Victor sold information about the operation to an ally of Castro, and the shipment was stolen.

The director lit his pipe. "How did you uncover Mr. Diaz's change of heart?"

The answer was Yenchi Baylin, but Gabe had promised to keep him out of it. "A source."

Dulles glared at Gabe through a pungent fog. "I could insist you name him."

"And I could quit."

The director pushed his wire-rimmed glasses up the bridge of his nose. "Respect for others is ideal. And irrelevant when dealing with the Soviets and their friend, Castro, none of whom fight by Marquess of Queensberry rules. Moral flexibility is how we avoid nuclear Armageddon. For some individuals, that flexibility can be troublesome. Are you comfortable with it?"

"More comfortable than Victor."

Dulles acknowledged the wisecrack with an avuncular grin. "We've been drafting a policy paper outlining our options for assisting Cuba."

Assisting, Gabe knew, was CIA-speak for *overthrowing Castro*. He took the silver cigar box from his briefcase and gave it to Dulles, who set it next to the blueprint and read the inscription on the lid. "Nicely done, Mr. Russo. Did you speak to your police contact?"

"I did. Your plan's a no-go."

With a forefinger, Dulles stroked his mustache—the pensive gesture, Gabe thought, of a venomous wizard. "Castro's April visit here distressed me. He went to Princeton—my alma mater, it pains me to say. I'm told the students behaved like Elvis Presley was in town, and the professors fawned over him as if he was about to endow a chair for each of them. I trust his next visit will be less pleasant."

If there was one thing Gabe had learned listening to the Ivy Leaguers from Special Activities and the Directorate of Plans, it was that they believed killing Commies was God's work. The silver box, he assumed, would be wired with explosives, and one day he'd pick up a newspaper and read the headline Castro Goes Boom!

The director lifted a file folder from a drawer. "We've discovered that a French freighter will deliver a shipment of Belgian munitions to Havana. Two operatives of ours in Mexico City claim they can get into Cuba and arrange to sink the freighter. Go watch over them until you're confident they're secure and on the up-and-up. Here's the information you'll need."

As Gabe took the folder, the director asked, "How's our friend Jack?"

"Running for president."

"Indeed he is. And there are things he can know and things he can't. Jack will be briefed by us in due course. All right, Mr. Russo?"

"Got it."

"Splendid," Dulles said.

◆ ◆ ◆

Driving to Georgetown, Gabe was bothered that the director seemed to know he was getting together with Jack. He could've been guessing; Dulles knew they were pals. Jack had recommended Gabe for the CIA job. Or maybe the agency had tapped his phone. If so, then they could be watching him and Cait. On the phone, Jack had invited Gabe to his house for breakfast. Gabe had suggested Martin's Tavern, saying that he missed their pancakes. Truthfully, Gabe felt sad being around Jackie. Jack had many qualities he admired. Cheating on his wife wasn't one of them. And now Été was in the States. Gabe assumed Jack was seeing her. He hadn't told Cait he'd known Été in Saigon. Cait was too perceptive and would've made the Jack connection. When Été had landed in New York, Gabe left Cait with the car and waited at customs. He'd filled in Été, who agreed to play along.

Nine years ago, Jack had met Gabe and Été on the same October evening. Gabe was drinking a beer at the rooftop bar of the Hotel Majestic, which had a view of the city lights glimmering on the Saigon River. Jack was alone at the next table. After seeing Gabe's marine uniform, he introduced himself and asked Gabe how he thought the war was going.

Gabe said, "Ho Chi Minh's guerillas are willing to die to get rid of France, and with their hit-and-run tactics, they'll drag out the fighting until the French get sick of it and go home. Their general, Giap, knows his business, and he's motivated. The French locked up his sister-in-law, wife, and little daughter, and the three of them wound up dead."

Their conversation drifted to the South Pacific, Jack talking about skippering a PT boat, Gabe about the hellhole of Okinawa. They had just arranged to meet for lunch the next day when Été entered the bar. "Who is *that*?" Jack asked, plainly bowled over by the shimmery sweep of her black hair and the exuberant curves of her body under a crimson silk tunic. Gabe said that Été was well known in Saigon. She had a reputation as a good-time girl, yet whenever Gabe said hello to her at the Majestic, she was sitting by herself reading a novel in French or English. Jack, who was a bachelor then, said he wanted to meet her. Gabe introduced them. Été and Jack looked at each other with such wanton hunger that Gabe excused himself.

The following day, at lunch, Jack said, "Never met a girl like Été. She's funny. And wise. One minute she's a teenager; a minute later, she could be a hundred years old."

"Hard to get elected to the Senate if you're in Saigon."

Gabe was kidding, yet the look on Jack's face was a blend of joy and regret. "I doubt Massachusetts voters would go for it, but it'd be nice to hang around."

◆　◆　◆

Martin's Tavern resembled a men's club—dark wood walls, muted lighting, and, even in the late morning, a distinguished array of gentlemen drinking at the bar, numbing themselves for another day of operating the machinery of government. Jack was seated in the Dugout, a small back room. The other booths were empty. After a waiter brought coffee and took their order, Gabe said, "I turned up a couple things. You know anybody named Ruby?"

"No. Who is he?"

"Beats me. I got a contact who maybe knows. Dulles has me traveling, and I can't talk to the guy until I finish my trip."

Jack stirred sugar into his coffee. "Your contact doesn't have a phone?"

"He has lots of phones. He's a bookie. So vice cops or the FBI could be listening in."

The waiter brought their food. Gabe watched Jack assault his eggs Benedict. Jack did everything fast. Like he heard a clock ticking in his head and time was running out. Perhaps it was his long hospital stays that made him feel closer to the grave. Or that his brother and sister were dead before they were thirty. Or that Jack had almost died in the war. Gabe understood that—the indelible lesson of combat: here one moment, gone the next.

Gabe said, "You got me looking for a film you hardly told me about."

Jack put down his fork. "I heard a rumor it's out there."

"You and a girl?"

Jack drummed his fingers on the table.

"I'm your doctor here. You don't lie to your doctor."

Finally, Jack quit drumming. "Me and a girl. She was a pro."

"Where was it?"

Jack put down his fork. "Havana, Las Vegas."

"Let's say you were set up. Who'd do that?"

"I haven't got a goddamn clue. The KGB honey-trapped Joe Alsop. Joe likes boys. That's the worst-kept secret of the Cold War. When Joe was in Moscow to interview Khrushchev, the KGB had a soldier pick him up, and the KGB photographed the action. They sent the photos to American journalists. Nobody wrote about them."

Gabe pushed his plate aside. "Havana and Las Vegas—that's mob territory. Not KGB."

"I probably met a few mobsters there. No one comes to mind. And I was on the Senate committee investigating labor racketeering. Saw a few there. But set me up?"

"Possible, isn't it?"

Jack leaned forward, his voice full of disgust. "All I'm sure of is that if Nixon's people get that film, they'll pass it to Republican newspapers, and they'll piss all over me. And if Lyndon Johnson, who I hear is looking for it and believes he can steal the nomination from me at the convention—if that prick gets ahold of the film, he'll run it at Boston Garden."

"Relax. If it's out there, I'll find it."

"Thank you, Gabe. Where's Dulles sending you?"

"Mexico City. And he said I can't tell you. You'll be briefed by him."

Jack laughed. "As soon as he thinks I'm going to win and let him keep his job."

"And build his monument. Speaking of monuments: Cait's pregnant."

Jack broke out the Kennedy smile. "That's great. Congratulate her for me. And let me tell you: if there's any perfect time in my life, it's my time with Caroline."

Gabe stood and placed a twenty on the table. Jack never carried cash. "You might consider cooling it with Été. If someone's trying to set you up, why help him? And Cait's friends with her. Women talk."

The Kennedy smile got brighter. "I'll take it under advisement."

CHAPTER 13

Greenwich Village
February 1960

On Friday, Caitlin was at her desk, writing on a legal pad, when the phone interrupted her. She answered it, and Howland said, "The pages you sent are extraordinary. You're keeping at it?"

Caitlin was excited to hear his voice, boyish and bright, which made her feel as if she were betraying Gabe, who spoke in the more somber tones common to detectives. Regardless of how she justified her feelings about Howland, Caitlin saw that behind her excitement was an unforgivable vanity. Gabe knew who she was; Howland knew only who she wanted to be.

Caitlin said, "I'm working, but I think I need to cut some of it."

"That's my job, kiddo. I'll be in New York next week. Bring the pages, and we'll have lunch."

"I'd like that." Howland had expressed such interest in her story that until she heard herself say these words, Caitlin hadn't considered that his greatest interest might be in her. She was flattered. Howland was urbane, accomplished, with a refined charm so unlike Gabe's. Yet in the next instant, Caitlin was insulted, wondering if Howland cared about her writing at all. So she added, "Call when you're here, and I'll try to make it."

"I'll do that," Howland answered, his voice less exuberant.

◆ ◆ ◆

That afternoon, Caitlin met Été for a walk. Since Été had returned from Hollywood, they had met twice for tea in her suite at the Algonquin. Today, with winter giving spring a tryout, Été wanted to walk in the Village.

"The writing goes well?" Été asked.

"Howland called to say he liked what I mailed him."

Children spilled out of the Little Red School House. Été watched them dash past her and through puddles of snowmelt. "You are fortunate. Howland is respected by magazine and book editors. If he likes your work, you will be published."

"I can't tell if he likes my work or me."

Été turned toward her with a grin that was both impish and wise. "If a man likes you for any reason, he wants to go to bed. It is the male's special form of stupidity."

If Caitlin wasn't married, sleeping with Howland would've been an attractive possibility. When she moved to the Village, she had slept with men far less appealing—a painter Winkie had introduced her to, an unpublished novelist she'd met at the White Horse Tavern, and a bartender at Fanelli's when she'd passed her martini limit. It had been fun, but after eight years with the nuns at Our Lady of Sorrows, Caitlin still suffered periodic twinges of shame about her behavior. "Suppose Howland has some kind of trade in mind?"

"Then you decide. But know this: If a man could make the best-seller list by fucking the bearded lady in the circus, he would. So men don't understand our reluctance. My advice: *croyez en vous*—believe in yourself. And wait for the man who accepts you with your clothes on."

Caitlin laughed. "Do they exist?"

"*Certainement*—after we train them. Now enough about Howland. How is Gabriel?"

"Traveling again. He should be back next week." Caitlin imagined his homecoming: Gabe atop her, each stroke driving Howland out of her head.

Été took a powder blue pack of Gauloises from her coat pocket. "Is your morning sickness bad?"

"It's not, but I'm always hungry. And dying for a chocolate milkshake."

"Is there a good place?"

"C.O. Bigelow. I've become a regular."

The pharmacy had a wood soda fountain. Été ordered tea and smoked a cigarette. Caitlin was halfway through her milkshake when cramps began to squeeze her stomach.

Été saw the pain register on her face. "There is something wrong?"

Caitlin gave her a five-dollar bill. "Can you buy me some Kotex and a belt and bring it to the bathroom?"

Sitting on the toilet, Caitlin spread her knees and looked in the bowl. Brownish-red clots of blood dotted the water. She knew what the blood meant. Her mind went blank. As if it wasn't her in this ammonia-scented room with a bare bulb above a cracked porcelain sink. Caitlin was shaking, crying without a sound. She cleaned herself with toilet paper. Été knocked on the door.

Caitlin couldn't bring herself to flush the toilet. Standing with her dungarees and panties gathered at her ankles, she flipped the hook from the eye latch. Été came in, taking a box of sanitary napkins from a paper bag. "It will be all right, *ma chère*."

Caitlin felt embarrassed as Été got the elastic belt and a napkin in place. Caitlin buttoned her pants. Été flushed the toilet. Caitlin winced at the sound of the rushing water.

At the curb, Été hailed a cab. "We can go to a hospital."

"My doctor's up by Union Square. I can call her if I have to. I want to go home."

In the apartment, Caitlin changed into a flannel nightgown and lay on the couch in the living room. Été saw a bottle of Courvoisier on a shelf of the hi-fi cabinet, filled a snifter with cognac, and gave the glass to Caitlin.

Caitlin took a sip. "Luck of the Irish."

Été sat in one of the armchairs. "Luck? What luck?"

"If something bad happened, my mom would say, 'Luck of the Irish.' She told me my grandmother started it. My grandfather was superstitious. Always had a four-leaf clover, Celtic cross, and a rabbit-foot in his pockets. One day, he's crossing a street and sees a penny, another lucky charm for his collection. He bends to pick it up and gets run over by a trolley. 'Luck of the Irish' is what my grandmother said after a cop gave her the news."

Été laughed, but her voice was tender when she said, "My mother had a miscarriage before I was born. You can still have a baby."

Caitlin closed her eyes. "I wanted this one."

CHAPTER 14

Miami Beach, Florida

Yenchi Baylin lived in Boca Raton, but his barbershop was in one of the stucco buildings on the southern tip of Miami Beach. Haircuts were handled on the first floor by a trio of old Jews. The manicurist was a curvy middle-aged Cuban with a beehive hairdo; when Gabe entered, he said to her, *"Hola, Inés. ¿Cómo estás?"*

"Bien, gracias, Gabriel. You want a manicure?"

He handed her a five-dollar bill. "Put it on account for next time. How's your family?"

"Everyone's well. Yenchi's upstairs."

Gabe went up the back stairway. He had known Yenchi since he was a kid. Gabe's father would give Gabe a dime to bet on the Dodgers, and he would bring it to Yenchi, who ran his book from the cellar of a deli on Church Avenue. Yenchi used to talk sports with Gabe, but as the World Series rolled around every year, he was complaining that "Winter is for suckers," and as soon as he'd socked away enough to buy the barbershop, he traded Brooklyn for South Florida.

"Celtics over Philly—ya gotta give seven points," Yenchi was saying, holding a phone in each hand and sitting at a bridge table. He was as round and pale as a snowman, and his yellow aloha shirt was so bright Gabe was tempted to put on his sunglasses.

Yenchi hung up both phones and peered at Gabe over his bifocals. "I hear Victor Diaz got himself a migraine."

"Getting shot in the head will do that."

The phones rang. Yenchi didn't answer them. "It ain't because I told you about Victor peddling information to his cousin?"

"No," Gabe lied, and suddenly the secrets he carried—and the lies he told to conceal them—were drowning him. But what were his choices? Scaring Yenchi and Cait. Or maybe putting them in danger.

"Victor lost big with me and never welched. All I did was take him across the street to Joe's Stone Crab for dinner, and after some gin and tonics, he blabs about this deal he'd done."

Gabe said, "You didn't do anything wrong. But I got a question. You know a guy named Ruby?"

"Victor asked me that. What're you up to, Gabie?"

"I'm doing a favor for a pal."

Yenchi unwrapped a cigar. "I know some Rubys, but I only know one who goes to Havana, and he's the one Victor asked about—Jack Ruby. If you see that midget prick, get the hundred clams he owes me."

"How'd you let that happen?" Gabe asked. "I figured you were too smart for that."

Yenchi shrugged. "Last September, he stops in for a haircut, saying he's off to Havana, and bets the Cubs against the Cardinals—Ruby's from Chicago. The Cards won; Bob Gibson pitched all nine. And I don't hear from Ruby again."

"Ruby's in Chicago?"

"Dallas. Ruby tells me he owns the Carousel Club. I ain't been there, but I'll give you twenty to one it's a strip club where they piss in champagne bottles and sell it for more than Dom Pérignon."

From his conversation with Jack at Martin's, Gabe was convinced that mobsters had made the film and had probably done it in a mob-owned hotel. That could be in Havana or Vegas. If Ruby was involved, that would narrow it down to Cuba.

Yenchi unwrapped a cigar. "If you need me to, I can ask around about Ruby."

Gabe got up, remembering that Church Avenue cellar fragrant with pastrami and sour pickles and Yenchi taking his ten cents' worth of action as if it was ten grand and giving him back his dime if the Dodgers didn't win. All at once, Gabe felt happy and sad. He wanted to tell Yenchi that he was going to be a father. Yenchi had a daughter once. Her senior year at Erasmus, she was killed in a car accident. Gabe didn't mention the baby. Bending over, he kissed the top of Yenchi's head with its sparse white hairs. "Ask carefully."

Gabe walked to his hotel. He wasn't as wary of the taxis on Collins Avenue. Nobody knew he was here. He had called Cait from Mexico City and told her when he'd be back. He said nothing about Florida. Gabe would have to get to Dallas, but now he wanted to go home. He had an early plane to DC, where he'd left his car, and a four-hour drive to New York. Ordinarily, on his longer trips, he missed Cait. This trip was worse than that. Now he missed his wife *and* baby. For Gabe, that he hadn't met his child was a technicality. His son or daughter was with Cait, waiting for him.

In his room at the DiLido Hotel, Gabe retrieved a three-ring binder from his suitcase and wrote a report on his twenty-four days in Mexico City. The operatives—cousins Luis and Alberto Rodríguez, ex-owners of a restaurant in Havana—were jowly men in their fifties, and how they could blow up a freighter in Havana Harbor escaped Gabe. The cousins spent their days at Café La Habana, downing espressos with steamed milk until the late afternoon, when they went back to their apartment. The sole contact the cousins had at the café was on Thursday, January 14, at 1320 hours, when a man in a seersucker suit with a blue Pan Am airline bag slung over his right shoulder stopped to talk to them. Gabe couldn't see the man's face. He wore a red baseball cap and aviator sunglasses. He left the bag under the table and walked away.

Gabe crossed the street to follow him, blending into the people streaming along the sidewalk, passing vendors scooping out avocados for guacamole and women peddling woven ponchos to camera-toting tourists. Gabe figured the man was paying the cousins, who had no other visible means of support. Dulles had likely approved the payments. Gabe assumed the man was CIA: seersucker was one of the Ivy League uniforms. But the man didn't move like a brainy college boy. He had the fast stride of a halfback in the open field. At the gate of the US embassy, the man stopped to chat with a guard and removed his cap. Gabe was too far away to see much except that the man's hair was unstylishly long and the color of wet sand.

Suddenly, the man stared in Gabe's direction, and Gabe started back toward Café La Habana. Glancing over his shoulder, he saw a crocodile cab—painted green and black with rows of white triangles like teeth—stopping by the embassy gate. A rear door of the *cocodrilo* opened, and a short, husky, pasty-faced man emerged. Gabe made him for a Russian. His shapeless gray suit could've come from Nikita Khrushchev's closet.

The Ivy Leaguer walked over to the Russian. Without exchanging a word, the two men crossed the street and went into a taco-and-enchilada joint. Gabe didn't know what he was observing, but he included it in his report. The Russian could be a source or a spy.

After sliding the binder into his suitcase, Gabe pulled out his pocket calendar and made a few notes about his conversations with Jack and Yenchi. Then he went next door to Wolfie's for dinner, ordering pot roast with key lime pie for dessert. Afterward, he strolled by the stores and movie theaters on Lincoln Road. Off to his right, Gabe spotted a sign for STEWART'S TOYLAND and couldn't resist. The first toy he saw was a miniature black piano. Gabe tapped the white keys. Perfect. It would be fine with him if his son was another Thelonious

Monk. For his daughter, Hazel Scott would do. Hazel could flat-out play and sang a version of "Autumn Leaves" that could break a statue's heart.

Standing at the cash register, Gabe couldn't remember the last time he'd felt so lucky.

CHAPTER 15

Greenwich Village

Caitlin was trying to eat a slice of cinnamon toast when Gabe called.

"Hey, Cait. I should be in on Tuesday by two."

She wanted to tell him about the baby. To blurt it out and let Gabe listen to her cry. Except Caitlin wouldn't dare tell him. Bad news was worse on the phone. And she wasn't ready for her husband to know that she'd failed. Gabe would comfort her, saying it wasn't her fault—they would try again. Caitlin knew that wouldn't help.

"I miss you," he said. "How's the baby?"

"Fine."

They said goodbye, and Caitlin dumped the toast in the pail under the kitchen sink. She reread her article. The words might as well have been hieroglyphics. She missed talking to Winkie, who was in Cleveland for an art show, and she didn't want to bother Été, who had already done so much for her. Friday after the miscarriage, Été had stayed over, sleeping on the couch. Saturday, Caitlin woke up sobbing. Été put her arm around her and didn't go back to her hotel until the afternoon. And on Sunday morning, Été returned with a dozen bagels.

Caitlin smiled through her gloom. "You're now an official New Yorker."

She brewed a pot of tea and, to be polite, ate a bagel. It was crusted with salt and tasted like her tears. When they finished, Été said, "I have to go. You will see your doctor?"

"Tomorrow."

"I can go with you."

"No, you've been so kind, and Gabe will be here the day after."

Été kissed her on both cheeks. "When I was a girl, my mother used to say, 'The world isn't kind, so friends must be.' It makes me happy to help."

In the shower, before her appointment, Caitlin saw the bleeding had stopped. She assumed this was a positive sign, and Dr. Hart confirmed it after completing a pelvic exam. Dr. Hart's gray hair was knotted in a long braid, and she had an air of unflappability that reminded Caitlin of the intrepid women in Willa Cather's novel *O Pioneers!*

Dr. Hart said, "Your uterus is clear. That's good. But you're disappointed and sad?"

"Yes" was all Caitlin could say, because she was afraid that if she spoke about her feelings, she'd start weeping.

Dr. Hart placed her palms on Caitlin's shoulders. "Nature has the final say in this matter—not you. And there's a reliable treatment for your sadness: nothing in the vagina for two weeks, and then you begin trying again."

Caitlin wanted to cry. "OK."

On Fourteenth Street, the bare trees along Union Square Park were silver in the icy light. Caitlin couldn't recall when she decided to continue walking on Sixth Avenue, but she didn't stop until she was in front of the red doors of Saint Joseph's. She hadn't entered a church since her mother's funeral Mass. Now, she went inside. The pews were empty. Her eyes were drawn to the fresco behind the altar—Jesus on the cross, with Mary kneeling at his feet. How did she bear it? Caitlin hadn't given birth, and her grief made it hard to breathe. Mary survived, thanks to the resurrection. Caitlin had no faith in eternal life. The best she could do was to murmur, "Hail, Holy Queen, turn thine eyes of mercy toward us, the poor banished children of Eve."

The next day, Caitlin scrubbed, mopped, and vacuumed the apartment. Cleaning made her feel that she was in charge of her day. She put fresh sheets on the bed. *Nothing in the vagina* didn't mean they couldn't play a game or two. She soaked in a hot bath. Drying herself, she practiced telling Gabe about the miscarriage. That didn't seem too difficult now. Perhaps the Mother of Mercy had taken pity on her. Caitlin dressed in black slacks and a pink cashmere turtleneck. She loved the softness of the sweater against her skin. Gabe had bought it for her at Bergdorf's. She looked out the living room window. A woman in a fur-collared coat was hurrying by the statue of General Sheridan and waving at a taxi on Grove Street. The cab kept going, and the woman threw up her arms.

Caitlin dragged a chair to the window and sat reading the *Times*, glancing out the window now and again to watch for her husband. At last, she saw Gabe striding alongside the park. He was carrying a suitcase with his left hand and a shopping bag with his right. Gabe crossed over to the sidewalk, and a yellow cab pulled up alongside him. The cabbie must have spoken to Gabe, because he turned toward the taxi, which was when Caitlin heard a loud *crack-crack-crack*, and Gabe stumbled backward as the cab sped down Grove Street.

As Caitlin ran down three flights of stairs, she told herself that while Gabe had been shot point blank, his wounds weren't necessarily serious, a bit of self-deception that dissolved when she saw him lying on the sidewalk, his legs splayed at awkward angles, his cap on the ground, and dark wet blossoms soaking the lapels of his new Harris Tweed jacket.

Caitlin knelt beside him and tore open his shirt, compressing the chest wounds with her hands and shouting at the mailman approaching with his bag, "Call an ambulance! The phone booth across the street!"

Gabe was gazing at Caitlin and mumbling. His blood was coating her hands and darkening the cuffs of her sweater. Calmly, as if the holes in his chest were no worse than the Thanksgiving he'd cut his thumb carving the turkey, she said, "I can't hear you, sweetheart."

Curling an arm around her neck, Gabe yanked Caitlin to him. "Take her."

"Take who?"

"Care of her. Or him."

The baby, he was talking about the baby. "We both will."

"I love," Gabe said, his voice a hoarse whisper. "I . . . love."

He let go and slumped against the building, his eyes going back in his head, his chest no longer rising and falling. Caitlin heard sirens on Grove Street. The winter seeped inside her, an aching numbness. She looked at her husband and tried to console herself with the fact that Gabe had died believing he would be a father.

CHAPTER 16

Normally, you can feel time pass. A yawn, a hunger pang, any sign that the present is moving on. However, for Caitlin, time wasn't going anywhere. For three hours, ever since the shooting, she had been lying on the couch in her living room.

"Cait?"

A cop was standing over her, holding his cap. It was Gabe's former partner, Danny Cohen. With his blond hair and doe eyes, he seemed too young to be wearing a captain's uniform.

Danny, his voice tentative, said, "You want to change your sweater?"

Caitlin glanced at the splotches of dried blood on the pink cashmere. "I don't."

"Can I help with the arrangements? Gabe buried his folks at Linden Hill in Queens."

Caitlin sat up. "His parents drove him crazy. Gabe used to laugh and say he wanted some peace and quiet when he was dead, so I should put him in Arlington. He's eligible. They gave him the Navy Cross after Okinawa."

Danny nodded. "I know a sergeant at the marine recruiting station in the city. He could steer me in the right direction."

"Thanks, Danny. And could you call Senator Kennedy's office? He'll help. And someone should tell him about Gabe. I'm not up to it."

Danny had been speaking softly, as if her loss required it, but suddenly his tone changed, hardening into the voice of a street cop. "Gabe was working for Kennedy?"

"They're friends."

Caitlin went to the windows and gazed out at Grove Street.

Danny said, "Crime scene guys are done. They drew a blank—no shell casings, nothing. I got the whole homicide squad chasing leads. You up to answering some questions?"

Caitlin felt woozy and wide awake. And she kept seeing Gabe on the sidewalk, bleeding.

Danny placed his cap on the back of the couch. "A witness got a partial plate on the taxi, and a radio car spotted it parked on Twelfth Street. Near the Holland Tunnel. The cabbie was in the trunk. Strangled. The poor guy probably picked up the shooter as a fare, and the shooter did him, then came for Gabe."

Caitlin was shivering. The cold air was leaking in. Gabe had promised to caulk the windowpanes when he got home. *He promised me . . .*

"Cait, a few weeks ago Gabe stops by the station house and asks me about the department's security detail for Castro. And says he's worried about you being followed. Now you tell me he's palling around with a senator who wants to be president, and some bastard hunts him down. What the hell was Gabe into?"

"I never knew. I accused him of working for the CIA. He said he was doing security for a private company."

"Q&D Relocation Services?"

Caitlin nodded. "How'd you know?"

"From the letterhead on a report he wrote. The address was a PO box in College Park, Maryland. I brought in Gabe's stuff. They're on your bed. Come take a look."

When Caitlin saw Gabe's suitcase on the bedspread, her eyes filled with tears.

Danny said, "We can do this tomorrow."

Caitlin lifted a three-ring binder off the suitcase and opened it.

"That's the report," Danny said. "Gabe was in Mexico City watching two cousins named Rodríguez." After taking the binder from her, he dropped it onto the bed. "I'll bring it to the station house. If Gabe was doing a job for the CIA and they get in touch, you say I've got it." Danny handed her the pocket calendar. "You keep this. Nothing in it helps. Gabe's .38 is in the suitcase. He had it on his hip. You're here alone; you should hang on to it."

"Don't bother. I've got one in the nightstand. And a license. Gabe insisted."

Danny pointed to the cordovan briefcase on the bed. "What d'you know about that? I grabbed Gabe's car keys and got it out of his trunk."

"I haven't seen it since before Christmas."

Danny flipped up the clasp and, using two fingers, gripped a High Standard automatic with a silencer by the barrel and held it up.

Caitlin stared at the pistol, feeling betrayed. What else was Gabe hiding from her?

Danny asked, "Where were you when you saw the briefcase?"

"Gabe was dropping off something on the Upper West Side. I don't remember the street. It was across from Riverside Park."

"I got to take it with me. Anyone asks you about it—"

Caitlin wasn't listening. Behind the suitcase was a shopping bag with STEWART'S TOYLAND printed on it. She sat on the bed and pulled out the miniature piano and held it on her lap.

Danny said, "Gabe stopped in Miami Beach on his way home."

Caitlin rocked back and forth. "He bought it for the baby."

Danny sat down. "You're pregnant?"

"I lost the baby, Danny. And I lost Gabe."

Danny put his arm around her. Caitlin was rocking faster and sobbing. Her throat ached as if it had been sandpapered, and she was furious and slapped the tiny keys of the piano, the discordant notes making no sense as she furiously slapped the keys, slapping them until the absurd music was as loud as the sounds of her grief.

CHAPTER 17

Arlington, Virginia

The gravestones glistened in the rain. There were a few dozen people at the ceremony. Jack couldn't see Caitlin; she was up front. It was hard to hear the navy chaplain over the rain. Jack held up his umbrella. His back throbbed. He wished he could use his crutches, but Americans were done with wheelchair presidents. They wanted youth and vigor. They wanted Elvis. His plane, christened the *Caroline*, was waiting to fly him to Wisconsin. The primary wasn't until April 5. Jackie was accompanying him. Jack needed all the help he could get. Protestants were everywhere in Wisconsin, and many of them seemed to believe Catholics practiced witchcraft.

The rain let up as the chaplain recited the twenty-third psalm. Jack looked out past the gray, leafless trees to the gravestones covering the hills. The cemetery was a testament to the stupidity of the men who started wars and the bravery of those who fought them. *Yea, though I walk through the valley of the shadow of death . . .* Gabe had lived in that valley. Now he was dead, and Jack had been asking himself why ever since the police captain had phoned his office. Some harebrained scheme in Mexico City cooked up by Dulles? Or for doing Jack a favor and tracking down that film? Jack had asked the captain how Caitlin was holding up. *Not well,* the captain had said, *especially on top of her miscarriage.* Jack hadn't felt so overwhelmed by guilt since his two men had died when *PT-109* was cut in half. For the last week his insomnia had been so bad he'd doubled up on the Nembutal.

When the chaplain finished, the marine officer in charge said, "Mrs. Russo, please rise."

Caitlin stood. Jack could see her reddish-brown hair spilling out from under a flat black hat. Beyond the casket, seven marines in dress blues fired three volleys toward heaven. Jack doubted he could find anyone he trusted enough to look for the film. He trusted Bobby, but his brother was no detective. Dad might know a guy, except Jack would have to tell him what had happened, and his father would dump a load of shit on him for being so careless. Caitlin knew cops. He couldn't ask her to recommend someone now—and maybe never if, after talking to Dulles, Jack concluded it was likely that Gabe had been murdered doing a favor for him.

A bugler played "Taps." If the Republicans or Lyndon had stills made from the film and got them out to voters, that bugle call would be fitting music for his candidacy. There was nothing Jack could do but push on. Besides, the higher the tightrope, the more alive he felt walking on it. Jack was a rebel angel right out of *Paradise Lost*. He had been cheating death since childhood and had avoided every pothole in his political career because all people ever saw was charming war-hero Jack with a sense of humor as dry as Manzanilla sherry, a glamorous wife, and an adorable daughter. And though Jack knew these were essential to his success, he resented that the public never saw the Jack whose body belonged in a junkyard, the Jack whose loneliness was impervious to the cheering of crowds and the sultry acrobatics of women, the Jack who knelt in church and prayed for relief from the agonies of his flesh and spirit.

Caitlin sat as the casket team of marines folded the flag. It was handed to the officer in charge. He passed the flag to the chaplain, who presented it to Caitlin.

The ceremony was over. Jack made his way up front. A green tarp was spread over the grave, and Gabe's blond-wood casket rested on brass railings above the tarp. Jack gazed at the raised Star of David on the casket. He could feel people watching him. Most of them were cops in NYPD uniforms. Aware that the department had enough Irish for its own Saint Patrick's Day parade, Jack was thinking that showing up for Gabe would pay off on Election Day, but as he approached Caitlin, he excoriated himself for his cold-blooded ambition, another sin to carry into the confessional.

Caitlin was standing and holding the flag. Her eyes were red rimmed. *First you mourn,* Jack thought. *Then you suffer.* He remembered that August afternoon in Hyannis Port when two priests delivered the news that Joe had died when his bomber exploded in midair. The sorrow Jack had felt was overwhelmed by his concern for Mother and Dad, who were devastated by the loss. It had been different with Kick. Jack had been a congressman then, and when he got the news, he felt nothing, as if suddenly he had stopped breathing, and, in the next instant, as he hung up the phone, he heard himself weeping. Nor was that the worst of it. That came later, with Kick filling his thoughts and the sadness etching itself into his heart, an unhealable wound.

"Gabe should've lasted forever," Jack said to her. "He was one of a kind. I'm going to miss him."

Something was going on behind her glassy-eyed stare, but Jack had no idea what it was—her grief, anger at him, perhaps both. "Nice of you to come," she said.

The police officer standing next to her extended his right hand. "Captain Danny Cohen, Senator. We spoke on the phone."

Jack shook his hand. "Yes, I appreciated the call."

Off to the side, Jack spotted Julian Rose, tall and broad shouldered in a tan raincoat and tan bucket hat. If Jack didn't know his history, he could've mistaken him for an aging college professor.

Danny said, "Julian wanted to talk to you a minute."

Jack moved on to him. Julian kept his hands in his pockets. "I appreciate you cutting the red tape for the burial."

Jack said, "Gabe was my friend—a real friend. They're rare in Washington. Do the cops have any leads?"

"No, but Danny's in charge of the case. If the shooter can be got, Danny will get him." Julian held himself perfectly still. Jack found it chilling to be so close to him. Julian said, "I started calling the mayors and county bosses around Jersey for you."

"Thank you, Mr. Rose. I love my father, but I'm not him. I promise you won't regret it."

"I hope not," Julian replied and went to stand with Caitlin.

It was raining again. Spasms of pain shot up Jack's spine. To steady himself, he dug the tip of the umbrella into the wet grass and began walking to the car waiting for him. It was a long walk. Jack stopped to rest and watched the rain splashing against the gravestones.

CHAPTER 18

Greenwich Village

Other than her trip to Arlington, Caitlin had left the apartment only once since Gabe was murdered—to water Winkie's ficus trees. Winkie was supposed to have returned from her show at the Cleveland Museum of Art last weekend. Caitlin had called her on Saturday, Sunday, and Monday. Winkie wasn't home. Her parents lived in Cleveland Heights, and Caitlin thought she was visiting them. She was desperate to talk to her about the miscarriage and Gabe. She got the long-distance operator on the line and called Winkie's parents. No answer. She kept trying. No one picked up. On this Tuesday morning, after filling an aluminum coffeepot with water and four scoops of Martinson's, she tried again.

"Why, hello," Winkie's mother said, her voice with the same high-pitched sweetness as her daughter's. "Our Hannah goes on and on about you. If I can ever drag my husband to New York, I'd love to meet you."

"Same here, Mrs. Lewison. Is Hannah in?"

"Hannah went skiing."

Mrs. Lewison had to be kidding. If she'd said her daughter had traveled to Mississippi with her pals from the Congress of Racial Equality, as she had three years ago, to register voters, Caitlin would've believed it. But skiing? Winkie was a klutz, and she was so scared of heights Caitlin had to hang the art in her loft because Winkie got the heebie-jeebies standing on a stepladder.

Caitlin asked, "Does Hannah ski?"

"She always wanted to, but Mr. Lewison and I can't take the cold. She met a nice boy at her show who skis, and they drove to Vermont. She left us a note. Mr. Lewison and I were there for her opening night—we didn't meet the boy—and the next morning we flew to Arizona to play golf. That's just like our Hannah, isn't it? She loves her vanishing acts."

"Yes," Caitlin agreed, but she was worried. Although Winkie maintained a religious devotion to her impulses, whenever she fell for a guy, she called Caitlin.

Mrs. Lewison said, "I'll let you go. This long distance costs a fortune. I'll have Hannah call you as soon as I hear from her. Bye-bye."

The receiver clicked. Caitlin listened to the coffee bubbling on the stove and decided her worrying about Winkie was nothing more than her adopting Gabe's tendency to worry as a way to hang on to him and that she was going cuckoo from loneliness. Julian had invited her to live with him, his wife, and his daughter in South Orange. Danny was in favor of it—at least until he knew why Gabe was killed. Caitlin had refused. She would've missed Gabe's suits in the closet and their brass bed, where she slept cuddling a pillow as if it were her husband.

Caitlin brought a cup of coffee to her study. Reed Howland was going to phone to check on her progress. The call had been scheduled before Gabe was murdered. Following the funeral, Caitlin planned to send a letter to the editor telling him about Gabe and saying it would be a while before she finished the article. Yet after rolling a sheet of onionskin into the typewriter, Caitlin began writing about her time as a policewoman. Recalling her past was easier than living in her present. For ten days she wrote and rewrote until she had nineteen double-spaced pages. Caitlin thought the pages were good. She wished Été was in town so she could get her opinion, but she had flown to Paris the night before Gabe was shot to do a series of lectures at the Sorbonne. All the piece needed was an ending. Caitlin had considered several of them. Now, she typed:

> On June 1, 1959, after shooting Kevin Walsh's mother, I resigned from the NYPD and married Gabe at City Hall, intending to become a writer and to start a family. I write every day at an old rolltop desk that my husband made new again, but the other part of my plan fell through. Three weeks ago, I had a miscarriage, and four days after that, Gabe was shot to death in front of our building. I don't know why. Neither do the police. They are still searching for his killer.

The phone rang. Caitlin dreaded having to tell Howland about Gabe, but he already knew about the shooting. "Caitlin, I spoke to Joe Alsop yesterday, and he'd heard from Kennedy about your husband. I'm terribly sorry. How are you?"

"Exhausted. Mourning should be an Olympic event."

"Well put. That's how it was for me when Marjorie died."

With Winkie and Été unavailable, Caitlin hadn't spoken to anyone about losing Gabe. Maybe it was that Reed Howland had lost his wife or that Caitlin believed if she didn't give voice to the thought jumble in her head, she'd lose her mind, but the words rushed out of her:

"I didn't grow up expecting the world to be kind to me. My father was murdered before I was born. I went to Catholic school until ninth grade, and the nuns told us we'd suffer on the path to salvation. But what did I do to deserve this violence in my life? I know it's ridiculous, except I can't stop feeling that it's my fault. The other night my dead mother showed up in a dream to talk me out of it. I'm a child. It's Christmas Eve. Lights are twinkling on our tree, but there are no presents under it. I start crying and ask my mother, 'Why me?' With the saddest expression I've ever seen on her face, she says, 'It happened to me. Why not you?' Is that it, Reed? The prosaic truth about suffering? No reason. Just 'why not me?'"

Caitlin hadn't expected to unload on Howland. Nor did she expect him to answer her question, so it was a surprise when he said, "Smart woman, your mother."

"When does the grief end?"

"It doesn't. Grief changes shape."

"To what?" Caitlin asked.

"Memories."

Caitlin was silent.

Howland said, "Take all the time you need with your piece."

Caitlin got another surprise. She laughed—not full out as if she were watching *I Love Lucy*. More like she was reading the bitter humor in O'Neill's *The Iceman Cometh*. "It's done. I was about to mail it to you."

"Splendid. I'll get going on it as soon as it comes in. And, Caitlin: I've been through this, and if you want to talk, call. And reverse the charges."

"That's generous of you," Caitlin said, feeling a surge of gratitude and dismissing her earlier suspicion that his interest in her was more carnal than literary.

Howland chuckled. "The *Saturday Evening Post* can afford it."

CHAPTER 19

Caitlin had promised Danny to keep her Detective Special handy and dropped the pistol, along with her mother's rosary, into her courier bag, so she was prepared for earthly and heavenly strife. What she wasn't prepared for was the walk to the post office and then up to New York Savings. Shockingly, Caitlin realized that life was moving on without Gabe, and no one on Eighth Avenue—not the portly man with an armful of suits going into the dry cleaner nor the freckle-faced woman holding a toddler's hand—had an inkling that her heart was shattered. Her grief separated her from the city—from the people bundled up against the cold and the rumble of the subway—and as Caitlin crossed Fourteenth Street to the bank, she thought that Manhattan may as well have been a deserted atoll at the ragged edge of the world.

She wasn't overly concerned about money. The rent from her duplex covered the rent on her apartment, the *Post* would pay her decently if her article was accepted, she and Gabe had socked away $3,000 for a down payment on a house, and Gabe had a $10,000 life insurance policy from the Marine Corps. That would be more than enough until she found work.

The policy was stored in the safety-deposit box they had rented a week before their move. Caitlin was shown to a private viewing room and opened the box. Tucked under their wills and the Marine Corps policy was another policy, this one from Metropolitan Life Insurance for $100,000. Caitlin had never seen it: Gabe had transferred their papers to the box, and she assumed he'd purchased the policy after learning she was pregnant. With the average family earning under $6,000 a year, the MetLife payout would take care of a mother and child for a while. Caitlin was grateful for the policy until she saw the date it had been issued: October 2, 1959. That was before her pregnancy, right after Gabe had started his new job, and now Caitlin was so enraged at him that if he hadn't been dead, she would've killed him.

She remembered accusing Gabe of working for that ghoul Dulles—and Gabe responding with a story about doing security for a relocation company. That was a lie, and now Caitlin felt betrayed: Gabe had damn well known the work was risky, which was why he bought the policy. Was he playing patriot? Or was the ex-marine and ex-cop addicted to danger? What, in God's name, was wrong with him? He was forever talking about taking their son or daughter to ball games and to hear jazz. Baseball, music, kids, a wife who could cook and would fuck him to sleep any night he wanted—that wasn't enough?

Caitlin brushed the tears from her eyes, then shoved the wills and policies into her bag.

Her final errand of the day was to water Winkie's ficus trees. The loft door had a lock for the doorknob and, higher up, a dead bolt. Caitlin unlocked the doorknob, but the dead bolt wasn't closed. She slid the door sideways and, after glancing inside, grabbed the .38 in her bag. The loft had been robbed. Bookshelves were turned over. The ficus trees had been dumped out of their clay pots. Caitlin closed the door and rushed downstairs to Fanelli's.

Farley, the daytime bartender, was drawing beers for the early birds. He was a retired firefighter with a vanishing hairline and arms like Popeye.

"Hey-ya, Cait," he said. "Hated hearing about Gabe. How goes things?"

"Best they can." Caitlin held out a dollar. "Can I have change for the phone?"

"Keep your dollar." Farley reached into his pocket and gave her four dimes. "Gabe was a good egg, and it was such a kick in the head when I heard because I just seen him."

"Gabe came in during the day?"

"Nah. I seen him a while ago through the window. He was going up to Winkie's."

Neither Gabe nor Winkie had mentioned that to Caitlin, which didn't add up. She took out the card with Danny's direct line at the Sixth Precinct and called him from the pay phone.

"Captain Cohen."

"It's Cait. I'm in Fanelli's. Winkie's place was robbed. Will you come over?"

"Lots going on here, and I can't leave for a routine B and E. I'll send a radio car."

"It's about Gabe. I'll wait outside."

In less than ten minutes, Danny pulled up in an unmarked car with a radio car behind him. The uniforms went up to the loft.

Caitlin said, "Bartender says Gabe went to see Winkie in January. I didn't hear about it from either of them, and I want to find out why."

"Ask Winkie."

"For fuck's sake, Danny, I'm not stupid. She was supposed to be here two weeks ago, and her mother says she went skiing in Vermont with a guy. How's your investigation?"

"We know Gabe was shot with a Colt .45 auto."

"Millions of those around."

Danny nodded. "And we got no leads on the shooter."

"What about that silenced pistol in Gabe's Chevy?"

"Nothing yet," Danny said.

Caitlin stared at him. Danny laughed. "Gabe used to swear you were a radar station."

"One of my many charms. Tell me."

"I told you before: in January, Gabe came by the station house asking about the department's security detail for Castro. I don't know what it means, but I been thinking about it."

The uniform cops came outside, and one of them said, "All clear up there, Captain. You want to take a look?"

Before Danny answered, Caitlin went through the doorway.

The loft was one large room with high steel-frame windows overlooking Prince Street.

"What a mess," Caitlin said, stepping over Winkie's mattress.

The bed was upside down, and the mattress had been sliced open. Sketch pads, books, and record albums littered the concrete floor.

Danny said, "This is no robbery. They were looking for something. That's why they pulled down the paintings—to look behind them."

Caitlin asked, "What could Winkie have that they'd want?"

"Gabe was here. It could be connected to him. Or those two guys who came to see me with ID from Q&D Relocation Services."

"That's the company Gabe worked for."

Danny said, "These guys looked like they'd come straight from the Yale Club. They wanted Gabe's notebook with his report from Mexico City."

"And you gave it to them?"

"I did," Danny said. "But Yale must be slipping. I'd had a copy of the report typed up for me. There was nothing in it that explains this." Danny stared at the phone on Winkie's worktable. The tabletop and telephone were dusty. "Come over a sec, Cait."

She joined him. Danny pointed at a rectangular space next to the phone. "There's no dust here. Did Winkie keep an address book by the phone?"

Caitlin nodded. "One of those metal flip-up indexes. It was moss green."

The apprehension on his face scared her. "Was your name in it?"

"Probably," Caitlin said, going toward the woodstove against a back wall that Winkie used for storage. "She might have hidden it."

Danny followed her. The loft was heated by radiators. The stove pipe running up the brick wall had come loose from the ceiling. The stove was pitted and rust crusted, which most likely explained why the robbers hadn't checked it. Caitlin tugged open the little door and retrieved what she expected—a spare key to the loft, Winkie's passport, and her emergency fund, five twenty-dollar bills. The phone index wasn't there, but Caitlin found a sheet of tracing paper and unfolded it. Danny read the paper over her shoulder:

To Premier Fidel Castro from the People of New York City, September 1960

Danny asked, "What's that?"

"Winkie can do engravings. I'm guessing she did this for Gabe. And it could be why her place got tossed."

Danny said, "Let me have her passport."

"Why?" Caitlin asked, suddenly afraid.

"It's got her date of birth, height, hair and eye color, and I can give all that to the Vermont State Police so they can track her down and we can ask her about the engraving."

Caitlin saw the apprehension on his face again. "It's not weird for Winkie to take off and be out of touch."

"Yeah," he said. "She's the artistic type."

Caitlin's fear heated up to anger. "Winkie's not the 'artistic type'! She's an artist. And artists need a change of scene once in a while. You act like something happened to—"

"Nothing happened to your friend, Cait. Please, give me the passport."

Caitlin handed Danny the passport and wished that she believed him.

PART II

CHAPTER 20

Lately, Jack thought, the Sunday suppers in Georgetown had become predictable, but this evening at his house would be different. He could feel the cheery sense of expectation as the guests entered the dining room, drinks in hand, their eyes as bright as the candles burning in the silver candelabras on the table. On Tuesday, he'd won the New Hampshire primary, the election season's first contest. Before New Hampshire, the polls had him tied with Nixon. Now, Jack had a slight lead over the vice president. For the moment, then, the electorate no longer considered Jack too young, too Harvard, and too Catholic for the presidency.

The senator was seated at the head of the table, with Ben Bradlee and his wife, Tony, to his right. Ben, who had been writing about the Kennedy campaign for *Newsweek*, asked, "Jack, you believe you're going to the White House?"

Jack waited for the butler to pour him another daiquiri. "Polls are snapshots in time, Benjy. There'll be more—not all favorable."

"And I would advise you not to lose a single primary," Joe Alsop said.

The columnist was correct, but Jack was tired of discussing electoral arithmetic. He liked Ben and Joe and had invited Dulles because he wanted to speak privately with the CIA director, but Jack was more interested in his literary guests. Earlier that day, he'd bumped into Ian Fleming as the author toured Georgetown with Oatsie Leiter, a local socialite. Jack was a fan of the James Bond novels, so he'd asked Oatsie to bring Fleming. Oatsie was chatting with Été, who had just returned from Paris. Jack planned to see her tomorrow at the Mayflower. It was safer seeing Été in DC. He'd been meeting a Liz Taylor look-alike in Manhattan. Été had come with Joe and Reed Howland, Joe's editor at the *Saturday Evening Post*.

The butler began serving. Jack saw that his wife, sitting at the other end of the table with Howland on her right, was leaning close to the editor. They were smiling at each other and talking. Howland was fair haired, with the lined, tanned face of a gentleman explorer—attend a society gala one night; discover a new continent in the morning. Jack had disliked him the second he'd arrived with Été on his arm—a necessary subterfuge, but seeing it irritated Jack, and he disliked the prick even more now as Howland lit Jackie's cigarette, and her fingers lingered on his hand holding the match.

Jack focused his attention on Ian Fleming. Like Bond, the author was partial to martinis and in the process of drinking his supper. By all accounts, Fleming had been a creative British intelligence officer during the Second World War, and Jack wanted to pick his brain. Polls indicated that Americans deemed Cuba a crucial issue, and Nixon had a shinier cold warrior résumé than Jack. Last July, in a model American kitchen at a trade show in Moscow, Nixon had gotten into a debate with Nikita Khrushchev about capitalism versus communism. A photograph of the vice president jabbing his index finger at the Soviet leader had cemented the impression that Nixon, as president, would be tough on the Soviets. Jack was intent on scuffing up that impression. Claiming that Eisenhower and Nixon had lost Cuba to the Commies would be his counterattack.

"Tell me, Ian," Jack said. "How would you get rid of Fidel Castro?"

Oatsie, seated between Jack and Fleming, had matched the author drink for drink, and she let out a long gin-scented sigh. "Really, is that dinner-table conversation?"

Fleming had an aristocratic face that paired nicely with the refined cut of his suit and his polka-dot bow tie, and he glanced at Oatsie with the disdain that Brits had reserved for Americans ever since the Sons of Liberty had dumped their tea into Boston Harbor. Turning to Jack, he said, "I suggest a disinformation campaign. Have your embassy disseminate mock reprints of scientific articles that claim fallout from American atomic testing collects in beards and renders men unable to function sexually. Castro and his gangsters would trample each other to get to their razors and walking around without beards is disgraceful for Cuban revolutionaries."

Fleming had delivered his flaky recommendation with the gravitas of a wartime briefing, so no one knew whether he was serious or joking. Then Jack began to laugh, followed by Fleming and everybody else except Dulles and his mistress, a brunette young enough to be his daughter. She was plain and skinny, but Jack, as obsessed with his weight as a fashion model, marveled at her appetite. She ate like a horse coming off a hunger strike: two steaks and three helpings of mashed potatoes, and upon finishing her vanilla ice cream in chocolate sauce, she dug into the CIA chief's dessert. Maybe Dulles was miffed about losing his ice cream, but he altered the mood at the table by observing, "Cuba won't be the next president's biggest problem with Communists and the Third World."

With an exaggerated twist of his fingers, as though performing a complex, technical feat, Joe Alsop fit a cigarette into an enamel holder. "It will be in Vietnam."

Ben Bradlee said, "Eisenhower announced he's posting more troops there."

Tony Bradlee, a pert blonde and a stickler for facts, corrected her husband. "They are advisers."

"Why send anyone?" Été asked. "To start another war?"

Jack sensed a fight coming, and no one replied until Joe, the self-anointed king of anticommunism, said, "To stop Communist imperialism in Asia."

Été asked, "And to make the world safe for General Motors?"

Jack thought that was a snappy comeback, but Joe appeared irritated and leveled his cigarette holder at Été as if it were a pistol. "Are you a Communist, my dear?"

Été, her face serene, replied, "When I was girl, we lived off Rue Catinat in Saigon, in a stucco villa the color of this candlelight. We had servants and a swimming pool. Every morning, before my French father went to his bank, he walked me to school. It was down toward the river, and we passed Notre-Dame Cathedral and the busy cafés and a flower stall full of blinding colors and the patisseries with caramel éclairs in the windows, and my father would buy me one. This was the Paris of the East, a paradise that comes to me in my dreams. My mother—"

Été looked around the table. Everyone was watching her. She touched the gold heart-shaped locket dangling from her neck on a chain. Jack had seen the locket before. Été even wore it in bed. Jack wondered if she was touching it for luck or for memory. Her dark eyes were glistening when she said, "My mother was Vietnamese. A pediatrician at Grall Hospital. Twice a month, she and I would get in her Citroën and drive to villages. The stink of those villages is also in my dreams, the garbage and buffalo dung. I remember the men missing arms or legs sitting against the thatch-roofed huts. They'd been wounded in the wars with Japan or France. The children were happy to see us. I'd hand out the almond cookies we baked for them. Most of the children were malnourished and had dysentery or malaria. They lined up for my mother. I saw babies die from dehydration in their mothers' arms. Their mothers wailed and refused to let go of their dead children. My mother contracted dengue fever in one of those villages. She was gone in a week. When I cried for her, I heard those village women. I hear them still. The peasants are sad enough without another war. If Ho Chi Minh and his Communists can help them, I'm for it. If the

Americans can, I'm for that too. Because in the villages, I never noticed that the solution to human misery was philosophy."

What a clever woman, Jack thought. With that final sentence, Été had shown the political bandying at the Sunday suppers to be exactly what it was—the intellectual posturing of the well fed, the irrelevant chatter of the lucky ones.

Nobody spoke. Jackie stood and gave Été a melancholy look full of empathy. Then, to reignite the earlier high spirits of the evening, she said, "I'll put on some music, and we can dance."

CHAPTER 21

Jack watched Reed Howland jitterbugging with Jackie across the wood floor of the dining room and wanted to punch the editor in the face. To add insult to injury, Jack had to help move the dining table into the carpeted living room. Now he was leaning against it to relieve his back pain. Howland carried all his weight in his shoulders and chest. Jack would've bet the editor had played football in college. And played it well. He danced with quick, agile steps and spun Jackie in circles, her dress flouncing up, revealing the shapely lines of her calves. Jackie had put a stack of 45s on the stereo. Jack listened to the sax and drums and recognized the song from the Bill Haley movie *Rock Around the Clock*. Jack preferred Cole Porter and Kurt Weill. Neither composer caused Jackie to swing her hips and smile with uninhibited joy. Seeing his wife, who had just discovered she was pregnant, shed her sedate shell in front of guests disturbed Jack. The Bradlees were fox-trotting, Joe Alsop was waltzing at double speed with Dulles's young mistress, and Fleming and Oatsie were stamping their feet as if waiting for a bus in the cold. Jack saw all of them sneaking glances at Jackie. Like they were spying on her in the shower. Jack thought his wife was making a fool of herself. Or was it of him? Either way, he liked thinking about punching Howland in the face.

Jack hadn't punched anyone since he was fourteen. It was on the porch in Hyannis Port. A plate with a brownie was on the arm of a wicker chair. Jack, who couldn't resist sweets, was finishing the brownie when his brother Joe came out. "That was mine," Joe said.

Jack grinned. "I didn't see your name on it." Joe had two years, two inches, and twenty pounds on him, and he shoved him. Jack had hit his brother in the mouth and taken off for the beach with Joe chasing him until Jack dove into the sound and swam away.

The next 45 dropped, a slow number by Connie Francis. Howland lifted his arms. Jackie took his hands. They began dancing a box step, gazing into each other's eyes. Jack couldn't believe his wife was pulling this shit. And he hated the song: "Who's Sorry Now?"

Jack retreated farther into the living room, where, on a couch, Été was talking to Dulles.

Été said, "Jack, I need to use the phone."

"Upstairs in the study. Second door on the left."

She looked at the CIA director. "Nice speaking with you."

"Likewise," Dulles said with a polite nod.

When she was gone, Jack asked, "Allen? Have a minute?"

Dulles followed him out to the walled backyard. Coach lights on both sides of the doorway illuminated the brick patio.

Jack got right to the point. "Why is my friend Gabe dead?"

"Because spying is dangerous business."

Jack said, "I had breakfast with Gabe the day you sent him to Mexico City."

With his thumb, Dulles stuffed tobacco into a briar pipe. "Gabe should not have informed you of his destination."

"You can't fire him now, Allen."

Dulles flicked open a lighter and lit his pipe. "You recommended Gabe to me for the position. I can understand how you could feel guilty. You're officially absolved."

Coldness and a casual relationship to the truth, Jack knew, were in the CIA director's job description, but Dulles had developed his exasperating haughtiness on his own.

Jack said, "Last week, the papers reported that a French cargo ship carrying munitions to Cuba blew up in Havana Harbor. Is the CIA going after Castro?"

Dulles puffed on his pipe, and Jack pressed on: "News reports claim Castro caught the two cousins behind it. He's got them in prison. You think they're not talking?"

Dulles took the pipe out of his mouth. "When the Democratic Convention makes you the candidate in July, you will get your briefing and find out what we are doing."

"The vice president attends your briefings. That puts me at a disadvantage."

"It does, Jack. Nonetheless, those are the rules."

"Are you looking into why Gabe was shot?"

Dulles said, "I couldn't tell you if I were. From what I hear, his widow and a police captain are curious about the incident. Speak to them. I have to go inside. I wouldn't want my friend to eat all those fine chocolates I saw in those candy dishes."

Jack, furious at Dulles's evasions, smiled to hide his fury. "She has quite the appetite."

"Yes, appetite, particularly for women, can be a problem, can't it?" the director replied with a smile of his own, cagey and poisonous, and, without waiting for an answer, went into the house.

CHAPTER 22

The bedroom was lit by the Victorian hurricane lamp on Jackie's dresser, the dim light tinted by the lavender glass.

Jack yanked off his tie. "You made quite a spectacle of yourself with Howland."

Jackie reached behind to unzip her dress. "How sweet, Bunny. You're concerned about my reputation."

Underneath the breeziness of her voice was a menacing note, and it reminded Jack of the wind picking up on Nantucket Sound right before a thunderstorm. He tossed his tie and suit jacket on a chair. "I'm running for president. And like it or not, you're running with me."

Jackie removed her dress and hung it in the closet, then stood in her black bra and slip and glared at her husband. "Yes, and who would want the royalty of Georgetown to gossip? You wouldn't contribute to that, would you?"

Her question had to be one of the most loaded in marital history. In lieu of answering, he went on the offensive. "You have a weakness for literary types, but you don't have to go public with it."

Her schoolgirl giggle infuriated him. "That's rich, Jack. You're jealous."

She shimmied out of her slip and, stepping over the puddle of silk on the needlepoint rug, closed the space between them. He saw that his wife's public mask was gone, the mildly curious gaze of her wide-set eyes replaced by something eager, feverish.

"Did my dancing make you angry, Jack?"

"Yes, it did."

She put her hand on the fly of his trousers. "Did it make you any-thing else?"

He gave her his broadest campaign smile. "Apparently."

She unbuttoned his pants, her hand slipping into his boxers. "Was that a funny question?"

"No, Jackie. Not funny."

She tightened her grip and tugged him toward the bed.

Later, as they lay facing each other, Jackie touched his cheek, saying, "Bunny, I'm scared I'm going to lose this baby. I don't want to lose another one."

In the lavender-tinged light, he could see the worry and sadness on her face, and, fleetingly, he grasped again how fragile she was and thought about how his girling had hurt her. Worse than his flash of guilt was the knowledge that he had failed her all while feeling powerless to control the impulse that had led to his failures. He felt ashamed and promised himself to do better, maybe even to stop. Tomorrow with Été would be his last hurrah.

"You'll be fine," Jack said. "You, me, Caroline, and the baby, we'll go to the White House in January."

She brushed the damp strands of hair from her forehead. "You sure, Bunny?"

"The polls are," he replied and hoped the polls were right.

CHAPTER 23

Greenwich Village

Danny walked into her apartment. "How you doing, Cait?"

"Better." That was a relative diagnosis. For the last two weeks, when Caitlin woke up in the morning, she no longer thought, *Gabe's dead.* That didn't start until she was in the shower. "On the phone you said you had news. Is it Winkie?" Caitlin had been dreading his arrival, believing he was coming to tell her Winkie had been murdered.

Removing his cap, Danny sat on the couch. "Nothing on Winkie. I reached out to the Vermont State Police, the cops in Cleveland Heights, and her parents. She's missing."

Even though Caitlin still expected the worst, she was relieved not to deal with it today.

Danny noticed an aqua suitcase over by the windows. "Where you going?"

She sat in one of the armchairs across from the couch. "Florida. On Saturday morning. To see Yenchi."

"The old bookie from Church Avenue. Gabe loved that guy."

"Gabe saw him the day before he got—" Caitlin avoided the word *shot*, as if not saying it could alter reality. She knew this was the lunacy of grief and hoped tracking down Gabe's murderer would stop it. "I called Yenchi and told him. He was upset and said he didn't talk about private stuff on the phone, but if I was ever in Boca Raton, I should come by his house."

"Cait, you shouldn't be working this case."

"Why not? You have a shooter no one saw and you can't find."

"You know something I don't?"

"I know Gabe bought a hundred thousand dollars of life insurance, so he thought—"

"What else, Cait?"

"Nothing." She was holding back the rest of it and felt guilty for lying to Danny, but he couldn't use what she had—not yet, maybe never.

Danny looked away from her. "Gabe was into things he shouldn't—"

"Things? What things?"

He slumped lower on the couch. "That .22 automatic with the silencer in Gabe's briefcase—I had a bad feeling about it and didn't log it in as evidence."

"Danny, anyone finds out, you could get kicked out of the department."

He turned his hat over in his hands. "When we spoke after Gabe got shot, you told me you saw the briefcase in December the night Gabe made a stop across from Riverside Park. I checked for open homicides up there and found one. In an apartment on the corner of Riverside and Eighty-Second. The vic's name was Victor Diaz. There was a jacket on him from Miami. He was thirty-nine, a pimp—first in Cuba, where he was born, and then he ran some high-end girls for the tourists in Miami Beach. The autopsy found three .22 slugs in his head. I test-fired the High Standard auto and did the analysis myself. The slugs were from the High Standard."

Caitlin resisted believing Gabe was an assassin—not the man who'd taught her how to protect herself from a bully of an NYPD trainer and refinished her desk and couldn't wait to be a father. Yet she knew Danny was telling the truth, and as horrified as Caitlin was by the revelation, she hated there was a part of her husband she hadn't known and never would. "Why would Gabe shoot him?"

"In Diaz's file there was a rumor attributed to a confidential informant. Diaz was allegedly selling weapons to Cuba. The CI didn't say if Diaz was working for Castro or against him. But remember I mentioned the report Gabe wrote in Mexico City?"

Caitlin asked, "The report the two guys from Q&D Relocation Services came to get?"

"Yeah. Gabe was watching these two Cuban cousins, and it was in the papers that Castro just had two cousins arrested for helping to dynamite a freighter full of munitions in Havana. And we have Gabe getting Winkie to do that engraving sketch. My bet: the CIA is going after Castro, Gabe was involved, and somebody shot him because of it."

Danny gazed at the windows across the room. It was getting dark.

Caitlin said, "Let me fix you dinner. I could use someone to cook for. And to help me celebrate."

"What's to celebrate?"

"The *Saturday Evening Post* bought my story." Last week, Caitlin had received a note from Howland: *First-rate job. We'll publish in late summer or fall. I'm fleeing winter. Off to scuba dive Lake Atitlán in Guatemala.* She was ecstatic until she began wishing Gabe could read the note.

"Mazel tov," Danny said. "And do me a favor—stay away from this case. This is a whole different kind of crime. Gabe would beat me stupid for not stopping you."

"I'm going to see an old man in Florida. That's it."

Danny was giving her the full cop stare.

"Spaghetti, salad, and garlic bread," Caitlin said and went to the kitchen.

CHAPTER 24

Milwaukee, Wisconsin

Jack woke up. He had to piss. The room was dark, and Jackie slept beside him. They had another ten days of campaigning in Wisconsin before the primary. Today, he had been to Gay Mills, Muscoda, Lancaster, and Milwaukee. Jackie had received bouquets of flowers; Jack had gotten a homemade bologna. The state was wall to wall with Lutherans and snowdrifts. In the taverns, the men eyed Jack as if he'd come to borrow a dollar for a drink. And Jack had to win this primary. To prove that an East Coast Catholic could get the midwestern Protestant vote.

His opponent was Hubert Humphrey, a Protestant senator from Minnesota. The farmers were backing him. If Jack lost here, the Democrats would conclude that Jack couldn't beat Nixon. Then Lyndon Johnson, the Senate majority leader, who had been doling out favors to party bosses for years, could call in his markers and grab the nomination at the Democratic Convention in July. Or the delegates might go with Stu Symington, a senator from Missouri, who had former president Harry Truman behind him. Truman hated Joe Kennedy and wasn't too fond of his sons. Like Lyndon, Stu was sidestepping the primaries and counting on the bosses. Worst of all, the delegates could nominate Adlai Stevenson again. Talk about humiliating. In 1952 *and* 1956, Adlai had lost to Eisenhower. But the liberals loved Adlai. Especially Eleanor Roosevelt. Queen Eleanor would probably push for Adlai in her My

Day newspaper column. She hated the Kennedys more than Truman did. Beginning when Joe Kennedy pressured her husband not to go to war with Hitler. Jack had disagreed with his father then, but he hated Eleanor right back. Eleanor and Adlai, two moralists out to redeem humanity. Jack figured the best he could do was prevent the Russians from punching a nuclear hole in America.

And now, he had to piss—bad. Which meant getting out of bed. The problem was Jack's spine felt as stiff as a crowbar, and he couldn't sit up. Careful not to disturb Jackie, he swung his legs from under the covers, held on to the headboard, and pulled himself to his feet. Light shone under the bathroom door. God bless his wife. She had left the light on for him. Jack shuffled across the hotel suite to the bathroom and lowered his pajama bottoms. A few drops, tinted with blood, splashed into the toilet. His urinary tract infection was back, along with his inflamed prostate. He needed antibiotics and a prostatic massage. Maybe he should call a doctor and Jacques Lowe, his photographer. What a campaign poster that would make: KENNEDY FOR PRESIDENT across the top, LEADERSHIP FOR THE '60S on the bottom, and, in the middle, Lowe's shot of Jack bent over with a kindly old doc shoving a finger up his ass.

He chuckled and tugged up his pajamas. A lightning bolt of pain shot through his stomach. Jack would've collapsed if he hadn't grabbed on to the sink. His immune system was on the fritz. From the Addison's. Colitis, with its pain and bloody diarrhea, came with it. He lowered himself to the cold tile floor and leaned back against the toilet.

"It hurts, Kick," he whispered and heard his sister laughing with Inga. It was 1941. Jack was assigned to naval intelligence in DC and shared an apartment with Kick. Inga Arvad was a Danish beauty and estranged from her husband. She had been a journalist in Europe, and a photo of her with Hitler led to rumors that she was a spy. Jack knew it was bullshit. They were inseparable until J. Edgar Hoover had FBI agents tail them, and the navy, worried about the romance, transferred Jack to Charleston, South Carolina.

Kick sat on the rim of the bathtub. She was bundled up in a royal blue wool coat with a yellow sash, and her honey-brown hair sparkled with snowflakes.

Wisconsin has itself some snow, doesn't it?

The pain hit Jack again. "Joe was supposed to do this."

That was Daddy's idea, and what do you expect? Joe was the oldest. But Joe couldn't get elected. He was too much like Daddy. Too opinionated. Too pushy. Always ready to fight.

"He must be pissed Dad has me running."

Joe is dead. He doesn't get angry anymore. And you should stop lying. Dad has you running? Are you kidding? Remember our walks with Inga in Meridian Hill Park?

Jack recalled looking at the *Cascading Waterfall* and standing there with Inga and Kick, the sun silvering the water. It was before the war, and all felt right with the world.

We passed the statue of James Buchanan, and you said he helped cause the Civil War—and you couldn't be a worse president than him. Admit it, Jack. You were thinking about the White House even then.

"I didn't plan on being this sick."

Kick pressed her palm against his forehead. *You don't have a fever. But you're too skinny, and you look sad. Why so sad?*

Jack waited for the calm between the lightning bolts. "My friend Gabe was murdered. He was doing me a favor, and someone shot him. His wife's a sweet girl, and now he's dead, and I've been wondering if it's my fault."

"The fault, dear Brutus, is not in our stars, But in ourselves, that we are underlings."

"I can quote Shakespeare, Kick. Just tell me. Did I get my friend killed?"

Life is unfair, isn't it, dear brother?

Jack was angry now—angry about Gabe and his own traitorous body and the icy winds in Wisconsin and that his sister wouldn't tell him the truth. In heaven, truth reigned. And clarity. That was the promise of heaven, wasn't it? No more mysteries, no more lies.

"Kick, tell me."

Her coat was losing its color. Jack watched his sister melting away until all he saw was the light shining down on the tile floor.

CHAPTER 25

Florida

As the jet descended through the clouds to Miami International Airport, Caitlin still couldn't believe that Danny had missed it. He used to teach a training class in homicide investigations, emphasizing that detectives tended to screw up by missing the obvious. But miss it Danny did, because Gabe was a creature of odd habits, and Caitlin knew every one of them.

For his birthday, she had given Gabe a Moroccan-leather holder that had a calendar insert you swapped out every year. Gabe never made notes on the calendar. He would remove it from its holder and write on the back of the insert flap. Danny hadn't removed the calendar. It was the first thing Caitlin had done, and now she reread the list in Gabe's blocky print:

J. GIRLS

VICTOR FILM

RUBY CAROUSEL

PHONE TAPPED/OFFICE BUGGED?

HOTELS? HAVANA? VEGAS

J, she assumed, was Jack. Caitlin remembered reading a piece in the *Saturday Evening Post* about Kennedy—"The Senate's Gay Young Bachelor"—that portrayed Jack as a prize catch for any woman. After he married Jacqueline, she suffered through a miscarriage and a stillbirth, and Caitlin had a memory of a Drew Pearson column, four or five years ago, that claimed the Kennedys were on the verge of divorce. That rumor disappeared, and since then Caitlin hadn't read a scandalous word about the senator, and why would she? No husband would be dumb enough to cheat on such a posh beauty—and certainly not a husband who wanted to be president.

The only other notation that made sense to her was *Victor*, most likely a reference to Victor Diaz, the man Gabe had shot. Caitlin didn't know why his name was paired with *film*. Yenchi might. He knew something. That had to be why Gabe had stopped in Miami Beach on his way home from Mexico City to talk to Yenchi. Gabe had also kept in touch with Kennedy. He might be able to fill in some blanks, though if the senator thought any of it could turn into a headline, he wouldn't talk to her. Caitlin would need more information to persuade him. She wished Danny could dig into this, but nothing on the list was in the purview of the NYPD except for Victor, and Danny had already risked his career to protect Gabe's memory from a murder investigation.

Caitlin was two hours early for her meeting with Yenchi, so after picking up a Corvair and map at Hertz, she drove across the causeway to Miami Beach and took Collins Avenue to Boca Raton, passing pink-and-cream hotels, beaches full of sunbathers, and fishermen casting lines off jetties that ran out into the bright-blue water. The air rushing through her open window was like silk on her bare arms, and for the first time since Gabe died, Caitlin felt as if she could take a deep breath. Reed Howland had the right idea about escaping winter. She wanted Reed to tell her about scuba diving in Lake Atitlán and, it embarrassed her to admit, to hear him praise her writing again.

This drive, Caitlin decided, was precisely what she needed, a respite from her grief. Then she saw clusters of Black men, women, and children on a strip of sand and realized that Florida belonged to Dixie, and the beaches were segregated. She felt the same anger as when she watched the news and saw white mobs screaming at the Black children in Little Rock. She recalled Gabe shouting at the TV—"What the fuck is wrong with people!"—and her grief returned, potent and blinding. Her head pounded, and when she spotted a red Coca-Cola machine at a Shell station, she pulled in, bought a bottle of Coke, and swallowed two aspirins.

As she waited for the throbbing to stop, Caitlin thought that, rationally speaking, it was doubtful that she would catch Gabe's murderer, and the search had more to do with her sorrow than her desire for justice.

It wasn't a comforting thought.

CHAPTER 26

Yenchi's wife, Hilda, was a brassy-haired, sun-broiled woman in a tennis dress, who, when Caitlin stepped onto the driveway and said hello, was watering the potted bougainvillea next to the front door of a ranch house.

Hilda said, "We were sad hearing about Gabie. Come, Yenchi can't wait to meet you."

They went through the gate of a stockade fence and around a kidney-shaped swimming pool. Yenchi, in an orange paisley cabana outfit, was sitting at a redwood table under a lime-green umbrella. He stood, smoothing the remnants of his white hair. He said, "Gabie's wild Irish rose. Sit, sit." He flipped up the tops of two bakery boxes on the table. "For lunch I got rugelach from Cohen's and their seven-layer cake for dessert."

Hilda looked at Caitlin. "Men, right? Yenchi, give her some coffee. If I don't water my plants, they'll fry."

Hilda left the yard. Yenchi filled two cups from a CorningWare pot. "The police ain't arrested nobody?"

Caitlin added cream from a glass creamer. "No leads. I'm trying to find some."

Yenchi nibbled a cinnamon-dusted rugelach. "I shoulda known it was gonna be bad for Gabie. When he was here in February, I say to him, 'You want me to ask around about this guy?' and Gabie says,

'Ask carefully.' That's the last thing he says to me. He shoulda been careful."

"What guy?"

"Jack Ruby."

Caitlin was as excited as a kid finding her first clue on a treasure hunt. "Does Jack Ruby have anything to do with an amusement park? Gabe wrote a note about him and a carousel."

"The Carousel. That's Ruby's strip club. In Dallas. Ruby placed a bet with me."

Caitlin drank some coffee. "Why was Gabe asking about him?"

All the sadness Yenchi felt over Gabe's death was on his face. "I'd bet he got the name from Victor Diaz, and I'm the one told Gabie about Victor. Does this got to do with Victor getting a bullet in his head? Was Gabie mixed up with that?"

"He wasn't," Caitlin lied. She had promised herself that whatever Yenchi told her, she wouldn't break his heart by telling him that Gabe had shot Victor.

Yenchi put the rugelach on the saucer. "I been thinking it's my fault. Last November, Gabie was in Miami Beach, and I told him about Victor telling me how he made big dough shipping weapons to the guys fighting Castro and then made a lot more by tipping off Castro's people to a shipment."

That solved a problem for Caitlin. If the CIA was funneling arms to the anti-Communists through Victor, and Victor double-crossed them, the CIA would want Victor gone. So she could almost forgive Gabe for the shooting. What she couldn't forgive—and this left her feeling selfish and guilty—was that Gabe had taken such a dangerous job and gotten himself killed.

Caitlin fished the calendar insert out of her courier bag and read over the list on the flap. "Why would Gabe write *film* next to Victor's name?"

"Before this weapons business, Victor did other work."

"Prostitutes."

"Bingo. Victor bet heavy with me and paid up. So I'd take him to Joe's Stone Crab. Great place. Fills up every night. And I seen a girl there, each time with a different fella, most of them old enough to be her father. She was a real angel face with a heck of a shape. And Victor says to me, 'That's Clara, my *Polaco*.'"

"*Polaco*?" Caitlin asked.

"Spanish for *Polack*. It's how Cubans call Jews from Europe. Victor says he's gonna put Clara in a movie. He ain't no Cecil D. DeMille, so it's gotta be that trash."

"Stag films."

Yenchi squinted at her, as if unpleasantly surprised that Caitlin had heard of them.

"I used to be a cop," she explained.

"Yeah, Gabie was proud of that." Yenchi took a newspaper clipping from his shirt pocket. "I told you, before Gabie went home, he says I should ask carefully about Jack Ruby, and that's how the story gets mixed in with Victor and Clara and Santo Trafficante."

"Santo—"

Yenchi put the clipping on the table. "I cut his picture from the *Miami Herald* for you."

Caitlin inspected a photo of a balding man in a suit, a narrow tie, and thick-framed glasses. "He looks like an accountant."

"An accountant with the soul of a dragon. Trafficante's a mobster from Tampa. He took over from his father. He had millions invested in casinos and hotels in Havana."

Caitlin said, "Which Castro seized."

"That's how this connects to Ruby. There's an FBI special agent name of Davenport. He chases mobsters in South Florida. This putz couldn't pick a winner in a one-horse race. He's into me for five grand, and I carry him in case I need a favor. The morning Gabe flies home, Special Agent Davenport shows up at my office to put two hundred clams on his debt. I say to him, 'If you know anything interesting about Jack Ruby, you can keep your money, and I'll write it off.' Davenport says, 'Make it three hundred, and I'll give you something good.' 'Done,' I say, and Davenport says, 'Ruby carries cash out of Cuba to the US for the mob.'"

"From the casinos?"

Yenchi nodded. "Ruby brings it home for them so the IRS don't ask about it. On one of his trips to Havana, Davenport says, Ruby visits Trafficante. See, after Castro grabbed the casinos and hotels, he locked up some mobsters in Triscornia, an immigrant station in Havana. Davenport says that in September, after Ruby went to Triscornia, he paid off one of Castro's flunkies to let Trafficante go from there. Trafficante came to Miami Beach. And lately, according to Agent Davenport, Trafficante has been asking about Clara."

Caitlin asked, "Was Trafficante one of Clara's clients?"

"Davenport says no. Trafficante has a reputation for loving his wife. The FBI thinks Trafficante has some unfinished business with Clara from Havana. And she's disappeared."

"Are there any photos of Clara?"

"I didn't ask Davenport about that."

"Could you?"

Yenchi said, "For you? Why not?"

Caitlin read Gabe's first entry: *J. Girls.* She had hesitated asking Yenchi about the senator because she didn't want to hear anything negative about him. She used to tease Gabe, saying that just because his friend Jack was Catholic didn't mean he walked on water. Yet Caitlin had liked the senator at Alsop's party. And reading about him in the papers and magazines, she had started to admire him with the same enthusiasm as Gabe. "Did the agent—or Victor—bring up any gossip about Jack Kennedy?"

"Nope. And I'll vote for Kennedy if the Democrats nominate him. After eight years of Eisenhower going in and out of the hospital, we could use a young, healthy fella with pizzazz in the White House."

Caitlin was relieved that Yenchi hadn't heard any dirt on Jack. Still, she wondered why Gabe had written that entry about *J* and *girls*.

Yenchi said, "It's hard for you without Gabie."

"He made me feel my life was a miracle."

"It'll be a miracle again."

Caitlin doubted this was true, but she appreciated his confidence.

CHAPTER 27

Greenwich Village

Monday morning, Caitlin was in her study opening her mail when she found a check from the Curtis Publishing Company, owner of the *Saturday Evening Post*. She stared at it in disbelief: PAY TO THE ORDER OF CAITLIN RUSSO $1,500. She was, finally, a well-paid professional writer, a dream come true, yet endorsing the check and filling out a deposit slip made it no more real. Maybe if Gabe or her mother or Winkie could see it. At least her last piece of mail, a postcard, made her smile. On the front was a deep-blue photograph of Lake Atitlán with a volcano in the distance, and on the back Reed had written: *Regards from Guatemala. I'll be in NYC, Friday 4/8. Lunch? Dinner? Will call.*

Caitlin placed the postcard against the base of her desk lamp. She was still looking at it when the phone rang. Caitlin picked up, and Viola Mauri, arts editor of the *Newark Evening News* and her best friend in high school, said, "How are you, Cait?"

"Moving along." The last time they spoke was the week after Gabe died.

Vi said, "There's a play opening at the Morosco, *The Best Man*, by Gore Vidal. It's about a presidential campaign."

"I read about it in the *Times*. Isn't Vidal running for Congress in Upstate New York?"

"That he is," Vi replied. "Want to review the play?"

"I would." Vidal had a connection to the Kennedys. His stepfather was Hugh Auchincloss, who, after divorcing Vidal's mother, had married Jackie's mother. Caitlin was thinking that some of that gossip about Jack and other women might have leaked into the play.

"We can't get in opening night," Vi said. "We have two tickets for either next Thursday or Friday."

"Will you come with me?" Caitlin asked.

"Can't. Too busy here. Take a friend. You want Thursday or Friday?"

"Friday," Caitlin said, deciding that she'd invite Reed.

Caitlin was going to see Danny at the Sixth Precinct station house, and as she crossed Bleecker, two bearded men came out of a bookstore arguing, and when one of them proclaimed, "Plato's an asshole!" Caitlin laughed. The check and Broadway tickets had cheered her up. Yet her laughter had a deeper cause—if today could be better than yesterday, then there was hope for tomorrow.

Danny had his feet up on his desk. He looked gloomy.

Caitlin pulled a box of coconut patties from her bag. "What's wrong?"

"My divorce is final. I'm officially a three-time loser."

Caitlin gave him the coconut patties. Danny peeled the cellophane off the box. "What'd Yenchi say?"

"Nothing we didn't know." Danny was far enough out on a limb not logging in the pistol Gabe had used to shoot Victor, and Caitlin didn't want to drag him further out. Telling him about an FBI agent who was a degenerate gambler and selling information to his bookie about smuggling cash into the country could put Danny in a bind and force him to report it. Caitlin doubted Danny knew anything about Jack Ruby and Victor's prostitute from Cuba whom Santo Trafficante was trying to find. Danny had chased mobsters, so the name Trafficante would get his attention. Caitlin planned to read up on the mobster in the library and ask Julian about him. She had to see Julian anyway. He was investing her $100,000 insurance payout, and she had papers to sign. Julian had been out of the rackets for thirty years, but he had an amicable relationship with the Abruzzis, a New Jersey family involved in numerous enterprises, at least half of which were legal.

Danny finished a patty and offered the box to Caitlin. She shook her head. "I came by to give you those and ask about Winkie."

"I spoke to the Vermont State Police again and her folks. No one's heard."

Like most people, Caitlin had a great capacity to believe what she preferred to believe, and even though an irksome voice in her head reminded her that the capacity for self-deception was infinite, she preferred to believe Winkie was alive.

As Caitlin walked up the steps of New York Savings, she noticed a telephone booth on Eighth Avenue and had a brainstorm. She deposited her check with the teller, then gave her fifteen dollars for a roll of dimes and a roll of quarters.

In the phone booth, Caitlin dropped a dime in the slot, dialed the operator, and asked her to find the number for the Carousel Club in Dallas and to connect her. The operator told her to deposit two dollars and ten cents for the first three minutes. On the third ring a woman answered.

"Is Mr. Ruby in?" Caitlin asked.

"No."

"Do you expect him soon?"

"No."

"Is there a good time to call?"

"Now's as good as any," the woman replied.

"You said he's not in."

"No, he ain't."

"Can I leave a message?"

"You might could, 'cept Mr. Ruby don't read messages."

The exchange could have been a comedy routine. "I'll try again," Caitlin said, then hung up and left the booth.

Across Fourteenth Street, a short man in a long coat and Greek fisherman's cap was standing by a hot dog cart and staring in her direction. Caitlin had no reason to believe he was observing her, other than a momentary flash of fear. No harm being careful. The library was at Forty-Second and Fifth, and instead of crossing toward the man, she went in the other direction, comforting herself by reaching into her bag to hold the checkered wood grip of her .38 Special.

CHAPTER 28

Georgetown
April 1960

Sitting in an Adirondack chair, Jack looked across the walled backyard to his daughter, in red overalls and a blue cardigan, skipping across a carpet of pink-and-white cherry blossoms.

The phone rang. It was on the armrest of the chair. Jack picked up.

"Darling," Jackie's mother cooed. "We saw you on the television last night. We're so proud of you."

Janet Auchincloss, a disciplined social climber, was a collector of bright things. Rich husbands with impressive pedigrees and mansions in Virginia and Newport were her favorites. Listening to his mother-in-law gush about his victory in Wisconsin, Jack had the impression that, given the chance, she'd display him in one of her curio cabinets as if he were a Fabergé egg. He listened to her with rising impatience. He had won nearly 57 percent of the vote, but that was because of his performance in the predominately Catholic districts. In the Protestant districts and in Madison, home to the flagship campus of the state university and a hotbed of liberalism, Jack had gotten his ass handed to him. So he would have to campaign in all the primaries to prove that he could win the general election, starting with West Virginia, a state that was 5 percent Catholic. His back hurt just thinking about it.

"I'll let you go, darling," Janet said. "Is Jacqueline in?"

"She went shopping for maternity clothes."

"You take care of her, Jack. We don't want another miscarriage."

"No, Mrs. Auchincloss, we don't." His wife had lost two babies. Now and again, Jack beat himself up for his lack of compassion in the wake of those losses. Even after he had confessed his failure and been absolved by Father Kerry at Saint Francis Xavier, his guilt worked on him like dry rot gnawing at a dock.

After saying goodbye, Jack dialed his office to check in with Evelyn Lincoln, his personal secretary for the last seven years. Listening to Mrs. Lincoln was relaxing. She was from Nebraska, with a voice as calm and flat as a prairie on a summer evening. "Nothing pressing, Senator. A Miss Fournier called. You hadn't mentioned her, so I put her off."

Mrs. Lincoln's best quality was her buoyant toughness. It was easy for Jack to picture her humming a show tune while skinning a buffalo. He relied on her to keep his schedule, official and unofficial. Fournier was Été's surname.

"Mrs. Lincoln, please get back to her and have the operator transfer the call here."

Jack put the phone into its cradle. He wanted to cool it with Été. It had been fun seeing her again, but now he'd lost interest. Losing interest was typical for him. The women were beguiling at first, a mystery to be solved. Jack studied them as they spoke, curious about their lives and enchanted by their minds. They were flattered by his attention, and while this approach was mostly successful, Jack never failed to be surprised that they wanted him because he offered little beyond his fleeting attention. His payoff was in that instant before sex began. At that instant, Jack felt at peace and worthy of love. The act itself distracted him from his conviction that he was nearly out of time, but often, before the finale, he floated up—and, watching the scene below, Jack was ashamed to be risking his future for these inane calisthenics. His girling was wrong; he knew it. Yet Jack couldn't quit. Why should he? Because soon after, he was lost again in the maze of his own emptiness and longing. Or because if it ever became public, it would destroy his chance at the White House and extract a dreadful price from Jackie, Caroline, and the new baby. Wasn't a man supposed to protect his family—even from himself?

The ringing phone startled him. He answered it.

Été said, "Hello, Senator. New York is dull without you."

"I've been busy in Wisconsin."

Été laughed, an ebullient and caustic sound that had intrigued Jack ever since meeting her in Saigon. "*Busy* is a word men use when their clothes are on."

Jack steered the conversation in a platonic direction. "How's the movie of *Au Revoir, Papa* coming along?"

"The producers want to cast Jean Seberg in the lead."

He had recently seen the actress when Jackie, the Francophile, had dragged him to see *Breathless*, a piece of French New Wave realism he'd enjoyed despite the subtitles. "Jean Seberg's a blonde from Iowa or Idaho. How can she play a Vietnamese French woman?"

"A beautician dyes her hair, a makeup artist reshapes her eyes with mascara, the propman hands her chopsticks, and voilà!"

Jack chuckled, and Été said, "They paid me well, so I wished them luck and went to work on my new novel."

Jack wondered if he was going to be a character in her book. Not an appealing prospect, but not as bad as what Caitlin and her police captain pal might dig up on him and women. "How is your friend Caitlin doing?"

"She left me a message that the *Saturday Evening Post* was going to publish an article of hers. I've called, but I haven't caught her at home."

Jack wondered what Caitlin was up to. There was nothing he could do about it—not until he had a plan. "I've got to run, Été. I'm off to Indiana, Arizona, and West Virginia. I won't be in New York for a while."

Été hesitated, then said, "Bonne chance."

"You too."

Jack hung up. Caroline was sitting cross-legged on the patio and throwing cherry blossoms into the air.

"Hey, Buttons," he said, pulling a bag of M&M's from the pocket of his chinos and waving it at his daughter.

Caroline scurried over. Jack shook out the M&M's into her outstretched palms and watched her hurry back to sit in a patch of sunlight.

CHAPTER 29

New York City

For Caitlin, a Broadway show had all the grandeur she recalled from Midnight Mass—the limestone walls lit by candles, the sparkling Christmas tree on the altar, the choir singing "O Come, O Come, Emmanuel." And this evening at the Morosco Theatre was just as glorious. The lobby was redolent with Broadway's version of frankincense and myrrh, an indigo haze of tobacco smoke sweetened by Chanel No. 5. An usher led Caitlin and Reed Howland to their seats in the orchestra, and they sat on plush crimson velvet and listened to the buzz of the audience until the curtain went up.

The Best Man opens during a presidential nominating convention in 1960. The two front-runners want the endorsement of the outgoing president, a bourbon-swilling caricature of Harry Truman. One candidate is a principled ex–secretary of state who resembles a Vidal favorite, Adlai Stevenson. The other is a senator, a take-no-prisoners brawler who resembles Vidal's bête noire, Richard Nixon. Five minutes into the first act, Caitlin knew Vidal didn't belong in the American pantheon with O'Neill, Arthur Miller, and Tennessee Williams. Yet the actors made the most of their lines, and the play was entertaining. Some current issues cropped up—the missile gap, for instance. And there were charges of mental illness, homosexuality, and adultery, but none of these, as far as Caitlin could tell, were tied to Kennedy.

◆ ◆ ◆

Frankie & Johnnie's was down Forty-Fifth Street from the Morosco. The steak house was packed. The open kitchen ran into the dining room with its scuffed hardwood floor and tables jammed together. Caitlin had provided the tickets to the play; Reed was paying for dinner.

When they were seated, he scanned the wine list. "Would you prefer a burgundy or a bordeaux?"

"Either one'll be fine," Caitlin replied, because she knew almost nothing about wine and hated appearing like a New Jersey hick, especially with Reed as a witness.

He ordered a burgundy, and the waiter brought a bottle, uncorked it, and poured a drop for Reed to taste. He nodded his approval. The waiter filled their glasses, took their order, and disappeared. They drank.

The wine tasted like the juice of black cherries and raspberries, and Caitlin emptied her first glass with little effort. When the waiter didn't appear to refill it, Reed poured her another. "You like writing for newspapers?"

"I like free tickets to Broadway, and reviewing was a way to get started writing."

Reed said, "You've made quite a start at the *Post*. I gave your piece to the managing editor—our toughest critic. He thought it was terrific and moved up publication to the June fourth issue. Are you working on anything else?"

"Contemplating a summer rental at the Jersey Shore."

That was true, yet it was more an evasion than an answer. What could she say? That she was trying to track down her husband's murderer? Reed was studying her as if he sensed that the shore was beside the point. Caitlin looked at him—his rugged face and the unruly waves of his hair, the finely cut gray flannel and striped tie—and thought Reed was one of those blessed souls born comfortable in his own skin.

She said, "I want to find out who shot my husband and why."

"Isn't that a matter for the police?"

Caitlin discovered the second glass of wine was as easy to drink as the first. "The police don't have any leads. And Gabe worked—Gabe said he worked security for a private company, but he—he was involved with the government."

"I still have some of my friends from the State Department, and I edit Joe Alsop at the magazine, and Joe knows everyone worth knowing in Washington. If I can help—"

The waiter arrived with their rib eyes and sides of creamed spinach and french fries. Reed ordered another bottle of wine.

Caitlin grinned.

Reed gave her a puzzled look. "Did I miss the joke?"

"I'm hoping to locate a prostitute from Havana."

Reed laughed. "Can't help you there."

Out on Eighth Avenue, it felt warmer to Caitlin than when they'd left the Morosco. She couldn't tell if it was the fickle April weather or if she'd had too much to drink.

"Walk you home?" Reed asked.

Caitlin decided it was the wine. "It's two miles." His offer had caught her off guard. Reed hadn't picked her up before the play: they'd met at the theater. Tipsy as she was, Caitlin could foresee the potential for awkwardness outside her building with him gazing hopefully at her, waiting for an invitation upstairs. Gabe had been gone for only three months, and romance wasn't in the cards, not with this grief-dazed widow. Caitlin looked up at Reed and saw an unmistakable melancholy behind his calm expression. Seeing it didn't change her mind about taking a taxi home alone. Not for lack of empathy. She wanted Reed to admire her work, not her body. If she'd worn high heels instead of her more sensible pumps, she'd have a good excuse—only a masochist walks two miles in heels.

"Forgive me," Reed said and smiled as sheepishly as a teenager who had spilled punch on his prom date. "I've made you uncomfortable. It's been six years since my wife died, and I'm still shocked she's gone. I know what you're going through, and I have no motive other than I seldom get to take a walk with someone in Manhattan. Please, let me get you a cab."

Caitlin was impressed by his perceptiveness, but she was embarrassed her feelings had been obvious and disappointed by her conceit. Did she really believe Reed couldn't find a woman in Philadelphia? And where did she get off thinking that he was chasing her? *She* had invited him to the show. He'd reciprocated by inviting her to dinner. She could've said no.

"Let's walk," Caitlin said.

Times Square, in all its neon glory, streaked the nighttime blue with swirling letters of orange, yellow, and green. The sidewalk was shoulder to shoulder with people, and Caitlin saw stories everywhere. A tall girl with curly red hair talking a mile a minute in a phone booth, and a middle-aged man, briefcase in hand, glancing over his shoulder before entering a peep show. These sights, like museum dioramas come to life, had always set a match to her imagination and fueled her love affair with Manhattan. Lately, however, she'd grown weary of this frenetic island and even the places the guidebooks described as *rich in historical charm*. After all, Gabe had bled to death in perhaps its quaintest neighborhood, and Winkie had vanished from a loft above a bar that dated back to the Civil War.

As her thoughts drifted to her hometown—the gas lamps glowing at dusk and the smell of burning leaves in the fall—she asked Reed, "Didn't you say you were from Philadelphia?"

He was looking up at the billboard of the Camel man smoking a cigarette and blowing smoke rings the size of storm clouds across Broadway. "Yes, during our lunch at Twenty-One. Why do you ask?"

"I've been thinking about where I grew up."

They veered onto Sixth Avenue. There were fewer people and cars, less noise, less light.

"Actually," Reed said, "I'm from a suburb of Philadelphia, Gladwyne. It's on the Main Line, a bastion of old Protestant money, where parents give more thought to naming their mansions than their children."

Caitlin heard a bitterness in his voice. As they passed a white-bearded man leaning against a van and drinking from a paper bag, she said, "I didn't mean to—"

"A girl looks like you," the man piped up, "say whatever you want. Trust me, he'll like it."

Caitlin was mortified. Even after Reed laughed, she was hesitant to ask any more questions. She didn't have to. Reed said, "My mother was related to the Drexels—investment bankers. She had the money; Father had the pedigree. The first John Howland arrived with the Pilgrims and signed the Mayflower Compact in Provincetown Harbor. Father was proud of that. I was sent to Mount Hermon for prep school—it's in Massachusetts—so I researched my illustrious ancestor and learned he was an indentured servant."

"Did you tell your dad?"

"At Christmas dinner. And my mother said, 'See, John, you're exactly like the first John Howland.' Father sulked. He was supposed to manage her money but preferred spending it, and she never forgave him."

Caitlin heard a nagging pain. She didn't know what to say. They walked three more blocks before Reed went on: "Like you, I was an only child who loved to read. At Mount Hermon, a teacher introduced me to Dostoevsky, and I got it in my head I wanted to learn Russian. I was anxious to leave the East Coast, and Berkeley had a Slavic-language program. Off I went to California, met Marjorie, and wound up in the Foreign Service. It was in Moscow where I saw real tragedy. What the Russians had suffered in the war. Their poverty was soul crushing."

On Grove Street, lights were shining in the windows of the apartment houses. Caitlin stopped in front of her building. "Here I am."

His smile was warm and, surprisingly, grateful. "Thanks for inviting me to the play. As for my monologue—"

"You know about me; now I know about you. And thank you for dinner."

His face appeared to float in and out of the shadows. "My pleasure."

Since the age of thirteen, Caitlin had kissed boys after dates. She would know it was coming when they stepped to close the gap between them. Reed stayed an arm's length away. Reaching out, he touched her upper arm. It was a friendly gesture, nothing more.

"Good night, Caitlin. And if you have any ideas for stories, don't hesitate to call."

She watched him walk back up Grove Street, and it wasn't until she was upstairs that she could admit that the lines on Reed's face were as intriguing to her as words on a page.

CHAPTER 30

Wyoming County, West Virginia

Jack emerged from the clammy darkness of the mine with a one-armed coal miner behind him.

"Senator," the miner said. "You got your nice suit dirty."

The cluster of miners, in coveralls and helmets, chuckled. They were staring at Jack as though he were an exotic bird who had landed there by mistake. Reporters and photographers were behind the miners.

"I'm in my work clothes," Jack said. "What would you think if I showed up in overalls?"

The miner replied, "I reckon you'd be out for Halloween."

Jack laughed. A miner called out, "You got anything to say, Senator?"

The miners' faces were smudged with black dust, and their expressions were stuck in that torturous land between hope and doubt. Hope that Jack could help with the fact that, as the need for coal had dwindled, two-thirds of the miners in the state had lost their jobs. And doubt that anyone in Washington gave a good goddamn that their families were starving. President Franklin Roosevelt had cared about these forgotten men—a lifetime sentence to a wheelchair taught lessons unavailable at Harvard. But FDR had died fifteen years ago. Jack had his son, Franklin Jr., campaigning for him in West Virginia, and to get out the Kennedy vote, his campaign was delivering envelopes of cash to the county bosses, who would push the faithful to the polls and hand out some walking-around money. Yet the miners, Jack believed, didn't give a shit about any of that. While their poverty may have been as foreign to him as Samoan cuisine, his pain-seared body had familiarized him with wishing for better days. All these men wanted to hear from Jack was that he thought they were as worth helping as the bankers and businessmen who circled the candidate like roosters after a hen.

"I know times are tough for you," Jack said. "But I'm optimistic about your future. In the next decade, our population will pass two hundred million. We'll need more energy—energy that can be created with coal in new plants and transmitted over cables to the homes of America as electric power. We can do this with federal help. And I will help."

Hundreds of townspeople had been hiking up from the town: men in ties and shirtsleeves, older folks using canes, women in cardigans and long skirts with children running beside them. As they arrived and ringed the miners, Jack said, "Many of your neighbors are out of work and forced to survive on flour, rice, and cornmeal. This is absurd in a country that produces enough food to feed the entire world. It is worse than absurd—it's the bankruptcy of our moral responsibility. And I know, as president, I can do better."

Jack couldn't tell whether his audience believed him. They were listening, though, standing still as the wind, laced with coal dust, blew across them.

"And I promise you," he concluded, "I won't forget what I've seen here."

Jack waded into the crowd; looking everyone in the eye; saying "Hello, good to meet you"; and shaking outstretched hands. He wasn't a natural politician. Ever since his 1946 run for Congress, he'd had to push himself. His curiosity helped—his interest in people whose lives were so different than his own. Like these West Virginians—the leathery-faced men, their calloused hands as rough as coconut husks; the women touching the sleeve of his suit coat; young women with timid smiles; older women, white hair in braids, every deprivation of their lives cut into their faces, and yet still believing enough in a kinder future to hear out a politician.

Campaigning offered Jack a reward beyond votes. As the crowd closed in, a familiar stillness came over him, the stillness of a perfect summer day on the Cape with Nantucket Sound as smooth as cobalt glass. His physical torments vanished. His lust quieted. His brother and sister weren't dead. Lyndon Johnson wasn't marshaling his allies to destroy him. Gabe hadn't been murdered. Caitlin and her cop friend weren't digging around the seamy edges of his life. Encircled by voters and tucked safely behind his magnetic smile, Jack dispensed an optimism he never felt, and using the alchemy of his presence made him feel useful and decent and like illness and death had stopped chasing him.

CHAPTER 31

Greenwich Village

As an afternoon rain fell outside her bedroom window, Caitlin tried to clean out Gabe's closet. She could smell the Royall Lyme Cologne clinging to his sport coats. Or thought she could. Memory of the dead was tricky. Her grief wasn't going anywhere. She wasn't ready to be in love again. Less lonely would do. Her date with Reed had persuaded her.

Caitlin touched a suit and withdrew her hand. The clothing would have to wait. On the floor behind the shoes was an olive drab footlocker, and she dragged it out. On top, below a decal of the Marine Corps insignia, Gabe had written: **GABRIEL RUSSO, 500 OCEAN AVE, BROOKLYN, NY.** Caitlin had never seen Gabe open the footlocker, but it must have been important to him, because he had the movers bring it to the Village. Yet she wasn't ready to look at Gabe's past and shoved the footlocker under the window.

She went downstairs to the wall of mailboxes in the vestibule. Jammed between her light bill and phone bill was an oversize envelope postmarked Miami Beach. She hoped Yenchi had sent her some info on Clara, the missing Cuban prostitute who connected Victor Diaz, Jack Ruby, and the mobster Trafficante. Cait had no idea whether this would lead her to Gabe's killer, but it was worth a try. Hope, even if unwarranted, beat hopelessness every time.

Someone knocked on the outer glass doors, startling her. It was a moment before she recognized Danny in his denim jacket and khakis. She rarely saw him out of uniform. Without it, he looked like a college boy.

"Hey," she said, stepping outside with him. The rain had stopped. She debated telling Danny about the short man in the long coat staring at her when she left the phone booth outside the bank. She chose not to. Three weeks had gone by, and Caitlin hadn't seen him again—and, what's more, grieving for Gabe, she often felt unsafe and distrusted her ability to perceive danger.

"I got some good news," Danny said. "A Vermont trooper showed Winkie's picture to a gas station attendant in Bennington, and the guy says he thinks he saw her in March."

"In March? If Winkie was in Bennington two months ago, she'd have been in touch with her parents by now. But I appreciate you telling me. And you didn't have to walk over. You could've called."

He glanced at his penny loafers. Caitlin noticed they were newly shined. Looking up, he said, "I thought we could get a drink at Fanelli's."

Men were funny, Caitlin thought. They ask you out with a statement, not a question. Safer for them, she figured, avoiding outright rejection. Caitlin would've enjoyed going out, but she didn't want to lead Danny on. She liked him. With his blond hair and liquid-brown eyes, he was appealing in that eternally boyish way, and, in theory, their friendship could take a romantic turn. But Danny was the head-over-heels type—thus, the hasty marriages and three divorces. And while Caitlin wasn't prepared to fall in love at the moment, she was less prepared for the responsibilities of being loved, the daily attentiveness, the unflagging devotion.

She said, "I'm tied up with work."

He wasn't buying her explanation. "I miss Gabe too."

"I know, Danny. Another time."

He was never affectionate with her, not even a hug at Gabe's funeral, so Caitlin was surprised when Danny kissed her cheek, and she stood there, feeling confused and abandoned and wishing he wouldn't leave as he disappeared down Grove Street.

Back at her desk, Caitlin found three five-by-seven prints of stakeout photographs in the envelope. Common to all three was a young woman, presumably Clara. In each photo, she was walking next to a different man, her long hair splashing over her shoulders in waves and wearing the same jersey dress that accentuated her curves. It was her face, though, even in black and white, that was striking. It was the face of a movie star: Ava Gardner and Sophia Loren came to mind. And there was more than beauty in her face, especially around the eyes, where Caitlin spotted an irrepressible intelligence.

In the first photo, Clara and a balding, thick-necked man in sunglasses were exiting a lobby with a spuming fountain in front of them. In the second one, Clara and a slick-haired dandy in a double-breasted suit were standing under a porte cochere with a hotel sign overhead—DEAUVILLE. The third photo was different. Clara was walking down wide stone steps next to a bent older man with a straw fedora and goatee. Behind them was a cream-colored stone building, and inscribed above the doors was TEMPLE EMANU-EL.

Caitlin doubted this man was a john, not the way Clara held his arm with both her hands, like a daughter supporting her elderly father. Yenchi might know. It was too early to call him at home, and Caitlin knew he wouldn't talk to her at work in case the cops had tapped his lines.

She placed the call at eight o'clock, and Yenchi answered. Caitlin said hello and thanked him for the photographs.

Yenchi chuckled. "Don't mention it. Whenever I cut FBI Agent Davenport some slack for a favor, he bets bigger and dumber."

"The picture in front of the temple. Who's the guy with Clara? He doesn't look mobbed up. Is he the rabbi?"

"Nah, the rabbi of that fancy joint, he's a big deal here. He wouldn't let himself be seen with a gal like that."

"Can you find out who the guy in that photo is?"

"I could ask. Some guys that go there bet baseball with me. This got to do with Gabie?"

"I can't say till I talk to her."

"I'll let you know how I make out. And, sweetheart, promise me you'll be careful."

"I promise," she said, studying the photograph and wondering if Clara had ever met Jack Kennedy.

CHAPTER 32

Wood County, West Virginia

Jack finished shaking hands outside the post office and walked to the station wagon. Kenny O'Donnell was in the back seat, reading the *Charleston Gazette*. Kenny, a war hero and Bobby's roommate at Harvard, had worked for Jack since his first campaign for Congress. Jack got in next to him. The driver was a native of coal country, with all his gray hair and half of his teeth. "Where to, Senator?"

"Take a ride, Smitty, and find me some voters."

Kenny said, "I spoke to Bobby. A new poll has Humphrey winning here sixty-forty."

"Jesus, in December I was beating Hubert seventy-thirty."

Smitty piped up. "Folks is finding out you Catholic."

Kenny passed the *Gazette* to Jack. "Thanks to Reverend Peale. "

Norman Vincent Peale was among the most famous clergymen in the country. He had visited West Virginia to warn his fellow Protestants, 95 percent of the state, that if a Catholic were elected president, he'd be more loyal to the Vatican than the United States. A recap of his remarks was on the front page of the *Gazette*. Jack flung the newspaper into the rear of the wagon.

Kenny said, "Hubert's not getting the nomination."

"No, but if he wins here, I might not make it on the first ballot at the convention. Then we'll have to fight for the nomination, and

Eleanor and her liberals will be waiting to kick me in the balls. She must be royally pissed that Franklin Jr.'s helping us."

The station wagon bounced along the potholed road, each jolt like a needle jabbing Jack's spine. It was a relief when Smitty pulled over. "There's a voter, Senator."

In front of a cabin with a tar-papered roof, a blond woman in a red cardigan and a thin, towheaded teenager were throwing a football back and forth.

Jack opened the door, and Kenny said, "One vote, Jack?"

"One person, Kenny."

As Jack went up past a rusty Nash Rambler with a busted headlight, the woman gave him a bright look of recognition. She couldn't have been more than thirty-five, but the sole remaining sign of her youth was her long ponytail. The boy eyed Jack as though he were coming to sell his mother a set of encyclopedias he didn't want to read. Jack raised his arms for the boy to throw him the football, and the boy threw him a tight spiral.

"Nice," Jack said, tossing back the ball. Pain shot up his leg, and he felt a flash of anger. He could barely throw a damn pass.

The woman watched him limp toward her. "You didn't have to trouble yourself none, Senator Kennedy. I'll be voting for you come primary day."

Jack smiled. "I appreciate it, ma'am. You are?"

"Dreema Parsons. That's my son Orton. Who should be getting on his sport coat so he can go pick up Sherri and get to the church supper."

Orton went inside. Jack saw a little Negro girl in a yellow jumper walking up the road.

"What you got there, LuAnn?" Dreema asked her.

The girl held out a plate. "Mawmaw sent y'all her corn muffins to thank you for your apple crisp."

Dreema accepted the plate. "You thank Mawmaw. And you might could take one of these off my hands?"

LuAnn took a muffin and scampered down to the road.

"Ma," Orton called, coming out onto the sagging porch in a tan plaid sport coat, a white shirt, and black pants. "I can't go. I lost my tie."

"Get over here," Dreema called back.

Jack waved for Kenny O'Donnell to join them. After introducing him to Dreema, Jack said, "Kenny, let me borrow your tie."

Kenny's long placid face was impossible to read. "My tie?"

Jack put a hand on Orton's shoulder. "Our friend here has a date."

Kenny undid his tie and held it out to Orton. "Don't know how," the boy said.

After taking the tie, Jack turned up Orton's shirt collar, tied a four-in-hand knot, and smoothed the collar. He looked at Dreema. "I've got to get out of that car and sit in a chair—if you'll let me borrow one. Could Kenny drop them off?"

Orton perked up. "Can he, Mama? I'll give him directions."

Dreema said, "I reckon a mother ain't the best chauffeur for a date. But I'll come get you at seven thirty. And be a gentleman, hear?"

With a fast "Yes, ma'am," Orton took off for the car. Kenny aimed a thin-lipped frown at Jack. Kenny was familiar with his habitual pursuit of the extracurricular, and Jack figured Kenny was worried that winning West Virginia was enough of a Hail Mary without Jack setting off a shitstorm of gossip by jumping this poor woman. Jack ignored the frown and followed Dreema to the cabin.

The main room was divided into a kitchen and a parlor, and the walls were ablaze with magazine covers. "They help with the insulation," Dreema said, opening the icebox and taking out a bottle of Dr. Pepper.

Looking behind the threadbare brown sofa, Jack saw a *Life* cover from 1953 with a photo of him and Jackie sailing, and one with Ernest Hemingway. Below the writer was a row of *Time* featuring Martin Luther King Jr. and several of FDR.

"Go on and set, Senator." Dreema put a tray with the soda, two coffee cups, and the plate of corn muffins on a low split-log table between the couch and a cane-back rocking chair.

The chair was similar to Jack's rocker in Georgetown. Dr. Travell had prescribed it for his back pain. Jack took a corn muffin. "Thank you, Mrs.—"

"Miss." Dreema sat on the sofa and poured the Dr. Pepper. "I was sweet on Orton's daddy in high school, and he was going to the war. That poor boy didn't make it off the sand at Normandy. And Orton, well, he's what a lot of wine and a little moonlight will do."

She laughed. It was a poignant sound, and as Jack ate, he wondered how, given her circumstances, she could laugh at all.

After a sip of Dr. Pepper, he said, "I'm curious. You're friendly with LuAnn's grandmother, and I saw miners of both races working together and joking with each other. Officially, West Virginia is as segregated as the Deep South. Yet it's so hateful down there. What's the difference?"

"With that coal dust on their faces, every miner's the same color. LuAnn's granddaddy and my daddy dug coal side by side. Our kids play together after school, and the grown-ups do for each other because we all in the same leaky boat. Why you ask?"

Jack was tired. The rocking had eased the tightness in his lower back. "To be president, a Democrat has to win the North and the South."

Dreema put her coffee cup on the tray. "Don't mean to get above my raising by dishing out advice, but if I's a politician, I'd only talk about the future. Voters like the future. It's when their wishes will come true. History's a sadder business. History's their real lives."

Dreema saw Jack looking at the book on the table—Eric Hoffer's *The True Believer*. She said, "Not being book read is living blind. I work lunches at the North End Tavern in Parkersburg, and the Carnegie library's nearby. I go most every day. The legislature's talking about putting a branch of the state university in Parkersburg. They do that, I'm gon' be a librarian. My Orton's an A student. He could use that branch. Plenty of children around here could. But long as our men dig coal and go to the wars, nobody don't give an owl's frosty ass about us. You get to be president, you might could do something about that."

The rocking was making Jack sleepy. "I will."

Her smile lit up her face, and Jack could picture her as a teenager, with that same blond ponytail and her green-blue eyes seeing a future she'd never have. After picking up the tray, Dreema went toward the kitchen. "You rest, Senator."

Jack closed his eyes and saw his PT boat in flames. That memory popped up at the oddest moments, and he seldom understood why. Now it made sense. The navy, Jack had discovered, hadn't ordered a search and had left him and his crew to die, relegating them to numbers on a casualty list. That the navy deemed him and his men expendable had infuriated him, and he believed Dreema was on a similar list along with millions of Americans. Kick was right. Life was unfair. Her death proved it. Jack had no illusions that he could rid the country of poverty, but something could be done. Imagine what Dreema could've been if she'd had a chance. Jack, as president, could create some of those chances. All he had to do was get the nomination and win the election. Jack was sinking into sleep when suddenly he felt despondent, thinking that a goddamn movie could stop him from making life less cruel for people like Dreema.

"Senator," she said, and Jack felt her hand lightly touching his shoulder. "Wake up. Mr. O'Donnell's here."

CHAPTER 33

Greenwich Village

This widow business was for the birds. Caitlin was astonished that emptiness could be excruciating. How could nothingness hurt? She bent to open Gabe's footlocker. The coat of his marine dress blues was folded on top. It was lunchtime, a convenient justification for her to leave and go to Fanelli's. Winkie's parents were paying the rent on their daughter's loft above the bar. As if that meant she would return. Danny had no leads other than that Vermont gas station attendant who thought he'd seen her. And with Gabe gone, it was unclear why Winkie had traced that greeting for Castro. Walking home, Caitlin noticed that spring had arrived, the flowers spurts of color in the window boxes of the brownstones.

Caitlin sat in her study sorting through the mail. It was preferable to digging through a dead husband's footlocker. She had donated everything in Gabe's closet to the Salvation Army except for his Brooks Brothers button-downs, which she occasionally wore to bed. The closet had been his present; the footlocker contained his past. Emptying it would be erasing Gabe forever. Caitlin picked up the stakeout photo of Clara and the older man on the steps of Temple Emanu-El. Last night, Yenchi had called. He hadn't been able to come up with a name for the man, and he was going to Kutsher's Hotel with his wife for a vacation.

"I'll ask around up there," he said. "I could get lucky. With all those Jews, the Catskills are a little Israel."

Caitlin hated waiting, but she had a plan: ask Julian about Santo Trafficante, figure out how to talk to Jack Ruby, and find Clara. All of it, she admitted to herself, was stumbling around in the dark, but Gabe used to say that when you didn't know what to do, you had to do something. Tomorrow she was supposed to meet Été for a walk in Central Park. She was looking forward to it. Now all she had to do was get through the evening. She'd start with *The Huntley-Brinkley Report.* A ringing telephone delayed her move to the living room. When Caitlin heard Reed Howland say hello, her spirits rose.

"I just got out of a meeting," he said. "The editor wants a story on the new youth culture at the beach. He says it's going on in Southern California—surfing, luaus, the kids lighting bonfires, and dancing like pagans. He got the idea from his teenage daughter. She saw the movie *Gidget* and can't stop talking about it. He wants the East Coast version. Did you rent that house?"

"In Belmar. From late July to mid-August."

"Does Belmar have a youth culture?"

"You mean teenagers ogling each other in their bathing suits?" Ordinarily, Reed was so serious with her that Caitlin was surprised by his laughter. She said, "There's surfing at the shore. And rock 'n' roll. My second year of college, I saw Bill Haley and the Comets in Wildwood."

"That'll do. I'll send you a contract. And an invitation. The *Post* has writers and artists down in the summer for a picnic."

His tone was businesslike, and Caitlin was disappointed by it. She should've been thrilled that her career was lifting off. Why did she expect anything else from this man? As Reed said, he had to run. Caitlin decided loneliness was a disease, and it was eating away at her sanity.

On TV, David Brinkley was saying the Humphrey-Kennedy primary battle in West Virginia was attracting a large turnout, and it would be close to midnight before all the votes were tallied. Seeing JFK on-screen talking to miners, Caitlin reconsidered her plan, focusing on how to arrange a conversation with Jack Ruby. She had an idea. There was nothing she could do about it at the moment, and she went into the bedroom and knelt over the footlocker, then removed the Marine Corps dress coat and pressed it to her face. It just smelled musty.

Under the coat was the rest of the uniform—trousers, belt, sash, and shoes. There was a metal canteen; a leather case with an Argus camera; a baseball mitt; a pack of letters, tied with string, that Gabe's mother had sent him while he was fighting in the Pacific; and a black cardboard box. Caitlin opened the box and saw a Baby Browning, a small gray automatic pistol. Caitlin checked the magazine. It was loaded, and she racked back the slide and pushed up the safety. No bullet in the chamber. The Browning was pristine. She sniffed the barrel and doubted the pistol had ever been fired. Why Gabe owned it was another of his secrets.

Placing the items on the floor, Caitlin knew she couldn't part with them. All that remained were nine faux-leather photograph albums. She pulled a purple one from the middle. Under the plastic on the first page was a cocktail napkin from the Three Deuces, and written on it, in looping letters, was *To the coolest cop in the city, Miles Davis*. That must've been Gabe's reward for not arresting the jazzman when he busted him with heroin. The next page was a Brooklyn Dodgers program from 1953, and across it, in neat script, was *Best Wishes, Jackie Robinson*. The other pages were empty. Caitlin smiled, thinking that Gabe wouldn't want to stick his gods in an album with mere mortals.

One more, she decided and took an album from the bottom. The cover was brown, with the marine insignia embossed on it. The pages held photographs of marines sitting on boulders, cleaning their rifles and lined up with the jungle behind them. The album shifted from the South Pacific to a city that, judging from the French signs on the baroque buildings, had to date to Gabe's time in Saigon. There were pictures of men and women in conical hats riding bicycles and motor scooters through streets jammed with traffic. On the last page was a single photograph. Careful not to tear it, Caitlin worked it free from under the plastic. The picture appeared to be of a rooftop bar. A glacial anger made her shiver. Jack Kennedy was sitting at a table and talking to someone across from him. Seated beside the senator and looking at him as if hanging on his every word was Été.

Caitlin grew dizzy and realized that she'd been holding her breath. She exhaled and inhaled.

And she still felt dizzy.

CHAPTER 34

Washington, DC

Ben Bradlee lit another cigarette. "Quit fucking worrying."

Dinner was over. Ben and Jack were still at the table. Jack was convinced he'd lose in West Virginia.

Ben crumpled up his empty pack of Kents. "Your last poll had you up in West Virginia."

Jack opened the *Washington Post* to the movie listings. "By two points. And I've gotten screwed before. You remember the 1956 convention. Adlai let the delegates pick his VP candidate, and I almost beat Kefauver."

"And your televised concession speech put you on the map. Last week you won the Indiana primary. You're going to win Nebraska and Maryland. By July—"

Jack cut him off: "The big boys won't give a damn if I win every primary. They'll get together at the convention and pick their candidate, and I doubt they want a young Catholic from Massachusetts."

"By July, you'll have so many delegates none of those backroom cigar chewers can fuck you."

Acting as if he hadn't heard Ben, Jack lowered the newspaper and turned toward the living room, where his wife and Tony Bradlee were talking on the couch. "Jackie, the movie of that Tennessee Williams play you wanted to see, *Suddenly, Last Summer*, is playing at the Trans-Lux. Let's go. It'll be a while before Bobby has numbers."

◆ ◆ ◆

Lead foot Johnny. Kick used to call him that as Jack sped around the Cape in their father's car and his sister bubbled with laughter. Now, Jack was speeding through Georgetown in his convertible, but no one was laughing. In back, Tony pressed a hand to her head in a futile attempt to keep her hair in place, and Ben cursed because as he tried to light a Kent, his matches died in the wind. From experience, Jackie knew that preserving her hairdo was hopeless. At every intersection, she jammed a low-heeled Pappagallo shoe against an imaginary brake until, unable to suppress her fear, she called out, "A red light means *stop!*"

Jack shouted, "If you're late for a movie, it means *step on the gas.*"

He parked on New York Avenue. They walked past the Plaza Theatre to the Trans-Lux with its glowing tower marquee. After going to the ticket window, Jack returned with bad news. "The movie started, and they won't let us in."

Ben said, "We can go to the Plaza."

Tony asked, "Don't they show dirty movies there?"

"Lucky us," Ben said.

The film, *Private Property*, was the story of two male drifters and a young housewife whose husband had no interest in her. For all Jack cared, the actors may as well have been speaking Turkish. After fifteen minutes, he was in the lobby, placing a collect call to Bobby, who was tracking the vote at the Kanawha Hotel in Charleston, West Virginia.

Bobby said, "You're winning with a sixty-forty split."

"How many precincts are in?"

"Ten. Out of two thousand seven hundred and fifty. Let's give it some time."

Jack gave it seventeen minutes, and Bobby said, "Votes from coal country are beginning to show up. No Catholics there, and you're winning."

"What's the vote total?"

"A couple thousand," Bobby said. "Turnout should be near four hundred thousand."

Jack laughed. "Let's give it more time."

"Good idea," Bobby said.

On the way to his seat, Jack stopped at the candy counter. He was so conscientious about his weight that during his campaign swings, he brought along a scale and weighed himself morning and night. His weight had hit 173; he preferred 170, not easy with all those political dinners. The main courses were usually inedible, but Jack had never encountered a bad slice of cake or scoop of ice cream. *Fuck it,* he thought and bought a Hershey's. He stuffed the squares of chocolate into his mouth, then eased his conscience by dropping the last row of the bar into a trash can.

"Any news?" Ben whispered in the dark.

"Not really," Jack replied, shifting in his seat to relieve the pressure on his spine.

His mind was racing. Jack had told Gabe and Ben he was worried about Democratic power brokers fucking him out of the nomination. That wasn't the whole truth. He knew Lyndon Johnson hated him and had sent his friends to tell reporters that Jack was dying of Addison's disease. His adrenal deficiency could be fatal, though Jack doubted Americans would pay attention to his health if he campaigned with his usual vigor. So Jack denied the charge, telling the press the bronzing of his complexion, a symptom of Addison's, was due to malaria, a response that emphasized his heroism because hundreds of thousands of sailors, soldiers, and marines had been infected with the illness during the war.

Nor was Jack sweating the rumors of his girling. One night, a blue-nosed busybody had seen him leaving one of his stopovers, but her story didn't fly with the papers. No mystery there. Bed-hopping was off limits to reporters. That was the rule, and a convenient one because a lot of the married guys in Congress, along with the reporters and editors who covered them, would hump a parking meter if you wrapped a skirt around it. A movie, on the other hand, would be trouble. Prints could be made from a movie and sold on street corners or shown in smut houses. Gabe had told him Caitlin was the sharpest woman he'd ever met, and with her and that police captain chasing Gabe's killer, and with Caitlin's friend Julian Rose making it impossible to intimidate her, who knew how it would go. If Gabe had been murdered searching for that film and Caitlin found out, she could be angry enough to talk to the press. Not that Jack would blame her. But if that film became public, he could forget about the nomination and his marriage.

The lights came on. Jack blinked and heard his wife say, in a tone of disgust familiar to him but one she never used in public, "That was a perfectly horrid film."

Back at the Kennedys', Jackie was showing Tony one of her priciest finds, an eighteenth-century walnut sideboard. As Jack sat on the couch and reached for the phone, Ben stood off to the side in the living room, writing on a notepad.

"Benjy, what're you doing?"

"It's for my memoirs. The night I knew you were going to be president."

Jack replied as he dialed the operator, "You better wait till I speak to Bobby."

When Bobby came on the line, he said, "You won. With over sixty percent of the vote."

Jack looked at Ben.

"Well?" Ben asked.

"Keep writing," Jack said.

CHAPTER 35

New York City

Easy to become an American, Caitlin thought, seeing Été standing by the West Seventy-Ninth Street entrance of Central Park. All you had to do was change clothes. In her white blouse with the Peter Pan collar, high-waisted jeans, and saddle shoes, Été looked ready to pledge a sorority.

The sun was buffing up the sky to an incandescent blue, and Été used a hand to shield her eyes against the light. *"Bonjour, ma chère."*

Caitlin had calmed down from last evening, but as she exchanged a double-cheek kiss with Été, her anger returned. Caitlin knew it wasn't fair to criticize Été for not telling her she'd met Kennedy in Saigon when it was Gabe who should have told her. Yet she was hurt that Été, who was supposed to be her friend, had kept silent, and the urge to lash out at her was hard to resist, so Caitlin held off mentioning the photograph.

They were walking through the Ramble, the woodland in the middle of the park, when Été said, "I'm moving to Quebec City."

"Why?"

Été brushed her long black hair away from her face. "My new novel refuses to speak to me. I write in French and need to hear it. Quebec is closer than Paris. You will come visit, yes?"

In a clearing off the trail, a woman with a face as wan and creased as rice paper was sitting on a rocky ledge above a pond, and the sight of her whispering to the Chihuahua on her lap gave Caitlin a nauseating preview of her future—alone, with a dog her only comfort.

"Hello?" Été said, stopping on the footbridge.

Resting her courier bag on the log railing, Caitlin retrieved the photograph from Saigon and held it out. Été gazed at it. "This is the bar on top of the Hotel Majestic."

Despite her best effort, Caitlin couldn't filter the sarcasm from her voice. "You forgot to tell me you knew Senator Kennedy?"

"Gabriel had me promise."

Caitlin dropped the photograph into her bag. She had assumed Gabe had asked her not to mention Kennedy. But hearing Été say it made her furious at Gabe for every one of his secrets.

Été touched her shoulder. "In France, *les journalistes* call me *La Jeune Fille Sauvage*, and in the wildness of my life, I am French. But a piece of my soul belongs to my mother, and she was a loyal daughter of Vietnam. At home, she kept an altar with candles, incense, and pictures of her ancestors. During Tet—the New Year—we placed fruit and wine on that altar to let our family ghosts celebrate with us. My mother taught we are responsible to the dead. I understood why Gabriel had me promise. His reason was not changed by his death. He didn't want you, the person he loved most, to think badly of his friend."

"Fuck his friend," Caitlin said.

"I was not the only one, *ma chère*. Jack has women everywhere."

That solved the mystery of why Gabe had written *J. Girls* on the back flap of his pocket calendar, but the revelation left Caitlin feeling uneasy. She didn't consider herself a prude. With the nuns' admonitions about lust ringing in her memory, Caitlin had eagerly surrendered her virginity her junior year of high school, and when she met Gabe, she was at the end of a fling with an aspiring novelist who was on the outs with his wife. However, Caitlin valued honesty above all else. Lying rankled her, and a serial adulterer would have to be a consummate liar. Dante sentenced adulterers to the Second Circle of Hell. Caitlin would've thrown them into the Eighth Circle with the hypocrites, thieves, and crooked politicians.

She said, "Why is Kennedy running around? He has an exquisite wife, and he may be the next president."

Été, her eyes opening wide, appeared thunderstruck by Caitlin's naivete. "King Solomon is remembered as a wise leader, and the Bible says he had seven hundred wives and three hundred concubines."

Caitlin's head was pounding. "King Solomon wasn't the great Catholic hope."

"Jack spreads hope while he lives behind a wall. He is *un politicien extraordinaire*. The people think he belongs to them, and he knows he belongs to no one."

Caitlin watched the stream bubbling over the rocks and under the bridge.

Été said, "These *relations extra-conjugales* you are so curious about. Do they have something to do with Gabriel's dying?"

"I don't know."

Été looped her arm through Caitlin's. "Let's get a coffee."

"And two aspirins," Caitlin said.

CHAPTER 36

New Jersey

With its bulldog coverage of local political high jinks, jazzy sports pages, and a highbrow arts section, the *Newark Evening News* was revered as the state's newspaper of record. The late morning was a madhouse in the city room—reporters shouting on the phone over the clacking of the wire service teletypes or pounding typewriters desperate to make deadline, with a miasma of tobacco smoke overhead that would've suffocated Caitlin if a gray-bearded bear of a man, sucking on an asthma inhaler, hadn't opened a couple of windows.

Viola Mauri, the arts editor, was in back. Vi was a bottle blonde with teased-up hair, and it would have been a cinch to mistake her for a truck stop waitress if you didn't know she'd graduated Rutgers Phi Beta Kappa.

"You feeling better, sweetie?" Vi asked, standing to hug Caitlin.

"Almost."

Vi backed into her squeaky swivel chair. "Your review of the Vidal play was tip-top. What're you doing in Jersey?"

Caitlin sat in a metal folding chair. "I'm meeting Julian for lunch."

"Word here is that Mr. Rose is talking up Kennedy for the nomination with the bosses."

"Julian doesn't consult me." In high school, Caitlin and Vi had been inseparable. They'd often double-dated—movies at the Maplewood, pizza burgers at Don's Drive-In, summer days down the shore. Yet even back then, Caitlin had never told her about Julian.

Taking a *Saturday Evening Post* from her courier bag, one of the prepub copies of the June fourth issue that Reed had sent her, Caitlin said, "And I wanted to give you this." After opening it to her article, THE LADY COP: TRIUMPH AND TRAGEDY, she passed the magazine to Vi.

When her copies had arrived, the unfairness of Gabe not being around when he'd been the one encouraging her to write had infuriated her. As she'd stared at her name on the page, her fury had dissolved into a manageable sadness, and she'd felt a sense of accomplishment and decided to bring a copy to Vi, who had been listening to her literary dreams since tenth grade.

Vi stopped reading and looked at Caitlin. "This is so good."

Her sadness returned in a less manageable form, and Caitlin might have lost it had a reporter not recalibrated the mood in the city room by jumping on the desk of the bearded asthmatic and yelling, "Rabbi, you circumcise my lede again, I'll stomp on your lungs."

Gripping the lip of his desk with both hands, the asthmatic jerked it upward, spilling the reporter onto the floor, drawing an "Attaboy!" from reporters who glanced up before they began typing again.

Caitlin asked, "Is he really a rabbi?"

Vi laughed. "You ever meet a rabbi named Kelly Conners?"

Rose Development Corp. was in South Orange Village, across from the public library. Julian was waiting for Caitlin in the conference room. On the black granite table were documents for her to sign, bottles of Dr. Brown's Black Cherry Soda, corned beef sandwiches on rye, and cartons of coleslaw and potato salad.

As they ate, Julian explained how the $100,000 from Gabe's life insurance was invested. "You have an account with my broker. There's money in the Templeton Growth Fund and stock in Walt Disney,

Coca-Cola, General Motors, Bristol-Myers, and IBM. You'll get a monthly statement, and you can reinvest the dividends or request a check. And I put you in a deal of mine—a garden apartment complex I'm building in Bergen County."

She gave him a suspicious look.

"What's with the look, Cait?"

The disapproval was plain in his voice, yet his face was expressionless, and Caitlin envisioned a younger Julian Rose—the raffish bootlegger with a cleft chin and a red carnation in his lapel, a man by turns debonair and savage, the man who had killed her father's killers.

She said, "Is this garden apartment deal an excuse for you to send me money? If it is, please don't. You've done enough. Bought Mom the house, paid my tuition. I'm doing fine. I have rental income, savings, and I'm selling magazine articles."

"Your dad died because I couldn't settle a fight between Abe Zwillman and the Abruzzis. It was a stupid fight. Prohibition was almost over, and bootlegging was finished. I was beside myself. Your dad was my friend, and your mother's pregnant with you. So I took care of my friend's family. I liked your mom—she was a gutsy lady—and later on I liked you." He smiled at her, a tolerant smile, but there was no forbearance in his tone when he said, "The deal's not an excuse, so let's not talk about it."

Caitlin looked at him, a softer, grateful look. She hesitated, knowing that Julian would be worried by her request. "Do you know Santo Trafficante?"

"I met him years ago in Havana. Why you asking?"

"I want to speak to him."

Julian wiped his hands on a paper napkin. "Is this about Gabe?"

"Sort of. Trafficante has been trying to track down a woman I want to talk to."

"Cait, Trafficante is a vicious SOB."

"So was his late father. I've been researching the family. They control gambling in the Tampa area. They also have ties to the Abruzzis."

"Who says?"

"In November 1957, Santo was arrested at that mob meeting in Apalachin, New York, and the Abruzzis also had people arrested there."

Julian dropped the napkin onto his paper plate. "Isn't your police captain friend investigating the shooting?"

"Danny has nothing. This woman—her name could be Clara—might know why someone would shoot Gabe. She knows mob guys and maybe a pimp who had ties to the CIA. Couldn't you ask around about my meeting Trafficante?"

"I could, but not if you're going to run around playing Sherlock Holmes."

Caitlin said, "I'm not. If I learn anything, I'll give it to Danny and back off."

Julian—ex-gangster, real estate titan, political operator—eyed her with all his formidable experience listening to 24-karat bullshitters. "How come pretty women always think men believe whatever they say?"

She got up and kissed him on the cheek. "Because you always do."

Before going back to New York, Caitlin drove out Valley Street, through South Orange Village and into Maplewood Township, and passed Memorial Park, where mothers and their young children were throwing pieces of bread to the white ducks gliding across the sun-silvered pond. There was a Norman Rockwell quality to the village and the town— the cheerfully painted Arts and Crafts houses and great shade trees. Growing up, Caitlin had longed to escape the placid rhythms of her life there. Now, exhausted by her losses in the city, she wanted to start over in a place where life was as predictable as the changing of the seasons.

Nevertheless, Caitlin knew there would be no peace for her until she caught Gabe's murderer. Yenchi still hadn't been in touch about the man with Clara outside the temple. If Caitlin could ID him, that might lead her to Clara. She was confident Julian would help her with Trafficante. When she spoke to the mobster, she'd need some idea of why he was interested in finding Clara. Jack Ruby might be able to shed some light on that. Caitlin had put off calling Ruby's club from her apartment. A pay phone was a better fit with her plan.

She had turned onto Springfield Avenue, a wide commercial strip, when, glancing in the rearview mirror, she noticed a Country Squire behind her. She thought it was the same station wagon with wood-grain-trimmed doors that had been trailing her on Valley Street, occasionally dropping behind a bus before reappearing again. The May sunlight was reflecting on the windshield, so she couldn't make out the driver. Country Squires were as common in the suburbs as crabgrass. Yet Caitlin, the erstwhile policewoman, believed that it was better to be safe than sorry, so she slid her .38 out of her bag onto the seat.

As the avenue crossed from Maplewood into Irvington, the Country Squire was behind a Good Humor truck, and she saw her chance to find out if she was being tailed. Hitting the gas, she flew by filling stations, a beauty salon, and a Chinese-takeout joint and abruptly turned into the parking lot of the Kless Diner. The Good Humor truck went by, then the Country Squire. She caught a glimpse of the driver, a man or woman with sunglasses and a bucket hat pulled low. Caitlin put the .38 in her bag and walked into the diner. The phone booth was outside the restrooms. She took out her change purse, dialed the operator, and asked to be connected to the Carousel Club in Dallas, Texas.

CHAPTER 37

Palm Beach, Florida

Jack was sitting at the long mahogany table in the dining room. The breakfast dishes had been cleared. His father sat at the head of the table. Bobby was across from Jack.

"How the hell did the Russians knock out our spy plane?" his father asked.

Jack said, "The CIA isn't talking, but I've heard the U-2s fly at seventy thousand feet, and for the last few years the Soviets didn't have the missile capability to hit them."

Bobby chuckled. "I guess they improved."

After the U-2 had been shot down on May 1, the United States had claimed it was conducting weather research. The Russians knew that was a lie because the CIA pilot, Gary Powers, had been captured along with film of their top secret military sites. Two weeks later, at a Paris summit to lessen Cold War tensions, Soviet premier Khrushchev demanded that President Eisenhower apologize for spying. The president refused, and Khrushchev canceled Eisenhower's scheduled visit to the Soviet Union in June.

"I'm not asking about missiles," his father said, aggravated, as if Jack was deliberately misunderstanding him. "I'm asking how Eisenhower let this happen."

Jack stared past Bobby to the glass french doors. He had come to his parents' oceanfront estate to relax in the sun and swim, but it was raining. "I can't get an official briefing. Scuttlebutt is that Dulles told Eisenhower if a U-2 crashed, it wouldn't be a problem because the pilot would die."

His father took the top off a box of Fanny Farmer candies. "I wouldn't trust that nose-in-the-air bastard Dulles as far as I could throw him. But, Jack, you didn't help yourself telling the press Eisenhower should apologize and call off the U-2s. Nixon and Johnson will kill you on that."

"That's old news, Dad," Bobby said. "Jack gave a speech in the Senate blaming Khrushchev for the failed summit, and he hit Eisenhower for losing Cuba to Castro."

Jack was drifting away, thinking that if the movie of him got out, none of this would matter.

"I'm off to Mass," Rose Kennedy said, walking in with a lace mantilla covering her hair and wearing one of her recent acquisitions from Dior, a brown silk dress with a matching jacket. "Can I interest any of you in joining me?"

Her husband smiled at her. "It's politics today, not God."

Her voice full of pained disapproval, Rose said, "Joe, it's God every day whether we like or not. And it's too early for you to eat candy."

Joe closed up the Fanny Farmer's, and Bobby said, "Mother, could you put in a word for Jack and the nomination?"

Rose dismissed the request with a wave. "Jack is going to be nominated. And he is going to win. You just make sure he keeps talking to the people on television. Jack is beautiful on television. And, boys, don't give Father a hard time, and sit up straight, both of you."

Jack and Bobby grinned at each other. And sat up straighter.

When Rose was gone, Joe started talking about Dulles again, but Jack was done listening. He wanted to swim, to lose himself in the water, but the rain wasn't letting up. Through the glass doors, Jack watched the rain.

CHAPTER 38

Dallas, Texas

Strippers were job-hoppers. Caitlin had heard about it from the girls during a temporary duty assignment with Vice on Forty-Second Street. That memory was the key to her plan. When she'd called the Carousel Club from the Kless Diner, the same unhelpful woman had answered. Rather than waste time asking to speak to Jack Ruby, Caitlin said, "Hello, this is Aileen McQuillan"—a name she'd borrowed from a classmate at Our Lady of Sorrows, because Ruby would have to be blind not to make her for Irish. "I heard you're hiring dancers. I'm in Florida, but I'll be in Dallas day after tomorrow. Can I stop by?"

"We open at noon," the woman had said. "Come at eleven, and let the boss look at you."

Caitlin flew from Idlewild, then landed at Love Field in the evening and took a cab downtown to the Adolphus Hotel. In the morning, after a room service breakfast of a danish and coffee, she bathed and reread the notes she'd made for her meeting. It took close to an hour with rollers, her new electric curling iron, bobby pins, and a can of Max Factor hairspray to create a fair approximation of a bouffant. To complement her cover story, she had gone to a secondhand store on the Lower East Side to buy an outfit—a low-cut black silk blouse, a leopard-print skirt, black suede stilettos, and a black satin pocketbook with a drawstring closure that was roomy enough to hide her .38 under a wad of Kleenex.

Inspecting herself in the mirror, Caitlin came down with a case of the jitters but convinced herself it was no worse than the Christmas pageant in eighth grade, when she had played Mary and somehow remembered her lines.

The Carousel Club was across Commerce Street from the hotel. It was above a barbecue joint, and not even the rising fragrance of charcoaled beef could obliterate the faint stink of cigarette smoke and spilled alcohol. The tables were close together and faced a stage and the bar. Except for a bartender, a young guy in a denim shirt who was slicing lemons, and a man sitting farther down with his back to her, the place was empty.

"Mr. Ruby?" Caitlin asked, approaching the man.

"Yeah," the man said, shifting around with a can of V8 juice in his hand. He was stubby and thick necked in a black double-breasted suit with wide gray stripes, and his thinning hair was slicked back to cover the bald patches.

"I'm Aileen McQuillan."

He gave her the once-over, a professional evaluation, not the stare of a lecher. "The dancer from Florida, right? Have a seat."

Caitlin sat as Ruby put the V8 can on the bar between *The Fat Boy's Book* and *Keep Slim and Trim with Domino Sugar Menus*. He saw her looking at the covers. "I exercise and follow them diets, but it ain't a battle I'm gonna win."

"You're not fat," Caitlin said.

Ruby's laugh sounded like he was gargling pebbles. "You're halfway hired, honey. Where'd you do burlesque in Florida?"

"Here and there," she said.

Suddenly, Ruby was suspicious, eyes narrowing. That's how Caitlin wanted it. And he kept his eyes on her when a busty platinum blonde in a G-string and with tassels on her nipples sashayed onto the stage, gazed around the empty club, and then disappeared behind the curtain. Caitlin glanced away from the stage as if she was mortified by the sight of the stripper.

Ruby noticed and rubbed her arm. Only for a moment, though, not like a guy on the make but in an attempt to reassure her. "We got other jobs, honey. Champagne girls keep their clothes on. All you gotta do is bat your eyelashes at the customers and pour champagne. If a customer offers you any dough to fool around, you tell me—I'll bust the pervert in the nose. I done it plenty. Jack Ruby takes care of his girls."

He was showing off for her, and Caitlin felt sorry for him. He reminded her of that sulky boy in school everyone avoided, and she believed he, like that boy, would welcome anyone, especially a woman, who asked for help. Earlier, at the Adolphus, standing before her bathroom mirror, she'd practiced transforming her face into a portrait of anxiety, and now she went into her act: "Mr. Ruby, please, please don't be mad at me."

"Mad, why would I be mad?"

"I'm not here for a job."

His expression hardened, and Caitlin said, "I'm really sorry. I'm no liar, but I want to find my best friend. She just up and vanished. Her grandfather told me she moved to Dallas and dances at a club on Commerce Street."

"OK, OK, don't get upset. What's her name?"

"Clara."

"Clara what?"

"Agüero," she said, a name she'd plucked off the shelf at the New York Public Library, confident that Ruby wasn't an aficionado of nineteenth-century Cuban poetry.

"Don't ring a bell. You maybe got a picture?"

Her handbag was on her lap, and, after loosening the drawstring, she slid out the five-by-seven stakeout print of Clara and the older man and placed it on the bar. Ruby studied it. "She's a looker, but I ain't seen her."

Caitlin had rehearsed this next part. Handle it wrong, and Ruby would mistake her for a cop or a hustler running a con. "Clara used to dance in Havana. She said she worked for a nice man, Mr. Traffic-something. Trafficson?"

Ruby grinned like he'd solved a riddle that would've stumped Einstein. "Trafficante?"

Bubbling with excitement, Caitlin replied, "Yes, yes, that's it. Do you know him?"

"Sure. The man's the salt of the earth. Don't put on no airs." He drank the rest of his V8 juice, then crushed the can in his hand, looking at Caitlin as if he expected her to applaud. She rewarded him with a coquettish grin. Ruby asked, "Where'd your friend dance?"

In the library, Caitlin had scrolled through microfilm of newspaper articles, noting the Cuban hotels that Trafficante reputedly owned out-right or with partners. She had memorized that list but now pretended she was having trouble recalling them: "Saint John's was one, and the Tropicana. I don't remember all of them. The Comodoro."

"The Comodoro?" Ruby flipped the V8 can into the sink on the other side of the bar. "She's a good girl, your friend?"

"Clara danced, but she wouldn't, you know, do things for money. Why?"

Ruby shrugged like a doctor reluctant to give a patient bad news. "The Comodoro, its reputation ain't that nice. Me, I doubt Mr. Trafficante's involved. He wouldn't have nothing to do with perverts."

Caitlin had to stop herself from pushing Ruby to talk. She was close—she knew it. But she remembered Gabe lecturing her class at the police academy on interrogation techniques: *Nothing makes somebody talk like silence. You don't extract information. You wait for it.*

Probably a full minute passed before Ruby said, "They make movies."

"Clara wouldn't—"

Ruby gave her a look that brought to mind a basset hound having a bad day. "Clara don't know, necessarily. Talk is there's a suite with a two-way mirror. Creepy bastards."

Bingo! Caitlin was tempted to ask if Jack Kennedy ever stayed in the suite, but that was too obvious. She said, "There must be a lot of famous people staying at the Comodoro—movie actors, politicians. Do they use the movies for blackmail?"

Ruby was staring at her. "Who knows what those creeps do."

Caitlin didn't turn away from his stare, didn't want him to wonder if he was being pumped for information. If he checked out her story with Trafficante, Caitlin would be on her way to New York before Ruby made that call. And if Julian arranged for her to meet with the mobster and Trafficante had spoken to Ruby, he'd be on edge when they met, and one lesson she'd learned as a cop was that it was easier to read a person on edge.

"I gotta shove off," Ruby said. "You hungry? We make a real nice hamburger here."

"No, thank you. I should go ask about Clara at the other clubs."

"You say Jack Ruby sent you, they'll pay attention. And you get a hard time, honey, let me know, and I'll give 'em what's what."

CHAPTER 39

Palm Beach, Florida

Jack, in light-blue swimming trunks, sat on a wicker chair, drying off in the sun. He recalled Joe and Kick standing in the pool while he took their picture. Kick had pasted the photograph into an album. Jack had looked at it last night when he couldn't sleep. It was from Christmastime, 1941. Joe had dropped out of Harvard Law to train as a navy pilot. Jack, beset by colitis, ulcers, and a deteriorating spine, had failed his military physical. At Jack's insistence, his father had pulled a string here and there, and presto—Jack was an ensign assigned to the Office of Naval Intelligence. The one depressing note was their sister Rosemary. Because of her wild mood swings, their father had sent her off for a lobotomy and she had to be institutionalized. Of course, none of them knew how the war would change everything. They couldn't know how lucky they were that Christmas.

Jack closed his eyes, and Kick, in her one-piece bathing suit printed with pink blossoms, emerged from the pool, leaving Joe behind.

Why the long face, big brother?

"Because a lot of voters don't like Catholics."

Kick sat on the chaise beside him. *Who does? Those fish sticks on Friday night are murder. Now tell me the truth.*

"How do you know I'm lying?"

Kick wrung the water from her hair. *I'm your conscience. And your best friend.*

"My conscience isn't my friend."

No one's is.

"Caitlin's going to call. I had Mrs. Lincoln give her the number here."

And Caitlin could be looking for that movie?

Jack nodded and looked at his brother standing in the pool. Joe was tan and lady-killer handsome and smiling like that Christmastime in 1941. And why not? He didn't know that in three years he'd be dead.

Jack said, "When *PT-109* sank, the crew was in the water all night. We were bushed, and I really didn't give a damn if I died."

What poppycock! You had so much to live for. You had a Harvard degree, you were famous for writing Why England Slept, *and Daddy had given us our trust funds.*

"The point is, Kick, I feel the same way now. The same emptiness."

That's ridiculous. Go to Green's Pharmacy for a banana split; you'll feel better.

"I did. Yesterday. It didn't help. Then I had a chocolate malt. And felt just as empty. So I gained two pounds, and today I have to starve myself."

I'm dead, Jack. I can't feel sorry for you. What's next? Mother didn't hug you enough?

"Did Mother hug us at all?"

Kick scowled. *And that's why you go girling?*

"No. It makes me feel healthy. And like I'm going to live forever."

What about ashamed? Doesn't it make you ashamed?

Jack grinned. "Sure. But who wouldn't trade shame for immortality?"

Incensed, Kick glared at him, her eyes a blue-gray fire. *Not funny, Jack.*

The phone on the low bamboo table next to him rang. Jack watched his sister dive into the pool and swim the breaststroke out to Joe. They linked arms and sank underwater.

"Hi, Caitlin," Jack said after picking up. "How're you getting along?"

Caitlin disregarded the question. "We should meet and talk. I can come to you."

Jack didn't want her to make a special trip to see him. With his success in the primaries and looking like a favorite for the nomination, reporters were tailing him, and one of those nosy bastards could ID her and start putting facts together. They wouldn't report run-of-the-mill adultery, but no news editor would be dumb enough to kill a story about the mob filming a presidential candidate with a hooker. Anxious to discover what Caitlin knew, Jack said, "Can we discuss it now?"

"Did you ever suspect the CIA of tapping your phone or bugging your office?"

"No."

Caitlin asked, "Could it be the FBI?"

"Why do you think such a thing?"

"Gabe wondered about it."

Her answer set his head spinning. The last thing Jack needed was that prude of an FBI director snooping on him. But even worse, if Gabe had told Caitlin about a tap, he could've mentioned the film he was chasing. Jesus, what a mess.

Hoping to learn more, Jack tried to draw Caitlin into a conversation. "Did you see the *Times* this morning? Democratic leaders in Essex, Hudson, and Middlesex Counties say their delegates will support me at the convention."

Caitlin said, "I did see that."

"If you talk to Mr. Rose, please thank him for his help."

"You can call his office."

"Caitlin, I feel terrible about Gabe, and if there's something I can do—"

"Meet me."

Peter Golden

Jack said, "I'm in Los Angeles tomorrow and then off to Chicago and Minneapolis. Two weeks is the soonest I can do. Mrs. Lincoln will call you with the details."

"Fine."

Trying to end the call amiably, Jack said, "Washington's a town where you say hello to a guy, he figures it's an invitation to stuff your ears with horseshit. One of the things I liked about Gabe: he never used two words when one would do. Obviously, it runs in the family."

"Yes," Caitlin replied and hung up.

CHAPTER 40

New York City
June 1960

The summer solstice was four days away, but the heat had arrived, and after a subway ride uptown, the air-conditioned lobby of the Carlyle Hotel was a relief. The white-gloved elevator operator wished Caitlin a good day as she stepped off on the thirty-fourth floor. Jack's secretary had told her the senator would be stopping here on a swing through the city, but after Caitlin knocked on the door, it was Jackie, in a lemon yellow cotton shift, who opened it.

Caitlin, expecting the senator or one of his staff, was startled. "Mrs. Kennedy—"

"Caitlin, yes? Jack said you'd be by. He's still out, but when he gets back, he'll take you over to campaign headquarters to get the research for your article. Please, come in."

Caitlin was glad the senator had concocted an excuse to explain her presence. In the sitting room, Jackie sat on the brocaded couch. Caitlin took the high-backed Victorian chair across from her. On the marble coffee table between them was a silver bucket with two bottles of champagne, four flutes, and a stack of magazines. On top was the *Saturday Evening Post* with Caitlin's piece in it. Jackie saw Caitlin looking at the cover—a richly colored painting of a mother photographing her daughter accepting her diploma at graduation.

"Your article was beautifully done," Jackie said, pulling a bottle of Veuve Clicquot from the ice. "So funny at times, and very moving."

"Thank you."

Jackie began pouring champagne. "Join me?"

Caitlin nodded. As a rule, she didn't drink at noon, but given the questions she had for the senator and sitting alone with his wife, whose pale complexion and dark, wide-apart eyes were even more arresting up close than in photographs, Caitlin was nervous enough to drink from the bottle.

"Cheers," Jackie said and drained her flute in several gulps.

Caitlin followed suit, and Jackie poured them another glass. "Jack had told me about your husband. I'm sorry for your loss. How are you?"

"Bad days, worse days." Caitlin had skipped breakfast, and the Veuve Clicquot went straight to her head.

Jackie took another long drink. "Terrible, just terrible. Have the police arrested anyone?"

"No." Caitlin had been flattered by her praise, but she didn't want to talk about Gabe, because those conversations were accompanied by the memory of her cradling his head in her hands and her fingers sticky with blood. So she asked, "How's the campaign?"

From a pocket of her shift, Jackie removed a pack of Salems and a matchbook. "Most of the time I'm tired and don't know where we are until I check the phone book in the hotel room. The crowds are getting bigger, and the women gape at me as if I'm a fairy-tale princess, and I stand there, afraid to move, and wish I could trade places with them—these wives with their houses and children and husbands who can't wait to get home for dinner."

Her voice was as high pitched and breathy as the peppier teenage girls Caitlin had taught. Unlike those girls, whose sentences collided like cars at a demolition derby, Jackie spoke as if weighing the impact of every word on the listener. It was tricky music, that voice, cannier than the wind-in-the-willows sound of it, and deciphering the meaning of her words would've been easier for Caitlin had she not finished another glass of champagne. Caitlin wasn't sure if Jackie was trying to create the impression that she aspired to be a hausfrau or hinting that she knew her husband played around. Maybe it was both.

"Ambition is a disease," Jackie said, lighting the Salem and blowing a stream of smoke at the ceiling. "And political ambition is the malignant form of it."

While Caitlin was wondering whether she was talking about herself or Jack, she added, "I'm being unfair. The bravest thing my husband does every day is get out of bed."

The meaning of this last statement escaped Caitlin until Jackie snuffed out her cigarette in an ashtray on the table, saying, "The pain, his back."

"From the war?"

"The war," Jackie replied, pouring the rest of the champagne into their flutes and turning the bottle upside down in the bucket. "Jack is easy to envy—unless you know him. Mummy warned me."

Jackie stared at Caitlin, whose mouth was set in that ambivalent territory between a smile and a frown. "You should see the look on your face. What are you thinking?"

Caitlin was loopy enough from the champagne to tell the truth. "How high class a family has to be for the mom to be called *Mummy*."

Caitlin thought Jackie might be insulted, but she started giggling. "Mummy is a class act, all right. I remember her threatening to smack a maid for folding laundered sheets and pillowcases incorrectly."

"There's a correct way?"

Jackie emptied her glass in three long swallows. "Mummy thinks so. And our teachers at Miss Porter's agreed. They supposedly taught us every correct thing a young lady needs to know. They were very prim and proper, so they skipped the part about the joys of the connubial bed."

Jackie was chuckling, a sweet, airy sound, and Caitlin couldn't tell if she was joking or referring to her situation. Été had said the senator had women everywhere, yet Jackie appeared perfectly happy, if a bit tipsy, talking to Caitlin. Being a campaign wife must be lonely, so in all likelihood Jackie welcomed the company, and her honesty with a stranger wasn't surprising. Strangers made the best listeners—no reputation to protect, no subterranean meanings to sour the conversation. And it was possible Jackie didn't know about her husband. Deceiving someone who trusted you was a snap. Hadn't Gabe deceived her about his work?

"I was going to order lunch," Jackie said, reaching to the floor and picking up a brown shoebox with **PAPPAGALLO** printed across the top in sky blue letters. "But I couldn't stand any more dreary salads."

She placed the box on the table and opened it. Inside were cellophane packages of Hostess CupCakes with white squiggles of icing across the chocolate frosting.

"Diet's over?" Caitlin asked.

"Let's call it a reprieve."

They were on their second round of cupcakes when Jackie turned to gaze out the window behind her to the treetops of Central Park. "You and I, we're members of an unfortunate club."

"Pardon?"

Turning back to Caitlin, Jackie said, "Your article, the miscarriage. It's hard to understand unless you've been through it."

Caitlin felt all her sadness about the miscarriage welling up. "The worst of both worlds. You don't get your baby, and you feel like you failed as a mother."

"Exactly." Jackie took the other bottle of champagne from the bucket, popped the cork, and filled their glasses. They both drank. Jackie was gazing at the park when she said, "Five years ago, I had a miscarriage—the next year, a stillbirth. A girl. I call her Arabella. She didn't have a birth certificate. And we didn't baptize her. But she—she's my Arabella." Jackie stared at Caitlin. "Cops keep secrets, don't they?"

"I do."

"I have to be careful and can't go to Los Angeles for the nominating convention." Jackie was silent for a moment, then said, "I'm pregnant."

"That's wonderful."

Jackie's face trembled. Caitlin thought she was about to cry. "I don't want to lose another baby. I can't. And Jack, Jack and I, we—"

A key jangled in the door, and the senator walked in—every hair in place, tie knotted, gray suit without a wrinkle.

"Sorry to be late," he said. "The breakfast at Pete's Tavern was sold out, and there were four thousand people outside."

Jackie said, "So you've nailed down the city's barfly vote?"

There was no irony in her tone, yet the senator heard something that made his grin vanish. An unpleasant stillness hung in the air. Caitlin was embarrassed. She also wondered if the unpleasantness was evidence Jackie knew about her husband's other women.

The phone rang on a stand by the door, and as Jack went to answer it, Jackie said, "That should be Caroline again. She wants to discuss her bedtime."

Jack said hello, and their daughter must have immediately launched into her pitch, because his face radiated a childish glee, like every day was a trip to the circus and life was forever.

"Buttons," Jack said, "Miss Shaw is in charge when Mommy and Daddy aren't home. Yes, we'll be home Sunday . . . all right, all right. I love you, Buttons."

When the senator came back, Jackie smiled slyly at him. "After you become president, I hope you do better negotiating with Khrushchev."

"So do I," he said, chuckling.

Caitlin smiled, more from relief than amusement. While the senator had been speaking to Caroline, Caitlin had been imagining Gabe talking to their daughter.

The senator said, "I'm taking Caitlin to the campaign office; then I have to be at NBC to tape my interview for *The Tonight Show*. I'll be here by eight."

Jackie stood, wobbling slightly. "Caitlin, I enjoyed our chat."

"Me too. And thank you for the champagne and cupcakes."

The senator gave his wife a quick kiss, and Caitlin couldn't decide if that was their usual goodbye or a performance staged whenever they had an audience.

CHAPTER 41

"Nine West Sixteenth," Jack said to the cabbie, who turned around and replied, "Jesus, it's you."

Caitlin saw the senator was in pain. His jaw was clenched, yet he conjured up a swell-to-meet-you smile. "Hello, sir. How're you doing?"

"Dandy now that I got the next president in my back seat," he said and, en route downtown, pontificated as if he were on *Face the Nation*. Two of his more rational suggestions: Jack should send Alcoholics Anonymous to Moscow to get Khrushchev off the vodka before he committed a nuclear idiocy, and because Castro already had a beret and a beard, Jack ought to buy him a set of bongo drums and get him a job playing for the beatniks at Cafe Wha?

Through it all, Jack kept repeating, "Interesting."

They got out of the taxi in front of a stately redbrick row house. Limping past the cast-iron gate to the basement entrance, Jack said, "This is my doctor's. The campaign-headquarters story was for Jackie. She worries about my treatments. Bobby thinks the Republican National Committee has been looking for my medical records, so this visit stays between us, all right?"

"Sure," Caitlin said, irritated that he must think she was stupid. The headquarters story was a credible explanation for why he was taking off with a potential bedmate. And Jack bringing her along to his doctor and requesting that she keep it a secret was probably his opening gambit for prevailing on her to keep the conversation they'd have to herself. That was a maybe. If Gabe had been murdered chasing down that movie, all bets were off.

◆ ◆ ◆

Inside the empty waiting room, Jack knocked on an oak panel door, and the woman in a lab coat who opened it—**JANET TRAVELL, MD**, according to the brass nameplate—had curly gray hair and the countenance of a no-nonsense kindergarten teacher.

"Senator," the doctor said, and Jack hobbled inside.

Caitlin, after three glasses of champagne, was in need of a lavatory, and she found one straight ahead. As she dried her hands with a paper towel, she heard an anguished cry, as if an animal was being slaughtered. She gripped the pistol in her courier bag. The cry came again. She opened the lavatory door a crack. The panel door swung in, and Jack returned to the waiting room. Letting go of her .38, Caitlin joined him.

The senator must have spotted the remnants of fear on her face because he said, "Injections in my lower back. They hurt."

And, evidently, made him feel better. His clenched jaw had been replaced by the relaxed expression of a man fresh from a rubdown, and as they went out, his stride was so limber that Caitlin could imagine him, long ago, bounding across Harvard Yard.

"Where would you like to talk?" the senator asked.

Her apartment would provide complete privacy, but Caitlin didn't want to give him the wrong idea. "I know a place. You'll even pick up some votes."

◆ ◆ ◆

Fanelli's had seemed like a prudent choice. Caitlin knew the bartenders and the regulars; reporters seldom drank there, and if one popped up, Jack's presence could be explained as an impromptu campaign stop. However, Caitlin hadn't anticipated that with the hot weather and most apartments lacking air-conditioning, people would be out, and as soon as the cab dropped them off on Prince Street, the senator was surrounded.

It started with the men and women, many of them mothers with young children in tow, lined up at the Italian-ice and hot dog carts on the corner of Mercer. Their ices and frankfurters were suddenly less important than meeting Jack Kennedy, and they jostled each other to get close. From the loading docks across Prince, men in sweat-stained work shirts wandered over, followed by secretaries in summery dresses from inside the warehouses who tilted side to side in their high heels as they darted over the cobblestones and between the cars and trucks. With the rubberneckers honking their horns and shouting "Kennedy!" traffic slowed—and then stopped when a burly driver hopped out of his tractor trailer and hurried over in a kelly green tank top with a white shamrock circled by the words **KISS ME I'M IRISH**.

As the crowd surged toward the senator, Caitlin backed up into the entranceway of Fanelli's and recalled the pictures in the papers of bobby-soxers mobbing Frank Sinatra outside the Paramount. But Sinatra was a singer. His love songs were intended to make women swoon. All Jack did was hold press conferences and give speeches on television about foreign affairs, the federal budget, and American leadership—hardly swoon-worthy subjects. But here he was besieged by admirers, shaking their hands and smiling as if Prince Street, with its abandoned factories and graffitied walls, was the only place he wanted to be. There was something sunlit about him, as though all those summers sailing on the Cape had soaked into his skin so that in the muggy overcast afternoon, he seemed to glow, a candle of many colors—reddish-brown hair, gray-green eyes, white smile.

To extricate him, Caitlin would require help, and she went inside. Farley, the bartender with the Popeye arms, was shooting the breeze with the hard-drinking soap opera fans watching *As the World Turns* on the TV above the bar. "Hey-ya, Cait. What's up out there?"

"I brought Senator Kennedy over, hoping we could talk privately in back, and now he's stuck. Can you bring him in?"

"Yeah, I love that guy. Boyce, let's go."

Boyce, a retired cop deemed an oddball by his bar mates for his beverage of choice, Jack Daniel's and chocolate milk, bore a resemblance to an albino gorilla. A minute after he and Farley went out, Boyce dragged in the senator by his arm, and Farley locked the door.

"I appreciate it, fellas," Jack said.

Boyce grunted and watched the soap opera. Farley drew two beers. "You're our man, Senator. These are on the house. Go on back, and I'll make sure nobody bothers you."

CHAPTER 42

"I apologize," Caitlin said when they were seated at one of the tables. "I didn't expect that."

Jack drank half the mug. Being idolized must be thirsty work. "Don't trouble yourself about it, and I appreciate the help extricating me. I suppose the crowds are because my campaign has accelerated. It's tiring, though."

As eager as she'd been to question the senator, now that she was with him, bringing up prostitutes and adultery made her uncomfortable. The plaid skirt and knee socks were long gone, but she was a Catholic school girl still.

"The Hotel Comodoro," Caitlin said. "It's outside downtown Havana."

"In Miramar. I've stayed there."

Caitlin drank some beer. She would've preferred a martini, a dose of courage with three olives. "The Comodoro has a suite."

"More than one, I'd guess."

"This suite has a two-way mirror," she said. "So if somebody had a camera—"

"Did Gabe tell you about—"

"He wrote a note about a movie," Caitlin said, "and I read it after he died. I've done some digging about the Comodoro. It's owned by a mobster, Santo Trafficante."

Jack was tapping a foot on the floor as if keeping time to his own private jazz combo. Caitlin found it nerve racking, like sitting across from a vibrating, oversize tuning fork. "Does Trafficante have the film?" he asked.

"I'm trying to meet up with him."

"Through Julian Rose?"

Ignoring the question, Caitlin pulled out the photograph of Clara and the older man from her bag and handed it to Jack. "Do you recognize the woman?"

He took a pair of horn-rimmed glasses from an inner pocket of his suit jacket and slipped them on. The horn-rims made him appear bookish and shy. "She's a prostitute?"

"Who may have worked at the Comodoro. Her name might be Clara."

Jack gave the photo to Caitlin. "I don't recognize her. Who's the old fellow?"

Caitlin put away the picture. "Don't know." She was starting to doubt she'd ever identify him. Last week, Yenchi had sent her a postcard from Kutsher's: *No luck in the Catskills. Will try again in Florida.*

Jack stuck his glasses into his jacket. "I may have met her. I don't remember much. I was in Cuba. A friend of mine said he knew some girls. It was late at night—"

"Senator, you're making it sound like a weak moment. I know it wasn't. It's a habit."

His voice was so casual he could have been commenting on the weather. "Last time I saw Gabe, we had breakfast at Martin's Tavern, and he warned me Été would tell you."

Caitlin finished her beer. "Été confirmed what I already knew. And truthfully, the whole thing makes my skin crawl. You have a wife and child. You're running for president."

There was a hint of the Kennedy smile. "You know the main thing you learn in politics?"

"How to lie?"

Jack laughed. "Lying you learn at prep school. In politics, you learn that if people could do better, they would. It's obvious, and no one wants to believe it. You see a three-hundred-pound guy waddling down the sidewalk puffing on a cigarette, you think he doesn't know he'd be better off losing weight and quitting smoking?"

"That's a convenient excuse for you," she hissed, thinking that a pint of beer, after too much champagne, didn't improve your self-control.

"Caitlin, why are you so angry?"

"Because I'm so disappointed in you."

"People will do that." His tone was somewhere between sarcastic and philosophical.

"You weren't supposed to."

Sounding more mystified than annoyed, Jack asked, "According to whom?"

"The millions of people who want you to be president."

"And they know me?"

"They believe in you," Caitlin said.

Jack took a deep breath, the lines deepening at the corners of his eyes, and Caitlin glimpsed the exhaustion beneath his glossy surface. "Don't kid yourself. The voters believe in who they want me to be."

He seemed as serious as when Caitlin saw him interviewed on TV, and her response, "That's not true," struck her as defensive and puerile.

"Here's what's true," Jack replied. "I'm richer than most voters. Smarter than some. And no better than any of them. Perhaps even worse."

He was so genuine when he spoke, and his words revealed a modesty about himself that Caitlin hadn't anticipated—she was inclined to believe him and wondered if his appeal to people was not simply that he was a good-looking, rich, urbane war hero with a photogenic family but also a sense that underneath his polished exterior, he was a realist about himself.

"I want to be president, not our Lord and Savior. It'll be hard enough with Lyndon Johnson trying to kill my nomination and Eleanor

Roosevelt endorsing Adlai Stevenson. If the Democrats choose me, then I'll have to beat Nixon, and he's smart and qualified. But if there's a movie and it gets out, my chances are nil. Will you look for it?"

"Gabe was doing that for you?"

Jack looked at his beer. The foam was gone. "He was."

"To catch Gabe's murderer, I have to find out why he was murdered. I have a friend, Winkie. Her real name is Hannah Lewison. She's an artist who did an engraving for Gabe about Fidel Castro. Winkie lived upstairs here. Her loft was torn apart, and she's disappeared. Danny, the police captain, thinks the engraving was part of a CIA assignment. Is Danny correct?"

"Caitlin, all I know is that Gabe was in Mexico City before he was shot."

"Then I need you to ask Allen Dulles what Gabe was doing and if he knows anything about Winkie."

"Allen will only talk to me if I'm nominated."

Caitlin asked, "Because if you're elected, you can fire him?"

"That's right. So we have a deal? You won't talk about the movie with Danny or Julian or anyone you don't have to, and you'll be in touch with me through my office?"

Caitlin stared at him. "For now."

"Unless Gabe died looking for the movie?"

"Unless Gabe died looking for the movie," she said.

CHAPTER 43

Boca Raton, Florida

Every morning, Yenchi unhappily followed his cardiologist's orders. A grapefruit and Special K cereal with skim milk. "Guys eat better in jail," he'd told his doctor, who pointed out that Yenchi was no kid. He was overweight, and his heart beat like a maniac banging on a snare drum. Then he'd sentenced Yenchi to forty daily laps in his pool. Yenchi, who believed physicians were God's earthly representatives, obeyed—less unhappily, because while swimming his awkward crawl, he relived the pleasures of breakfasts gone by, two glazed apple fritters from Walt's Bake Shop and three espressos.

On this morning, his sugary, caffeinated memories were obliterated by his thoughts of Gabie. Yenchi couldn't shake his sadness. He hoped the info he'd given Gabie on that no-good pimp Victor Diaz hadn't gotten poor Gabie killed. And he regretted telling Caitlin about Ruby and Trafficante and sending her those stakeout photographs. If Caitlin dived into the middle of this, all kinds of things could happen, none of them pleasant.

At least the vacation at Kutsher's hadn't cost him a dime. That was his wife's doing. Thirty years before, Hilda had helped Yenchi start his book. He never would've figured those canasta-playing grandmothers with their rhinestone-crusted cat-eye glasses for gamblers. But Hilda had an eye for suckers. The old babes were bored. They were all dolled up after getting new dye jobs in the beauty parlor, and though their husbands complimented their upgraded hair, they refused to take cha-cha lessons and just wanted to play gin rummy in the cardroom. The husbands placated their wives by doling out wads of cash, and Hilda persuaded the ladies it was fun to bet baseball. Because they were largely from New York and New Jersey, the team the wives knew was the Yankees, who paid Hilda and Yenchi's hotel tab by losing the next five out of six. That was the good news. The bad news: Hilda said, "Yench, I forgot how much I liked making book. When we get home, I want to work with you in Miami Beach."

For the last two weeks, Hilda had arrived at the barbershop with him, and, in between taking bets over the phone, she criticized the barbers for failing to sweep up after every haircut and Inés the manicurist for failing to button her blouses sufficiently to hide the prominent swells of her breasts. The barbers, who cut enough hair to cover the mortgage on the building, grumbled about quitting, and so did Inés, whose breasts made the customers smile.

Yenchi wanted to tell Hilda that it'd be better for everyone if she'd stay in Boca, except what man ever nixed his wife's plans and came away happy? The barbershop and his book were closed Mondays. Weekends were his busiest time, and maybe he could talk Hilda into taking off Saturday and Sunday. That would work nicely for him. Unfortunately, bookies as adept as the Yench never kidded themselves about the odds, and at best he calculated his chances of getting a break from his wife were three to one against.

Nonetheless, it was worth a try.

PART III

CHAPTER 44

Los Angeles, California
July 1960

In a suite on the ninth floor of the Biltmore Hotel, Jack slumped in a chair, reading a draft of the acceptance speech he'd give if the delegates nominated him for president. The speechwriter, Ted Sorensen, a young lawyer with the weary gaze of an old pastor, stood by the chair, cleaning the lenses of his black-framed glasses with his tie.

"'We stand today on the edge of a New Frontier,'" Jack said, quoting from the speech. "That's a good slogan." He gave the pages to Sorensen. "Trim the Catholic paragraph, and emphasize my backing of public education."

Sorensen departed, and Jack turned his attention to Bobby. His younger brother was standing with a phone to his ear and the exaggerated frown that appeared whenever he was enduring a lecture from their father. For Jack's critics, Joe was an irresistible target—rapacious Wall Street speculator, bootlegger, and appeaser of the Nazis who was attempting to buy his son the White House. Former president Harry Truman, who had resigned as a delegate to the convention claiming it was fixed by Kennedy's backers, had made the wisest crack: *It's not the pope I'm afraid of, it's the pop.* Still, Joe and Rose Kennedy wanted to be in town for their son's nomination, and they were holed up at the

Beverly Hills estate of Marion Davies, erstwhile mistress of the late newspaper publisher William Randolph Hearst.

Bobby held out the phone. "He wants you."

Jack got on, and his father said, "My reporter friends tell me there's lots of delegates saying they should nominate Stevenson because of his experience. I told the reporters Adlai's a weak sister, which is why he needs his nursemaid Eleanor Roosevelt."

"Dad, I'm not sure it's a great idea to vilify Adlai and Eleanor off the record."

"Vilify! I don't vilify any of these fuckers! And tell Bobby and Teddy to lock up the southern delegates or Lyndon will steal them—Texas is as southern as fried chicken."

"How's Mother?" Jack asked.

His father wasn't fond of anyone derailing his train of thought, and, before slamming down the phone, he made a pitch for paternal fealty. "Mother's praying for you and says you should do everything I tell you to do."

Jack returned to the chair.

Bobby looked at him. "What's bothering you?"

Jack considered telling him about the possible existence of the Comodoro movie. Ever since speaking to Caitlin—going on four weeks now—Jack had walled off the idea of the movie, as if it concerned someone else, but it kept popping up like the memory of his PT boat in flames. He had rented an apartment on a quiet street away from downtown, and he'd passed some time there with Marilyn Monroe. If he couldn't be good, he could be careful. Once Marilyn was gone and Jack was soaking in a hot bath, his thoughts drifted to the Comodoro— Jack in bed gazing across at a wall mirror edged in gilded fleurs-de-lis, or was it two-way glass with a movie camera behind it? No, Jack wouldn't tell Bobby. He didn't want to discourage him with the work he had left to do corralling delegates. And while this was how Jack justified his silence to himself, in the back of his mind there lingered a humiliating glimmer of truth. He was ashamed to admit he was powerless to stop himself from risking so much for so little.

"Jackie Robinson's bothering me," Jack said.

Bobby sat on the bed across from his brother. "Why? Because he supported Humphrey in Wisconsin? Hubert lost."

Jack shook his head. "I spoke to Robinson three weeks ago in Georgetown. He's still pissed off I met with the governor of Alabama. And after Robinson lets me have it for not understanding the Negro situation and I agree that I don't, I told him about a professor I had who used to tell his students that the Irish Potato Famine was the worst tragedy ever to reach our sacred shores."

Bobby said, "All those Catholic immigrants ruining his nice Protestant country."

"And Robinson says, 'One name I got called when I broke in with the Dodgers was *smoked Irishman.*'"

"Maybe Robinson liked the story," Bobby said. "You saw his column last week in the *New York Post* saying you were willing to learn."

"Half the NAACP and Eleanor Roosevelt must've missed it. Eleanor was down by the pool here, in a hat and long dress like a Puritan sunbather, assuring reporters I can't win the Negro vote. To the starry-eyed tribe of liberals, I'm Jefferson Davis. Meanwhile, who's Nixon—the second coming of Abraham Lincoln? Don't they understand a Democrat can't become president without the South? In '52 and '56, Adlai got his ass kicked by Eisenhower, and that was with Adlai winning Alabama, Georgia, Mississippi, and the Carolinas. I'm fucked without those states, and I still publicly supported the lunch counter sit-ins. The Democratic Platform Committee outlaws discrimination and gives the attorney general the power to beat the shit out of the crackers if they don't like it."

Jack was disgusted by his own whiny ranting. If Catholicism, and his life, had taught him anything, it was that everyone had a cross to bear, and Jack believed it should be borne with your mouth shut.

Bobby said, "The segregationists hate the civil rights plank of our platform. Some southern delegates are refusing to pledge to any candidate, and with others supporting Lyndon, it'll be harder to get you nominated on the first ballot. After that—"

"Chaos. And maybe the bosses will pick a candidate, and a lot of them don't like me."

"Jack, you have to talk to—"

"No, not that silly bastard."

A knock sounded on the door, and Bobby said, "That's CC. He's why I came up. Let's go in the other room, and you convince him to help me."

Cecil Colewater, a scion of nouveau poor Virginia gentry, had been a year behind Jack at Harvard, where he'd edited the *Crimson*, and had gone on to fly P-51 Mustangs for the US Army Air Corps. After the war, he married a wealthy older widow from New Orleans, then moved into her Garden District mansion and plundered her fortune to buy newspapers across the South. His weekly editorials, signed *CC*, ran in his papers and were critical of the federal government for imposing its will on the states, pointedly with respect to integration. He wrote with tasteful disdain, though it was rumored that he had financed a series of vicious, unsigned pamphlets distributed by the Ku Klux Klan, the thrust being that the United States would be better off if Negroes and Jews went elsewhere.

"Senator," CC said, walking toward Jack with a broad grin. He was slender and narrow shouldered and outfitted in the summer uniform of the upper-crust good old boy, a bow tie and seersucker suit. After Jack and CC shook hands, they sat on opposite ends of a curved sofa while Bobby stood apart, leaning against the console television.

Brushing a fine gray-blond forelock from his high forehead, CC said, "Senator, your brother says you may require some assistance."

"Call me Jack. And yes, I need more southern delegates to support my nomination."

"Well, Jack," CC replied, his tone so contemptuous it sounded as though he'd said, *Listen up, asshole.* "That civil rights plank has put an awful fright into folks."

"CC, the plank stays no matter who gets the nomination."

"True, except you were behind this one. And it's plain ugly—halting any discriminating in voting, schools, housing, and letting the Justice Department poke its big nose in where it doesn't belong. You're fixin' to eviscerate Jim Crow."

Jack dragged up a smile from somewhere, and his stomach flip-flopped when he said, "Come on, CC. Do you agree with every word in your papers?"

"I don't. That doesn't change the fact folks are scared Negroes will overrun the South, becoming mayors, police chiefs, and what have you. How will folks protect their daughters and wives with Negroes doing as they please?"

Jack's head was pounding, and he almost snapped, *Bring back lynching.* He didn't say that, yet his response, to his mind, was equally atrocious. "You know the game. What's written in a platform hardly anyone reads and what a president does are two different things."

"Yes indeed, but your civil rights plank has been disowned by nine states down South. I own newspapers in every one of those states, and it's no brag to say down there I've done more than most to elect governors and congressmen. I can steer those fellows in any direction I want, because their instinct for self-preservation exceeds their devotion to causes. I could work for your nomination if you don't make me look like God's own fool."

"You could?"

"Sure enough," CC said, his voice resonant with oily splendor. "I'll talk to the big party boys and the delegates, and after you're the candidate, your campaign could reserve space in my papers. My readers would be hospitable to you talking about closing that missile gap, bringing some down-home justice to Castro, aid to farmers and the poor. And there'd be editorials seconding your proposals."

In a perfect world, Jack thought, he'd instruct CC to stick his news-papers up his ass. Regrettably, political ambition was the enemy of per-fection, so with a moral and physical nausea rising in him, Jack asked, "And the price of this space?"

"Two hundred thousand dollars."

Jack wasn't shocked. His father frequently remarked he'd never met a man who wasn't for sale. Jack just hadn't expected the price to be so high.

"No," Bobby said. His face was impassive, but Jack knew that was the mask his brother donned to hide his outrage. "A hundred thousand, not a penny more."

CC slowly got to his feet. "I reckon that'll do. I've seen some of my friends at the grill. Bobby, come on down with me, and we'll talk to those boys."

Bobby looked at his brother, who nodded.

"Jack," CC said. "It's been a pleasure, and I'm betting you'll be nominated."

Jack couldn't bring himself to stand and shake his hand. "I hope you win that bet."

When they had left, Jack went into the bathroom and knelt in front of the toilet. His stomach contracted. Nothing came up. He raised his head from the bowl. Kick, in the red-white-and-blue-striped dress fash-ionable among young Kennedy supporters, was sitting on the pedestal sink with a flagrant look of disapproval on her face.

Jack, that man is a gargoyle.

"Correct," he said and, wrapping his arms around the toilet, began to vomit.

CHAPTER 45

New York City

Caitlin got into the front seat of the Chrysler Imperial. Julian was staring up at West Fourth. "See that short, squat guy on the corner?" he asked.

"In the blue blazer and white duckbill cap?"

Julian said, "That's him. He's been nibbling a pretzel and watching your street for ten minutes. It's a hot day for all that salt with nothing to drink. Have you seen him before?"

"No. And half the people in the Village stand around navel-gazing."

Julian pressed a button, lowering his window. "Let's say hello to him."

As the car started up Grove Street, the man blended into the crowd heading for the subway and vanished down the steps of the Christopher Street–Sheridan Square station.

"You see him again," Julian said, "lock yourself in your apartment and call Danny."

"I'll do that." With Gabe she'd learned it was no use arguing with a man about his desire to protect you. Even so, she'd never forgotten the man who'd appeared to be tailing her on MacDougal Street last December.

Julian drove onto West Fourth, and Caitlin asked, "Why did Trafficante agree to talk?"

"The Abruzzis asked him. As a favor to me. It's good business to make the Abruzzis happy, and if Trafficante's looking for this Clara, he'd want to know what you know."

"Trafficante doesn't know you?" Caitlin asked.

Julian shrugged. "By reputation—my old reputation."

Down Canal Street, on the border between Little Italy and Chinatown, four Cadillacs with long, high tail fins were parked in a delivery zone outside a store. Across the storefront windows, in elegant script, was the name **A. KAPLAN**, and each of the six nattily attired male mannequins in the windows held a highball glass in one hand and a cigar in the other.

Julian pulled alongside the Cadillacs. "Since Carlo Gambino began shopping here, it's like Brooks Brothers for mobsters. Go in and ask for Mr. Trafficante."

Unnerved, Caitlin asked, "You're not coming?"

"Trafficante will say more if you're alone, and you'll be safe. Nobody likes making the Abruzzis unhappy."

Entering the shop, Caitlin's impression was that, with its club chairs and red oak herringbone floor, it could've been one of those snobby clothiers in London—except for the clientele. Men, redolent with an overdose of cologne, were slipping in and out of suit coats, their gold watchbands catching the overhead light, while others gathered at the wall display of Dobbs fedoras, the choice of sartorially minded hit men, because a fedora, worn low, made it more difficult to identify a shooter.

She asked a salesman, with a tape measure draped around his neck, if Mr. Trafficante was around, and he pointed at a staircase next to the dressing rooms.

Upstairs was a room with tables, sewing machines, and overhead fluorescent lights. Trafficante was inspecting a shiny gray sharkskin suit coat on one of the tailor's dummies when Caitlin came in and introduced herself.

"A pleasure," he said, his face with all the joie de vivre of a poached salmon.

Trafficante moved two chairs from the tables, and they sat. Caitlin handed him the stakeout photograph with Clara and a balding, thick-necked man in sunglasses exiting a lobby with a fountain in front of them. She knew the man was a mobster. She had seen his picture on microfilm at the library when she was researching Trafficante. Caitlin didn't want to show him the photo with the old man outside Temple Emanu-El. Trafficante might not know about the man, and Caitlin wasn't there to provide new information.

"Do you recognize these people?" she asked.

Trafficante studied her, his eyes black pinpoints behind his glasses. "I don't, but I recognize the hotel. It's the Fontainebleau. In Miami Beach."

Keeping her tone sweet and girlish, Caitlin said, "Could you take another look?"

Trafficante gave her the photo. "You ask questions like a cop."

"How's that?"

With more than a hint of impatience, Trafficante said, "Like you know the answers."

Caitlin attempted to sound contrite. "You caught me. The man is Sam Giancana. Walter Winchell says you and Giancana are the top mobsters in the country."

Trafficante grunted disdainfully. "Winchell's a gossip columnist. You can't trust nothing that louse writes. Next thing he'll be saying is Elizabeth Taylor's gonna marry Khrushchev."

Caitlin laughed, light and airy, like the mobster was the wittiest comic alive. "The way she goes through husbands, she might get around to him."

Trafficante responded with a small grin, as if grinning violated a sacred vow.

"The woman's name is Clara," Caitlin said. "She worked at the Comodoro. You owned that hotel, and I heard one of the suites in the Comodoro had a two-way mirror so you could watch couples in bed."

Trafficante sighed, letting his boredom show. "I owned the Comodoro. I didn't work there."

"Clara was a prostitute," Caitlin said.

Trafficante put some muscle in his voice. "The only woman I chase is my wife. Got it?"

Caitlin was gratified she'd gotten a rise out of him. It proved she had his attention. "I wasn't implying you were Clara's john. But I heard a rumor there was a movie of her with a man—and you knew about it and are trying to find her."

That brought another reluctant grin from Trafficante. "That's some rumor. There's nutcases that'll swear Martians land in their yards. You don't believe that, do you?"

"I don't. But do you know about the movie and Clara?"

Caitlin wasn't expecting a truthful answer, yet even liars as experienced as Trafficante could make a mistake, an unplanned expression or abrupt twitch, that gave them away. Trafficante brushed a hand over what remained of his hair, but that wasn't the mistake she was counting on. It was that he was eyeing her angrily and holding himself still, like a cobra in a basket, and before he spoke, Caitlin was convinced the movie was real, Trafficante wanted to get his hands on it, and Clara possibly knew where it was.

"You like rumors?" Trafficante asked. "You should talk to Jack Kennedy about Giancana. I hear Jack gave Sam a bag with a quarter million bucks in hundred-dollar bills so Sam's friends could pass out cash to voters in the West Virginia primary. That's a smart move for Sam. It don't hurt having a guy in the White House owing you."

Trafficante was staring at her, and she stared right back, saying, "If someone had a movie of the president with a prostitute and kept it private, wouldn't he be owed a favor?"

Trafficante ignored the question. "You asked me what I know, so here it is, and then I gotta go. I know there's an FBI agent in Miami who gambles more than is good for him, and he owes his bookie, and that's where you got the stakeout picture of Giancana. Jack Ruby called me, so I know some gal—you, I'm guessing—went to see him asking about the Comodoro and a prostitute. I know you and your husband used to be cops, and somebody shot him. And I know I had nothing to do with it."

Caitlin was inclined to believe him about Gabe, because she couldn't think of a reason Trafficante would want him gone.

"There's one more thing," Trafficante said. "I know the Abruzzis a long time. But they don't scare me enough to let you go poking around in my business."

Caitlin had wondered how long it would take him to threaten her. She had anticipated being frightened, and she was, but her rage exceeded her fear, so as Trafficante got up to leave, she played her trump card, Julian's murderous past. "You know Julian Rose?"

Trafficante flinched. "You think I'm afraid of him?"

Caitlin smiled sweetly. "Of course not. I just think everybody's afraid of being dead."

Trafficante looked at her. Finally, he said "Yeah" and went down the stairs.

CHAPTER 46

Hyannis Port, Massachusetts

Through the bay window, Jack saw Caroline and Jackie holding hands and heading for the beach. He wanted to go with them, but he was stuck in his house while the director of the Central Intelligence Agency briefed him on the world's trouble spots. That morning, Dulles had flown on a private plane to Barnstable Municipal Airport, where Bobby was waiting to drive him to the Kennedy compound. Bobby couldn't attend the briefing. It was classified and restricted to the nominees for president and vice president. So far, Jack had heard nothing he couldn't have read in the *New York Times*.

Jack asked, "How serious is our missile gap?"

Dulles removed his wire-rimmed glasses, rubbed the bridge of his nose, and then put the glasses back on. "The Pentagon would have a better handle on that."

Jack had asked the question to see if Dulles was there for some straight talk or to fulfill an obligation, and obviously it was the latter. Jack knew from two sources, a CIA officer and a casual dalliance who typed reports for the Senate Armed Services Committee, that the U-2 photographs indicated the United States was well ahead of the Soviet Union in the production of intercontinental ballistic missiles. But because Dulles hadn't answered, Jack was free to use the missile gap in the campaign to criticize Eisenhower and Nixon for falling behind the Soviets.

Jack said, "Let's go sit on the porch of my parents' house. You'll like the view."

Watching the two men walk across the grass, past boys and girls playing tag, one could have concluded that a tall, white-haired, pipe-smoking grandpa had dropped by to visit his grandchildren. Even Jack, with his discerning eye for images, might have reached that conclusion had he not been aware of the director's fondness for the cloak and the dagger.

"Gorgeous," Dulles said when they were seated on the porch with Nantucket Sound sparkling before them.

Jack knew the CIA director wasn't going to like his questions, yet he had to ask them to keep Caitlin looking into the movie and to find out who murdered his friend. "Allen, who shot Gabe Russo?"

"Honestly, I don't know."

"What was Gabe doing for the CIA in Mexico City?"

Dulles unrolled a black tobacco pouch. "Covert operations are not on our agenda."

"If I give what I know to Ben Bradlee, he can write a story for *Newsweek* about the CIA shitting in its shoes. That'll give me another excuse to kick Eisenhower and Nixon in the balls."

Dulles dipped his pipe into the pouch. "That's beyond the pale, wouldn't you say?"

"Interesting phrase, *beyond the pale*. In Ireland, the English had pales driven into the ground to delineate the area of the king's rule. If you went beyond them, your fate was in the hands of surly Irish peasants—my ancestors."

As Dulles lit his pipe with the flick of a lighter, Jack said, "The polls have me trailing Nixon. But the second you read a poll, it's out of date. I'm going to win, Allen, and I assume you want to stay on as director."

Dulles was puffing smoke like an overworked steam engine. Then he took the pipe out of his mouth. "The agency set up a security company for Gabe, and he investigated agents and assets to make certain they were safe and hadn't been co-opted by our adversaries. He was in Mexico City investigating two operatives."

"The cousins Castro arrested for blowing up a ship?" Jack asked.

"Gabe went down to see if they were being watched by the Cubans or the Soviets. According to the report we retrieved from Gabe's suitcase, they weren't."

"Gabe had a friend, Hannah Lewison. She did an engraving for Gabe. What was it?"

With a knowing, condescending smile, Dulles said, "You've been talking to Gabe's wife and the police captain."

"That doesn't change my question, Allen. Or that Hannah Lewison is missing."

"I never met Miss Lewison. She engraved a cigar box from Tiffany, a gift for Castro to mark his visit this fall."

"And what's going in the box?" Jack asked. "Plastic explosive?"

"Nothing. It was a flight of fancy of mine. We couldn't neutralize Castro in New York."

Jack felt the muscles in his lower back spasm and wished Dr. Travell was around with her needle. "How developed are the plans to get rid of Castro?" If it happened prior to Election Day, Jack doubted he'd win, because he wouldn't be able to blame Eisenhower and Nixon for letting Cuba go Communist.

"One function of the CIA is to explore options. That's all I'm at liberty to say."

"Fair enough," Jack said. "But nothing you told me accounts for Gabe being murdered."

Dulles knocked the ash from his pipe by tapping the bowl against his hand. "People working in intelligence neither think nor behave as everyone else, so discerning motives is dicey. I doubt it was the box. No one knew about it except Miss Lewison, and I'd wager her disappearance is a coincidence. It could be someone from Gabe's past as a detective. There was one other incident, involving a Victor Diaz, an operative arranging for small arms to be delivered to Castro's opposition. The guerillas requested the weapons, and we delivered them. Gabe was a self-starter, and via an informant he discovered Victor was double-dealing, and we had Gabe neutralize him in Manhattan."

"And Diaz had no network that would go after Gabe?"

"I had agents check into that in Cuba," Dulles said. "They drew a blank. And that police captain, Danny Cohen, Gabe's friend, had the NYPD chasing the shooter, and they haven't arrested anyone." Dulles glanced at his watch. "We ought to make a statement to the press."

As they started back toward Jack's house, Dulles pocketed his pipe, and Jack asked, "You'll be going to Texas to brief my running mate?"

"Lyndon has promised me a tour of his ranch."

"Have fun," Jack said.

"*Fun* is contemplating Lyndon as vice president," Dulles replied. "He has a less-than-sterling reputation as a team player. I suppose it's safer to have him as your VP than leave him in the Senate to rip apart your legislative proposals. But I wouldn't discount the residual bitterness Lyndon feels about losing the nomination to you."

"Something he's done?" Jack suspected Dulles preferred Nixon and wondered if the director was trying to sow some discord into his campaign.

"It's an impression. When I spoke to Lyndon to arrange the briefing, he told me—and I'm quoting—'I got more pussy than that skinny rich boy ever thought about getting.'"

Dulles was chuckling, and Jack joined in, but he was wary. Was that a reference to the Comodoro movie? Was it coming from Lyndon, or was Dulles putting the screws to him to ensure that, if elected, Jack would be too afraid of what he knew to put him out to pasture? Caitlin had told him Gabe had wondered if his phone line was tapped. That would be disastrous, so Jack decided to go right at Dulles. He asked, "Is the CIA tapping my phones?"

Dulles stopped walking. So did Jack, and the director was glowering at him when he said, "I'd have no part in that. If anyone is listening to your conversations, it would be J. Edgar Hoover's FBI agents. The CIA doesn't spy on our citizens."

That would be a relief, but Jack couldn't be sure Dulles was leveling with him. Jack had ordered his office and homes swept for bugs, and all of them were clean. Yet the CIA could have pressured the phone company to identify his phone lines and tapped into them. The same was true of Hoover, and the FBI director could be trouble, though Hoover was even more frightened of forced retirement than Dulles.

Dulles smoothed his white mustache. "When I had dinner at your home with Ian Fleming, we spoke privately, and I mentioned appetite. The overriding problem with it is that there are no secrets in Washington. People see or hear things, and they gossip. And if we were to be honest, we'd have to confess that neither of us has been restrained in satisfying our hunger."

"Any suggestions on how to handle the fallout?"

Dulles said, "You could try a broach from Van Cleef & Arpels."

"Jackie prefers eighteenth-century antiques."

"Pricey."

"Very," Jack said.

CHAPTER 47

Boca Raton, Florida

On a blazing Saturday morning, the Yench caught a break. Hilda had rejected his suggestion she take off the weekends, yet today—*blessed are You, O Lord our God*—she went to Palm Beach with a girlfriend to help her choose a gown for her son's wedding.

As soon as Hilda had backed out of the driveway, Yenchi drove to Walt's on South Dixie Highway, where he bought two glazed apple fritters and Walt filled his thermos with espresso.

A real breakfast, and then Yenchi could do whatever he wanted at work. He'd knock off for a while in the afternoon, shoot the shit with one of the barbers while he got a trim and Inés gave him a manicure, and then he'd take her to lunch at Joe's.

To celebrate his freedom, he decided to swim in the raw. As he stripped in the sunroom, the phone rang. When he answered it and Caitlin apologized for bothering him at home, the day lost some of its luster. He wished she'd drop the whole thing already. What good could it do? And a lot of bad could happen.

Caitlin asked, "Have you had any luck identifying the goateed man with Clara?"

"I crapped out," Yenchi said. "But I'm working on it, and so is Hilda. The woman knows half the Jews in South Florida, and those

Jews know the other half. I'll buzz you the second we find out who he is, OK? I gotta run."

Poolside, Yenchi drank the espresso and devoured one of Walt's masterpieces, savoring the crispy sweetness of the crust and the syrupy apple filling. Then, out in his driveway, Yenchi thought he heard a car door close. He froze. Was Hilda home? Did she forget something? She'd crucify him for the coffee and cake. Yenchi stared at the gate of the stockade fence, waiting for it to open. Nothing. Yenchi was relieved, figuring he'd heard his neighbor coming home.

His fear, along with the sugar and caffeine he'd been missing for months, had given him such a jolt of get-up-and-go that he set aside the second fritter and jumped into the pool.

CHAPTER 48

Greenwich Village

Saturday night, the window fans in Caitlin's apartment blew the wet heat through the rooms and made her feel as if a tropical storm was coming. She quit packing for her three weeks in Belmar and went for a walk on Eighth Street. The tourists and beatniks were out in force. There were waiting lines for the sidewalk portrait artists. Caitlin carried her .38 in her courier bag, but there was no sign of the short man in the blue blazer and duckbill cap. On Astor Place, a shirtless old man, bearded like Santa Claus, was yodeling for an audience of three wild-eyed teenagers drinking from bottles of Thunderbird wine. Caitlin tried to recall why the Village had fascinated her. The arty, bizarre novelty of it? Up on the fire escapes, where people were waiting for a breeze, she saw the glow of their cigarettes in the darkness and remembered quiet July evenings in South Orange catching fireflies in a jar. As the teenagers answered the yodeler by howling like coyotes, Caitlin knew that when Gabe's killer was caught, she would go home.

At a newsstand, she bought the Sunday *Times* and stopped at the Cedar Tavern for a beer and to read the paper. An article datelined *Hyannis Port, MA* stated that CIA director Dulles had spent two and a half hours briefing Senator Kennedy, their talk focusing on Cuba. Caitlin had phoned the senator's office on Friday following her meeting with Trafficante and left a message for him to call her. Now that he'd met with Dulles, she hoped he would. Tomorrow she had to catch the noon train for Philadelphia to attend the *Saturday Evening Post* picnic.

Early the next morning, Caitlin continued packing for the shore. She piled clothing onto her bed, weighing each choice before arranging it in a suitcase. She smiled, recalling Gabe teasing her that she packed as if preparing to invade a country. Six months after losing Gabe, Caitlin concluded that Reed Howland was right. Grief didn't go away—it became memories.

In the bathroom, she loaded up her makeup case. Breck shampoo, Coppertone suntan lotion, Jean Naté splash. She kept at it until the cabinet under the sink was cleaned out and two items remained in the medicine chest: the beige plastic clamshell containing her diaphragm and a tube of contraceptive jelly. She could always pick up a guy in a boardwalk bar, a piquant detail for a story on youth culture at the beach. An amusing fantasy but not part of her plan.

Caitlin packed the diaphragm and jelly anyway, an act of wishful thinking.

CHAPTER 49

Hyannis Port, Massachusetts

Mrs. Lincoln had given Caitlin's message to Jack, but he didn't want to call her from his house in case the CIA or FBI were listening, and he had been too busy to leave the compound. Friday had been a blur of meetings with advisers, where they discussed the latest Gallup poll, which revealed Americans viewed relations with the Soviet Union and Cuba as the country's gravest problems. After lunch, it was back to the meetings until it was time for a sail on Nantucket Sound and finally dinner with the Kennedy brothers, sisters, and their children.

Saturday, Jack breakfasted with Jackie and Caroline, then assembled a Mickey Mouse kite and flew it with Caroline and her cousins. After meeting with Dulles, Jack greeted the hundreds of well-wishers on Irving Avenue outside his house until the film crew was ready in his parents' living room, where Jackie was filming a campaign ad in Spanish, a pitch to the Mexican community in Texas.

Jack was bowled over by his wife's performance. She gazed at the camera as if it were her oldest friend, her face as glorious as summer light and all her formidable intelligence visible in her eyes. While Jackie was fluent in Spanish and French and spoke passable German and Italian, Jack was a dismal linguist, and he envied Jackie's facility with languages, much as he envied her effervescent remoteness. His wife was a radiant island in a leaden sea, and Jack, unable to take his eyes off her, realized that he resented how her existence forced him to hide who he was, to keep his raging lust a secret, to live an artfully constructed life. Ever since prep school, sickly, lonesome Jack had given his lust free rein without concern for consequences. What changed him? What made him care? It was the presidency and Jackie and Caroline, the prize he wanted and the people he couldn't afford to lose. It was also why he couldn't stop wondering whether Caitlin had discovered anything about that movie.

"Was I all right?" Jackie asked her husband when the filming ended. He kissed her cheek. "Perfect."

At home, Jack polished off half a leftover roast chicken, but it didn't touch his hunger. Jackie brought out a quart of ice cream. Three scoops of vanilla with hot fudge made him sleepy. Jack limped upstairs for a nap. He couldn't bend to untie his shoes. Jackie helped him. He unzipped her dress and kissed her long neck. Then they were on the bed, and she was above him, both of them frantically chasing that small miracle. They arrived together. Jackie lit a cigarette, and Jack slept until Jackie shook him, saying that he had to get ready for dinner.

Sunday, the Kennedys were scheduled to attend ten o'clock Mass at Saint Francis Xavier. Millions of Americans might be skeptical about putting a Catholic in the White House, but they expected their presidents to consult with God. At seven, before Jackie and Caroline were awake, the chief of the Barnstable Police called, and Jack picked up.

"Sorry to bother you," the chief said. "We got a big crowd waiting for you and Mrs. Kennedy at the church. My guys will help you get inside."

Jack thanked the chief and saw his chance to call Caitlin. He put on a sweatshirt, chinos, and sneakers. Jackie kept a Lalique crystal bowl full of coins on the kitchen counter, and he grabbed a handful. Mist was swirling up from the sound, and the well-wishers weren't out yet. He went down Longwood Avenue to the News Store, where he liked to take Caroline and his nieces and nephews for candy. Next door was the post office and, on the wall in back, a pay phone. He got the operator on the line, recited Caitlin's number from memory, and dropped in some coins. Her phone rang twice before Jack heard her say hello.

"How're you coming along?" he asked.

"The movie exists," Caitlin replied. "And I'm almost sure Trafficante is looking for it."

"Did he say why?"

"He said Sam Giancana got cash from you to get out the vote in West Virginia. Giancana figures you owe him, and he'll have some influence at the White House if you win. Trafficante, I assume, also wants some influence, and he thinks the movie will give it to him."

Jack was suddenly angry. "I'll lose the election before I'll do a damn thing for those bastards."

"Giancana handing out the money, doesn't that compromise you?"

She sounded shocked, and Jack said, "West Virginians are drowning in poverty. The cash was for the county bosses. Some of it sticks to them, and the rest they pass out to the poor if they go to the polls. It's an old story there. I'd bet Humphrey's people did it. We just did it better."

"You told me you didn't know any mob guys."

"I don't, Caitlin. The campaign used a go-between with Giancana." Jack doubted it was prudent to mention that the go-between was a young divorcée he was sleeping with.

"Did you bring up wiretapping with Dulles?" she asked.

"He denied it," Jack said.

"Do you believe him?"

"Maybe," Jack replied. "The man is a professional liar."

"What did Dulles say about Winkie?"

Jack said, "That's your friend, Hannah Lewison, who did an engraving for Gabe for some nutty plot that went nowhere? He knew nothing about her disappearance, which had to be a coincidence."

Caitlin said, "When Gabe was lecturing at the police academy, he told our class that detectives working a case should consider a coincidence a situation you don't understand yet."

Jack chuckled. "That sounds like Gabe. But Dulles didn't appear to know anything about Hannah."

"And Gabe? What did he say about Gabe?"

"Before he was shot, Gabe was in Mexico City checking on a couple of operatives." Jack hesitated, remembering the first time he'd met Caitlin. It was at Joe Alsop's, and later Jackie said that she resembled pictures of Kick. Caitlin did remind him of Kick, though not because of their passing resemblance. It was that Kick had been capable of unshakable devotion. Caitlin had the same capacity. It was evident in her single-minded pursuit of Gabe's murderer. When he let himself think about it, Jack felt humiliated that Caitlin knew about the prostitute. He knew she condemned him for it—and for his affair with Été. Were Kick alive, she would've judged him as harshly. Yet Jack still would've trusted his sister. Just as he trusted Caitlin, and he didn't want to hurt her by telling her that Gabe killed Victor Diaz, so his answer fell between a lie and the truth. "Dulles mentioned Gabe was involved in a stickier situation."

"I heard about Diaz from Danny. Did Dulles have anything to add to that story?"

Jack said, "As far as the CIA could determine, no Cuban or Soviet agents went after Gabe for Diaz. Have you considered that the movie and Gabe have nothing to do with each other?"

"Yes, but all I have to go on is a woman in a photo, so I'll follow that lead and see where it goes."

"Caitlin, with Trafficante involved, is it safe? Gabe would never forgive me for putting you in harm's way, and I won't forgive myself if something happens."

"If I need protecting, I have Danny and Julian."

"Is there anything I can do?" Jack asked.

In a voice somewhere between a joke and a rebuke, Caitlin replied, "Don't make any more movies."

CHAPTER 50

Wyncote, Pennsylvania

Stepping off the train in Philadelphia and getting into a taxicab, Caitlin still imagined that the *Saturday Evening Post* picnic would bear some resemblance to an outing that Norman Rockwell would have painted for a *Post* cover, complete with a blanket spread on the grass and a woven-wood food hamper.

However, when the taxi dropped her at the Curtis Arboretum, carved from the estate of Cyrus H. K. Curtis, the late owner of the magazine, she discovered that the event was more society wedding than summer picnic.

Under an enormous pink-and-white-striped tent was a pastel-and-cream-colored crowd of women and men in silk, cotton, and summer wool. They were standing and talking or sitting at tables with center-pieces of marigolds and impatiens. On one side of the tent a string quartet was playing on a raised stand. On the other side was a buffet of chafing dishes with salmon, braised chicken, sliced beef, and a medley of vegetables. Beside it was another buffet with cakes and pies, and the rest of that side was taken up by a bar with three bartenders in white jackets.

Caitlin ordered a gin and tonic and felt out of place as the party eddied around her until she saw Reed approaching with his graceful strides. In his khaki poplin suit and burgundy tie, with his lined face deeply tanned and his wavy hair sun streaked, he looked like a cross between an Ivy League professor and a mountain climber.

"Quite the little picnic," she said.

Reed shrugged. "It's a bit much, isn't it? But I'm glad you made it. The publisher wants to meet you."

Caitlin held up her drink. "Let me get ready."

"No hurry. Want to take a walk?"

Smiling, she said, "First things first," and after finishing her gin and tonic, she set the glass on the bar and followed Reed out of the tent and down a corridor of towering oaks. The simmer of conversation and the music faded away. The gravel path ended at a field lit a shimmering green-gold by the sun. Caitlin gazed across the field.

Reed said, "A penny for your thoughts."

"You'd be overpaying." The dark woods past the field could've come right out of *Grimms' Fairy Tales* and made her uneasy. She turned to Reed. "On the train, I began thinking about my mother not remarrying after my dad was murdered, and now I can't stop."

"No boyfriends?"

Caitlin glanced away from him. "Monday nights, Mr. Murphy, a sweet older widower, a retired milkman, used to take her to bingo at church. It didn't dawn on me till high school that they weren't just playing bingo. I asked her about it, and she said, 'Go do your homework.'"

Reed laughed softly. "Can't say I blame her for that answer."

Caitlin sighed. "I don't blame her for anything. Mr. Murphy died my sophomore year of college. I went to the funeral with her, and she didn't shed a tear. The next night, out of nowhere, she said, 'I cried all I'm ever going to cry for your father.' After that, no more bingo. She ran a hospital cafeteria, came home, watched TV, and filled an ashtray with her Pall Malls. My mother lived in exile from the world, and I worry it's happening to me."

Quietly, as if sharing a secret, Reed said, "Whenever I felt lost after Marjorie died, I made myself consider the facts. And for you the facts, other than your grief, are your writing career is flourishing, and you're investigating what happened to your husband. That's not exile."

Caitlin shut her eyes, holding back tears, not wanting to cry in front of Reed. "I walk through the Village, and mothers are wheeling baby carriages through Washington Square, and couples are having coffee at Caffe Reggio, and it's as though I'm locked in a glass cage. I see the living, but I'm not part of them."

"It becomes easier, Caitlin. I promise. Let's get something to eat, and I'll introduce you around, and when you're ready to go, I'll drive you to the train station."

"I'm sorry for going on like that. I didn't even ask about you. You're well?"

"I am. I'm going kayaking in Maine, and I plan to write about it. I haven't written in a while."

Caitlin gave him a playful smile. "Well, if you need an editor—"

Reed returned her smile. "I'm sure I will. When do you leave for the beach?"

"Tomorrow."

"Give a call at the office," Reed said. "If I get the piece done, I'll send it along if you have the time to read it. How's the investigation going?"

"Still haven't found the prostitute from Havana. But I did find out Gabe was on assignment in Mexico City before he was shot. And he wrote a report about it. That might be worth digging into."

"It could be a fascinating story," Reed said. "You should make some notes and let me look at them."

At the moment, Caitlin couldn't tell him about the CIA, Victor Diaz, Kennedy, and Trafficante or anything about Clara. Yet, depending on why Gabe was murdered and who shot him, there could be a story for her to write. "Let me think about it," she said.

CHAPTER 51

New York City

At dusk, with a merciful summertime wind blowing off the rivers, Caitlin exited Penn Station. Her mood had improved after talking to Reed and hearing the publisher and several editors compliment her writing, so she rode a crosstown bus and got off on lower Fifth Avenue to take one of her favorite walks through Washington Square Park and down MacDougal.

After passing under the marble arch, she strolled by the bench-sitters, dog-walkers, hand-holders, and drunk stumblers and veered toward the fountain, where kids splashed in the water and an older group gathered on the steps listening to a girl with flowing hair playing a guitar and singing "House of the Rising Sun."

On MacDougal, people were going somewhere in a hurry or nowhere in particular—happy, noisy shadows in the neon-burnished twilight. Caitlin hadn't avoided the street since she'd been followed by the man in the fedora and overcoat, nor was she concerned by the man in the duckbill hat that Julian had spotted allegedly watching her building. Yet her bag was slung across her body with the flap unfastened, making it easier to get to her .38, and she used the storefront windows as mirrors to scan the reflection of anyone walking behind her.

Skirting the crowd outside Cafe Wha?, Caitlin went down the slope of Minetta Lane to Sixth Avenue, then over to West Fourth and onto

Grove. The street was deserted. To her left, someone, a silhouette in the darkness, came out of Christopher Park. Caitlin was wary. The silhouette was across the street from her. Her wariness was replaced by a sense of longing as she gazed at the lights in the apartment houses and saw men, women, and children moving by the windows, a backlit portrait of family life.

Somewhere, a dog barked. Caitlin glanced over her shoulder. The silhouette had crossed to her side of Grove and was sixty or seventy feet away. She hurried toward the double doors of her building. There were footsteps now, coming at her fast. The glowing carriage lamps on either side of the doors seemed as far away as Saturn and Jupiter.

Caitlin was aware of her fear. It wasn't real, though. It belonged to someone else. A woman onstage. The footsteps were right behind her. Remembering what Gabe had taught her in that Chinatown gym, Caitlin tucked her chin against her chest so the silhouette couldn't grab her around the throat, and then, spinning around, she threw her left elbow upward in the direction of the footsteps while pulling her .38 out of her bag with her right hand. She was lucky. The silhouette was her height. Her elbow struck his chin. He staggered back, uttering words in a language she didn't understand. Caitlin screamed "Get the fuck away!" and started to raise her pistol, cocking the hammer with her thumb. He charged at her. She caught a glimpse of his pallid face in the light of the carriage lamps—eyebrows as thick as caterpillars and mean, beady eyes. Before she could squeeze the trigger, he shoved her. Falling backward, Caitlin clutched the .38, and as her back hit the sidewalk, she fired twice at the bullnecked man above her, the gunshots ringing in her ears. She missed, but he turned and ran toward West Fourth.

Caitlin was shaking when she let herself into her building, raced up three flights of stairs, and went into her apartment, then shut the door and threw the bolt—shaking still when she sat with her back against the door, gasping for air and holding her pistol tight.

CHAPTER 52

Sunday evening, Danny was asleep on his couch in his uniform. He was beat after eight hours at the station house reading reports and semiplastered due to a single-malt sleeping potion from Scotland. That was why he didn't answer his phone until the seventh ring.

"Danny?" Caitlin sounded frightened.

"What's wrong?"

"Come over, please."

"Ten minutes," he said, pulling up his tie and unwrapping a stick of Wrigley's Spearmint.

Danny lived in a one bedroom above a shoemaker on Saint Mark's Place, and it was a quick ride to Grove Street. When he arrived, four radio cars, their cherry lights flashing, were on Grove Street from West Fourth down to Waverly.

"What's going on?" he asked the uniform standing on the steps of Caitlin's building.

"I just spoke to a lady on the first floor. Real upset, she is. Two bullets through her window fucked up her fancy tin ceiling. We're doing the canvass. So far there ain't no witnesses."

Danny said, "Keep me apprised. I have a friend on the third floor, and I'll talk to her."

Caitlin let Danny in and walked to the kitchen. "Coffee?"

"Black."

Danny sat at the small round table. Caitlin filled their cups, put the pot back on the stove, and sat at the table. "I was attacked. He knocked me over."

"You hurt?"

"I'm not, but I shot at him and missed."

Danny unbuttoned his coat. "You didn't miss your neighbor's ceiling."

"Is she all right?"

Danny nodded and sipped his coffee. "You get a look at him?"

Caitlin had a sheet of notepaper on her laminated aqua place mat. "I wrote a description."

She gave it to him, and he read aloud: "'Accent, maybe Eastern European.' What's this word you wrote?"

"It was the only word I could make out. It sounded like *suka* or *shuka*."

Danny stuck the paper into his coat pocket. "Any idea why'd he come after you?"

Caitlin shrugged.

Apprehensive about her safety and exasperated by her reluctance to give him the straight scoop, Danny let his exasperation seep into his voice. "Julian Rose called me last week and says he saw a guy watching your apartment. Is that who attacked you?"

"Julian saw somebody eating a pretzel. It was nothing. He shouldn't have called you."

"Cait, Julian's scared for you. And he says you went to meet Santo Trafficante. Why're you talking to that scumbag?"

Caitlin pointed at Danny's tie clasp, a gold-plated PT boat with **KENNEDY** inscribed on it. "Where'd you get that?"

"Catholics and Jews in the precinct got together on this Dollars for Democrats program. I coughed up twenty bucks and got the clasp. Now could you cut the crap and level with me?"

Gabe had told Danny his wife was an angel where you could see her and a kidney-punching heavyweight where you couldn't. Danny hadn't seen her pugilistic side, but when he added that Caitlin should start at the beginning, it was the fighter who answered him: "At the beginning! The beginning was my husband dying with his head in my lap! Then you told me Gabe killed Victor Diaz on the Upper West Side while I sat in his car. How's that for a beginning? Or should I add Winkie doing that engraving about Castro for Gabe and disappearing to who knows where?"

Her cheeks were flushed. Danny said, "What did Yenchi tell you in Florida?"

"Yenchi told me Victor Diaz was a pimp who gambled and that he was arranging shipments of weapons the CIA was sending to the anti-Castro people in Cuba. Gabe met Diaz through Yenchi. One night at dinner with Yenchi, Diaz let it slip that he was making money by tipping off Castro's boys to the shipments. Yenchi told Gabe, and the CIA had Gabe shoot Diaz. I confirmed this with Senator Kennedy. He spoke to Dulles."

"Why would Kennedy tell you about a conversation with the director of the CIA?"

"He was friends with Gabe and feels responsible for him working there."

Danny didn't believe her. There had to be more to it, perhaps involving Kennedy. But Caitlin wasn't going to tell him until she was ready. Or until she had to.

She said, "Dulles told Kennedy the cigar box was part of a scheme that went nowhere. Nor did Dulles know why Gabe was killed. He had agents check it out, and there was no network with any interest in paying back Gabe for Diaz."

"Where does Trafficante fit in?" Danny asked.

"Trafficante had a ton of money invested in Cuban hotels and casinos, and when Castro chased out the Americans, Yenchi said Trafficante had couriers smuggling millions in cash into the States. There's this call girl, Clara, a Jew from Cuba, who worked for Diaz in Miami. Yenchi heard a rumor that Trafficante was looking for her. I wondered if she was smuggling his money and took off with it or gave it to Diaz, and if Gabe knew about it. Whatever Clara was doing, she's gone. I spoke to Trafficante to figure out if he's trying to find her. He is. And I want to find her first. Yenchi and his wife are helping me by asking around about her."

Danny felt the hole in her story, yet he couldn't see it. "And how is this tied to Gabe?"

Caitlin replied sharply, "It may not be. But do you have any better leads?"

"I don't, Cait, but all you have is a theory and no facts."

"Here are the facts. Clara knows Diaz, Yenchi, Trafficante, and maybe Gabe. I want to know whatever Clara knows."

Her courier bag was hanging from her chair, and she removed the stakeout snapshots of Clara and spread them on the table so Danny could look at them.

Caitlin said, "I didn't tell you about these when I came back from Miami. You'd taken a risk deep-sixing the pistol Gabe used on Diaz, and Yenchi got the photos from an FBI agent, and I didn't want you near him. He's a gambler and into Yenchi for big money."

"Who is this bearded guy with her by the temple?"

"Yenchi didn't recognize him," Caitlin said.

"Did you go to the temple and ask the rabbi?"

Caitlin said with a forced laugh, "Ask a rabbi about a call girl?"

"Last I checked, rabbis are men. You could fly down and ask the rabbi yourself and then go see what Yenchi's really doing."

"I trust Yenchi. Gabe was like a son to him. Are you suggesting I leave town?"

Danny sighed, more impatient than tired. "Isn't it possible Trafficante sicced this guy on you?"

"Possible."

"And because the guy blew it, you think Trafficante's going to quit?"

"In the morning, I'm going down the shore for three weeks, so if somebody shows up, I won't be here."

Danny said, "To Belmar. Four twelve Seventeenth Avenue."

Caitlin looked shocked. "How do you—"

Danny tapped the wall calendar next to the table. "You wrote it in right there. Anybody else know?"

"Just me," she said with a faint smile. "And you."

"Good. I'll clean up the mess here, and I'll have a radio car on Grove Street tonight."

Caitlin reached across the table and touched his hand. "I appreciate it, Danny."

"Give me a buzz if you need anything." He stood, grinning. "Don't forget your pistol. And try not to shoot your neighbors."

CHAPTER 53

Seventy-two hours after Caitlin was attacked, Danny was in his office at the station house, and he was stuck. The canvass of Grove Street and the surrounding area hadn't turned up any witnesses, unsurprising to Danny because after fifteen years of questioning people about shootings in busy subway stations and barrooms, he concluded you could machine-gun half the city and no one would pay attention unless you were shooting at them. To protect Cait from the investigation—the law doesn't give you a prize for accidentally shooting up your neighbor's ceiling—Danny had shared her description of the attacker with a few of his beat cops and detectives, saying it was a personal matter, an attempted rape of a woman friend who was reluctant to file a complaint. But his men hadn't located anyone.

Why Cait had met with Trafficante puzzled Danny. And he couldn't understand how this Cuban prostitute was connected to Gabe, who never went near hookers. Plain and simple, her story didn't add up. The Sixth Precinct's detective squad had worked Gabe's case, but apparently the shooter was invisible. The way Danny saw it, neither Gabe's killer nor his motive was local. If Danny had the power, he would've focused the investigation on Diaz and his double-dealing on the weapons shipments to Cuba, shipments the government would have to deny. Dulles may have told Kennedy no one wanted payback for Diaz, but why believe him? The CIA was a fairy-tale factory. Danny was sure there was more going on than either Cait admitted or knew. Yet she could've annoyed Trafficante enough that he'd drop the hammer on her, and Trafficante was one of her problems Danny thought he could solve. When Julian Rose had called him about the guy watching Cait's building and her meeting with Trafficante, he'd given Danny his number in New Jersey, which Danny had scribbled on his desk blotter, and now he dialed it.

Julian's secretary put him on hold, and seconds later Julian came on. "Is Cait all right?"

"Yes and no," Danny replied and launched into a recap of the attack and everything Cait had told him afterward.

Julian asked, "You got a suggestion?"

"A talk with Trafficante."

Julian said, "I'll get right back to you."

And in under five minutes, he did. "You around tonight?"

"I can be," Danny said.

"What's your address?" Danny told him, and Julian said, "I'll pick you up at eleven thirty. Leave the uniform at home."

That night, as Danny showered and dressed, he tried not to let his loathing of mobsters knock him off balance. He'd seen their greed and violence up close, and it was unforgivable, even in a man like Julian Rose, who had retired from the game and was heralded in the press for donating millions to charity. Julian lived large on his bloodstained fortune while decent people—like Danny's late father, who spent forty years pushing racks in the Garment Center—worked their asses off and pinched pennies till the day they died. Gabe had told him Julian was 100 percent legit, though sometimes he let the Abruzzis invest in his real estate deals. Danny was disgusted that Julian would partner with those animals, yet he did have one redeeming quality, a quality Danny shared with him: he loved Cait. However, while Julian was a stand-in for her father, Danny, since Gabe's death, had imagined himself with

Cait, which left him feeling guilty. Gabe had been his best friend, and Danny felt as if he was plotting to steal his wife. Not that they'd be together anytime soon. Cait wouldn't even go for a drink with him.

At eleven thirty, Julian pulled up in his Chrysler Imperial, and Danny got in. Neither one spoke until they were at a red light uptown. With more ire than he intended, Danny asked, "Why'd you set up that Trafficante meeting for Cait?"

Julian, with his salt-and-pepper hair, wine-dark tie, and silver collar pin, would've been a portrait of the affable businessman in prosperous middle age had it not been for the iciness of his gaze. Seeing it, Danny knew that if Trafficante had gone after Cait, Julian would kill him or have him killed by his occasional real estate partners, the Abruzzis.

Julian said, "Cait would've found a way to see Trafficante and gotten in over her head. She has her dad's sweetness, but push comes to shove, she's like her mother, tough and stubborn. I did have the Abruzzis warn Trafficante she shouldn't be bothered."

"You figure he listened?"

"Let's find out," Julian said.

At the Park Central Hotel, Julian gave the doorman his car key and some cash. The Mermaid Room was off the lobby, and in the smoky light, Danny saw several couples at the circular bar in the middle of the lounge. Above the bar, four green sculptures of mermaids were anchored to the ceiling. Trafficante was seated on a mustard-colored banquette in back. A younger man with his hair slicked back in a duck's ass sat to his right in a chair. Danny recognized him. It was Matt Calvetti. He lived in Brooklyn, but most evenings he was in a Greenwich Village bar or coffeehouse arranging to supply the Sheridan Square dealers with heroin. His acne scars and broken nose were useful for scaring beatniks.

"*Buona sera*, Santo," Julian said.

Trafficante set his cup in its saucer. "Hello, Julian. It's been a while. Who's your pal?"

Matt got up, moving close to Danny. He smelled like he'd been dipped in a vat of Aqua Velva aftershave. "That's the legendary Danny Cohen. A Jew cop. They got Jew cops in Florida, Mr. Trafficante?"

Quietly, Trafficante replied, "Matt, why don't you have a drink at the bar?"

"You got it, Mr. Trafficante. But I gotta ask something." He looked at Danny. "Cohen, what the fuck's wrong with you? Didn't your mother tell you to be a doctor?"

Danny drove a fist into Matt's stomach. Doubling over, Matt sank to his knees. Danny grabbed his chin and tilted up his face. "And your mother told you to be what? A shitbird with a stomachache?"

Danny let him go. Matt was giving him his hard-guy stare from the floor. Trafficante, buffing his eyeglasses with a napkin, said, "The bar, Matt. Before he hits you again."

Matt got going. Julian sat in a chair. Trafficante slid on his glasses and glanced up at Danny. "You can beat it too."

Danny sat in the other chair. "Don't sweat it. I'm not with the Federal Bureau of Narcotics."

Trafficante frowned. "Julian, since when do you like cops?"

Julian chuckled. "Since I was bootlegging and used to buy them by the bushel."

Trafficante nearly smiled. "You two want a drink?"

Julian nodded at the cup and saucer. "What're you drinking?"

Trafficante said, "Ovaltine. Hot malted milk. Helps me sleep."

Julian shook his head. Danny said, "I'll pass."

Bending toward Trafficante, Julian said, "Caitlin, who came to talk to you. She was attacked outside her building."

Danny was watching Trafficante. Nothing showed on his face. Trafficante said, "This Caitlin and me, we been asking around about the same girl, a Cuban hooker."

Julian bent closer. "She told me that."

Trafficante said, "If I ain't finding her, Caitlin won't. I don't got no ill will for her. Now, the punk bookie in Miami Beach and that bust-out gambler of an FBI agent giving her stakeout photos, they can fry in hell. But that ain't Caitlin's fault."

Julian said, "That's correct. It isn't her fault."

As a cop, Danny had encountered unregenerate rapists and murderers, pure evil with arms and legs, and Julian's expression was as malevolent as any Danny had ever seen on the faces of those human catastrophes.

Trafficante said, "This Caitlin, I know, is important to you, and—"

"Correct again, Santo. She's important to me."

Trafficante said, "And I wouldn't have nothing to do with hurting her."

"If you did," Julian said, "you'd have two problems."

Trafficante asked, "And my problems are here at this table?"

"Right here," Julian replied.

"I see them," Trafficante said.

Julian stood, and Danny followed him out of the lounge.

"It's not him," Julian said.

"I got that feeling."

Julian said, "I was hoping it was him. I could've fixed it if it was him."

"I'll keep an eye on Cait."

"Both eyes," Julian said.

CHAPTER 54

Belmar, New Jersey

For Caitlin, this summer at the Jersey Shore was like every other summer before it, beginning in childhood when her mother rented a place in Sea Girt and lasting into high school, when she waitressed at the Essex and Sussex Hotel in Spring Lake. Her assignment was to write about the changing youth culture, but nothing had changed at Bradley Beach and Lavallette. Teenage boys bodysurfing and clustering on the sand to watch the girls rub baby oil on their bodies. Radios playing a concert of Americana: Phil Rizzuto exclaiming "Holy cow!" as Mantle homered; news that Woolworth's in Greensboro, North Carolina, responding to the sit-ins, had integrated its lunch counter; and a silly new song, "Itsy Bitsy Teenie Weenie Yellow Polkadot Bikini." Caitlin hadn't spotted any of the skimpy swimsuits until, two blankets away, a girl with short brown curls pulled a University of Michigan sweatshirt over her head to reveal a purple bikini. A paunchy man with white zinc cream on his nose was in a chair glowering at her over his *Guns & Ammo* magazine. She said, "Relax, Mister. When you guys blow up the world, it won't matter what I'm wearing."

During those summers, Caitlin was often on the boardwalks in Asbury Park and Seaside Heights. They were also unchanged. Lights glazing the evening with gold, and the sunburned crowd trying their luck at the ring toss or playing miniature golf while children darted onto the Tilt-A-Whirl, their cheeks puffy with saltwater taffy. Caitlin stopped at Kohr Bros., and she was seven years old again with her cone of vanilla frozen custard, and then, looking out at the couples strolling across the moonlit sand, she was seventeen and kissing her boyfriend, their mouths sweetened by cotton candy.

Caitlin delayed going to Cape May until her second week. She hadn't been back in ten years. She walked the side streets of Victorians. The house at 505 Hughes Street was ringed by the pink hydrangeas she remembered from high school. It had belonged to her boyfriend's grandparents. Graeme Baird had been captain of the swim team and had the bluest eyes Caitlin had ever seen. He and Caitlin were in love, meaning they were unable to be apart for an hour without longing for each other, and one Saturday night in August when Graeme's grandparents were visiting relatives in Scotland, they decided to go all the way. Graeme had swiped his older brother's copy of *Sex Technique in Marriage*, and they worked their way through the book. On Sunday morning, walking to Mass at Our Lady Star of the Sea, they passed another house Caitlin would never forget. A young mother was on a porch swing cooing at the baby in her arms as a muscular crew cut man watched from the doorway. Graeme said, "I hope that's us someday." Caitlin nodded, but a husband and children were so far in the future she couldn't see them. The future she could see was writing and living in Greenwich Village, an unencumbered future of adventure as joyous as her summers at the shore.

In retrospect, Caitlin knew, her imaginings had sprouted from her wish to dodge adulthood. Yes, she had become a writer in the city, but the rest of it—being a cop and chasing broken kids, the murder of her husband, searching for his killer and the film of a presidential candidate and a prostitute, getting assaulted and shooting at her attacker—were not the adventures she'd had in mind. The next summer, Caitlin had broken up with Graeme. She never thought of him without recalling the hurt she'd caused. A year ago, she'd heard that he'd married a girl from

San Jose, and they had two daughters and three Pontiac dealerships in Northern California.

Now, as Caitlin left Hughes Street, she envied Graeme's less adventuresome life.

◆ ◆ ◆

Other than the bikini, Caitlin had seen nothing new. Perhaps the young people weren't so different from their elders because the shore attracted families whose summertime rituals, from where they swam to their preferred seafood shack, were handed down like heirlooms. Caitlin would make this observation in her piece, yet she needed the latest in youthful obsessions, so she drove to Wildwood. Since the 1940s, jazz greats like Count Basie and Tony Bennett had performed there, and in the 1950s, rock 'n' roll came to town, a transition celebrated on TV when Dick Clark broadcast his *American Bandstand* from the Starlight Ballroom.

Caitlin found a space on Pacific Avenue. A pair of teenage girls with big hair and an overdose of eye shadow were outside a liquor store. Caitlin asked them the best place nearby for music. They gazed at her floral sundress as if it was a space suit, and one of them said, "Go up to the Rainbow Club."

The club was hot, crowded, and loud. A band was playing on the stage, and kids were dancing or sitting at the tables, talking, laughing, and chugging beer from plastic cups. The drinking age in New Jersey was twenty-one. Caitlin estimated half the kids didn't qualify. Rules were not really rules down the shore. Caitlin wanted a gin and tonic, but she had a long ride to Belmar ahead of her, and she came away from the bar with a bottle of ginger ale and a cup. In back by the cigarette machine, a pudgy teenager was sitting alone at a table for two. He looked as lonely as Caitlin felt. She went over to him. "May I sit here?"

He stared up at her as if startled by the question. His hair was short except for a tuft in front that had been butch-waxed up like a fence post.

"I'm Caitlin," she said, sitting down. "What's your name?"

"Bruce."

Caitlin poured the soda into her cup. "I can't drink it all. Will you share it with me?"

"Thank you."

Caitlin slid the bottle to him, and he drank. His round baby face was tan, but his arms were pale. She remembered the pudgy boys in high school who never removed their sweatshirts on the beach. Bruce was studying the dancers.

Caitlin asked, "Do you like to dance?"

"I don't have anyone to dance with."

Caitlin smiled. "Yes you do. Come on."

Bruce was transformed by the music, a fast, swinging number, "At the Hop." He jitterbugged with such speed and grace, swinging her around as if she were weightless, that Caitlin, no slouch on the dance floor, was mesmerized. Several girls in their vicinity, much to the dismay of their partners, stopped dancing and watched him.

"You're terrific," Caitlin said when the song ended. "Who taught you?"

Bruce, too shy to meet her eyes, said, "My older sister."

Onstage, a man with a microphone announced, "Ladies and gentlemen, please welcome Cameo-Parkway recording artist Chubby Checker."

A teenager in a checked sport coat and tie appeared with a glad-to-be-here grin. The band began to play, the drums going hard. He was singing "The Twist." Caitlin had heard Hank Ballard sing it on the radio, but she hadn't even heard of Chubby Checker. He was turning the song into a dance she hadn't seen, sliding his feet side to side and swinging his arms. Bruce and Caitlin followed his lead, and all around them the crowd began twisting wildly.

Cheers erupted when Chubby Checker finished. Caitlin, leading Bruce off the floor, said, "I have to go. Thank you for dancing with me. I saw a lot of the girls watching you. You should ask one to dance."

Caitlin kissed him on the cheek. Bruce smiled and headed back to the dance floor.

Caitlin went out with two guys behind her, who were laughing drunkenly. The girls with the big hair had moved under a streetlight. They had company—two guys on motorcycles at the curb doing their impression of Brando in *The Wild One*: tilted Johnny caps, black leather jackets, existential scowls. One of them called out, "Mike, how was the show?"

Mike was one of the drunks behind Caitlin, and he called back, "Funny, man. That lady there was dancing with Fat Bruce. Hey, lady, why didn't ya dance with me?"

Caitlin picked up her pace, her hand going into her courier bag.

He laughed. "Lady, I'm talking to you."

Caitlin was past the liquor store when a hand clamped on her shoulder. "Lady—"

Caitlin spun toward Mike, pulling out her .38 and using her body to shove him against the building. Her mind was blank as she pressed the muzzle of her pistol against his neck. He raised his arms. "I'm sorry, lady. I—" She could hear the fear in his voice. He was maybe eighteen or nineteen, tall and skinny with an Elvis pompadour. Caitlin lowered the pistol and went to her car. Her hands shook on the steering wheel. It was a minute before she could drive away.

CHAPTER 55

Quebec City, Canada
August 1960

"How are you?" Jack asked.

Été was stretched out on her bed, cradling the phone between her neck and ear. "I'm well. And you?"

"Hyannis Port has been a nice break, but I'm going to Washington tomorrow for a special session of the Senate. Then it's off to campaign."

"I've been reading about the campaign. Yesterday there was an article on the poll, predicting you will lose to Vice President Nixon by six percent."

Jack said, "Polls are like fog. Thick before dawn, gone by breakfast."

Été had slept naked, and the breeze wafting through the open french doors of the balcony was cool on her skin. "I thought you were calling for—what is it Americans say? A *pep talk*?"

Jack laughed. "That's what we say, but it's not why I called. I was hoping to convince you to fly to Washington and check into the Mayflower so we could visit."

Now it was Été's turn to laugh. "Visit? This is *un euphémisme, non*?"

"It's the language of a gentleman."

Été said, "It's an appealing invitation, but I have company. An enthusiastic gentleman. He's out buying croissants."

Jack said, "So then tell me about the novel you're writing."

Été removed a cigarette from the pack of Gauloises on the bedside table. "I thought you would say you had a meeting and must hang up."

Sounding perplexed, Jack asked, "Why? Does no hotel mean we're not pals?"

Été decided against the cigarette. She hadn't had her coffee yet. "You will try again."

"Perhaps, but in the meantime I could use someone to talk to. Tell me about the novel."

Été stuck the cigarette in the pack. "It is about a Venetian woman in the eighteenth century. For now the title is *Les Confessions de Marina Morosini.*"

"And what did Marina confess?"

Été said, "Her aristocratic family would not pay the dowry to secure her a suitable husband and sent Marina to a convent on an island. Marina was a voluptuous beauty, and she considered the convent a prison. To rebel, she had an affair with an older man, the French ambassador to Venice, and one day Casanova visited the church on the island, and she arranged to sneak out and began sleeping with him. Eventually, Marina persuaded another young woman to join her, Casanova, and the ambassador for a *ménages à quatre.*"

Jack chuckled. "Marina sounds like a fun girl."

"*Absolument.* But her joie de vivre is not the point. The novel is about sex as a rebellion against the tyrannical expectations of parents and society—and our search to be loved for who we are with our imperfections, not who we pretend to be to please others."

Jack said, "Are you suggesting I should read your book when it's published?"

"I did not say that, but you understand my Marina, don't you?"

After a long pause, Jack said, "I understand Marina. And now I do have to get to a meeting. Good luck with the novel."

"And bonne chance with the campaign," Été said and hung up. She went into the bathroom, and afterward put on a peach-colored chemise and stepped out on the third-floor balcony. Below was a white-graveled courtyard and a rock garden with the orange-and-yellow flames of begonias rising among the stones. She had been content in Quebec City. Speaking French in the shops or during dinners at Le Château Frontenac when her publisher or agent or a Parisian friend came to town had reignited her imagination, and renting an entire house had been the correct decision. Her privacy was precious to her. As she'd told Jack, her companion was enthusiastic and, better yet because Été had been too long without a lover, insatiable. He was a strange one, though. All he wanted to talk about was her time in New York City, what she did, her friends, why she left. When he had unzipped his valise to remove his shaving kit, she'd noticed a large pistol and asked him about it. He had laughed, saying Canada was famous for bear hunting, and he might give it a try. She knew he was lying, and it unsettled her. She was thinking about asking him to leave when she heard footsteps in the bedroom and turned. Her lover was coming out to the balcony, but he wasn't carrying a bag from *la boulangerie*.

"No croissants?" she asked.

He towered over her and bent to kiss her, his hands roaming under her chemise. Her arms were around his neck, and he lifted her off her feet, as if to carry her inside, but instead he broke free from her arms and, in one swift motion, dumped her over the railing of the balcony.

For a split second, Été had the giddy weightless sensation of a child leaping off a diving board into a pool. In the next second, as she plunged headfirst to the rock garden, her giddiness soured into terror. She had to do something, but what? Then her head hit stone. She didn't even have a chance to scream.

CHAPTER 56

Hyde Park, New York

Ask Jack, and he'd tell you Eleanor Roosevelt had been shoving a spear up his ass ever since she realized he wanted to be president. In print she lambasted him for ducking the censure vote on that scurrilous Communist hunter, Senator Joseph McCarthy, and she stated she doubted Jack could separate his Catholic faith from the duties of the presidency. During a televised interview, where her British-boarding-school voice enunciating every syllable gave her opinion the ring of unassailable truth, Mrs. Roosevelt declared Jack unqualified to be president and said she was distressed by his father allegedly trying to buy him the election.

Jack understood her animosity. She was a true believer in the verities of liberalism, while he was more skeptical about the human capacity for goodness, a residue of his Catholicism, his grisly experience in the South Pacific, and his knowledge of the rough treatment dished out to the Irish by the Roosevelts' tribe, the Protestant elite. He groused about her criticism to Jackie and his prep school pal, Lem Billings. Publicly, he kept his mouth shut. The widow of FDR, with her record of championing the poor and downtrodden, was perhaps the most admired woman on earth. Liberal Democrats would have put her up for sainthood if they believed in such quaint delusions as God. Jack would need the liberals to beat Nixon, and the blowback from his father denouncing

FDR in public for dragging the country into war with Hitler had taught Jack the wisdom of silence.

That wisdom didn't preclude him from sending Mrs. Roosevelt a letter claiming her charge about his father's spending was false and, if she couldn't prove it, she should retract it. In her syndicated My Day column, Mrs. Roosevelt repeated his denial. Jack informed her he wasn't satisfied. Mrs. Roosevelt proposed mentioning it again in My Day. Jack rejected her proposal, writing her he was willing to let it go and, in a pitch for her support, added that he hoped they would "get together sometime in the future to discuss other matters."

A week later, perhaps wanting the last word or to take Jack down a peg or two, Mrs. Roosevelt fired off a telegram to him, playing with the title of his book *Profiles in Courage* and jamming that spear so far northward Jack felt as if the tip was in his mouth:

> My dear boy . . . I have found in a lifetime of Adversity that when blows are rained on one, it is advisable to turn the other profile.

Now that Jack was the Democratic nominee, they had to patch up their differences. Mrs. Roosevelt had been helping her neighbor, Gore Vidal, in his long shot race for Congress, and Gore told Jack he was talking him up to her. Gore had a flair for self-importance, so Jack didn't know if he was telling the truth. Yet he was invited to the grounds of FDR's birthplace and grave site to address a crowd on the twenty-fifth anniversary of FDR signing Social Security into law. Mrs. Roosevelt asked if, prior to his speech, Jack would lunch with her. He agreed, but two days before they met, Mrs. Roosevelt's thirteen-year-old granddaughter Sally fell off a horse and died. When Jack heard the news, he discovered his shock and sadness about Joe and Kick were never far away. He offered his condolences to Mrs. Roosevelt, suggesting they reschedule lunch. Mrs. Roosevelt, no stranger to the hectic schedules of presidential campaigns, demonstrated how resolute she could be by insisting that Jack come on Sunday as planned.

Val-Kill, her stucco-and-fieldstone cottage, was two miles from FDR's family home. Jack went around back to knock on the door of a screened porch, and Mrs. Roosevelt came out. Her steel gray hair was under a hairnet, and her shapeless dress was wrinkled.

Jack said, "I appreciate you meeting me at such a terrible time."

Her eyes were piercing behind the thick lenses of her glasses, and Jack could see every day of her seventy-five years on her face. "Life marches forward, doesn't it?"

She didn't wait for an answer and led him to a book-lined alcove off the living room. They sat across from each other in chintz-covered chairs. Between them was a small round table with a lacy cloth and a silver coffeepot, cups, and saucers. As Mrs. Roosevelt poured the coffee, she said, "You know something of suffering and loss, don't you, Senator?"

Jack spooned sugar into his cup. "I do."

"Then, as president, imagine all the people you can help. But you appear rather hostile to our more open-minded Democrats. Why is that?"

"Because I don't believe *realism* is a curse word."

"Nor do I," she said. "But we ought to keep the right thing in mind even if circumstances prevent us from doing it. Adlai Stevenson is a man who subscribes to this principle."

That had been her angle from the start, a job for Adlai. A small price for her support. With her interviews on radio and TV, her speeches at rallies, her column appearing six days a week in newspapers across the country, and her articles in magazines like *Vogue* and *Reader's Digest*, she was a one-woman political machine.

Jack said, "There will be room for Adlai in my administration."

Mrs. Roosevelt nodded approvingly. "Dear boy, I trust you haven't been discouraged by the polls."

"I'd prefer Gallup had me up by six points instead of down."

Mrs. Roosevelt said, "Tom Dewey was ahead of President Truman by six points right before the election, and Truman won. We will beat Vice President Nixon."

Jack had seen Mrs. Roosevelt as puritanical and distant. Yet here she was, mourning her teenage granddaughter yet maneuvering to secure a friend an appointment and attempting to convince a presidential candidate to embrace her idealism by offering her substantial assistance. She was a queen who had held on to her crown through an indomitable will, political savvy, and hard work, and Jack thought if a movie of him with a hooker ever became public, she'd shrug and instruct him to take his lumps and get on with his campaign.

Mrs. Roosevelt set her coffee cup on the saucer. "I'd like to clear the air between us."

Jack knew what was coming. Even though Senator McCarthy drank himself to death three years ago, she was going to bring up the censure vote. Like all compassionate and vengeful people, Mrs. Roosevelt had a memory as long as her life.

She said, "I understand you were in the hospital and had undergone a troublesome surgery on your back. I am not unsympathetic. But the lives McCarthy ruined with his Communist witch-hunting was unconscionable. You could have released a statement supporting the censure, and I remain disappointed you did not."

Her stare, Jack thought, could freeze a forest fire. But he knew the rules of this game—look away first, you lose—so he stared right at her and told her the truth. "Senator McCarthy was a personal and family friend, but that's not why I didn't censure him. McCarthy was an Irish Catholic. Like my biggest supporters in Massachusetts. They're primarily blue-collar people with dirt under their fingernails. I'm not sure they cared why McCarthy was ranting and raving, but they recognized the manicured men criticizing him, the same ones who have derided the Irish for generations because they prayed at a different church."

Still staring, she replied, "You are saying it was politics?"

"Meaning no disrespect, Mrs. Roosevelt, your husband wasn't above politics. You publicly supported a federal antilynching bill; President Roosevelt did not. Did he believe lynching Negroes was acceptable? No, but he needed the southerners in Congress to back his programs. You supported letting the Jewish refugees from Hitler on that ship, the *St. Louis*, land in the United States; President Roosevelt said no. Why? He was no fan of the Nazis. Because in 1939 he knew from public opinion polls Americans wanted nothing to do with refugees in general and Jewish refugees in particular."

Her stare softened. "Well, Franklin was a magnificent president, but he wasn't perfect."

Jack couldn't resist teasing her. "I suspect he would've been perfect had he listened to you."

Her smile was enchanting, a smile retrieved from the best moments of her girlhood. "My dear boy, I've often thought that very thing myself."

CHAPTER 57

Belmar, New Jersey

Caitlin stood at the newsstand in the lobby of the Surfside Hotel, staring at the front page of the *New York Times*. She read the Associated Press report twice, but the words didn't change.

> THE "SAVAGE YOUNG WOMAN" OF FRENCH
> LETTERS DIES
>
> QUEBEC CITY (AP)—Goncourt Prize–winning
> novelist Été Fournier, whose wild nights in Saigon
> and Paris were as famous as her international best-
> seller *Au Revoir, Papa*, was found dead in the court-
> yard of her rented house by the owner of the property.
> She was 28.
>
> Quebec City police spokesman François Gagnon
> stated that "Été had been dead for approximately 36
> hours, and her head injury suggests she died from a
> 12-meter fall off a balcony."
>
> According to investigators, neighbors saw no one vis-
> iting the house, and the balcony railing was intact.

No note was left, and at present Coroner Edouard
Côté has reached the "presumptive conclusion" that
her death was a suicide.

Caitlin's mind rebelled at the idea that Été had taken her own life.
A few weeks back, Été had sent her a note from Quebec: under a line
drawing of her smiling face, she'd written, *I'm happy here. So is my novel.*

There was a phone booth across from the newsstand. Reed said she
could call him collect at the office anytime.

After accepting the call, Reed said, "I read about Été and would've
phoned, but I didn't have your number. How're you doing?"

"I'm in Belmar. Do you want to go to the beach tomorrow?"

Reed hesitated. She wondered if he felt she was inviting him to
cross the boundary between professional and personal. That wasn't her
intention. She was heartbroken about Été, and imagining spending
another Saturday by herself made her desperately lonely. To put his
mind at ease, she said, "Reed, I could use some company."

"Let me have your address," he replied. "I can be there around
noon."

Late the next morning, as Caitlin packed a cooler, the doorbell
rang. From the kitchen she looked through the living room and saw
Reed on the other side of the screen door. He was wearing a white polo
shirt, black bathing trunks, and a red baseball cap with a white *P* on it.

She let him in, and the silence was becoming awkward when Caitlin
asked, "You're a Phillies fan?"

He grinned, deepening the beguiling lines around his eyes and
mouth. "Tragically, yes. One of the masochists of Connie Mack
Stadium."

Caitlin hadn't anticipated feeling nervous around Reed, but swimming and sunbathing together was more intimate than a business lunch
or Broadway show. She excused herself, saying she had to put on her
suit. She went into the bedroom and chose the shell pink two-piece

over the beige one-piece, telling herself she wanted to feel the sun on her stomach and back. Then she told herself to stop lying. There was no law against wanting a man to admire you.

An hour later, they were sitting on beach towels under an umbrella, eating roast beef sandwiches and discussing Caitlin's Jersey Shore piece. Their discussion ended as they finished the sandwiches. They were quiet until Caitlin said, "I don't believe Été killed herself."

Reed removed his aviator sunglasses. "Why's that?"

"Été was a compulsive note writer. In her suite at the Algonquin, she taped them to the mirror, the sink, her desk. She wouldn't leave for good without leaving a note. Her neighbors claimed they didn't see any visitors. They must not have been paying attention, because Été didn't go long without male company. And she wrote me from Quebec. She was doing well."

Reed drank the last of his Coca-Cola. "When I was working at our embassy in Moscow, my best friend shot himself. I couldn't believe it. My reaction to the news about Été was similar. She was so brave in her writing and had survived a horrendous past, and in July I read that interview with her in the *Times* where she said her new novel was rolling along. Novelists firing on all cylinders don't commit suicide. If you want to go to Canada to see if there's a story, I could get the magazine to cover your expenses."

Caitlin took the empty bottle from him and put it in the cooler. "The night before I came here, I was attacked outside my apartment."

"What? Were you hurt?"

Caitlin said, "I had my pistol with me and chased him off. But now I'm thinking: Gabe is murdered, a friend of mine disappears, I'm assaulted, and Été is dead. Coincidences? Or a situation I don't understand yet?"

"Last you told me, you were going to get a report Gabe wrote in Mexico City."

"I have other research to do." In three days, she was going to drive from Belmar to Newark Airport and fly to Miami to track down Clara. She wished she could tell Reed how a prostitute might connect to Gabe and the CIA, Cuba, a dead pimp, Trafficante, and Kennedy.

Reed was peering at her as though he knew she wasn't telling him the whole story. However, he didn't question her. "Why don't we go for a swim?"

They swam the crawl side by side, out past the bodysurfers, and then floated on their backs, the sun on their faces and the gulls a brilliant white in the sky. When they grew tired, they swam in and lay on their towels until they were warm enough for another swim. It was the type of day at the shore Caitlin recalled, golden sunlight on a gray sea and not a care in the world. There was one disquieting moment. On their last walk in from the ocean, a wave broke behind them, staggering Reed and knocking Caitlin off her feet. Reed reached into the water to help her up. She grabbed him above the wrists. He pulled, and as Caitlin stood, she let go. Reed lurched forward, his right hand pressing against her left breast.

"I'm—" he sputtered. "I'm sorry."

Caitlin laughed. It was her all-purpose laugh, a placeholder until she could determine how she felt about something. As they walked up the hot sand, Reed said, "I've heard about a great seafood place here, Dave and Evelyn's. May I buy you dinner?"

Caitlin determined she'd been more amused than embarrassed and, accompanied by a comic roll of her eyes, said, "To make up for your impropriety?"

Now Reed laughed. "If that's what it takes."

At the bungalow, Caitlin showered first. When she left the bathroom in a terry cloth robe with a towel wrapped around her head, Reed had cleaned out the cooler and retrieved a knapsack with a change of clothes from his car. Caitlin gave him a fresh towel and washcloth and went to the bedroom to dress and comb the tangles out of her hair. The bungalow had thin walls, and Caitlin could hear Reed in the shower.

She had missed the sound of Gabe showering. That sound meant they might be going out for the evening or, if they stayed home, she wouldn't be alone. For a tingly second, Caitlin pictured Reed soaping his broad chest. Then she put up her hair in a damp loose bun and dressed for dinner.

CHAPTER 58

Dave and Evelyn's was a pine-paneled joint with doo-wop playing over the speakers, but the food was delicious, which was why the tables were filled. Caitlin and Reed drank muscadet with their lobster tails, coleslaw, and baked potatoes, rarely stopping to talk because they were so hungry. Reed did tell her his kayak trip in Maine had been rained out, and Caitlin described the couples twisting at the Rainbow Club, leaving out that she pulled her .38 on a drunk kid, because she didn't want Reed to think she had lost her mind.

They were too full for dessert, and as Reed paid the check, Caitlin asked, "Would you like me to make us some coffee?"

Reed checked his watch. "I've got some time. That would be nice."

They walked down to the ocean. Above the beach an iron railing ran the length of the boardwalk, and sun-browned teenage girls in sleeveless blouses and shorts were perched on it, watching the knots of teenage boys swaggering over the boards.

"The railbirds," Caitlin said. "I used to be one of them, waiting for the boys to notice us."

Reed stopped and, in the most serious tone she'd ever heard from him, replied, "I doubt you had long to wait."

Even in her pale-green shift with spaghetti straps and standing in the cool briny air, Caitlin felt as if her blood was heating up to a boil. She could critique her appearance like a catty art critic eviscerating a painting—too many freckles, for instance, especially after a day in the sun, and her thighs were too fleshy. Still, Caitlin knew she was pretty. She just thought Reed hadn't noticed.

Flustered, Caitlin said, "Most of the boys were too shy to talk to us," which was sufficient to get them walking again.

As they came up Seventeenth Avenue to the bungalow, a reddish glow was spreading over the rooftops. Caitlin asked Reed to sit in one of the scallop-backed chairs on the porch, then went inside, through the kitchen, and to the bedroom. In her makeup bag, the clamshell case with her diaphragm was wedged between the Cutex nail polish and Jean Naté splash.

She was watching Reed through the screen door when he turned. "Is the coffee ready?"

"I didn't put it on," she said.

"Is something wrong?" he asked.

Caitlin held open the door. Reed didn't move. She opened the door wider. When she didn't step onto the porch, he stepped inside. The sleeves of his button-down were rolled up. Caitlin rubbed her hand down one of his muscular forearms, the silky hairs gold from the sun.

As if apologizing for his delay in interpreting her signal, Reed said, "I've never quite understood feminine desire."

Her voice braver than she felt, Caitlin said, "You're not supposed to understand it. You're just supposed to appreciate it when it shows up."

He kissed her, slow and gentle, one arm around her shoulders, the other reaching back to close the front door. Caitlin was worried that taking off her clothes would start her ruminating about Gabe. It didn't, and, lying on the bed, she felt miraculously light, as if she'd shed a suit of armor. Reed, bare chested and without his madras Bermudas and boxer shorts, was beside her, touching her, kissing her everywhere. For Caitlin, it was her eagerness to begin that rang the bells of guilt in her head. She tried to block out the bells, but they clanged louder as Reed, hovering above her, asked softly, "Is it all right?"

It was a gentlemanly question, but Caitlin, perhaps from nervousness, couldn't help herself and let out a little laugh. "I hope it'll be better than all right."

"I'll do my best."

She had forgotten the sudden thrill of the connection. Reed moved with a disciplined patience, like a man of experience and proper breeding. But that wasn't what Caitlin wanted. She wanted to let herself go and drown in that exquisite darkness. She was done with loneliness, wasn't she? Done with grief. Wasn't that why Reed was in her bed? To pursue the erotic paradox with him—to be lost and found at the same ecstatic instant?

Locking her arms around him, she moved faster. Time passed or didn't pass. Caitlin couldn't tell. Nor did she care. His breathing quickened, and then he was calling to her. He sounded far away, as if he was standing on the sand and Caitlin was swimming well out from shore. She heard herself call back to him. The satiny darkness enveloped her, and, after a while, she rested her head on his chest while his fingertips traced circles on her back.

CHAPTER 59

Why Danny Cohen was driving along the ocean in Belmar with the champagne light of dawn peeking over the horizon was a question with two answers.

One: he woke up on his couch at four on Sunday morning with an all-American hangover, popped two aspirins, and concluded that to protect Cait, he had to check on her.

Two: he missed Cait. Even when Danny didn't see her, he liked knowing she was in New York. The sorry-ass truth was Danny had been harboring a crush on her ever since Gabe had introduced them. Forget her Irish-lassie beauty; all that did was catch your attention. Who she was, that was the reason. A stalwart friend. She'd seen Danny through his divorces, often telling Gabe to bring him for dinner. And when Cait loved a man, she loved him completely. Gabe used to say he must've pleased God in another life because He sent him Cait. And now look at her, hunting Gabe's killer as if obeying one of her wedding vows.

Danny slowed to scan the house numbers on Seventeenth Avenue. His plan was simple. Stake out Cait's place for a couple of hours and, if she didn't come out, knock on the door and take her to breakfast. Odds favored Cait giving him holy hell for keeping tabs on her. Danny was prepared. He'd blame Julian for insisting on it, because as far as Danny could tell, Cait never got mad at Julian.

He spotted 412, a bungalow the color of dried apricots with a small open porch. Danny drove past. Two cars were in the crushed-seashell driveway: Cait's Chevy Bel Air and behind it a dark-green Triumph with Pennsylvania plates. Did women ever own British sports cars? Danny hoped so. He wrote the plate number on a chewing gum wrapper.

Down the block from Cait's, Danny set up on the opposite side of the street. He would be able to see anyone coming out, and he had binoculars to take a closer look. A milk truck went by the bungalow—and a woman in a housecoat with curlers in her hair walking a sheepdog. The dog lifted his hind leg to water a tree. Danny was wishing he could use the same tree when Cait's front door opened. Bringing up the binoculars, Danny turned the focus knob, and what he saw made his heart sink.

A man in a red Philadelphia Phillies cap, a white shirt, and madras shorts came onto the porch with a knapsack slung over his shoulder. He was in his late thirties or early forties, about six feet tall, athletic build and stride, one of those ruggedly handsome sons of bitches. Before getting in the Triumph, he waved at the doorway. Danny shifted the binoculars to Cait. All she wore was a T-shirt. She waved as he ducked into the Triumph and backed out of the driveway. Cait closed the door.

Danny put the binoculars on the seat. He was fuming, feeling as if Cait was cheating on Gabe, but he knew the truth. Danny wanted her, and she wanted someone else. And he couldn't talk to Cait now. She'd think he was acting like a jealous boyfriend, and she'd be right.

Danny would go to the station house and run the plate. Maybe the guy was a jerk. Maybe he still had a chance with Cait.

CHAPTER 60

Miami Beach, Florida

As Caitlin spoke to the birdlike blue-haired secretary at Temple Emanu-El, she recalled how her mother used to warn her that everyone was half as smart as they thought, which was how rich boys went broke and single girls got pregnant. Her plan had been to show the rabbi the photograph of Clara and the bent older man and ask if he recognized either of them. An unannounced drop-in was a cop trick. It was easier to read a person's initial reaction and to judge if he was lying. However, Caitlin had failed to consider the possibility that the rabbi would be out.

"Rabbi's at the Doral Country Club," the secretary said, her fingers resting on the keyboard of a humming electric typewriter. "Playing in a charity golf tournament. Tonight he's leaving for a vacation in Europe. He'll be back in early September."

Caitlin brought out the photograph of Clara and the man on the steps of the temple. "Have you ever seen these people?"

The secretary peered at the stakeout photo. "I haven't, but he's too old for her."

"I agree," Caitlin said.

◆　◆　◆

The late-afternoon sun had heated the air until it was as thick as custard, and after the short walk to her rented Chevy, Caitlin's seersucker blouse was damp with perspiration. Yenchi's bookie joint, above a barbershop, was just south of the temple. Only one barber was in. He was sitting in his chair, using two fingers to wax his droopy white mustache. To his right, the manicurist was behind a nail table reading *Diario Las Américas*, her dark beehive hair visible above the newsprint.

"Excuse me," Caitlin said to the barber. "Can you tell Yenchi Gabe's wife is here?"

The barber spun his chair toward her, and the manicurist lowered the paper. Both of them were giving her an odd look. The barber shuffled past the nail table, opened a door, and called, "Hilda, come down."

The barber returned to his chair, and Yenchi's wife came through the doorway, looking like a harried accountant, half-glasses low on her nose and an adding machine tape in her hand.

A little sadly, she said, "Caitlin, honey, you're here to see Yenchi?"

Caitlin felt the bad news coming in the pit of her stomach before Hilda said, "Yenchi passed away. Six weeks ago. He had a heart attack in the swimming pool."

"Mrs. Baylin, I'm—"

"Every day I tell him, 'Yench, you're too old for apple fritters and espresso and cigars,' but does he listen?"

"I'm so sorry," Caitlin said.

"I appreciate that, honey, but I gotta get back upstairs. Sandy Koufax is pitching tonight, and the Jews are betting like he's Moses with a fastball."

Caitlin said, "I spoke to Yenchi after you got home from the Catskills. He was asking around about this woman I'm looking for, Clara, and he told me you were helping him."

Hilda glanced toward heaven as if to make sure her late husband could hear her. "Yenchi, I swear to God, was missing most of his brain. He never asked me about any Clara."

Caitlin showed her the stakeout photograph. "Yenchi gave me this. Does the woman or man look familiar?"

"Never seen them," Hilda replied. "And I don't know what my Yenchi was talking about. I gotta go. Call me at home if you want."

Caitlin noticed the manicurist watching Hilda with a contemptuous smile. Caitlin looked at the manicurist, who disappeared again behind her newspaper.

◆ ◆ ◆

A fiery breeze was blowing through the palm trees, and Caitlin heard the coconuts clicking above her as she sat in her car across from the barbershop. She was shocked Yenchi had lied to her. Had he cut a deal with the FBI agent who owed him money? Was it a favor for Trafficante? No way to know. And why didn't the manicurist bother to hide her contempt for Hilda? Did she merely dislike her? Or did she know something? The shop closed at five. Caitlin decided to wait an hour for the manicurist. She had already checked into a motel by the airport and had a ticket for a morning flight to Newark. Resting her head on the back of the seat, Caitlin thought about Reed. She had spoken to him twice before leaving Belmar. He was at a convention of magazine editors in San Francisco now. She missed him, which made her feel guilty, as if she was abandoning Gabe. Jesus, how screwy could she get? Wasn't missing Reed a sign her grief was receding after seven months? So what was the problem? She still felt Gabe watching over her—that was the problem—because suddenly, at the strangest moments, she imagined Gabe could see her in bed with Reed.

The manicurist emerged from the shop in a low-cut violet dress. She looked like an aging pinup girl, but time hadn't beaten her yet, and she moved toward the bus stop with a slinkiness that was closer to dancing than walking. Caitlin got out of the car and hurried to step in front of her. The manicurist stopped, clutching her straw pocketbook against her breasts as if Caitlin was a purse snatcher.

"Can we talk?" Caitlin asked.

The manicurist didn't answer, and Caitlin said, "Please, Gabe was my husband and—"

"*Un buen hombre*, Gabriel. He always pay me for a manicure and say, 'Inés, I don't have no chance to get one.' I feel bad when I hear about your Gabriel."

"Then talk to me, Inés. I'm trying to find his killer."

"If that cow who owns the shop see us talking, she'll fire me. I need my job."

"There's a restaurant across the street," Caitlin said. "Let me take you to dinner."

"A drink. I got to get home to my daughters."

At Joe's, they found seats by themselves in the woodsy barroom. Inés ordered a Cuba libre. Caitlin hadn't heard of it, but she ordered one, believing it would make Inés more comfortable with her. She was relieved it was a rum and Coke with lime juice.

"You knew Yenchi well," Caitlin said.

Inés drank as if she'd just run a marathon. "He is my boss."

An obvious, meaningless answer. Caitlin waited until Inés was down to the ice cubes, and she said, "Another one?"

"*Sí.*"

Caitlin signaled the bartender by pointing at Inés's glass. He brought her another Cuba libre. As Inés drank, Caitlin asked, "Did you talk to Yenchi much?"

"Every day."

Caitlin went into her bag, retrieved the photo of Clara and the goateed man, and placed it on the bar. "Did Yenchi ever say anything about these two?"

Inés snickered. "What Yenchi say to me is '*Vamos a joder hoy por la noche.*'"

"I don't speak Spanish," Caitlin said.

Moving her head close to Caitlin, Inés whispered, "He say, 'Let's fuck tonight.'"

Giggling drunkenly, Inés moved away. Caitlin couldn't tell whether Yenchi was being crude or Inés was sleeping with him. Inés saved her the trouble of asking by saying, "Yenchi *un toro con grandes cuernos.*"

Caitlin said, "*Toro* is bull, yes?"

"*Sí,* and Yenchi a bull with big horns." Inés was down to the ice cubes again, and her eyes were glassy.

"You and Yenchi?"

Inés nodded. "His wife, that *vaca,* she don't do nothing for him. My husband in Cuba, he goes make revolution, and I hear Batista's police arrests the families of *Comunistas.* I come here. Yenchi give me a job and later help me buy a house. I know he not divorce his wife, but she don't come to the shop then, and my children is safe."

Caitlin said, "Why would Yenchi lie to me about his looking for Clara?"

Inés jabbed her index finger into the photo of Clara as if impaling her on a blade. "That *puta.* Her *chulo,* Victor Diaz, bring her to Yenchi, and Yenchi get *demente.* He can't get her enough. I catch them at our hotel room. The whore run away, and I yell at Yenchi he an ungrateful fool. I give him for free whatever he want, and he go paying for it. We make up, but he would keep chasing that young *puta* if she didn't disappear. He want you to find her."

"Why didn't he look himself?"

Inés said, "Because her uncle, the man in your picture, threaten Yenchi."

"Threaten him how?" Caitlin asked.

"In a letter, Yenchi say. I never read it."

"Do you know where the letter is?"

"Maybe in the hotel room," Inés said.

"Yenchi's dead. He has a hotel room?"

Inés shrugged. "There's a few months still paid. The manager give him a deal. He gamble and owe Yenchi money."

Caitlin, nervous the answer to her next question would be *no,* sipped her Cuba libre for courage. "Do you have a key?"

Inés shook her head. "The man at the desk give it to me when I go."

"Will you take me to the hotel and let me check the room for the letter?"

Inés said, "I have to be home for my daughters."

"Call them. There's a pay phone by the ladies' room. After the hotel I'll drive you home. You won't have to take the bus. That'll save you time." Caitlin went into her wallet and held out a dime in the palm of her hand. "Please, Inés. Help me find who killed my husband."

Finally, Inés took the dime.

The hotel was a mile from the barbershop, on a broad avenue with the ocean on one side and hotels, like a pastel row of art deco birthday cakes, on the other. The room was on the third floor. It smelled of cigar smoke. Inés sat in the one chair, her eyes wandering from the ceiling to the unmade double bed. Caitlin was glad the hotel didn't take cleaning seriously. Beneath the windows was a table littered with sports pages from the *Miami Herald*. Under the newspapers were a cigar clipper and a walnut ashtray with a layer of ash and blackened wood matches. Next to the desk was a brass swing-top trash can. She put the trash can on the desk and removed the top. Inside were a *TV Guide* and cigar wrappers.

Caitlin checked the drawers in the dresser and the night tables. Nothing. She went into the bathroom and turned on the light. Black-and-white-tiled floor and walls, and a white sink with a black ceramic trash can under it. Caitlin dumped the trash into the sink. A flattened tube of toothpaste, a can of shaving cream, and a snowstorm of paper scraps. There was writing on the scraps in blue ink. She sifted through them, then picked up two triangular wedges of paper with a yellowy squiggle of glue on one side. The backflap of an envelope, she guessed, fitting the two pieces together, and there it was, a return address: *A KORN 7 WAIT STREET, GLENS FALLS, NY.* At last, here was a solid lead, and she stuck the pieces into her courier bag. She was sure the paper in the sink was the threatening letter from Clara's uncle, which Yenchi had torn up. She collected the paper from the sink and sat on the floor, arranging the scraps as if doing a jigsaw puzzle, and she felt euphoric as the pieces formed enough words for her to understand the gist of the letter:

STOP WHAT YOU DOING WITH CLARA WILL TELL YOUR WIFE ARTHUR

Caitlin dropped the scraps in her bag and went into the room. Inés was still sitting in the chair. Her face was streaked with tears and mascara.

She said, "Yenchi go off with a whore, and I miss him. Am I *loco*?"

Caitlin knelt, taking a Kleenex out of her bag and wiping her cheeks. "No, you're sad. Let me take you to your daughters."

Inés put her arms around Caitlin. She began to sob. Caitlin held her until she was quiet and helped her out of the chair.

CHAPTER 61

Greenwich Village
September 1960

The minute Caitlin arrived home from Newark Airport, she went to her study and called long-distance information and asked for the number of Arthur Korn—"That's Korn with a *K*"—on 7 Wait Street in Glens Falls, New York.

She felt her excitement rise until the operator said, "We have no listing under that name."

"Are you sure?"

"Honey," the operator replied before breaking the connection, "I been reading since first grade, and there ain't no listings for Korn with a *K* or a *C* in Glens Falls."

Caitlin had planned to confirm Korn's address and then pay him a visit and ask about Clara. Now, as she checked the AAA atlas in her study, her plan didn't change. She'd drive to Glens Falls in the morning, a little over two hundred miles away, according to the atlas, and knock on his door. It was possible he didn't have a phone or it was listed under the name of his wife or a roommate. If no one answered the door, she'd sit on his place until he showed up.

Her Jersey Shore piece needed polishing, and she wanted to send it off because she didn't know how long she'd be in Glens Falls. She raised the window to air out her study. Below, in Christopher Park, a guy in a beret and sunglasses sat on a bench playing a saxophone. Caitlin recognized the song, "Groovin' High," from one of Gabe's albums, but the guy sounded closer to a third grader practicing scales than Charlie Parker.

The polishing went smoothly, and Caitlin was placing the typed pages in an envelope when the phone rang. It was Viola Mauri, her best friend from high school who oversaw the arts section of the *Newark Evening News*.

"Hi, sweetie," Vi said. "I'm in the city. Want to go to Sevilla for dinner? Say, six o'clock?" That was their usual spot, a Spanish restaurant on Charles Street.

"Six it is," Caitlin said and, after hanging up, wrote out the address of the *Post* on the envelope, adding *Attention: Reed Howland* and sticking on the stamps.

On the way, she dropped the envelope into a mailbox and noticed her guilt had been supplanted by an optimism that had been missing ever since Gabe had died.

◆ ◆ ◆

Sevilla was a fixture in the Village with its homemade sangria, roomy booths, and Spanish artwork brightening the dark walls. Caitlin and Vi were sharing the specialty of the house, a pot of paella a la Valenciana, an aromatic mix of chicken, sausage, shellfish, and saffron rice.

"What were you doing in the city?" Caitlin asked.

In the light of the hanging Tiffany lamp, Vi's bleached, teased-up hair was platinum. "My niece started her job as a researcher at *Newsweek* and moved into a studio on Third Avenue. I promised to buy her a couch. And I wanted to talk to you."

"About?"

Vi refilled their glasses from the plastic pitcher of white sangria. "I got approval to hire an assistant arts editor starting in January, and I want to hire you."

"That's so nice of you, Vi, but I've never worked at a newspaper."

"Sweetie, if it was that hard, there wouldn't be a million journalists."

Caitlin laughed, and Vi said, "I could use a buddy in the middle of the asshole boys' club. You can have days off if you want to freelance for magazines."

"I've been thinking about moving back to Jersey. When do I have to let you know?"

"Mid-November," Vi said. "If you don't take it, there's like twenty people at the *News* who want me to hire one of their idiot cousins."

CHAPTER 62

Walking to Grove Street in the evening-blue light, Caitlin felt the coming autumn shoving summer aside.

"I've been waiting for you," Danny said.

He was parked outside her building, sitting behind the wheel of his black Thunderbird with the top down. In his brown suede jacket, he appeared younger than in his captain's uniform and less taut, the cool blond boy you hoped would ask you to dance.

"How'd you know I was home?" she asked.

"The saxophonist in the park is one of my undercovers. He's been watching your place."

"And me?" Caitlin hadn't intended to sound so annoyed. She appreciated Danny protecting her but wondered if he had a cop watching her in Belmar and had seen Reed. She wasn't ready to tell anyone about Reed, least of all Danny.

He ignored her question. "Hop in. We might have the piece of shit who came after you. I was talking to one of my detectives, Lev Rifkin, whose parents are from Odesa. That word you remembered him saying, *suka*. It's Russian. Means *bitch*."

The Allerton Hotel, a turn-of-the-century stone building, was a cheap Village way station for bohemians. Up in the second-floor hallway, residents were being interviewed by a uniform and a detective. The smell from the communal bathroom was so bad Caitlin was breathing through her mouth as Danny led her to a uniform guarding a closed door.

Danny asked, "You found him, Jonesy?"

"I did, Captain. I got a complaint from the manager that the vic was behind on his bill. He'd been here eight months. I checked the room, and there he was."

"What else?"

Jonesy said, "The vic was got like the army teaches you to kill a sentry. Get in back of him, cover his nose and mouth with a hand so he can't shout, stab him in the kidney, then cut his throat. And the vic must've known him. He was filling two beer mugs when he got it. And none of the people living here saw nothing. The medical examiner sent Phillie over."

"Good job," Danny said, and Jonesy opened the door. The overhead light was weak. A detective was dusting the dresser for prints, and another one was bagging the beer bottle and mugs. A bald, stooped man in a tie and shirtsleeves was standing over the body.

Danny said, "Whatta we know, Phillie?"

The bald man cackled. "*I* know there's some rigor in this fellow's neck and jaw, and I estimate he hasn't been gone more than a couple hours."

Caitlin had been standing behind Danny, who gently ushered her toward the body. The man was on his back, reddish-brown blood under him staining the threadbare carpet. His throat had a black half-moon of a gash, and the front of his white shirt was dark with dried blood. Even with the grimace of the dead, it was a face Caitlin would never forget: bushy eyebrows; high, wide forehead; flattened nose; and the beady-eyed glare of an angry animal.

"That's him," she said.

A detective in a fedora and trench coat and rubber gloves came over from the dresser, holding up a plastic evidence bag. His eyes were bloodshot.

"What do you got, Lev?" Danny asked.

"Three passports: Mexican, East German, and Russian. All with different names. I'd say he's an intel agent. I went to the lobby and called a buddy at the FBI, and he says they been keeping tabs on some of these jerks, but the stiff on the floor wasn't on their radar."

Caitlin asked, "Did you check the stamps for February?"

Lev eyed her as if he was surprised that she had the gift of speech, and Danny said to the detective, "I was gonna ask the same thing."

"I checked. In February, his Russian passport was stamped entering and leaving Mexico City and then entering New York. He hadn't left since then."

Lev went back to work. Caitlin said, "Danny, that's when Gabe was in Mexico and here."

"Yeah, it is. Let's go to your place and talk."

In her apartment, they sat on the living room couch. Caitlin asked, "Could Trafficante have ordered a hit on the guy?"

"Whacking an intel agent? That's above Trafficante's pay grade. And Julian and me, we convinced him—"

"You talked to Trafficante?"

Danny said, "We told him it was in his interest not to go near you. Did you hear anything in Miami that could be connected to the Allerton?"

"No. The rabbi wasn't around, and Yenchi's mistress said Yenchi was never helping me locate Clara. Yenchi was one of her johns until her uncle wrote him a letter threatening to tell his wife if he didn't cut it out."

Danny laughed. "Hope I'm that frisky when I'm his age."

"Yenchi's out of the frisky business. He drowned in his pool."

Danny thought about that for a moment. Then he said, "Trafficante could've had that done. He was pissed off at him for sending you those FBI stakeout photos. Did they do an autopsy?"

"All I heard was Yenchi had a heart attack while he was swimming."

Danny asked, "Could the uncle be involved?"

"Unlikely. From his picture, he looks too old for a fight, and his mistress says he didn't confront Yenchi in person."

"Then what's your next move?"

"I have the uncle's address, and I'm going to Glens Falls in the morning to talk to him."

"Cait, I still can't see how Clara ties in to Gabe."

She was prepared for his skepticism. He'd been a cop his whole adult life. Half-truths were a language he understood, and she knew omitting the movie skewed the logic of her story. Yet she had an answer for him, and she liked to believe Clara would lead her not only to the Kennedy movie but to Gabe's killer. "I told you right after I was attacked: Clara knows Diaz, Yenchi, Trafficante, and maybe Gabe. Whatever Clara knows, I want to know."

Danny retrieved a fifth of Jameson's from a shelf of the hi-fi cabinet, brought the bottle and two shot glasses back, and set them on the low brass table and poured the whiskey.

Danny said, "I still don't see how Clara knits this whole thing together. And going upstate alone is a crummy idea. Whoever did the Russian might make a run at you."

"Maybe. But I'll be careful."

"Fuck *maybe*, Cait! No fucking *maybe*!" Danny knocked back a drink, then said, "The Cleveland cops called. They found Winkie."

Caitlin went numb. Danny gave her a shot glass of Irish whiskey. She drank. When she was done, Danny set the glass on the table. Softly, he said, "Winkie was in a trunk in Lake Erie. The trunk came up, and a tugboat crew fished it out. The Cuyahoga County medical examiner estimates she's been dead since February, right after her art show."

Caitlin wanted to cry. She didn't feel sad, though, only a spooky numbness.

Danny said, "She was strangled, and all her fingers were broken. Cops out there believe she was being tortured during an interrogation."

Caitlin heard herself ask, "Why would—"

"Probably Gabe was being followed. Somebody figured out he was working for the CIA, and he was seen going to Winkie's loft, and they broke in to find out what Gabe was doing there. They were on the right track. Winkie did do that engraving for Castro's cigar box, which was key to an assassination plot. But when they didn't find anything after tossing her loft, they figured out how to grab Winkie and wanted to make sure she was telling them the truth."

Caitlin pictured Winkie as she had last seen her, with her short coppery hair and freckles. In her mind, Winkie looked too young to be dead.

"I have to go to Glens Falls, Danny."

"I'd bet the guy who killed the vic at the Allerton is involved in Winkie's murder. And he's still out there. Which is why going to Glens Falls is stupid."

"Winkie's murder is another reason I've got to go."

"Take my car. If somebody's watching you, he knows your car and plate. I'll take your car and follow you to the bridge to make sure you're not being tailed."

Caitlin nodded.

"Don't tell anyone where you are. And check in with me. I'll stay on your couch tonight, and we can go out together in the morning."

"Thank you," she said and then walked to her bedroom, closed the door, changed into a nightgown, and went to sleep.

She woke with a start. The alarm clock glowed in the dark. It was midnight. On the wall was a birthday present Winkie had given her last year, a framed etching of the fountain in Washington Square Park in full watery bloom. Caitlin made her way to the wall in the dark. She ran her fingertips over the steel frame. Winkie had made the frame. Winkie must've been so frightened while that bastard broke her fingers, the fear even worse than the pain and then those murderous hands around her neck. Caitlin sat on the bed in the dark for a long time.

And she wept.

CHAPTER 63

Houston, Texas

Jack crossed the lobby of the Rice Hotel and entered the Crystal Ballroom. He was about to address hundreds of Southern Baptist ministers, many of whom suspected he intended to move the pope into the Lincoln Bedroom. Following his speech, he would answer their questions, and the evening would be broadcast on TV. As he walked down the center aisle alone, the ministers stared at him, and except for the whisperings of the press corps in back, an uncomfortable quiet hung over the ballroom. Even Bobby and the ballsiest of Jack's Emerald Isle band of vote-chasers, Kenny O'Donnell, had objected to him accepting the invitation, arguing that some of the ministers would try to flay him for the cameras, and Ted Sorensen, as he'd drafted the speech, worried that if Jack screwed up, Nixon would ride the anti-Catholic vote into the Oval Office.

Jack had heard his Catholicism could cost him more than a million votes, so he believed that he had to confront the religious issue. Whether a meeting of the Greater Houston Ministerial Association was the wisest forum to do it was unclear, but Jack's rule was that if you don't know what the fuck to do, do something. That rule had saved his life when *PT-109* sank, and it had brought him here to win over an audience of pasty-faced tight-asses who made Boston Brahmins look like opium-eating beatniks.

Jack took his seat on the dais. The leader of the association asked everyone to stand for a prayer, and Jack seethed. The hypocrisy of the ministers was galling. God-fearing men who hated other God-fearing men. In that moment, as never before, Jack hoped Caitlin would take care of business and his private life would remain private so he could prove to every bigoted son of a bitch that a Catholic—and an Irish Catholic at that—could damn well be president.

The prayer concluded, and Kick hissed in his ear, *Ask them, Jack.*

Your timing's lousy, Kick.

Ask them why our brother Joe was good enough to die in a war for them, but you're not good enough to be president. We're both angry about it. So ask them!

Anger doesn't win elections.

You're the angriest of us all, Johnny boy. But all anyone ever sees is your smile.

Smiles win elections.

At the lectern, Jack was speaking with the measured tones of a professor, but his message was a left hook aimed at any minister who preferred splitting theological hairs to compassion and progress: "The hungry children I saw in West Virginia, the old people who cannot pay their doctors' bills, the families forced to give up their farms—an America with too many slums, with too few schools, and too late to the moon and outer space. These are the real issues which should decide this campaign. And they are not religious issues."

Jack heard the words coming out of his mouth, but it was as if he was hearing a disembodied voice. He was distracted by the image of his brother Joe floating above the suspicious faces of the ministers. He was seated in the cockpit of his B-24 Liberator with his rakish grin. Joe had been on his mind ever since the shock of reading about Été's suicide. His brother had volunteered to pilot a bomber loaded with TNT that would be radio-guided to a target in France after Joe parachuted out. It was a mission bordering on insane, and Jack believed Joe wouldn't have volunteered if he wasn't chasing a medal as part of his lifelong competition with his younger brother, who had been decorated for saving his *PT-109* crew.

Now, with Joe staring at him, Jack assured the ministers that he believed in the absolute separation of church and state. "This is the kind of America I fought for in the South Pacific and the kind my brother died for in Europe. No one suggested then that we may have a *divided loyalty.*"

Usually, Jack had a feel for how his speeches were being received. Not tonight, though. Tonight, as he expressed his hope that religious intolerance would end and pledged that if elected president, he would "preserve, protect, and defend the Constitution," he might as well have been addressing the figures at Madame Tussauds wax museum. So at the end the enthusiastic applause surprised him. After gathering up the pages of his speech, he backed away from the lectern, and when he looked up again to take questions, Joe's image exploded in midair just like his plane.

CHAPTER 64

Glens Falls, New York

Glens Falls was fifty miles north of Albany, in the foothills of the Adirondack Mountains. After Caitlin checked into the Queensbury Hotel, she picked up a city map at the front desk and went to find Arthur Korn, walking to Wait Street under a canopy of autumn-gold elms. Number 7 was a white-brick cottage with two large oblong windows on the first floor and two smaller ones on the second. The shades were drawn. Caitlin didn't see a garage. She rang the doorbell. No one answered.

Back in her room, she phoned Danny at the Sixth Precinct. He wasn't in. Caitlin spoke to the duty sergeant and left a message for Danny with the name of the hotel and the phone number. Then she called Reed at the magazine.

"I was beginning to think I'd never hear from you again," he said in the half-joking tone of a man concealing bruised feelings.

A bit defensively—after all, they'd made love three times in Belmar—Caitlin replied, "I've been chasing a lead. How was your convention?"

"I missed you," he said.

"I've missed you too," she replied, embarrassed by the longing in her voice. "I miss you right now."

"Then you've made my day," he said. "I've been going over your beach story. It's quite good. I could bring the edits to you. We could have a weekend together."

Caitlin, recalling Reed hovering over her in bed, was tempted to invite him to Glens Falls. The invitation was on the tip of her tongue, but she'd promised Danny not to reveal her location. "I'm moving around. Hang on to them. The post office is holding my mail. I'll let you know when I'll be in the city."

He was silent, and Caitlin hoped she wasn't discouraging him. "Will do. But a phone call once in a while would be appreciated."

"I will, Reed."

For nearly a month, Caitlin staked out 7 Wait Street. No one went in or out. To avoid attracting attention, she watched from either end of the block. She saw men leaving for the paper mill carrying lunch pails, children going to school, women unloading groceries from their cars. She considered asking one of the mill workers if he knew Arthur Korn but decided against it. If she made him suspicious, he could call the police, forcing Caitlin to lie about why she wanted to speak to Korn. Even worse would be if he contacted Korn. Clara had to know Trafficante was trying to find her, which was why she'd disappeared, and she'd probably told Korn, who might be scared into relocating if he heard a stranger was searching for him.

Caitlin felt foolish watching an empty house for so long, but she knew Gabe would approve. While they were dating, he staked out a rapist's apartment for three weeks, and when Caitlin suggested he look elsewhere, Gabe said, "There's a famous statue of a guy sitting on a rock with his chin on his hand." Caitlin replied, "*The Thinker*, by Rodin," and Gabe said, "Rodin could've named it *The Cop* if he'd stuck one of the statue's thumbs up his ass. That's the job. Sit around with your thumb up your ass till you see what you need to see." The next night, Gabe had arrested the perp.

To preserve her sanity, Caitlin took breaks—lunch at the Woolworth's counter, then a stroll through the bustling downtown, where she bought a new novel, *To Kill a Mockingbird*, and a biography of James Joyce. She ordered dinner from room service and read and watched television. Sleep evaded her. She hung on to its foggy rim for hours, thinking that ever since Gabe was murdered, she'd been buried in the past. On her Sunday walks around Glens Falls, Caitlin had seen families going to church and realized how desperately she desired a future of her own. Maybe Reed was a start.

In the mornings, she had breakfast in the hotel dining room and read the *New York Times*. Kennedy was getting beaten over the head with the pope. Par for the course, Caitlin thought. No shortage of tribal animus in America. *Mockingbird* was such a loathsome depiction of racial hatred it made the comments about Kennedy being in cahoots with the Vatican seem quaint.

Caitlin was surprised that Nixon, with his reputation as a no-holds-barred opponent, didn't subtly refer to Kennedy's Catholicism during that first televised debate. On-screen, the vice president was wan, his face sweat streaked, and he was frequently hesitant when he spoke. Kennedy was tanned and confident, and Caitlin had never felt so proud of being Irish and Catholic. She even set aside her disgust with Kennedy and his bedmates and her anger about the possibility Gabe had been shot tracking down a film for him. Whatever problem Kennedy had below his waist didn't harm him above his neck. And the debate, Caitlin recognized when it was over, had a deeper resonance for her than tribal pride. Kennedy's theme, that Americans weren't living up to their potential and the country needed to start moving again, seemed to be directed at her as a challenge to stop floundering and to create the life she wanted. With his spoken and unspoken elegance, Kennedy rekindled her faith in a sunnier tomorrow, while Nixon, defending the status quo, recalled her most dismal memories of yesterday.

Caitlin's mother, who'd dropped out of high school to help support her family, had had a habit of citing clichés as if she were sharing exalted, original insights, a habit that had irritated her studious daughter, a fixture on the dean's list in college. Years later, Caitlin understood that clichés were clichés because they were generally true, and among her mother's favorites was "Smart's OK; lucky's better." And on this afternoon, with Caitlin on the verge of abandoning her search for Arthur Korn, she was about to discover the truth of that platitude.

She had walked past 7 Wait Street to Bay Street, where she'd parked across from a brown-brick building with white pillars. A sign hanging above the pillars identified the building as the HEBREW COMMUNITY HOUSE, and a craggy-faced man in a red-and-black-checkered lumberjack shirt stood on the grass, raking leaves. As Caitlin went by him, he said, "How are you today?"

She stopped. "Fine, thank you."

Nodding at the community house, he gave her a neighborly smile. "I've seen you walking from my office window. I'm Rabbi Birnbaum. Are you new in town?"

Because she was going to leave in the morning, Caitlin figured she had nothing to lose by admitting, "I came to see Arthur Korn, but he's not home."

"You're a friend of Artie's?" the rabbi asked, straightening the yarmulke bobby-pinned to his graying hair. His skullcap had the same red-and-black pattern as his shirt. Who knew? Caitlin thought. Yarmulkes for Jewish lumberjacks.

"I'm a friend of his niece Clara," she said, assuming that if lying to a rabbi was a sin, it was venial, not mortal. "Clara moved, and I can't find her."

"Never met Artie's niece," the rabbi said.

"Do you know where I can find Mr. Korn?"

Rabbi Birnbaum rested his hands on top of the rake. "Artie had a friend from Europe, Ed Werner, living on Wait Street. Ed had a remodeling business, and Artie stayed at his house and worked with him for ten years or so. Artie came to services sometimes."

"Is Ed Werner around?"

The rabbi shook his head. "Ed passed away in March. He left the house to Artie, and he sold it to a family with a daughter coming back from Colorado. I hear Artie went to Albany to open a pipe shop. Artie liked making tobacco pipes. Beautiful things in briar and cherrywood."

Caitlin didn't want to encourage him to ask any questions by showing how excited she was by the information, so keeping her voice casual, she thanked him and went on her way.

At the hotel, the desk clerk gave her a message that Danny had called. Caitlin stuffed the message slip in her bag. She would call him from Albany.

CHAPTER 65

Albany, New York
October 1960

While the attendant gassed up her car on Route 9, Caitlin went to the pay phone and found a listing for Artie's Pipes & Tobacco in the yellow pages.

She asked the attendant for directions and wrote them in her notebook. It was late afternoon when she reached Albany. Turning on State Street, she drove past the granite capitol looming above the grimy brick buildings downtown. She parked two doors from the DeWitt Clinton Hotel and walked down the hill to a row of shops on South Pearl. Artie's was between a vacant storefront and O'Brien's Luncheonette. In the window, pipes were arrayed like dueling pistols on crimson velvet. Caitlin recognized Korn from the stakeout photo—his stooped shoulders, white goatee, and straw fedora, which, inexplicably, he wore indoors. He was standing at the cash register with several men in line. The sign on the door said that Artie's opened at nine. Caitlin would come back then. Korn would be more likely to tell her about Clara if they were alone.

◆ ◆ ◆

The lobby of the DeWitt Clinton had a mural of Dutch settlers trading with Indians and a malodorous scent of larceny—men in club chairs speaking furtively in corners, the legislators in suits that should have been donated to the Salvation Army, and the lobbyists in fine, buttery wool, all of them with the omnivorous looks of men plotting to give the taxpayers as fair a deal as the settlers gave the Indians.

Once in her room, Caitlin was too tired to unpack or undress. She lay down for a catnap and woke up two hours later. Danny should be home by now. She placed the call and, when he answered, said, "Danny, Clara's uncle is in Albany."

As if he hadn't heard her, Danny said, "I've been pondering."

He sounded as if he was drinking as he pondered. "What're you pondering?"

Danny said, "How I always wanted to take a girl to Coney Island for a ride on the Ferris wheel. None of my ex-wives when we were dating would go. They said it was sappy."

"It is sappy."

"Yeah," he agreed. "But I should've known not to marry them if they wouldn't go. My last wife told me she did enough giving me top-shelf pussy."

Caitlin laughed. "Top shelf? Did she have her drinking and screwing mixed up?"

"She did plenty of both and not always with me. That's probably why I couldn't convince her riding the Ferris wheel is romantic."

"Overly romantic, Danny. Which is why it's sappy."

"Cait, you would've went with me."

"If I wasn't married to your best friend," she said.

"Gabe was luckier than me in that department, but when you're done with this, you'll come with me to Coney Island?"

Caitlin considered mentioning that she was involved with Reed and then thought this wasn't the time. "Sure. And we'll go to Nathan's for a hot dog and orangeade."

He didn't answer. Caitlin heard a bottle clink against a glass. Danny said, "Julian called me this afternoon. He was talking to Kennedy about the election, and Kennedy says if he hears from you, would he ask you to contact his office. He wants to talk. Cait, why're you mixed up with him?"

"Because he wants to know why Gabe is dead."

"Be careful," he said and no longer sounded drunk. "Where you staying?"

She told him the name of the hotel and read the number to him off the phone dial.

After a pause, Danny said, "We can't go to Nathan's till after the Ferris wheel. You don't want to get sick up there."

"No," she replied. "That's definitely not romantic."

In the morning, the wind was blowing leaves across the sidewalk as Caitlin walked down to the luncheonette. Men were on the stools at the counter, talking or reading the paper. Caitlin brought her coffee and cider doughnut to a table by the front window and watched the doorway of Artie's. Korn arrived. Caitlin waited three minutes, then went into the shop. The biting aroma of tobacco was as thick as fog.

Korn, a slight man in an oatmeal-colored cardigan, looked up from behind one of the glass display cases of pipes and boxes of cigars. He had the face of an underfed hawk—sunken cheeks and a small beak of a nose.

"May I help you?" he asked, the echo of Europe in his accent.

"My name is Caitlin Russo, and I'm trying to find your niece Clara."

His dark eyes appeared to have taken a close look at the world and disliked most of what they'd seen and were now adding Caitlin to the list. "I don't got no niece."

"Mr. Korn, I know about Clara and the letter you sent Yenchi."

"I tell you, Miss, I don't got no niece."

"Please, Mr. Korn, I just want to ask Clara if she knows anyone who knew my husband. He was murdered, and I want to find who shot him. I know Clara had nothing to do with it. I'm no threat to her. But Santo Trafficante is. I found you, and I'm one person. Trafficante has lots of people on his payroll, and sooner or later they'll locate you and Clara."

Korn tugged up the left sleeve of his cardigan and held out his arm. Tattooed on his forearm, in fading blue ink, were the numbers *149593*.

"You know what this is?" he asked.

Her mother had told her about a Polish woman, Jan, who worked with her at the hospital cafeteria. Jan was as tiny and nervous as a hummingbird, and she had come to America after the war with numbers on her arm. "I think so," Caitlin said.

"The Nazis give me these numbers at Auschwitz and send us to Birkenau. I was scared at Birkenau. Until my wife and two daughters die. Then I wasn't scared no more."

"I'm—"

"You come here to scare me?" he said, his voice managing to be simultaneously flat and ferocious. "Birkenau don't scare me. Not the guards, the gas chamber, the ovens, the stinking piles of dead, none of it scare me. So you, Miss, you don't scare me at all. Get out."

As Caitlin was leaving, a heavyset priest with a pipe in his mouth was entering. He held the door for her.

"Thank you, Father," she said.

CHAPTER 66

During the day, Caitlin staked out the shop, and in the evenings she tailed Korn on foot as he walked north on State Street past the town houses and taverns with the **KENNEDY FOR PRESIDENT** posters in the windows. He lived in a four-story rooming house with graffiti, in swirls of pear-green paint, marking the stone facade. She watched his place from a bench across the street, her head turtled in her camel hair coat against the cold, and after eleven days with no sign of Clara, Caitlin felt like Zippy the Chimp roller-skating in circles on *Ed Sullivan*.

At least it gave her a chance to consider what Kennedy had told her. When they'd spoken, he had been in New York City and preparing for his fourth and final debate. His office provided her with his number at the Carlyle and asked her to call at ten in the evening. Jack answered the phone. Caitlin congratulated him on his debate performances and the newest polls, which had him leading Nixon by three points.

Jack thanked her and asked, "How're you making out?"

"Closer than I was."

"I have some information for you," he said.

"I read in the *Times* Dulles briefed you again before the debates."

Jack said, "Dulles didn't get into specifics, but I got the feeling plans to remove Castro have progressed. Then my campaign—without consulting me—released a statement to the press with me saying we should assist Cubans who want to dump Castro. Bobby heard a rumor Nixon blew his stack when he read it. Americans want us to get rid of him, and Nixon knows defending Eisenhower's public stance of leaving Castro alone hurts him. I'm guessing Nixon can't advocate for taking out Castro because he knows about a classified operation to do precisely that."

"Senator, how does this help me find the film?"

She could hear the impatience in her voice. Apparently, so could Jack. "I'm grateful for your help, Caitlin. And you may tag me as self-serving for saying this, but I doubt Gabe was shot because he was looking for the film. Not with this covert action in motion, and who knows how long it's been going on. Have you heard about your missing friend, Hannah?"

"Hannah's dead."

"I'm sorry to hear that," Jack said. "What happened?"

"She was pulled out of Lake Erie. The Cleveland Police say she was tortured. Danny believes it's because Gabe had her engrave the cigar box to blow up Castro. And Danny doubts Trafficante's involved. He thinks it's the Russians protecting Castro. I was attacked outside my building, and my attacker was Russian."

"Jesus," Jack said. "Are you all right?"

"I am, but my attacker turned up with his throat cut at a hotel in Greenwich Village."

Jack was silent.

"Senator?"

Caitlin heard him sigh. Then he said, "The other information I have for you is about Été. I spoke to her the day she died. She was her jolly self, telling me about her new novel and a man visiting her. It doesn't make sense she killed herself. Maybe her visitor was involved."

When Caitlin didn't answer, Jack said, "Été was too much a survivor for suicide. I don't know if it's connected to this other business, but I want you to quit looking for the film. If Nixon or Lyndon's people had it, they'd have released it by now. I'll take my chances."

"I can't quit. Looking for the film is my only shot at finding who murdered Gabe." Caitlin wasn't sure she still believed this was true.

Actually, sometimes she doubted the film would lead anywhere. But it was all she had, so she wished it was true, because finding who murdered her husband was a parting gift to Gabe and her path to the kind of future she could have shared with him.

"Caitlin, when my boat went down, two of my crew died. Those deaths stay with you, and I don't want you in danger for some mistake I made. Quit looking."

"No," she said.

"Caitlin—"

"It's late, Senator. Good night."

Caitlin wasn't unaware of the potential danger. With people being killed for reasons she didn't understand, she occasionally felt afraid, and, without a conscious thought, her hand went into her courier bag to rub the grip of her .38 as if it were a rabbit-foot. Yet it wasn't as bad as the fear she'd felt after Gabe died. Grief, Caitlin had discovered, contained a unique terror. Lose the beloved at the center of your world, and you were like a planet knocked loose from its orbit, but physical fear had nothing to do with your predicament. In fact, during her worst nights after burying Gabe, as she'd wrestled with the demons of insomnia, Caitlin had regarded her own death as a cure.

As she returned to watching Korn, Caitlin mulled over Kennedy's call with Été. She could imagine Été mentioning her visitor to Kennedy to get a jealous rise out of him, but she couldn't picture her flinging herself off a balcony. Été liked drama, not opera. Then what happened? Another murder? Reed had said the magazine would pay her expenses if she wanted to go to Quebec City and look into it. So at lunchtime, Caitlin went to the DeWitt Clinton and phoned Reed from her room. They spoke at least once a week, affectionate conversations, ending with how they couldn't wait to see each other. Not this time, though. Without naming Kennedy, Caitlin said, "I heard from a friend who spoke to Été right before she died, and he told me she had company. A lover, it sounds like. There could be a story for me to write."

"I can't assign any new pieces this month," he replied and then complained he had meetings all afternoon and three articles to edit that were due tomorrow, and even though it was October, Philadelphia was doing an excellent imitation of winter. He concluded his woe-is-me litany by saying, "I need some sun."

Caitlin said, "I've always wanted to see the coral reefs in Jamaica."

"I hear they're splendid," Reed said. "I have to go. We'll speak soon."

Caitlin blamed his curtness on overwork and went back to her stakeout. She was in her car, her eyelids heavy with fatigue and boredom, when a car pulled up outside the pipe shop. Her eyes popped open. It was a cranberry-colored Packard with a slatted front grille and with spare tires mounted on the sides. Caitlin's mother had owned a Packard in the 1940s. Caitlin hadn't seen one in years. Just as intriguing was the driver, a nun in a habit and gold wire-rimmed glasses, who went into the shop. Caitlin recalled the pipe-smoking priest who had held the door for her and guessed the nun was picking up tobacco for him. Yet when she came right out without a package, Caitlin decided to tail her, a decision based more on her desire to escape the drudgery of the stakeout than her belief the nun would lead her to Clara.

The Packard rolled out of downtown, onto a broad avenue, and through a prosperous stretch of the city, the homes reminiscent of English-country manors and medieval castles. Farther up, the Packard stopped at a red light. On the corner was an imposing cream-and-brown-brick building with cement columns and the name THE VINCENTIAN INSTITUTE carved into the stone above the columns. Caitlin would've sworn it was a post office designed by a mailman with delusions of grandeur until she realized it was a Catholic school. Nuns were standing in the doorways as teenagers streamed past them, the girls in blue blazers, plaid skirts, and knee socks; the boys in the same blazers with blue ties and black trousers.

When the light changed, the Packard turned left, and two blocks later, it turned right into a warren of the working class, the two-family houses so close together everyone could watch their neighbors eating in the kitchen. One house was the exception—a high, wide, rectangular redbrick house with a glassed-in porch. The nun was parallel parking across from it. Caitlin backed up to give her room. She saw nuns moving on the porch and guessed it was a convent. The nun fit the Packard into the space, then went up the steps to the porch. Past the house, girls were playing hopscotch on the sidewalk. They waved at a young woman approaching them. Her shoulder-length hair, a glimmery brown, was pulled away from her face by a black headband, and she wore a dove gray dress and charcoal gray cardigan with a shawl collar. Smiling at the girls, she kept walking until she noticed Caitlin watching her through the windshield. She stopped. Caitlin recognized Clara's heart-shaped face from the FBI photographs, the impeccable beauty of it and the eyes like polished onyx.

Caitlin double-parked and got out. "Your uncle told you who I am?"

"He told me who you said you were. That is not the same thing, is it?" Her accent was a blend of Cuba and Europe, a merry lightness with a sadder melody below it.

Caitlin said, "I just want to talk."

"Why did you follow Sister Cecilia?"

"Because I'd never seen a nun go into a pipe store."

"She was picking up money from Uncle Arthur. He wants I should buy a better winter coat. He knew you were watching him, and he didn't want to come and bring you here."

"You work at the convent?" Caitlin asked.

Clara ignored her, glancing back at the girls on the sidewalk.

Caitlin said, "Like I told your uncle—"

"He's not my real uncle. He was my father's friend."

"It wasn't that hard to find you, Clara. I may be able to stop Santo Trafficante from looking."

Clara turned toward her. "The Sisters of Mercy have a house for older nuns a block from the convent. I do chores for them and live there. Part-time I teach Spanish at Vincentian. Uncle Arthur thinks it's clever to hide a Jewish girl with nuns and Catholic students. He arranges it with a customer, a priest."

"Is there a place you'd be comfortable talking?"

"There's a deli," Clara said. "We can walk."

Caitlin smiled to show she wasn't offended. "You don't trust me."

"Enough to talk," Clara replied. "Not enough to get in your car."

CHAPTER 67

At this hour, between lunch and dinner, they had their choice of seats. Clara chose a table in back.

"It's my treat," Caitlin said. "What do you recommend?"

"The Vincentian. The owner names the sandwich after the school because the kids like it. It's a triple-decker with corned beef. We should share."

The ancient waiter, in a black dinner jacket, was as surly as a mugger. He took their order and brought their Dr. Brown's sodas—black cherry for Caitlin, cream for Clara.

Caitlin started with a casual question, nothing to put Clara on the defensive. "Your family was from Germany?"

"Hamburg. Why do you want to know this?"

Caitlin said, "Because somewhere in the details of your life, I might hear something that will lead me to who murdered my husband, Gabe."

As Clara studied her with the hard-eyed intelligence Caitlin had noticed in the FBI photos, the waiter delivered their sandwich. Clara began to eat, and Caitlin took a bite. The Russian dressing was a wondrous concoction with a light touch of garlic and horseradish.

Clara drank some soda. "Do you have a picture of Gabe?"

Caitlin held out her wallet. In the plastic insert was the snapshot Danny had taken on her wedding day. Gabe was in a suit and standing next to her outside city hall.

"I don't recognize him," Clara said. "I thought you afraid he was a client of mine."

Caitlin put away her wallet. "I wasn't."

Clara glanced at her plate as if expecting to discover the answer to a mystery in her sandwich. Then she looked up. "In 1939, we come to Havana on a ship, the *St. Louis*. Mama; my brother, Max; and me. Life is terrible for Jews in Hamburg. The Nazis lock Papa in Dachau and steal his import-export business. In a letter, Papa says he will join us in Cuba. Max is a baby. I'm five, and the voyage is an adventure. There are children to play with. And a swimming pool. When we sail into Havana Harbor, the passengers hug and cheer. Then we hear the Cuban government cancels our visas—no more Jews from Europe. Some people get off. No one knows why. On the third afternoon, we're on the lower deck. Mama has me hold Max and says she will get us off the ship."

"What did she do?"

"There is a Cuban, a tall, bony police officer with a long pointy nose. He reminds me of anteaters in the Hamburg zoo. He's looking at Mama. She is a very beautiful woman."

"Like you."

Clara shrugged. "Mama is also smart. She speaks five languages. She taught herself English because she helps Papa in his business, and he imports from America. I watch her talk to the anteater. I know she's not paying him. We have dollars Papa saved, but Mama sewed the bills in my and Max's teddy bears. The anteater, Colonel Tomás López, takes us in a motorboat to Havana. We stay at a poor hotel with many Jews. Then he moves us to an apartment in Vedado, a richer area. Every Wednesday before going home to his wife and children, the anteater comes. Mama tells me to take Max outside. A half hour later he is gone. The *St. Louis* returns to Europe. A lot of passengers die in the camps. Mama traded her body for our lives."

Clara sighed, tired and sad all in one sound. "When I'm older and understand, I feel happy Papa never finds out."

So far, Clara's story was irrelevant to Gabe's murder, but Caitlin didn't want to interrupt her. At first, it was a tactical decision: let a person ramble, they'll tell you everything. Then she got caught up in the story, sensing its tragic end and wanting to hear it. Why? The same reason drivers slow to look at a car wreck? No, not that. It was because after losing a husband and two friends, Caitlin was worn out by the loneliness of her grief, and listening to Clara, she felt less alone knowing she wasn't the only person bullied by fate.

"Your father didn't get out of Dachau?" Caitlin asked.

Clara laughed, and the cruel irony in her laughter was chilling. "Oh, the Nazis release him. Also Uncle Arthur, who was a tobacco importer until the Nazis steal his warehouse in Hamburg. Uncle Arthur has contacts in Rome. The Italians aren't killing Jews. Papa goes with Uncle Arthur, his wife, and daughters. For a few years, Papa sends Mama letters. Then the Nazis deport the Jews in Rome to Auschwitz. When the war is over, Uncle Arthur writes to say Papa dies in the camp from typhus. I cry even though remembering Papa is like staring in the sun, a hot, blank light. My life goes on like nothing changes. Mama is a seamstress and later owns a dress shop. Max and I start at public school; then Mama pays for a private one where they teach in English. She dreams we will all leave for America."

"Why didn't you?" Caitlin asked.

"We are illegal in Cuba and can't get new passports. The anteater promises to help. He lies. He doesn't want to lose Mama. But he loses her. She dies. Leukemia. I'm seventeen and in school; Max is in school and works cleaning up at the Cine Gris, so he can see movies for free. He wants one day to work in Hollywood. We need money. I sell the dresses in Mama's store. The anteater comes. He gives Max money and says go to the bakery and bring back a dozen Torticas de Morón, the shortbread cookies we like. Max goes, and the anteater says, 'You will do as your mother did for me.' I say, 'What do you mean?' By then, I have two boyfriends. I know what he wants but not that he will slap my face and push me on the couch to get it. When it's over, he says, 'That is what I mean.' He leaves. The next day, I talk to Victor Diaz."

Caitlin looked at her sandwich. The thought of taking another bite made her stomach turn. "How did you know Victor?"

"Before Castro, Havana is a circus, and Victor Diaz is like a famous clown. His picture is all the time in *Diario de la Marina* and the *Havana Post*, laughing and drinking at the Hotel Presidente or the roof garden of the Ambos Mundos. He has the face of a baby, and his suits are the color of grapefruit or limes. Everyone knows Victor—doormen, bartenders, dealers in the casinos, movie stars, mobsters, police, and soldiers. Victor sells what men like to buy, and he was popular with his girls. The men who do this work, they want their girls to perform for them. Not Victor. He desires men. And he is generous. I first meet him at Mama's shop when he brings three girls to buy them dresses."

Caitlin said, "And Victor took care of the anteater."

Clara smiled. It was a broad smile, pure delight. "He is found shot in an alley near the Plaza de Armas. The newspapers say he is paralyzed. So I work for Victor. His girls don't work the streets. They go to fine hotels or to mansions in Miramar. Victor charges a lot, and he pays fair. He has a doctor examine us, give us diaphragms, and teach how to check men for disease. In those days, I dye my hair red and use a pencil to make freckles. Not as many freckles as you, but I feel better when I look in the mirror. It isn't the real me doing this, do you understand?"

"I do."

Clara said, "I hate lying to Max. I say I am a hostess at the Hotel Nacional and buy him a movie camera. This makes him happy. And I save money. To take us to America. I plan to ask Victor to get us the papers. In America maybe I do different work."

"When Victor sent you to the Hotel Comodoro, did you recognize Senator Kennedy?"

Lowering her voice as if scared someone might hear her, Clara said, "From American magazines. Another girl comes with me. Senator

Kennedy is with a friend. The girl is for him. I am for the senator. He is polite but gets to business quickly. The friend pays, and we go."

Caitlin asked, "When did you find out about the film?"

Clara stared at her hands, rubbing them together as though they were cold. "I don't know there is filming." Clara looked up, her eyes bright with tears. "I tell you I buy Max a movie camera. I know he has a job at a photograph studio. I don't know the owner develops film for men making sex movies. Bad men, men like Santo Trafficante. And I don't know the owner teaches Max how. I couldn't know this."

Caitlin asked, "Your brother developed the film of you and Kennedy?"

Nodding, Clara wiped her eyes with her napkin. "Max comes home screaming I am a *jinetera*, a whore. I am ashamed my brother sees me like this and want to tell him why I sell myself. But he throws the reel of film on the floor and runs out. He disappears. I am frightened and look everywhere he goes. Two days later, a policeman comes. Max's body washes up on a beach in Old Havana. He was beaten and drowned. I call Victor. He is sometimes in Miami. I tell him about Max and the film and beg him to get me to Florida. He does. I work there. Then I hear Victor is murdered in New York and Trafficante wants the movie of the senator and he is searching for me. I write to Uncle Arthur, and he comes, and I go away with him."

"Do you know who murdered Victor?" Caitlin asked, checking to make sure Clara had no inkling that Gabe had pulled the trigger.

"I think men sent by Trafficante. Like the men who kill Max. But there are rumors about Victor. I hear them from the older girls. They say Victor works for the CIA and has a boss the girls call *El vaquero Americano*. The American cowboy."

Caitlin was furious, thinking that Gabe was the cowboy and this was another detail he hid from her. Then Clara added, "I never meet him. This is before I see Senator Kennedy."

"Do you remember the year?"

"Nineteen fifty-eight. Maybe a few months before."

Caitlin relaxed. Gabe hadn't started working with the CIA until 1959. And the movie had nothing to do with him shooting Victor. In all likelihood, Danny was right when he speculated that the CIA was going after Castro, Gabe was involved, and, when the Russians found out, they had Gabe killed. "Clara, what happened to the film?"

"I burn it."

"Trafficante still wants the film, and the men he sends to find you won't believe you burned it."

Clara snapped, "Why not?"

"Because I don't. You're smart like your mother and probably figured the film would keep you safe. You could trade it to Trafficante if he'll leave you alone. That's not how it will go. The only way Trafficante can be sure you don't have the film is if his men torture you, and if you hand it over, you're a loose end, so they'll kill you anyway."

Clara stood. "Thank you for the sandwich."

"Wait," Caitlin said sharply, taking a pad and pen from her bag, then writing her address and detaching the page and holding it out to Clara. "Think about what I told you and talk to Uncle Arthur. You've suffered enough, and I don't want you to suffer more. If you mail the film to me, I'll phone your uncle and give him the name and number of a man who will make sure Trafficante won't bother you."

"And how will he do that?" Her tone implied that it was impossible and Caitlin was lying.

"He was once a man like Trafficante," Caitlin said. "He knows other men like that who will do as he asks. And there is a police captain helping him. This captain is not a man Trafficante will want to upset."

Clara smiled sweetly. "You could give me that information now."

"And you could give me the film."

"I burn it," Clara said, taking the page and walking out of the deli.

CHAPTER 68

Greenwich Village

After retrieving her accumulated mail from the post office, Caitlin planned to phone Reed to let him know she was in the city. However, on top of the pile, under the thick rubber bands, was a picture postcard of the Liberty Bell. On the back Reed had written:

> My apologies for my brusqueness last we spoke. An overdose of work and the inclement Philadelphia weather, and a longing to relive our day and night in Belmar were to blame. I'm off to hunt for sunshine. Can't stop thinking of you. Will call soon.

Caitlin was disappointed Reed was away but glad he was anxious to see her. She sifted through the mail, dropping the junk into the wastebasket and writing checks for the bills. Danny had called earlier. She was going to stop by the station house, but Danny said he needed a break, so they were meeting in Washington Square. Caitlin walked up Waverly Place under a hard-blue late-October sky. In the park, the leaves were thinning flames of orange, copper, and gold. Boys with patchy beards and girls with long ironed hair sat on the stone rim of the fountain and scowled at the women in mink coats who crossed over from Fifth

Avenue to let their poodles relieve themselves. Danny was sitting by himself on a bench. His uniform didn't invite company.

"Did you miss your car?" Caitlin asked, handing him the keys to his Thunderbird.

"Missed you more," Danny replied.

Caitlin had missed him, too, yet didn't want to give him the wrong idea, so she answered him only with a smile and sat on the bench.

Danny gave her the keys to her Chevy. "It's on Waverly. Behind where you left mine."

"I saw it. Thanks."

Danny slid the keys into his pocket. "Clara say anything useful?"

"I don't know yet. She never met Gabe. But there was a rumor another CIA officer—they called him the American cowboy—was handling Victor Diaz. It was before Gabe joined the agency. Is it possible that since Diaz was taking money from the Americans and Castro's people, this CIA officer was also playing both sides?"

"You got crooked cops," Danny said. "Why not crooked spies?"

"Agreed, but I don't know where to begin. That's why I asked you to bring the report."

Danny passed her a file folder. "I haven't read it since February. Maybe you'll see something I didn't." Gabe had written the report following his trip to Mexico City. Caitlin had found it in his suitcase after he was shot. Danny had had the foresight to have the report typed up before two CIA agents appeared at his station house to collect the original.

As Caitlin got up off the bench, Danny said, "I sent a photo of the dead guy at the Allerton to the Cleveland cops. They spoke to a couple witnesses that ID'd him as being at the February art show. I'm sure he murdered Winkie. Remember, the guy who murdered him is somewhere. You see anybody suspicious, promise me you'll call."

"I promise, Danny."

◆ ◆ ◆

Back in her apartment, Caitlin sat at her desk and read the report, listing the details that caught her attention on a legal pad. Gabe had spent twenty-four uneventful days in Mexico City. He was watching two middle-aged Cuban cousins, operatives for the CIA who were assisting with plans to blow up a European freighter loaded with munitions, destined for Castro's men, in Havana Harbor. Every day, the cousins sat in the same café and spoke only to each other, except for Thursday afternoon, January 14. A man in a seersucker suit with a Pan Am airline bag on his shoulder stopped to talk to them. Gabe couldn't see his face. He wore a red baseball cap and aviator sunglasses. He put the bag under the table and walked off.

Gabe wrote: *Assume he is CIA. Seersucker popular with Ivy Leaguers. Tailed him, but he doesn't move like a brainy college boy. More like a halfback in the open field. He stops at the gate of the US embassy, chats with guard, removes cap. Too far away to make out his face. His hair is long and the color of wet sand.*

Nearby, she read, a short, husky pasty-faced man emerged from a taxi with a straw sombrero on his head. He wore a baggy gray suit. Gabe believed he was Russian. The Ivy Leaguer walked over to him. They didn't greet each other and crossed the street and disappeared into a taco-and-enchilada joint. The Russian, Gabe wrote, could be a source for the CIA or a KGB agent.

Caitlin looked at her list: *Cuban cousins. Payoff. Red baseball cap. Aviator sunglasses. Athletic Ivy Leaguer. Long hair the color of wet sand. CIA officer goes to eat with a short, pale Russian.*

She read the report again. And again.

CHAPTER 69

Bethlehem, Pennsylvania

Come along, Kick says.

Jack is dreaming, and he's in no mood to see Kick. He needs his rest. Tomorrow he continues his push for the Keystone State's thirty-two electoral votes. Usually his dreams are as drab as charcoal sketches, but Kick's tunic is gold, and red holly berries are in her hair. The color piques his interest, and he lets his sister lead him to their parents' Hyannis Port home—site of those Kennedy touch football games his campaign uses to perpetuate the myth of his vibrant health. Now, a big white tent sits on the lawn, and music, as soft as the summery sea breeze, fills the air.

Jack asks, "Whose party is it?"

Taking his arm, Kick walks him into the tent, where hundreds of people drink, talk, and pluck hors d'oeuvres off trays borne by waiters in tuxedo shirts and bow ties. Across the tent Jack sees his mother in a wheelchair, talking to his brother Teddy and his sisters Eunice, Jean, and Pat. His father, scowling, stands behind the wheelchair and holds its handles.

Jack laughs. "Dad has a new job."

Nothing new about him pushing Mother around.

A young man in a navy blue blazer and white slacks and an auburn-haired young woman in a wedding gown approach his parents.

"Kick, that's—"

Caroline. She just got married.

Jack is stunned by the sight of his grown daughter. And amazed he survived so long with his Addison's disease. He asks, "The handsome young guy's the groom?"

Your son, John Jr.

Eager to congratulate his daughter and to meet his son, Jack heads for them. Kick stops him by grabbing his elbow. *They can't see you, but Jackie can.*

His sister steers Jack to his left, toward his wife. Time has been kind to Jackie. She is still as slender and elegant as a tea rose.

"Dance with me, Jack."

As they dance to a classical piece, Jack asks, "What song is this? It's beautiful."

With the fetching smile of a schoolgirl, Jackie replies, "'The Wild Rover.'"

Jack may not recognize the music, but it's a waltz, not an Irish drinking song. "You're making fun of me. Because you think I'm a philistine."

"And because I love you," Jackie says.

She vanishes. The music turns brassy, pounding. At his feet, Nikita Khrushchev performs a Russian squat dance, beaming at Jack, extending a hand up to him.

Jack says to Kick, "A couple weeks ago, Khrushchev was banging his shoe on his desk at the UN to protest the Soviets being accused of crushing Eastern Europe."

Kick grins. *His mood's improved since then. He wants to dance with you.*

"My back. I can't."

Fidel Castro, in olive drab military fatigues, glides across the floor like an ice-skater and kisses the top of Khrushchev's bald head.

"Jesus Christ," Jack says. "Let's go."

Kick presses a fingertip to his forehead, and they are transported to the foaming edge of Nantucket Sound. The beach is crowded with women in bras and panties. Normally, women in lingerie would catch Jack's attention, but these women are faceless, indistinguishable from each other, and as lifeless as mannequins.

All your conquests, Jack.

Jack knows he's a hero to Kick, and he is floored by her cutting tone.

Go make a movie with them, Jack. And ask Caitlin to look for it. Maybe get her killed.

"I told Caitlin to quit looking."

Your girling is dumb. Dumb, dumb, dumb.

Jack doesn't need his sister to criticize his behavior. He is ashamed enough that he can't control himself. Feeling guilty and irritated, he asks, "What the hell's going on here?"

You're dreaming, and in our dreams we stand naked before ourselves.

"Does everyone in heaven spit out that pretentious crap?"

We read a lot. Most of the angels were librarians or owned bookstores.

His sister skips from the beach to the top of the hill. Jack follows her into a shining green field. He has no idea where they are. Heaven? Ireland? The Land of Oz?

"Kick, where's Bobby?"

Talking to a judge in Georgia to get Dr. King out of prison. Those cretins threw him in a cell for a traffic ticket.

"I called his wife, Coretta, and then I got the governor on the case."

Smart politics, Johnny.

"Even better, it was the right thing to do."

They ramble on and stop at the interior of a diner—a lunch counter with stools and booths with gray Formica tables. Richard Nixon sits in a booth, eating a hamburger.

He looks so young, Jack.

"He is. That was thirteen years ago. We were congressmen and invited to McKeesport, Pennsylvania, to debate labor law. Afterward, we went to that diner. We were friends and talked all the time. He was brilliant. I invited him to my wedding, but he couldn't make it. I hear when I almost died at the Hospital for Special Surgery, Dick broke down in tears. Did I beat him in the election, Kick?"

His sister giggles. *I'll never tell.*

"You enjoy torturing me, don't you?"

I'm your little sister. Of course I do.

Kick runs through the field. Jack chases her. The sky is gauzy with a cold drizzle. In the distance, Jack sees an old fieldstone church.

"Kick," he calls. "Where are we?"

When his sister goes by the church and into a cemetery of weathered gravestones, Jack knows they are in Derbyshire, England. Tears press behind his eyes. Kick stops at her grave.

You never visit me, Jack.

"Because I prefer believing you're alive."

✝

IN LOVING

MEMORY OF

KATHLEEN

1920–1948

WIDOW OF MAJOR THE

MARQUESS OF HARTINGTON

KILLED IN ACTION & DAUGHTER

OF THE HON. JOSEPH KENNEDY

SOMETIME AMBASSADOR OF THE

UNITED STATES TO GREAT BRITAIN

JOY SHE GAVE; JOY SHE HAS FOUND

Jack, his voice breaking, asks, "Did you really find joy?"

Don't be so sad, Johnny. I'm always here, and I still love you.

Someone has set a small stainless steel shaving mirror against the left side of her headstone. Jack hasn't seen one since the war. He bends to retrieve it, but his back locks up.

Kick laughs, a sunny musical sound. *You never could resist a mirror.* She hands it to him. His reflection is baffling. Jack was forty when Caroline was born. She has to be in her twenties now. Which means Jack is in his sixties. Yet he looks the same as the night in October 1960 when he landed at the Allentown-Bethlehem-Easton Airport.

"Kick, my hair isn't gray."

No, it isn't.

"Why isn't my hair gray?"

Kick hugs him, a fierce parting hug. *Jack, I've missed you so much.*

When Jack opened his eyes in his bed at the Hotel Bethlehem, he wasn't sure whether he was among the living or the dead. Then he felt the familiar cramping in his stomach. His colitis was acting up. That was the blessing of pain. It lets you know you're alive.

PART IV

CHAPTER 70

Greenwich Village
November 1, 1960

Morning frost clouded the windowpanes of her study as Caitlin reread Gabe's report from Mexico City. She had read it every day since Danny had given it to her and hoped her conclusion was wrong. She considered discussing it with Danny, but cops liked facts, not speculation. The apartment buzzer sounded. She looked out the window. A mailman, not the regular one, stood on the steps. Danny wasn't always warning her to hear himself talk. Her courier bag was hanging from her desk chair, and she fished out her .38, then tucked it in the waistband of her dungarees and covered it with her sweater.

"Special delivery," the mailman said, handing her a cardboard packet.

Caitlin thanked him. The packet was postmarked Albany and banded in packing tape. She used a paring knife to pry it apart. Inside was a reel of film and a handwritten note:

> Please tell phone number and name of the man who
> can tell Trafficante to go away from me. Please tell this
> to Uncle Arthur. His store number is 518-555-3806. I
> don't trust very easy. I am trusting you. Clara.

Before contacting Julian, Caitlin had to see the film. She walked to Big Lou's, a cubbyhole of a used-camera shop on Seventh Avenue.

Big Lou was one of those Village characters everyone seemed to know, yet no one remembered how they knew him. He was never without his black-and-green tartan beret or his sense of irony. Big Lou was five feet tall.

Caitlin put the reel on the counter. "What will play this?"

Big Lou inspected the reel. "It's sixteen millimeter. A reconditioned Bell & Howell will do the trick. You can have it for sixty with the case and the manual."

Caitlin paid and went home in a cab. She positioned the projector on her desk and plugged it in, then followed the diagrammed instructions, placing Clara's reel on the top arm, feeding the film through a series of sprockets, looping it around the empty bottom reel, and switching on the motor and lamp. After drawing the curtains to darken her study, she sat in her chair and turned the clutch knob to start the movie.

A ghostly image appeared on the bare wall. To focus the image, Caitlin rotated the lens until the ghost became Clara. She was standing over the ornate metal footboard of a bed with a come-hither pout, slipping off the shoulder straps of her camisole and revealing her high, round breasts. Even in murky black and white, her beauty jumped out as though she were a backlit painting. Clara's right hand disappeared into her G-string, and her face contorted in a laudable imitation of passion.

Caitlin discovered she hadn't completely outrun the nuns at Our Lady of Sorrows. She had to stop herself from glancing away from the wall. Whoever was filming behind the two-way mirror had to be to the right of the bed because the point of view shifted to a bare-chested Senator Kennedy lying with his head propped up on pillows. For an instant, the back of Clara was visible. Her G-string was off, and she mounted the senator. The camera pointed at him. His eyes were closed, and his face was as serene as a sleeping child's. Clara's long hair swayed in and out of the picture as she rocked on top of him.

Anger boiled up in Caitlin. Working vice at the NYPD, she had come to loathe the prostitution racket, the sadistic johns and the pimps beating their girls in the street. However, this was worse for Caitlin because she knew Clara's story—a child refugee from Hitler, a father dead in the camps, a mother dying young, a teenager taking care of a younger brother by selling her body to protect herself from a shit-bag police officer intent on taking it for free. And here was Kennedy, a rich Harvard man and Pulitzer Prize winner, a war hero and senator—the gilt-edged best of America—taking advantage of Clara's heart-wrenching life and risking his aspirations in a scene that struck Caitlin as more pathetic than erotic. She still admired Kennedy the candidate—his intelligence and humor, his clearheaded take on issues, his unapologetic Catholicism and willingness to confront bigots, and that luminous, undefinable quality marking him as the man to lead his country across the New Frontier. Perhaps Été had been right. King Solomon was so wise, who gave a damn about his thousand women? Caitlin would vote for Kennedy. But as she watched Clara climb off him and the film ended in quivering white light, Caitlin doubted she could erase these images from her memory or would forgive Kennedy for his weakness.

After rewinding the film, Caitlin switched off the projector. She was opening the curtains when the phone rang. She answered it, and Reed said, "You're home!"

"For about a week. How was your trip?"

"Sunny. I just landed at LaGuardia. Can I come by? I'd love to see you."

"That would be nice," Caitlin said.

"Let me go get my bag. I'll see you soon."

Caitlin hung up, wondering if she should call Danny. No need to bother him. She wanted to see Reed on her own.

CHAPTER 71

When a woman sleeps with a man, Caitlin thought as Reed entered the apartment and hugged her, she becomes a keen interpreter of masculine nuance. After Reed let her go and looked at her, a shadow of disappointment crossed his face, as though he had expected her to be waiting for him in a negligee instead of a crewneck sweater, Levi's, and moccasins.

Reed, removing his felt hat and velvet-collared overcoat, hid his disappointment behind a bland cheerfulness.

"Let me put those in the closet," Caitlin said. His fedora and overcoat were identical to those worn by the man following her last December on MacDougal Street. A mystery solved? Or had she, in the disorienting wake of losing Gabe, Winkie, and Été, finally relinquished the last of her reason to grief? The man on MacDougal had lit a cigarette, and Caitlin had never seen Reed smoke.

Sensing her remoteness, Reed asked with a pronounced formality, "May I sit?"

"Yes, do. Drink?"

Reed sat on the sofa. "Early, isn't it?"

"In New York, not Paris." Caitlin smiled at him, a summer-at-the-shore smile. She wanted Reed relaxed. "I have cognac, vodka—"

"Cognac, please."

Liquor bottles and glasses were lined up on a shelf of the hi-fi cabinet. Caitlin poured Courvoisier into two snifters, brought one to Reed, and sat in an armchair across from him. If he was put out she hadn't joined him on the sofa, he kept his feelings to himself and raised his snifter. "To seeing you again."

Leaning over the low brass table, Caitlin touched her snifter to his, sipped some Courvoisier, and put the glass on the table. "You're tan."

Reed rolled the cognac in his snifter. "I'm sorry I disappeared like that. I knew you'd call, and I missed you, and maybe that's why the weather had me so blue."

Caitlin understood she was supposed to say she had missed him too, but she was looking at the sofa cushions, the burnt umber fabric with tiny orange hexagons, and thinking about the afternoon she and Gabe had bought the couch at Gimbels. "Do you smoke?"

Reed seemed perplexed by the question. "Are you all right?"

Caitlin ignored his question. "I have a pack of cigarettes in the bedroom and wondered if you'd like one with your cognac."

"Marjorie used to get after me to quit. And I did—frequently. I quit for good in January. It was my New Year's resolution."

That meant Reed could've been following her. "Where'd you get your tan?"

Reed drank some Courvoisier. "Acapulco."

"I've never been to Mexico."

"You'd like Acapulco. Gorgeous beaches surrounded by cliffs. Perhaps we could go sometime."

"How about Mexico City?"

"It has its charms," Reed said.

"You like Mexico City, do you?"

Caitlin heard her accusatory tone. Evidently, so did Reed. He placed his snifter on the table. "What's bothering you? If you want me to go—"

Caitlin stared at the rug, a beige-and-rust checkerboard, and felt trapped in a vortex of anger. She and Gabe had bought the rug the same day as the sofa. "I want you to stay." She picked up the courier bag next to her chair, then pulled out papers and dropped them onto the table. "That's a copy of the report Gabe wrote in Mexico City. The report you were so interested in when I was at the *Post* summer picnic. You asked me to take notes on it and show them to you."

"Caitlin, we were discussing a story idea."

The vortex spun faster. "Here are my notes. Gabe observed a man in a red baseball cap and aviator sunglasses—like you wear. A very athletic Ivy Leaguer with long hair the color of wet sand. He dropped off an airline bag to a pair of Cuban anti-Castro operatives in a café and then had lunch with a short, husky Russian, most likely a KGB officer."

Reed gaped at her as though she were speaking Sanskrit, and Caitlin got up, glaring at him. "That Russian came after me, and the next time I saw him was in a hotel with his throat cut. Turns out, he tortured and killed my friend Winkie."

Going into the bag and gripping the .38, Caitlin remembered the Stoic philosopher she had to read in college declaring that anger was a temporary madness and any actions springing from it were insane. Did Caitlin give a shit about a toga-draped Roman sage? Not then, and definitely not now. She leveled the pistol at Reed.

He stood, the expression on his face evenly divided between fear and outrage. "Have you lost your mind?"

"I found the Cuban prostitute. She told me her pimp, the late Victor Diaz, worked for the CIA and Castro, and he had a handler known as the American cowboy. Like Victor, he worked both sides. And that man, the man in the report, the man who shot Gabe, is you, isn't it?"

Inching forward, Reed said in a soothing voice, "It's not me, Caitlin. I understand losing Gabe has been horrific for you. Like losing Marjorie was for me. Such a loss can make you think bizarre things. Please, put down the gun."

She was wondering if he was telling the truth when Reed lunged. He was quick and strong and tight against her, so Caitlin couldn't strike him. She was struggling to hold on to the pistol grip when she realized Reed wasn't trying to take the .38 from her. He had clamped one hand over the hammer to prevent it from firing while the other pressed the cylinder release and then the ejector rod. His knowledge of revolvers and his ability to unload one in the midst of a tussle persuaded Caitlin he was lying. As the bullets clinked onto the yellow pine floorboards, she let go of the pistol; pushed off Reed and rammed an elbow under his chin, staggering him backward; and then ran into her bedroom and turned the lock on the doorknob.

Caitlin was at the nightstand when she heard a loud thump against the door. Reed was kicking it. There was another louder thump. The latch fell out of the doorframe, and the door flew open. Reed walked in, holding a big .45 automatic at his side, the same type of pistol that had killed Gabe. "Sit with your legs on the bed and your back against the headboard."

Caitlin did as he ordered, fighting against her panic. Reed, his hand going under his olive corduroy suit coat, tucked the .45 into his waistband, then sat on the bed and slid close to her so she didn't have the space to hit him with any force. Caitlin saw sadness in his jade green eyes—a sadness, she knew, without mercy. He was planning to kill her.

Telling herself to relax and concentrate, Caitlin asked calmly, "Why did you shoot my husband?"

"I didn't intend to. You and I had our lunch at Twenty-One, and I liked you. I hadn't liked a woman in years, since Marjorie. And you were eager to write and, I believed, talented. And pretty. I'd been keeping tabs on Gabe for a while."

Caitlin hated hearing him use her husband's name. "Why?"

"New hires at the CIA intrigued me. I knew Gabe spotted me in Mexico City. I doubted he could pick me out of a lineup, but I had to check. I was watching your street, and when I drove past him in the cab, he looked over. I could tell he recognized me and . . ."

Reed didn't finish the sentence. Caitlin asked, "You work for us or the Russians?"

"For myself."

Caitlin said, "Not that I really know you, but I can't see you doing this for money."

"I don't. It goes back to 1946. I was at our embassy in Moscow. There was no CIA, only an intelligence group. My job was to nose around and write reports for the State Department to pass on in Washington. Over twenty million Soviets had died in the war, and the Nazis had destroyed the country. Stalin and his boys were monstrous, but the average citizen wasn't—they were suffering. My reports suggested we should cool the Cold War rhetoric. Not a popular view in Washington, and I was transferred to Paris. Marjorie was with me, and we had a ball until her cancer diagnosis."

Reed stared past Caitlin to the wall, then said, "In the evenings, Marjorie liked to walk around the lake in the Bois de Boulogne. One evening, from the woods, someone shot at me. A professional. He used a silencer. Except he missed and hit Marjorie. She died instantly."

"And you think the CIA was responsible?"

"Perhaps. I was sharing my opinion of the Cold War with reporters off the record. That could explain it. Or it could've been the KGB. I also discussed the corrupt Soviet officials I'd seen with reporters. Whoever did it, I decided to make both sides pay."

"By becoming a murderer?"

Reed said, "Like your husband? I assume Gabe shot Victor Diaz. What was his justification? A paycheck? I wasn't just out to avenge Marjorie. We and the Soviets are dangerous hypocrites, and both should be punished for their arrogance. We pontificate about countries' right to self-determination, and in Cuba we're trying to overthrow Castro, sending in weapons and training insurgents in Guatemala. I saw them with my own eyes. And Moscow crushes any country that wants independence, like Hungary, and slaughters thousands of civilians in the process. And if anybody gets out of line in the Soviet Union, they go to labor colonies or prisons. The Russian who killed your friend and attacked you, I told him to leave both of you alone. But he had other masters in the KGB who I assume wanted to know why Gabe was visiting Winkie and whether you knew what your husband was doing. That Russian paid, though. I made sure of it."

Caitlin hadn't understood why Reed had put away his .45. Now she did; he was going to use a knife—less noise that way. The trick was to keep him talking until she had no choice.

"What about Été?" she asked.

"That was regrettable. She saw the pistol in my suitcase and began asking questions."

Caitlin was trembling when she snapped, "And you talk about hypocrites! Été didn't do a damn thing to you. I didn't either, for that matter, and I'm next. Is that part of your Cold War strategy? Murder a husband, fuck his widow, then murder her?"

Reed didn't answer. Caitlin dredged up memories of Gabe, her mother, Winkie, Été, and the saddest movies she'd ever seen—*Imitation of Life*, *The Best Years of Our Lives*—any memory that would bring tears to her eyes.

Sighing, Reed patted her knee. "I wish you wouldn't cry."

Slowly, so he wouldn't interpret her movements as aggressive, Caitlin put her left hand on his shoulder, leaning forward and pressing her left cheek against his face. As she whispered "I could've loved you," she used her right hand to draw Gabe's Baby Browning from her back pocket. She had kept the pistol in the nightstand. It fired a small-caliber bullet, small enough that shooting a man the size of Reed in the chest wouldn't stop him from grabbing his .45 and killing her, so Caitlin thumbed off the safety, shoved the muzzle under his chin, and fired. The sharp crack hurt her ears, the barrel sparks made her blink, blood wet her cheeks. Reed pulled away. She clung to him, an image of Gabe dying on the sidewalk flashing behind her eyes as she fired into Reed's throat; fired again into his neck and head, a piece of his scalp flying off; and fired until she heard the click of an empty chamber and her hand, face, hair, and sweater were covered with his blood.

Caitlin let Reed go. He fell onto his back. She removed his pistol from under his suit coat. His face was a mess. His breathing was shallow. He moved his head and looked at her. She wasn't ready to call Danny. She was waiting for Reed to die.

CHAPTER 72

"Where is he?" Danny asked, closing the apartment door.

"The bedroom." Caitlin went to the brass table by the sofa. "First take a look at these."

Two pistols and an ivory-handled switchblade were on the table.

Caitlin said, "Run the ballistics on the .45; the slugs will match the ones dug out of Gabe. I'd bet that knife was used on the Russian at the Allerton Hotel. And I shot Reed with the Baby Browning. I found it in Gabe's footlocker."

Wistfully, Danny said, "To celebrate our first year as partners, Gabe took me to Peter Luger for steak, and I gave him the Browning. He never carried it."

"Lucky me," she said. "It saved my life."

Since phoning Danny and telling him what happened, Caitlin was aware she was in motion yet felt as if it was someone else in her body. They walked into the bedroom. Reed was half on, half off the bed, lying on his back, his arms flung wide, his feet on the floor, his hair caked with blackish-red blood, his features stippled with powder burns, and his head pockmarked with bullet holes.

"Jesus," Danny said.

With her rage gone, the horror that she had taken a life was real to her. She absolved herself with the knowledge that Reed had planned to kill her, so her response was an act of self-defense. But remembering her time with him in Belmar made her queasy.

"Excuse me a minute," she said and walked out to the bathroom.

Standing at the sink and looking in the mirror, she soaped a washcloth and cleaned the blood from her cheeks and forehead. She thought seeing her face in the glass would make her feel more like herself. It didn't. Could that woman in the mirror have slept with the man who murdered her husband? Could she have been so blind and needy? Yes. And yes. Would she ever be free of that shame? No. What was the appropriate punishment? Hamlet's mother, Queen Gertrude, married the king who murdered her husband, and Shakespeare didn't let her off the hook; he made her drink a cup of poisoned wine. The Bard could be vindictive, couldn't he? Caitlin had an idea for a cocktail, and she laughed out loud. Shakespeare's Martini, three olives and a pinch of hemlock. Was suicide more sinful than screwing your late husband's killer? Probably for Catholics. Only one choice here. Confession.

"Cait, you good?"

He was behind her.

"Danny?"

"Yeah?"

"Danny, I—"

He rested his hands on her shoulders and spoke to her reflection in the mirror. "One morning this summer I drove to the shore to check up on you. I saw him leave the bungalow and ran the plate on his car. He came back a solid citizen."

Caitlin let out a sad little chuckle. "Spying on me?"

"You mad?"

"Embarrassed. How could I have—"

"You didn't know, Cait."

She was trembling. Danny rubbed her shoulders. "Let's go over your story again, and I'll get somebody here to take your statement and some guys to process the scene."

"Do I have to talk about Belmar?"

"How you spent the day with your editor, and he drank too much at dinner and couldn't drive home. You can say that."

Reaching up, Caitlin held his hands and stared in the mirror. It was her, and it wasn't her. "Thank you, Danny."

CHAPTER 73

Hyannis, Massachusetts
Election Day: November 8, 1960

The phone rang. Caitlin didn't remember falling asleep. The bedside lamp was on, and the paperback of *Doctor Zhivago* was in her hands. She answered on the fourth ring.

"Hello," Jack said. "They held the room for you?"

"They did." Caitlin glanced at her watch. It was a quarter past ten. "Is the election over?"

"It's not. How are you? I've been following the story about that nut Howland in the papers."

Caitlin sat up. She was still wearing her turtleneck and jeans. "I'm fine. The tabloids couldn't find me. I was staying in New Jersey with Julian and his family. And I've been cleared on the shooting."

"You did the world a favor. One less murderous bastard. And the woman who had the film, she's safe?"

Caitlin said, "I put her in touch with Julian. She won't have any trouble with Trafficante."

"I can meet you on the beach behind the hotel in fifteen minutes. By the yacht club."

The Yachtsman Hotel was booked with journalists covering the election. Caitlin worried that they'd be seen and someone would ask questions. "Is that safe?"

Jack chuckled as if he didn't have a care in the world. "The press doesn't have time to be nosy. They'll be writing stories or getting drunk. Most likely both."

His lack of concern annoyed Caitlin. She knew Jack was mystified by his tattered self, yet sometimes she wondered if he had a single nerve in his body. "OK," she said.

Downstairs, Caitlin could hear Huntley and Brinkley on the TV in the barroom. The manila envelope with the reel of film was in a pocket of her camel hair coat. She exited through a side door and crossed the sand toward the Hyannis Yacht Club. The windows of the club restaurant were lit up, and couples were drinking and laughing. Caitlin wished she was eating the cannelloni at Grotta Azzurra with Gabe. Scratch that. She'd settle for roasted chestnuts from a cart if Gabe were alive. Roasted chestnuts every day if God would give her Gabe back . . .

Caitlin was listening to Lewis Bay lapping at the shore when Jack came out of the parking lot in front of the yacht club and joined her on the beach. His face was visible in the moonlight, and he was smiling. "Lyndon called to tell me I'm getting my butt kicked out west, but we're going gangbusters in New York and North Carolina."

"Sounds like the perfect vice president. "

"He wins me Texas, I'll bake him a cake."

The wind blew off the bay. Caitlin hugged herself against the cold. "Driving up, I heard on the radio you had a big lead."

Shivering, Jack stuck his hands in the pockets of his topcoat. "The Northeast returns. The lead's smaller now. I was glad to get out of Bobby's house. They're all so goddamn nervous."

"Not you?"

Jack laughed bitterly. "Haven't you heard? I'm a war hero. Getting nervous is bad for my image."

Caitlin gave the envelope to him. "This would be worse."

Jack stared at the dock of the yacht club. The planks were silver in the moonlit bay. "My brother Joe and I used to sail out there. Kick too. I remember feeling like those summer days would last forever. Joe's been dead sixteen years, Kick for twelve, and I keep wondering—where did those summers go?" The wind ruffled his hair, making him seem so young. Jack held up the envelope. "Caitlin, I can't tell you how relieved I am Gabe didn't die for this. I hate that I got him involved with the CIA. I didn't recruit him. We were talking about the agency, and he asked me if I could help him get a job."

"I don't blame you. I couldn't talk Gabe out of working there."

"But you're still angry at me."

"Disappointed. I like your wife. She's brave. Her miscarriage, the stillbirth, the campaign and being pregnant, you being gone so much— it has to be hard for her. And I worry about you."

Jack eyed the sand, digging up a seashell with the toe of his shoe. Caitlin was angered by his impervious calm, as though his balls routinely getting the better of his brain was in the natural order of things. "Maybe the reporters hold back," she said. "But what if a biographer writes about it? Or one of the women? Like Warren Harding's mistress."

Jack grinned. "Nan Britton. I read it. They used to get together in a White House closet."

"It's nothing to grin about. If you wind up in a memoir like that, I'll bet your daughter will have some questions for you. Won't that be fun?"

As intended, mentioning Caroline got his attention. He looked at her, the lines deepening at the corners of his eyes.

"Why, Jack?"

He shrugged. "I can't explain it."

"Try."

So softly it was difficult to hear him over the wind, he replied, "I'm hungry all the time. And I can't—I can't get full."

"I like you better like this."

"Sad?"

"Honest," Caitlin said.

Jack was gazing at the dock again. "Honest doesn't always get the job done, does it?"

Caitlin didn't answer. Jack looked at her.

"It doesn't," she said.

Jack smiled at her. "On a lighter note, J. Edgar Hoover called to tell me what he knew about Reed Howland and Été. He asked me how I knew her, and I told him we'd become friendly years ago when I was in Saigon."

"Sounds like he was blackmailing you."

"Edgar wants to keep his job. I'll keep him for as long as I can stand him."

Jack handed Caitlin a laminated card. "Win or lose, there's going to be a press conference at the armory. Here's a pass. If I lose, I'm still a senator, and if you want a job in Washington—"

"I had an offer to be the assistant arts editor at the *Newark Evening News*. I'm going to take it."

"That's wonderful. Good luck with it." Jack started to go, then pivoted back toward her. "Caitlin, losing someone you love doesn't mean your life is over."

"It just feels like it."

Jack was silent, then said, "I suppose it does, but here's what I know. The dead love you forever." He raised the envelope. "Thanks for this."

Caitlin knew she should be polite. She chose honesty instead. "I did it for Gabe."

Jack glanced out to where he used to sail with his brother and sister. "I know that. And like you, I wish Gabe was here."

Caitlin watched him walk toward the yacht club until she realized he was gone and she had been staring at the darkness.

CHAPTER 74

At 4:00 a.m., Jack crawled under the covers with the election in doubt. Five hours later, as he sat on the bed in his pajamas, his speechwriter and press secretary stopped in to tell him he had unofficially racked up 285 votes in the Electoral College, making him president-elect. After his aides departed, Jack went into the bathroom to shave. As he flicked at his soapy cheek with a straight razor, it struck him as vaguely unreal that he was about to line up behind George Washington and Abraham Lincoln.

At breakfast, he felt more presidential. Along with his gray suit, he was wearing the colors of the flag—a white shirt and a blue tie with red polka dots. And Caroline called him *Mr. President.*

As he ate his bacon and eggs, Jackie, eight months pregnant, shifted uncomfortably in her chair. "Jack, when is the press conference?"

The sun shone through the window behind her, and her dark hair and pale complexion glowed. "Not till Nixon concedes. "

Jackie gazed at the lace tablecloth, and Jack marveled at her ability to vanish before his eyes, as if she could summon the fog from the sea and surround herself in mist. That would have to stop now. It was lousy politics for a First Lady to disappear. Especially one so young and pretty and clever and stylish.

Out in the brisk salt air, Jack hoisted Caroline onto his back and gave her a piggyback ride across the lawn, pain shooting up his spine like fireworks.

"Daddy, Mommy says we have to move. I don't want to."

"Why, Buttons?"

"Because I'll miss you."

"I'm going too. I wouldn't leave you."

"You won't?"

"Never," he said.

By noon, Jack was sitting in Bobby's living room with his brother, his sister-in-law Ethel, and several aides, their eyes glued to the television set.

"What the fuck is this?" Jack asked.

"Merv Griffin hosting a game show," Bobby said. *"Play Your Hunch."*

Jack grinned, but his voice had a sarcastic edge. "You're a fan?"

Before Bobby could reply, Merv Griffin was replaced on the TV by Nixon's press secretary reading a congratulatory telegram from the vice president to the senator. As the results flashed on-screen, Jack remembered when he and Dick had been friends, and he imagined how rotten he must feel losing such a close one.

Bobby said, "Let's go, Jack. We're taking a family picture at Dad's."

With his palms on the arms of the chair, Jack pushed himself to his feet, his back still aching. "I'll meet you."

He returned to his house, opened a door in the kitchen, flipped a light switch, and descended the stairs into the cellar. Across from the furnace was a floor safe. It had belonged to the previous owner. Jack hadn't used it until last night. He spun the combination knob and removed the envelope. Cuba had once been his playground. As president, that island would be a colossal pain in the ass unless the CIA got rid of Castro before Inauguration Day.

Jack brought the envelope outside, waving off the Secret Service agents shadowing him and going into his side yard, where a gardener had been burning leaves in a row of smoldering barrels. Jack was ashamed Caitlin had seen him in this carnal circus act, and he tossed the envelope into one of the smoking barrels, then picked up a can of Kingsford charcoal lighter fluid from the ground and squirted the fluid into the smoke. An orange blaze flared up. He closed his eyes. For Jack, the fragrance of burning leaves was as joyful a part of autumn as football. Yet the season hollowed him out. He hated leaving the ocean to go away to school, and he hated his goodbyes with Kick.

Jack remembered the fall he was sixteen and Kick was thirteen. His sister was miserable because she was being shipped off to the Noroton Convent in Connecticut to receive a religious and secular education.

Kick said, "Mother won't be happy until I'm a nun."

They were walking home from downtown Hyannis. Jack had taken her for an ice cream soda at Megathlin's Drug Store, but his sister had just poked the scoop of vanilla with her spoon.

"Kick, I'll be at Choate, and I can visit you."

"If I'm a nun, I can still jitterbug at nightclubs, can't I?"

"Let's ask Mother."

Kick giggled and took his arm. "Brother, I love you."

Jack opened his eyes and saw the flames erasing the record of his Cuban debauchery.

"I love you too, Kick."

President-elect. That's impressive. I remember when you had pimples.

"Kick, I should've died so many times. When I was a kid. In the South Pacific. On a trip to Europe and the Far East. After my back surgery. Is this why God let me live? To be president?"

How do I know? God has no time for the dead. He can barely keep up with the living.

"Once I'm in the White House, we can't talk. Everybody will say I'm losing my mind."

Oh, stop. People know the Irish talk to ghosts, and they voted for you anyway.

Jack laughed, and the wind blew the smoke from the fire past him.

At his parents' house, his brother Teddy was standing on the porch and called down to him, "We're all here except Jackie. She went for a walk on the beach."

Jack negotiated his way down the hill through the dune grass toward the choppy gray sound. Jackie was coming toward him on the sand, her pregnancy swelling her tan raincoat. *Dear God, let this baby live, please.*

When his wife reached him, she said, "I knew you'd win, Bunny."

He kissed her cheek.

"Jack, it's going to be different now."

He smiled. "Yes, we'll live in a bigger house."

Her expression was flat, and Jack realized his wife was in no mood for jokes.

She said, "There will be so many people around us. Your staff, the Secret Service, reporters. People will be watching us."

"That's the job, Jackie."

"Yes, so we will have to be different—with each other."

His wife was staring at him. Jack knew what she wanted to hear, but he doubted it was possible. He'd try, though. He could do that. "It will be different."

The wind whipped her hair across her face.

He said, "I promise. It will."

She rewarded his promise with a kiss on his lips. Jack took her hand, and together they went up through the dune grass, the gulls crying as they wheeled overhead.

CHAPTER 75

Under a cinderblock sky, the motorcade drove down South Street. Men and women in their Sunday best stood five deep along the route, pressing forward to get a closer look while state troopers spread their arms to keep them out of the road. The lead car was a white Lincoln. Jack was in the front seat. Caitlin saw him through the windshield. She was standing near a cluster of campaign workers wearing KENNEDY FOR PRESIDENT buttons and waiting by the doors of the redbrick armory.

When the Lincoln stopped, Jack got out. No hat, no topcoat, just a gray suit and that winning smile. Next to him, a Secret Service agent, checking for threats, looked up at the flat roof of the armory, where photographers were yelling for the president-elect to hold still so they could take his picture. Jackie emerged from the car, her pregnancy partially hidden by a purple double-breasted coat, and followed her husband through an excited gauntlet of well-wishers. Caitlin couldn't tell if Jack spotted her through the crowd. He did nod in her direction, but he was nodding at everyone. Jackie saw her, though. At the entrance, Jackie turned to Caitlin. Rolling her eyes like a teenager impatient with the tedious rituals of adults, and referring to their tipsy conversation at the Carlyle, she said "Got any champagne?" and then disappeared into the armory.

Caitlin was reluctant to go in. She had stayed up late watching the returns and dozed on and off until she gave up on sleep and showered and dressed and bought the *Boston Globe* in the lobby and walked to the Mayflower Restaurant in Hyannis. She had coffee and cinnamon toast and read the paper. Evidently, Julian retained his clout in New Jersey. Jack had lost fourteen of twenty-one counties but narrowly carried the state. After breakfast, Caitlin meant to drive to New York. Instead, she wandered over to the armory, telling herself she was curious. That wasn't the whole truth. Caitlin was seeking a finale, a demarcation line separating yesterday from today, even though she knew that no such line existed. And this knowledge, that she was pursuing an illusion, explained her reluctance. Caitlin had helped Jack and found Gabe's killer, and her payoff was a guilty conscience and nightmares about shooting Reed. She should pack up and leave. But Caitlin was cold from standing outside, and illusions, after all, were not so easy to renounce.

Inside the armory, reporters, cameramen, and supporters were applauding as Jack wended his way through the audience and stepped onto the rostrum to give his speech. His parents and brothers and sisters sat behind him. Caitlin recognized the actor Peter Lawford. He was married to one of Jack's sisters. She remembered seeing Lawford with Frank Sinatra and Steve McQueen in that war movie Gabe liked, *Never So Few*. They had seen it in Times Square. Caitlin couldn't recall the theater. Either the Paramount or the Rialto. It made her sad she couldn't remember, another piece of her life with Gabe slipping away.

Jack stood at the microphone. Jackie was standing to his right, smiling at him as he spoke about the future in a clipped voice of high seriousness, but Caitlin was only half listening. She was distracted by the faces of the crowd. All of them looked at Jack as if they were seeing, for the first time, the dazzling embodiment of the dreams immigrants carried here—in Jack's case, a dream three generations old, when another Kennedy, fleeing the Potato Famine, traded his Irish farm for the slums of East Boston, and now his great-grandson would live in the White House.

Jack concluded his speech and grinned, then glanced over at Jackie and said, "So now my wife and I prepare for a new administration and for a new baby."

As reporters peppered him with questions, Caitlin left the armory. She was surprised to see Danny standing outside. More surprising was how happy she was to see him. In fact, when she thought about it, she was usually happy to see Danny. "What're you doing here?"

Danny said, "You promised to go to Coney Island with me."

"That's in Brooklyn, not Hyannis."

"I caught a ride with some Irish cops who want to see their hero. Can I get a lift home?"

"Of course."

The sun was out, and Caitlin's spirits rose as she walked with Danny to the hotel. At the corner, a redheaded girl with pigtails pedaled past them on a tricycle, going somewhere in a hurry. Jack, it appeared, was already getting the country moving again. That's what he promised during the campaign. A better America where even a Catholic could get elected president, and the hungry would be fed, and one day we'd all dance on the moon.

Down on Ocean Street, the wind was blowing off the water. Caitlin and Danny paused to watch a yellow fishing boat leaving the harbor. Life would be better for her too. Her past would no longer stand in the way of her present. She would lock Gabe away in that inviolable chamber of her heart where she stored the memories of her mother. The rest of her she'd save for another husband. Gabe would approve. Jack was right. The dead do love you forever. You can't lose them.

After marrying, Caitlin would return to Jersey. It would be an easier ride to Newark and her job at the newspaper. There was a Dutch Colonial on Burroughs Way in Maplewood she'd always admired. It was next to a public grammar school, so she could spare her children the swinging rosaries of the nuns. Caitlin would plant rosebushes in her yard, and her husband would set up a grill and a kiddie pool. Life would be good there. Eight tranquil years would pass by in a bright turning of seasons, with Jack and Jackie and Caroline and the new baby in the White House, and the First Family would happily grow older with all the other families in America.

It was coming. This better time. Caitlin was sure of it as she stood next to Danny in the sunlight, watching the boat move across the blue water and all the way out to the horizon.

A NOTE ON SOURCES

As is typical of historically inspired works of fiction, *Their Shadows Deep* was written against the background of events that were widely reported in the news at the time of their occurrence. While the names of real people appear, all the actions and dialogue concerning these people are products solely of the author's imagination and are not intended to depict actual scenes or to change the fictional nature of the book.

Anecdotes and historical quotes appearing in *Their Shadows Deep* were sourced and inspired by the following books, articles, historical papers, and public records.

Two aspects of this novel deserve special mention.

The first is JFK's imaginary conversations with his sister Kick. Despite the millions of words written about JFK, his inner world remains something of a mystery—partially obscured by his enduring heroic image, his murder and the lingering national grief, and the incomplete record he left us of his deepest feelings, which he generally hid behind a pose of detachment.

However, historian Arthur Schlesinger Jr., a former special assistant to President Kennedy, never believed he was detached. In a foreword to *Of Poetry and Power: Poems Occasioned by the Presidency and by the Death of John F. Kennedy*, Schlesinger claimed that this pose was to protect JFK from the waves of emotion that threatened to overwhelm him and make it impossible for him to cope with the disheartening realities of his life.

There were many of these: his poor health since childhood; the frequent hospitalizations, failed surgeries, severe back problems, and chronic pain; his conviction that he would die young; the deaths of his brother and sister in their twenties; and his reckless sexual behavior. Ted Sorensen, a JFK adviser and speechwriter from his days in the Senate until JFK's murder in Dallas, speculated in his memoir, *Counselor: A Life at the Edge of History*, that JFK was, at times, ashamed of his recklessness, and he must have had his share of dark nights of the soul about his infidelities.

All this gave JFK, once he became a public figure, ample reason to project an image at odds with his inner reality. In *Their Shadows Deep*, I have tried to illuminate this reality, and I used Kick to do it, because, as Kennedy family biographer Doris Kearns Goodwin observes, she was the only sibling that he could level with about his insecurities.

Second, I should mention the alleged film of JFK and the fictional Clara in the Santo Trafficante–owned Comodoro Hotel.

In *Havana Nocturne: How the Mob Owned Cuba and Then Lost It to the Revolution*, author T. J. English describes the suite at the Comodoro with its two-way mirror and how, in the late 1950s, Trafficante had watched JFK with prostitutes. According to English, Trafficante would excoriate himself for missing the opportunity to blackmail JFK by recording him on film.

Trafficante was not only one of the most powerful mobsters in the United States; he was one of the smartest. He died in 1987 at the age of seventy-two at the Texas Heart Institute in Houston and not in a prison cell or a hail of bullets, an impressive feat for a Mafia don. Apparently, the CIA believed he was clever enough to help assassinate Fidel Castro because, as Trafficante told the House Select Committee on Assassinations, he was recruited for that task.

I believe Trafficante was too shrewd not to collect evidence that could be used to blackmail a senator as well-known as JFK, whose face frequently appeared in magazines, who had nearly become the 1956 nominee for vice president, and who was talked about as a potential presidential candidate in 1960. Furthermore, one of Trafficante's Cuban operations was producing stag films. Finally, and perhaps most important, using pictures to compromise men in power had been done before—and by a man whom Trafficante knew, Meyer Lansky.

Anthony Summers, a biographer of FBI Director J. Edgar Hoover, maintains that Lansky had come into possession of photographs that revealed Hoover's homosexuality, and Lansky used that evidence to protect himself from FBI investigations, an arrangement that was widely known among mobsters.

I maintain that Trafficante had JFK filmed at the Comodoro. His later denial of the film's existence—and a prime motive for destroying it—makes perfect sense given the attention focused on him in the aftermath of the JFK assassination. In 1979, the House Select Committee on Assassinations concluded, contrary to the findings of the Warren Commission, that Lee Harvey Oswald had been part of a larger plot. The committee report could not prove who had participated in the assassination but stated that Trafficante and Carlos Marcello, a crime boss based in New Orleans, "had the motive, means, and opportunity to assassinate President Kennedy."

With the passing of time, among some who believe that the assassination involved a conspiracy, Trafficante and Marcello have emerged as likely participants.

SOURCES

Andersen, Christopher. *Jack and Jackie: Portrait of an American Marriage.* New York: William Morrow and Company Inc., 1996.

Andrews, Evan. "Fidel Castro's Wild New York Visit." History. Updated August 31, 2018. www.history.com/news/ fidel-castros-wild-new-york-visit-55-years-ago.

Bigart, Homer. "Winner's Pledge: Family Is With Him As He Vows To Press Nation's Cause." *New York Times*, November 10, 1960.

Bradlee, Benjamin C. *A Good Life: Newspapering and Other Adventures.* New York: Simon & Schuster, 1995.

————. *Conversations with Kennedy.* New York: W. W. Norton & Company, 1984.

Brinkley, Joel. "Mexico City Depicted as a Soviet Spies' Haven." *New York Times*, June 23, 1985.

Byrne, Paula. *Kick: The True Story of JFK's Sister and the Heir to Chatsworth.* New York: Harper Perennial, 2017.

Caputo, Philip. *10,000 Days of Thunder: A History of the Vietnam War*. New York: Atheneum Books for Young Readers, 2005.

Cartwright, Gary. "Who Was Jack Ruby?" *Texas Monthly*, November 1975.

Casanova de Seingalt, Jacques. *The Memoires of Casanova*. Translated by Arthur Machen. New York: G. P. Putnam's Sons, 1894; Project Gutenberg, December 2001. https://www.gutenberg.org/files/2981/2981-h/2981-h.htm#linkB2H_4_0019.

CBC Radio. "John F. Kennedy Was Given Last Rites 5 Different Times: Only 1 of Those Times Followed the 35th U.S. President's 1963 Assassination." Under the Influence. February 24, 2022. www.cbc.ca/radio/undertheinfluence/john-f-kennedy-was-given-last-rites-5-different-times-1.6362855.

Central Intelligence Agency. "E Street Complex Sign with CIA Seal." Artifacts. Accessed January 18, 2020. www.cia.gov/legacy/museum/artifact/e-street-complex-sign-with-cia-seal/.

Christopher Moran. *Ian Fleming, James Bond & the Public Perception of the CIA*. Library of Congress, and Sponsoring Body John W. Kluge Center. Filmed June 2, 2011. Video. https://www.loc.gov/item/2021688692/.

Cirile, Marie. *Detective Marie Cirile: Memoirs of a Police Officer*. Garden City, NY: Doubleday & Company, 1975.

Clarke, Thurston. *JFK's Last Hundred Days: The Transformation of a Man and the Emergence of a Great President*. New York: Penguin Press, 2013.

"Coal & the Kennedys 1960s–2010s." Pop History Dig. Accessed March 2, 2020. https://pophistorydig.com/topics/coal-and-kennedy-family/.

Dallek, Robert. "The Medical Ordeals of JFK." *The Atlantic*, December 2002.

———. *An Unfinished Life: John F. Kennedy, 1917–1963*. New York: Back Bay Books, 2004.

Damore, Leo. *The Cape Cod Years of John Fitzgerald Kennedy*. First Soft-Cover Edition. New York: Four Walls Eight Windows, 1993.

Deitche, Scott M. *The Silent Don: The Criminal Underworld of Santo Trafficante Jr.* New Jersey: Barricade Books Inc., 2009.

DocsTeach. "John F. Kennedy Academic Record at Harvard, 1940." National Archives and Records Administration. Accessed March 4, 2020. http://www.docsteach.org/documents/document/john-f-kennedy-academic-record-at-harvard.

"Eleanor Roosevelt to John F. Kennedy, January 29 1959." In *Eleanor Roosevelt, John Kennedy, and the Election of 1960: A Project of The Eleanor Roosevelt Papers*, edited by Allida Black, June Hopkins, John Sears, Christopher Alhambra, Mary Jo Binker, Christopher Brick, John S. Emrich, Eugenia Gusev, Kristen E. Gwinn, and Bryan D. Peery. Columbia, SC: Model Editions Partnership, 2003. https://erpapers.columbian.gwu.edu/browse-jfk-documents.

English, T. J. *Havana Nocturne: How the Mob Owned Cuba and Then Lost It to the Revolution*. New York: William Morrow, 2008.

Find a Grave. "Kathleen 'Kick' Kennedy." Accessed January 25, 2022. www.findagrave.com/memorial/3491/kathleen-kennedy.

Glikes, Erwin A., and Paul Schwaber, eds. *Of Poetry and Power: Poems Occasioned by the Presidency and by the Death of John F. Kennedy.* New York: Basic Books Inc., 1964.

Goldfarb, Ronald. "What the Mob Knew About JFK's Murder." *The Washington Post*, March 14, 1993.

Grassi, Ralph. "When Wildwood Rocked." Funchase. Accessed Jun 9, 2021. www.funchase.com/Images/Rocks/When%20 Wildwood%20Rocked.htm.

Grose, Peter. *Gentleman Spy: The Life of Allen Dulles.* Amherst, MA: The University of Massachusetts Press, 1996.

Halberstam, David. "The Vantage Point Perspectives of the Presidency 1963–1969. By Lyndon Baines Johnson." *New York Times*, October 31, 1971.

Hamilton, Nigel. *JFK: Reckless Youth.* New York: Random House, 1992.

Harrison, Mim. "Jackie Kennedy's Prowess as a Polyglot." Accessed May 11, 2021. American Bilingual. www.americathebilingual.com/ jackie-kennedys-prowess-as-a-polygot/.

Hart, Jeffrey. "Yes, the Mob Killed Jack Kennedy." *Herald-Journal* (Spartanburg, SC), January 25, 1992.

Havemann, Ernest. "Mobsters Move In on Troubled Havana and Split Rich Gambling Profits with Batista." *Life*, March 10, 1958.

Healy, Paul F. "The Senate's Gay Young Bachelor." *Saturday Evening Post*, June 13, 1953.

Hellman, Geoffrey T. "James Bond Comes to New York." *New Yorker*, April 13, 1962.

Herken, Gregg. *The Georgetown Set: Friends and Rivals in Cold War Washington*. New York: Vintage Books, 2014.

Hersey, John. "Survival." *New Yorker*, June 17, 1944. www.newyorker.com/magazine/1944/06/17/survival.

Hersh, Seymour M. *The Dark Side of Camelot*. Boston: Little, Brown and Company, 1997.

History.com Editors. "U.S.-Soviet Summit Meeting Collapses after U-2 Spy Plane Shot Down." History. Updated May 19, 2023. www.history.com/this-day-in-history/u-s-soviet-summit-meeting-collapses.

HUM Images. *Vice President Nixon Points a Finger Towards Premier Khrushchev*. Photograph. Getty Images. Accessed October 9, 2018. www.gettyimages.co.nz/detail/news-photo/nixon-points-a-finger-towards-premier-khrushchev-to-make-a-news-photo/1371455479.

Hunt, Thomas. "Jack Ruby's 1959 visit to Havana." *Informer: The Journal of American Mafia History* 2, no. 4 (October 2009).

———. "The Capone of New Jersey: Abner 'Longie' Zwillman." The American Mafia: The History of Organized Crime in the United States. Accessed August 1, 2022. https://mafiahistory.us/a026/f_zwillman.html.

"JFK's 1960 Campaign: Primaries & Fall Election." The Pop History Dig. Accessed January 2, 2020. https://pophistorydig.com/topics/jfks-1960-campaign/.

"John F. Kennedy to Eleanor Roosevelt, December 11, 1958." In *Eleanor Roosevelt, John Kennedy, and the Election of 1960: A Project of The Eleanor Roosevelt Papers,* edited by Allida Black, June Hopkins, John Sears, Christopher Alhambra, Mary Jo Binker, Christopher Brick, John S. Emrich, Eugenia Gusev, Kristen E. Gwinn, and Bryan D. Peery. Columbia, SC: Model Editions Partnership, 2003. https://erpapers.columbian.gwu.edu/browse-jfk-documents.

Kantor, Seth. *Who Was Jack Ruby?* New York: Everest House, 1978.

Kearns Goodwin, Doris. *No Ordinary Time: Franklin and Eleanor Roosevelt: The Home Front in World War II.* New York: Simon & Schuster, 1994.

———. *The Fitzgeralds and the Kennedys: An American Saga.* New York: St. Martin's Press, 1987.

Kennedy, John F. "Acceptance Speech, Hyannis Armory, Hyannis, Massachusetts, November 9, 1960." John F. Kennedy Library. Accessed July 22, 2024. www.jfklibrary.org/archives/other-resources/john-f-kennedy-speeches/hyannis-ma-acceptance-speech-19601109.

———. "Address to the Houston Ministers Conference, 12 September 1960." John F. Kennedy Library. Accessed July 22, 2024. www.jfklibrary.org/learn/about-jfk/historic-speeches/address-to-the-greater-houston-ministerial-association.

"Kennedy vs. Nixon: The First 1960 Presidential Debate." Uploaded September 26, 2020. YouTube video. Originally filmed September 26, 1960. www.youtube.com/watch?v=AYP8-oxq8ig.

Kessler, Ronald. *The Sins of the Father: Joseph P. Kennedy and the Dynasty He Founded.* New York: Warner Books, 1996.

Khrushchev, Sergei. "The Day We Shot Down the U-2." *American Heritage* 51, no. 5 (September 2000).

Kiger, Patrick J. "The Health Problems JFK Hid From the Public." History. May 2, 2023. www.history.com/news/the-health-problems-jfk-hid-from-the-public.

Kinzer, Stephen. "When a C.I.A. Director Had Scores of Affairs." *New York Times*, November 10, 2012.

Kirchick, James. "Joe Alsop and America's Forgotten Code." *The Atlantic*, February 15, 2017.

Klein, Edward. *All Too Human: The Love Story of Jack and Jackie Kennedy.* New York: Pocket Books, 1996.

Lacey, Robert. *Little Man: Meyer Lansky and the Gangster Life.* Boston: Little, Brown and Company, 1991.

Leaming, Barbara. *Kick Kennedy: The Charmed Life and Tragic Death of the Favorite Kennedy Daughter.* New York: Thomas Dunne Books, 2016.

Levine, Robert M. *Tropical Diaspora: The Jewish Experience in Cuba.* Princeton, NJ: Markus Wiener Publishers, 2010. First published 1993 by University Press of Florida (Gainesville, FL).

Levingston, Steven. "Jackie Robinson and JFK on Civil Rights: Two Men Divided by a Common Country." *Andscape*. June 5, 2017. https://andscape.com/features/jackie-robinson-jfk-on-civil-rights/.

Levy, Brian. "Havana Surprise: Discovering Jewish Cuba." *The Jewish Chronicle*, March 11, 2018. https://www.thejc.com/life-and-culture/travel/havana-surprise-discovering-jewish-cuba-ngyu98ew.

Loftus, Joseph A. "Kennedy Is Given a Secret Briefing by C.I.A. Director." *New York Times*, July 24, 1960.

Logevall, Fredrik. *JFK: Coming of Age in the American Century, 1917–1956*. New York: Random House, 2020.

Lowe, Jacques. *JFK Remembered: An Intimate Portrait by His Personal Photographer*. New York: Random House, 1993.

Maier, Thomas. *Mafia Spies: The Inside Story of the CIA, Gangsters, JFK, and Castro*. New York: Skyhorse Publishing, 2019.

Matthews, Christopher. *Jack Kennedy: Elusive Hero*. New York: Simon & Schuster, 2011.

———. *Kennedy & Nixon: The Rivalry That Shaped Postwar America*. New York: Simon & Schuster, 1996.

McCullough, David. *Truman*. New York: Simon & Schuster, 1992.

Michaelis, David. *Eleanor*. New York: Simon & Schuster, 2020.

Nixon, Richard M. *Six Crises*. Garden City, New York: Doubleday & Company, 1962.

O'Donnell, Kenneth P., David F. Powers, and Joe McCarthy. *"Johnny, We Hardly Know Ye": Memories of John Fitzgerald Kennedy.* Boston: Little, Brown and Company, 1970.

Olanoff, Lynn. "John F. Kennedy Drew Huge Crowds During 1960 Visit to Lehigh Valley." Lehigh Valley Live. November 17, 2013. www.lehighvalleylive.com/breaking-news/2013/11/john_f_kennedy drew_huge_crowd.html.

Oliphant, Thomas, and Curtis Wilkie. *The Road to Camelot: Inside JFK's Five-Year Campaign.* New York: Simon & Schuster, 2017.

Pace, Eric. "Joseph Alsop Dies at Home at 78; Political Columnist Since the 30's." *New York Times,* August 28, 1989.

Pait, T. Glenn, and Justin T. Dowdy. "John F. Kennedy's Back: Chronic Pain, Failed Surgeries, and the Story of its Effects on his Life and Death." *Journal of Neurosurgery* 27, no. 3 (July 11, 2017). https://doi.org/10.3171/2017.2.SPINE151524.

Parini, Jay. *Empire of Self: A Life of Gore Vidal.* New York: Doubleday, 2015.

Perrottet, Tony. "The Covert Casanova Tour in Venice." *Perceptive Travel* (June 2011). www.perceptivetravel.com/issues/0611/venice.html.

Phillips, Hart. "Batista and Regime Flee Cuba; Castro Moving to Take Power." *New York Times,* January 2, 1959.

Phillips, R. Hart. "75 Die in Havana as Munitions Ship Explodes at Dock." *New York Times,* March 5, 1960.

"Photo Gallery: JFK's Armory Speech in Hyannis." *Cape Cod Times*, November 4, 2016. www.capecodtimes.com/picture-gallery/news/local/2016/11/04/photo-gallery-jfk-s-armory-speech/682246007/.

Pietrusza, David. *1960: LBJ vs. JFK vs. Nixon: The Epic Campaign That Forged Three Presidencies.* New York: Union Square Press, 2008.

Princeton University Library. "Fidel Castro visits Princeton University." Library Archives. Accessed January 18, 2020. https://universityarchives.princeton.edu/2012/10/fidel-castro-visits-princeton-university/.

"Remarks of Senator John F. Kennedy at Charleston, West Virginia, April 11, 1960." David F. Powers Personal Papers, Box 33, "Economic Issues, Charleston, WV, 11 April 1960." John F. Kennedy Library. Accessed July 22, 2024. www.jfklibrary.org/archives/other-resources/john-f-kennedy-speeches/charleston-wv-19600411.

"Remarks of Senator John F. Kennedy at Glenwood Park, West Virginia, April 26, 1960." Papers of John F. Kennedy. Pre-Presidential Papers. Senate Files, Box 908, "Glenwood Park, West Virginia, 26 April 1960." John F. Kennedy Library. Accessed July 22, 2024. www.jfklibrary.org/archives/other-resources/john-f-kennedy-speeches/glenwood-park-wv-19600426.

"Remarks of Senator John F. Kennedy at Morgantown, West Virginia, April 18, 1960." Papers of John F. Kennedy. Pre-Presidential Papers. Senate Files, Box 908, "'Coal by Wire: The Key to Coal's Future,' Morgantown, West Virginia, 18 April 1960." John F. Kennedy Library. Accessed July 22, 2024. www.jfklibrary.org/archives/other-resources/john-f-kennedy-speeches/morgantown-wv-19600418.

"Remarks of Senator John F. Kennedy in the Senate, Washington, D.C., July 2, 1957." Papers of John F. Kennedy. Pre-Presidential Papers. Senate Files, Box 784, "Algeria Speech." John F. Kennedy Library. Accessed October 8, 2018. www.jfklibrary.org/archives/other-resources/john-f-kennedy-speeches/united-states-senate-imperialism-19570702.

Report of the Select Committee on Assassinations of the US House of Representatives. Washington, DC: United States Government Printing Office, 1979. Accessed July 11, 2024. www.archives.gov/research/jfk/select-committee-report/part-1c.html#trafficante.

"Reputed Old-Time Mafia Don Santo Trafficante Jr. Dies in Hospital at Age 72." *Los Angeles Times*, March 19, 1987.

Robin, Corey. "The Professor and the Politician." *New Yorker*, November 12, 2020.

Schlesinger, Arthur M. *A Thousand Days.* Boston: Mariner Books, 2002. First published 1965 by Houghton Mifflin (Boston, MA).

"Senator John F. Kennedy to Eleanor Roosevelt, January 22, 1959." Papers of John F. Kennedy. Presidential Papers. President's Office Files. Special Correspondence. Roosevelt, Eleanor, June 1958–November 1960. John F. Kennedy Library. Accessed July 22, 2024. www.jfklibrary.org/asset-viewer/archives/jfkpof-032-006#?image_identifier=JFKPOF-032-006-p0012.

Server, Lee. *Handsome Johnny: The Life and Death of Johnny Rosselli: Gentleman Gangster, Hollywood Producer, CIA Assassin.* New York: St. Martin's Press, 2018.

Silberklang, David. "St. Louis." In *Encyclopedia of the Holocaust*, vol. 4, edited by Israel Gutman. New York: Macmillan Publishing Company, 1990.

Sorensen, Theodore C. *Counselor: A Life at the Edge of History*. New York: Harper Perennial, 2008.

———. *Kennedy: The Classic Biography*. New York: Harper & Row, 1965.

Stout, David. "Janet Travell, 95, Pain Specialist And Kennedy's Personal Doctor." *New York Times*, August 3, 1997.

Summers, Anthony. *Official and Confidential: The Secret Life of J. Edgar Hoover*. Reprint, New York: Open Road Media, 2012. Kindle.

Thomas, Evan. *The Very Best Men: The Daring Early Years of the CIA*. New York: Simon & Schuster, 2006.

Travell, Janet G. Janet G. Travell recorded interview by Theodore C. Sorensen (January 20, 1966). John F. Kennedy Library Oral History Program.

"Truculent Texan: Jack Ruby." *New York Times*, October 6, 1966.

Van Gelder, Lawrence. "Batista, Ex-Cuban Dictator, Dies in Spain." *New York Times*, August 7, 1973.

Varela, Julio Ricardo. "The Time Jackie Kennedy Spoke to Voters in Spanish." Latino USA. October 27, 2015. www.latinousa.org/2015/10/27/the-time-jackie-kennedy-spoke-to-voters-in-spanish/2015.

Watts, Steven. *JFK and the Masculine Mystique: Sex and Power on the New Frontier.* New York: Thomas Dunne Books, 2016.

Whalen, Richard J. *The Founding Father: The Story of Joseph P. Kennedy: A Study in Power, Wealth and Family Ambition.* New York: New American Library, 1964.

White, Theodore H. *The Making of the President 1960.* New York: Harper Perennial, 1961.

Wikipedia. "1952 United States Presidential Election." Last updated June 1, 2024. https://en.wikipedia.org/wiki/1952_ United States_presidential_election.

———. "1956 United States Presidential Election." Last updated June 22, 2024. https://en.wikipedia.org/ wiki/1956_United_States_presidential_election.

———. "1960 United States Presidential Election in New Jersey." Last updated June 13, 2024. https://en.wikipedia.org/ wiki/1960_United_States_presidential_election_in_New_Jersey.

Withers, Bill. "A Conversation with Bill Withers." West Virginia Public Broadcasting. Uploaded December 14, 2007. YouTube video. www.youtube.com/watch?v=q1xQv6GhNSs.

ACKNOWLEDGMENTS

Novels don't come to life without the writer receiving assistance from many quarters, and here are some of the people to whom I owe a large debt of gratitude.

At Writers House, my intrepid agent, Susan Golomb, and her always helpful assistant, Sasha Landauer.

First and foremost at Lake Union, an imprint of Amazon Publishing, Danielle Marshall, editorial director; Adrienne Krogh, art director; Shasti O'Leary-Soudant, cover designer; Jen Bentham, production manager; Karah Nichols, production manager; copyeditor Mindi Machart and proofreader Anna Barnes; and Rachael Clark, marketing manager.

For his incisive commentary, humorous asides, and boundless enthusiasm, David Downing of Maxwellian Editorial Services.

Comments by early readers of *Their Shadows Deep* were invaluable, beginning with the wise suggestions of Marlene Adelstein. Later on, my novel benefited from the sharp eyes of Howard Dickson and Howard Sperber.

Two fine novelists whose insights and encouragement were tremendously helpful, Lisa Wingate and Laura Lane McNeal.

For over thirty years I have looked forward to my discussions, on events large and small, with the writer James Howard Kunstler, who is always available to either inform me or make me laugh.

For their research assistance: Lewis Abrams, LCSW; Corbin Apkin, archivist, John F. Kennedy Presidential Library; Professor Frankie Bailey, School of Criminal Justice, Rockefeller College of Public Affairs and Policy; Graeme R. Newman, distinguished professor emeritus at the School of Criminal Justice, University at Albany; Professor Mangai Natarajan, John Jay College of Criminal Justice; Roland J. Graves Sr., for his recollections of the Vicentian Institute and Albany in the 1960s; Deborah DeMarco Pakonis, for her memories of the Jersey Shore; Fancsy Pakonis, for her research on the training of nuns in the 1950s; forensic scientist Dr. Lowell Levine, for his insights on the autopsy of JFK; and supervisory park ranger Franceska Macsali-Urbin and park ranger Raymond Delamarter, for pointing out important details of JFK's visit with Eleanor Roosevelt at Val-Kill Cottage.

Others have also been of immeasurable assistance: Susan Novotny, owner of the Book House of Stuyvesant Plaza and Market Block Books; my sister and brother-in-law, Frann and Eric Francis; my friends Tracy Richard and Bruce Davis, Carol and Joe Siracusa, Ellen and Jeff Lewis, and David Saltzman.

I'd also like to send a heartfelt thanks to all the salespeople I met as I visited bookstores who reminded me why I wanted to be a writer in the first place.

I owe a tip of the hat to the morning coffee club for their wisdom and hilarity: Frank Commisso, Paul J. Goldman, Roland J. Graves Sr., John Graziano Jr., Jeanee Jarvis, John Mastrianni, and William A. Toomey III.

And finally to my wife, Annis G. Golden, for love beyond measure.

ABOUT THE AUTHOR

Photo © 2023 Ben Golden

Peter Golden is an award-winning journalist, novelist, and historian. His novels include *Comeback Love, Wherever There Is Light,* and *Nothing Is Forgotten.* The author lives with his wife near Albany, New York.